VIEBURY GROVE

BOOK II OF THE
METHOD 15/33 SERIES

SHANNON KIRK

SUSPENSE PUBLISHING

VIEBURY GROVE
A *METHOD 15/33* THRILLER
by
Shannon Kirk

PAPERBACK EDITION
* * * * *
PUBLISHED BY:
Suspense Publishing

Copyright 2020 Shannon Kirk

PUBLISHING HISTORY:
Suspense Publishing, Paperback and Digital Copy, May 2020

Cover Design: Shannon Raab
Cover Photographer: iStockphoto.com/ pancho6
Cover Photographer: iStockphoto.com/ enviromantic
Cover Photographer: Danish Abbasi (studio background)

ISBN: 978-0578633077

BOOKS BY SHANNON KIRK

METHOD 15/33 SERIES
METHOD 15/33 (#1)
VIEBURY GROVE (#2)

THE EXTRAORDINARY JOURNEY OF VIVIENNE
MARSHALL
IN THE VINES
GRETCHEN

SHORT STORY ANTHOLOGIES
THE NIGHT FLOOD
SWAMP KILLERS
NOTHING GOOD HAPPENS AFTER MIDNIGHT (2020)
BORDER NOIR (2020)

~Dedicated to all rogue scientists

PRAISE FOR VIEBURY GROVE

"*Viebury Grove* is a blistering and bracingly original thriller that squeezes suspense out of every single page. Shannon Kirk's sterling follow-up to *Method 15/33* features a colorful and original hero whose set her sights on an especially fiendish group of villains. A smooth noir reminiscent of Lisa Gardner effectively mixed with the feel of a John Wick film, this is reading entertainment of the highest order that is simply not to be missed."

—Jon Land, *USA Today* Bestselling Author of the *Murder, She Wrote* Series

"Watch out world, Lisa Yyland is back, and this time she'll make sure no one escapes her personal take on justice. *Viebury Grove* is a delicious story for every reader who likes their thrills mixed with vengeance."

—Victoria Helen Stone, Bestselling Author of *Jane Doe*

"In this sequel to the original and riveting *Method 15/33*, we find Lisa Yyland eighteen years on, and perfecting her revenge on the Center Ring, the sex traffickers who kidnapped her and who continue to abuse and murder young girls. It's Lisa's story, but it's also the story of victims and abusers and what goes on behind locked doors to satisfy the depravities of the rich and famous. Shannon Kirk writes with a vivid awareness of the suffering of innocents, and along the way I was certain she'd penned the story in her own blood using a strand of barbed wire for a quill. It's that good."

—James R. Benn, Author of the *Billy Boyle World War II* Mysteries

"Lisa is back! The heroine of *Method 15/33* is all grown up and kick-ass cool. And in *Viebury Grove*, Lisa is on a mission—so hold on tight—you're in for a hell of a ride. From the visceral and shocking opening to the final chapter, Kirk's writing has such energy, conviction and style, it's irresistible."
—Margaret Murphy, Dagger Award-Winning Author of *Weaving Shadows*

"It began with *Method 15/33* and now nearly two decades later this deeply disturbing and dark thriller series continues with *Viebury Grove*. A complex plot and excellent characterizations drive the story, and I promise you will not be able to put it down. An amazing series simply keeps getting better."
—D. P. Lyle, Award-Winning Author of the *Jake Longly* and *Cain/Harper* Thriller Series

"Shannon Kirk is an unstoppable talent. Gorgeous writing and risky storytelling combine in this darkly twisted and endlessly surprising tale of revenge delayed—but not denied. Timely, thought-provoking, and completely crazy-good original."
—Hank Phillippi Ryan, Nationally Bestselling Author of *The Murder List*

SENSITIVITY WARNING

Dear Readers, while in keeping with the *Method 15/33* theme of vigilante justice, please note that this book contains rape, violence against women, and human trafficking.

YOU DON'T KNOW WHAT I FEAR

I have a fear
Of untamed, unknown
I turn,
The hiding from truth,
Of senses, no, I will speak in code
The subdued touch, the tame sight,
The limits of sound, of taste,
I bear,
In defiance of-
Vacuums of space,
Dark holes of nothing
Unrelenting, vengeful fear
An eternity of zero worth

~SCK, 2/24/17

VIEBURY GROVE

BOOK II OF THE
METHOD 15/33 SERIES

SHANNON KIRK

14

CHAPTER ONE
A NEW CONDITION FOR LISA YYLAND
AGE 34

In this moment, I question who I am, if I stand, if I fly, if I crumble. I wonder if I'm nothing, perhaps only sound or light, something disconnected to what tethers me down to the ground. But this would not explain how I know I am holding her. So I try to focus. Try to turn off emotions that turned themselves on in shock.

Her blood drips from my fingers and forms webs in the V's at the joints. I've just removed my hands from the puddle she spilled—released from her back where the silent bullet exited.

Leaves carpet the earth: reds, oranges, burnt browns, yellows, the same colors matched in the still full canopy. We're in the height of fall, the season for leaf peepers. The air is hot, but perhaps the temperature I feel is from our run—the one cut short when the SUV turned the corner, looking like all the other luxury vehicles in this Massachusetts seaside village.

I relive the preceding minute in microscopic detail: a black SUV turned from Harbor Lane onto Beach Street, the back, tinted window, driver's side, rolled down, and I looked to my running companion, the woman now on the ground, but who was a minute ago upright and jogging—she was clicking at a playlist on her iPhone. In the simple turn of my head to her and the shift of my eyes to her iPhone's screen, I must have missed seeing the nose of a gun point in her direction from the rolled-down window of the turning SUV. Next, without any sound associated with any cause, she collapsed back-side-wards—like a dying giraffe. As the SUV accelerated out of town, her iPhone rolled and is somewhere under an out-of-bloom hydrangea bush, which happens to be scraping my Achilles right now. I'd set the security mode on her iPhone to three minutes when I gave it to her last Christmas: meaning, three minutes until a password is required. It's been two minutes since she last pressed a button, assuming I've correctly calibrated the timing in my shock.

I need her phone. Can't let cops, can't let anyone, seize it when they come.

I missed getting the license plate number of her murderer. An unforgivable mistake. *Would they be so stupid to have traceable plates? Maybe I missed nothing.*

The front of her holds no evidence of a bullet. It is her open back. Her open back on the gravel of this running path. I dropped to my knees, only two minutes ago, pushed her on her side, saw pebbles in the wound, and rocked her into my arms, hyperventilating myself into a literal breathtaking confusion. Nearly all switches of emotions in my mind turned themselves on, without my permission. *Who is screaming?* I believe it is me.

The harbor is behind. Boat bells and boat traffic continue. The ducks in the inlet, low in low tide, waddle to high grass in the salt marsh, as if the world didn't stop spinning, as if Hell didn't ride into town and rain terror and judgment and merciless evil on me, on Mother dying on the ground with rocks stuck in her flesh, dirt rattling in her burst spine. I must turn emotions off and command my own mind, control this situation.

Perhaps I hear sirens. Perhaps a woman is racing to me from her own run; I believe she's in a pink tennis skirt. Closer now, bending in my face, her white visor atop white hair reads Saleo Country Club. She's yelling at me to "Relaaax," which does no good, does the opposite, by infuriating me. No amount of yelling could revive who lies limp in my arms. "Relaaax," she says again. "Relaaax, Relaaax, Relaaax." The way she says it, with her Boston accent, spreading out the "A" like *mayonnaaaise*, causes my eyelids to sink, my nostrils to flare. Her Saleo Country Club visor shades her black sunglasses.

Saleo requires club members to wear only white. She's in pink.

Saleo Country Club, ten minutes up the road, away from Fry Rock

Beach, to which we were running. Saleo, where CEO's, corporate execs, judges, certain politicians, and sycophants play golf and rule the world. This is how Mother has described Saleo, snarling through deriding adjectives the way she does. *Did.*

I need to focus. I need to not feel this. I need to turn emotions off. I need to set Mother down and grab her phone without anyone seeing.

Cars slam to skidding stops on my left side. A vintage Mercedes. A new BMW. Several Volvos and SUVs. An old Audi; I think of my son Vantaggio. Vanty is away at his first year of college, safe at Princeton with Sarge, the man I pay to protect him. Vanty's own Audi is in the student parking lot.

I'll call Vanty, no, I'll call Lenny, ask him to check on our son, our Vanty.

Wedding Park with its looping, tree-lined, stone-dust running path, baseball diamond, white rotunda, and jungle-gym borders the harbor on my right side. Nannies, who moments ago were gossiping on benches while children hurdled down slides, packs of fashion joggers, and an entire yoga class congregate on that side. Noises, murmurs, screams swirl with the colorful leaves into a kaleidoscope of blurred senses.

I fix my sight on one cloud. I have been through traumas before. I can go cold. *Go cold.* I count the bumps and bulges: 11 nodules of cumulus, not a speck of darkness, not a storm cloud. I could paint this cloud, first with a flesh underbelly, adding contours by way of whites and the lightest of light gray, perhaps an infinitesimal brushstroke of blue. Studying the pixels of bright colors around me, I fight every switch that turned itself on inside me. Fear, I push off. Anger, I jam shut. Hatred, sadness, grief, disbelief—all off. I go numb. I go dead inside. I cannot feel this for her.

None of this was supposed to happen. None of this was part of the plan. This is a massive deviation.

A tug on my sweatshirt string pulls me down, so I bend closer to her mouth, in which blood stains her perfect white teeth. When my ear reaches there, I hear her gurgle and choke on the loss of viscosity of life.

"Judge Rasper," Mother whispers between gags.

"What? Who?" I say, even though her words are as clear in my head as if I spoke them myself. I want confirmation, for I feel a new condition swelling in me. Feel the plan is being remapped to add an extra layer. My plan has been in the works for eighteen years: a plan to expose those at the very center of what happened to me eighteen years ago. And now I'm sure Mother snooped, got caught in my web, and will die for it.

"Judge Rasper," Mother says. "Connected to your kidnapping." She rolls her eyes into her head, which falls fast over the back of my forearm. Gone. *She is gone.* A storm of emotions overcome me again. I see nothing but white, and my throat, my lungs, burn from no oxygen. I must fight myself, I cannot spiral. I focus on painting the cloud. *The cloud, the cloud is my anchor.* I work all the emotional levers, again. *Again.* Hardest of all, but I manage with a straining force: Guilt, I turn off. This is my fault she's gone. Emotions all off.

I set her down.

I grab her iPhone in a magician's swipe.

Pink Skirt is a little too keen on watching how I stuff it in my sweatshirt's belly pocket.

CHAPTER TWO
LISA YYLAND: CRAZY

In one of the thousands of self-defense videos I've studied over the years, a bodyguard said that if someone is following you, act crazy. He suggested you talk to yourself, bang on things, bug-eye your eyes, talk in a southern accent to an invisible kitten on an invisible leash, whatever, anything to make yourself seem nuts. Sometimes, this bodyguard had said, "Crazy don't want nothing to do with no crazy." I asked Nana to clarify this further for me, given my lifelong unwillingness to keep emotions on and truly understand such nuances. Nana explained, "Acting crazy is action and words disassociated with the actions and words of others around you." That made more practical sense to me, and it's a method I'm going to employ right now. I'm thinking crazy might keep these onlookers and the woman in a pink skirt away from me.

I brush Mother's corpse cheek. I stand, each muscle, each joint, one at a time, like the relentless metal alien in *The Terminator* coming back to life, as a vessel. Mother's head flops from the rumble on the path as onlookers crowd around. Her cheek, her better profile side, embeds in the gravel.

I take a long intake of air through my nostrils, eyes closed.

All is off.

I am me again.

A red leaf pastes to the glue of her blood on the reinforced toe of my retrofit right Nike, the tip covering two prosthetic toes. The

19

'relaaax' woman in the pink skirt is leaning in on me; maybe she's a nurse because she's the only one in the forming crowd not cowering or crying or screaming or punching a smartphone for 911.

"Honey, I need you to walk with me now. Walk here, breathe," Pink Skirt is saying. She's got a medical-type grip on my forearm, the kind that says *I will treat you* while also saying *I'm in control.* But she will not control me.

I press as many buttons as I can on Mother's iPhone in my sweatshirt pocket, even though only ten seconds have passed since I last revived her bytes. I am becoming increasingly cognizant of an urgent need to hack into her phone and read her emails, breach her home office and read her lawyer notes, and find whatever information she has on this Judge Rasper and how he's connected to her murder and what happened to me when I was sixteen.

Pink Skirt's grip is now too firm, too in control. I scan her face: mole on left temple, white hair, hairline thicker and farther forward than on most women her age. *A white wig?* Hard to tell under the pressing of her white Saleo visor. She's late forties, wrinkly nose, dripping dollops of cellulite on her arms where a true tennis player's biceps and triceps would be defined—hers are more like the scoops of penuche fudge Nana ladles with her wooden spoon. Her outfit is professional, looks new. While keeping one hand gripping my right arm, she sets her racket on the ground, taking care to toe kick the handle so the butt end faces me, and Mother on the ground behind me.

I twist from Pink Skirt's grasp and unclip and swish my long— nearly touching my tailbone—and extra thick—aided by a woven-in-place synthetic tuft—hair in slow swings, showcasing the shine and heft of my do. I'm swishing my real and fake hair, as if this is the crazy purpose for this whole event: a chance for me to show off my locks down at the harbor. But this is not the purpose of my synthetic hair.

I speak without making eye contact with anyone, sending a disconnected gaze to spaces between screaming people. "Can someone see to it that Mother cleans up her wound, give her a Band-Aid, and send her home," I say in a cool cadence. I open my eyes wide to that one unstormy cloud above, while trotting backwards out of the throng, away from Mother's body. "Please, now, Mother hates a mess. Let's help her clean up."

Read emails on Mother's phone. Get to her notes in her home office.

Two men in golf shirts reach for my arms, hold me in place, even though I'm covered in blood. I shake them off. While distracted by the men, and too consumed in playing crazy, Pink Skirt swoops in and drags me away. In a second, she is able to hold me firm, pushing me up against the wide trunk of an old tree.

"Call an ambulance. She's in shock. I'll hold her here," she calls back to the crowd.

Get your shit together, stop miscalculating, control this. No grief.

She locks both of her elbows. With her arms straight, she presses me into the trunk by holding me at the wrists. Bark of the oak is rough through my sweatshirt, and she's got me pinned, her body weight leaning into the press. I believe she may be trained in subduing people, because she's eliminated the use of my hands and my ability to reach her head, where I need to get to disable and control her.

I catch her eyes. We stare. She smirks. Nobody else can see her smirk. She whispers,

"Give me your mother's phone, Lisa, and tell me where all her notes are, and we won't touch Vanty."

Now I know I will hurt her.

She looks down to my sweatshirt pocket. "Now," she says, indicating Mother's phone. But she'll have to release her grip on my wrists to take the phone or allow me to hand it to her. I see her hesitate, considering me.

Sirens are definitely starting at the station.

It is futile to use my strength to fight to free my arms. Instead, I knee her crotch, so as to disrupt her balance. When she pops her ass back and bends her elbows, I rotate my arms in her wrists, breaking the grip at the thumbs, her weak spots. With my arms free, in one quick swoop, I knock off her sunglasses and visor, slam my palms to the sides of her face, jam thumbs in her eyes, and claw my fingers into the hard cartilage of her ears. Nails digging.

Now I own her. I twist her head, which will go where I direct so long as I have my thumbs in her eyes. I push her back; she stumbles and falls.

I run.

I'm past Mother's body by several yards now, rising up the hill that leads to her house.

Although I'm trained in several martial arts in anticipation of the plan I'm in Massachusetts to execute, I recall how Mother used to make me watch self-defense videos after I was kidnapped. The building blocks of my maternal lessons have been contoured by what to avoid, what to fight, what is ugly, how to plan, and the supremacy of efficiency. These have been valuable lessons.

Valuable lessons.

Thank you, Mother.

I pause at the top of the hill across from the park and note how Pink Skirt has crawled to her racket. She covers her mouth while talking on a cellphone; the web of her racket is tucked under her arm, the handle definitely pointed toward me.

The crowd swivels their heads to watch me, then her, then me. Pink Skirt watches from under the sunglasses she must have jammed back on her face while she crawled. She's pointing further up the road in my direction—like she knows where I'm headed. I take out Mother's iPhone, press camera, zoom in, snap. Beyond the crowd, past the harbor, and since I'm on higher ground, I see the blue and red roof bars on cop cars alight at the station house. They're coming.

I got to go. Go. Get Mother's notes.

CHAPTER THREE
LISA YYLAND: MOTHER'S NOTES

No doubt Nana would stop me and caution that a normal person would be suffering several confusing layers of emotional deterrents over what just happened. At age thirty-four, I have been a student of her instructions enough times to understand this much. But I haven't got time for humanistic lessons now. Girls' lives are at stake. This plan has a critical timing component. If we want to save a house of human trafficking victims, subject to the worst kinds of torture, and also capture their captors and their powerful customers, we must execute my plan over the course of the next two days. This ring of monsters is indeed connected to the small ring of fools who kidnapped me. And that connection is the thread I've picked and pulled since I freed myself to get to where we are now. I've spent eighteen years finding clues for the who, the what, the when, and the where, and eighteen years acquiring assets to trap them all in the act, allowing them zero legal wiggle room for denials or defenses. How Mother got herself involved, found this Judge Rasper—who she says is connected—I have no clue.

But nothing is going to stop me. Not Mother's murder. Certainly not emotions. Nothing. Because we will not get another chance.

I sprint down a trailhead through the woods that will empty on a street, closer to Mother's house. My father won't be there. He's been a *dear departed* for one year. An emotional stew is boiling in the back of my mind when I consider all this, feels like swirling in my cerebellum, bees in my temporal lobes. But I kill all this violent head energy and increase my running pace.

Mother's Audi is parked in the driveway. I wish her license plate wasn't so damn memorable: SHARKK. Anyone could follow her, find her with a plate like that. Anyone could have seen me driving it last week. I re-clip my real and fake hair into a loose twist, taking care not to yank on the thicker and fake strands at the base of my neck. I scowl at the SHARKK license plate.

Progressing to the back of Mother's granite home with the cathedral-ceiling kitchen and an office in a turret, I smooth a hand over my re-clipped hair. I ignore the sight of blood staining the chest of my sweatshirt, the reinforced tips of my Nike's, and the tops of my shins. Mother's blood, not mine.

Mother lives here, *lived here*, with her maid-chef, a polish woman in her late thirties: Barbara. Barbara's staff quarters are in the carriage house out back, beside the garage, which I see now as I circle Mother's house down the driveway and enter her backyard, heading for the rear mudroom. Salty air wafts over the hill as if it followed me, reminding me of the proximity of the sea.

Barbara is dead, gunshot through the posterior scapular region of her thorax, the heart side. She is crumpled on the steps of the back porch—arms up over her head: the telltale signs of execution. I sort of expected this on my run from the harbor. I'd had a faint hope they'd leave Barb be. And of course, no. I focus on the gray-blackness of the slate tiles, the dustless corners, and the angles of light cross-hatching the foyer. I do not look at Barbara.

Execute the plan. Don't fail like you failed to save Dorothy all those years ago.

The back door is open. I step over Barb's body. The house alarms are not blaring; the intruder must have made her punch the code at gun point.

Mother's cat, Vanessa, is arched and hissing toward the spiral stairs that lead from the kitchen to the right-wing basement, which tells me Barbara's murderer is still within. I note, too, a footprint larger than mine, Mother's, and Barb's. The footprint is fading in a sunspot on the foyer's slate floor. One footprint, barely visible, but fresh, perhaps minutes old. Size: Men's 11, likely boot, likely black.

I don't have time to deal with this murderer; he is obviously here looking for the same information I must find. Whatever Mother stumbled upon, these monsters want it erased from the planet, from Mother's mind, her phone, and her notes. I need to find those notes before the cops get involved and wreck things. I'm unsure who in law enforcement is involved—we know some are but not their identities—in the scheme we hope to unravel. We, myself and my small team.

I slide over to a doorless mudroom off the foyer, to a bank of security monitors I insisted Mother install last year. I study all the screens, which show every room in the house. *Cornered murderer, trapped himself in Mother's basement laundry room.* He's frozen, appears to be listening. I assume he heard me enter. I press the house speaker.

"Drop your weapon. The house is surrounded. Do not move," I say.

He mutters something, but there's no sound on these monitors. He bangs a gun on his thigh. He is stupid.

Sirens grow louder the longer time passes.

"Put your fucking gun on the dryer now, Asshole!" I shout into the speaker.

He does as told, holding his arms up in the air and walking backwards.

"Freeze. Do not move another inch!"

I look out through the back door. Barb is lumped and lifeless. Although I should, I do not have time to disable and punish her stupid asshole murderer. He hasn't moved. Still in the laundry room believing he's trapped. I figure I have four minutes to find what I need. The cops will figure out who Mother is and where she lives, how I twisted Pink Skirt's head and ran here, soon enough. I should have snapped her neck.

On my way up to Mother's turret office, I pull off my bloody clothes and kick off my bloody shoes. My prosthetic toes are secure and can tolerate less reinforcement. Along the way, I gather from Barbara's laundry basket, which she'd set on a coffee table, a folded gray T-shirt that reads "NOPE," my SEVEN jeans, and a towel. I wipe blood from my legs, throw the towel to a corner, and change as I walk. Mother's gardening Keds become my shoes. I slip into them, tie, and climb the stairs.

Mother's office is a total wreck. Mr. Stupid Asshole in the laundry room tried here first, but didn't find what he needed. And of course he didn't, he wouldn't know how Mother documents her thoughts and findings in a series of notebooks she designed to look like old books. On the walls of her office are floor-to-ceiling shelves of what appear to be volumes of historical English law, but really include, intermixed amongst real books, her years of notes. She wanted it this way because, as she said in the past, "The confidentiality of what I do must be obscured, even to myself, sometimes. And so in books, and in front of me always, my clients' confidences and my thoughts about them will be hidden in plain sight. And don't you, Lisa, don't you ever think to touch any one of them. Attorney-client privilege must be respected."

Mother could be rather severe like this. But she's dead now, so it would be impractical to follow rules that no longer apply, to me.

Stupid Asshole pulled a couple of decoy books from the shelves, saw they held nothing but old world font of legalese, not Mother's handwriting, and moved on.

I grab the last three books, following Mother's coded dating convention, which she scripted in white cursive on the binding of each volume. From one, a thin, paper moleskin notebook falls out. Speed scanning the last few weeks of her handwriting in it, I see the names "Velada" and "Mariana Church" and "Judge Rasper" and "Dentist" or short-hand for them all, "V" and "Mariana" and "J.R." and "Dentist", but often written on the same page. I don't have time to read all the actual entries. I know enough. "Velada" and "Mariana Church" tell me she stumbled on the hive that is part of my plan. But this "Judge Rasper" is new information. And I have no idea what the "Dentist" refers to.

I'll figure out Rasper's role and this "Dentist" from the inside. Stay on course. Execute the plan. We'll start today. Early. Control from the inside.

My own iPhone is in a locked safe in my bedroom in the right wing, the other side of the house, back by the kitchen. I pick up Mother's cordless to dial the cell of the retired FBI agent I have working at my consulting firm—who happens to be the same man who helped me save me eighteen years ago. Special Agent Roger Liu. As I'm dialing, I read a Post-it taped to Mother's computer of all her passwords.

"Liu," he answers. If he were at our home office in Indiana, he would have answered, "15/33, Inc."

"Listen," I say, as I rip up the Post-it of passwords. "Mother found or heard of Velada. Mother's been shot. Dead. Mariana Church is in her notebook. Something about a Judge Rasper and a dentist..."

Pounding on the stairs interrupts me. The room I'm in shakes with the vibration, for this is the old side of the house. I drop the cordless on the desk and Mother's moleskin on a cushy, swivel armchair and brace myself. Mother's iPhone is now in my jean's back pocket.

I look up to watch Stupid Asshole climb the stairs.

I swivel the chair so the cushion holding the notebook faces me. The back of the chair faces the door, where Asshole now stands, barring my exit. Behind me is a closed window, but at twenty feet up, I'm in the range of risk for serious injury or death if I jump; my Keds are not shock absorbent, and there are no exterior ledges to allow for a proper parkour to the ground. Asshole is a foot and a half taller than me.

Liu's voice yells from the desk cordless, "Lisa, what is going on? Lisa...fuck...Lisa..."

"Notes now," Asshole says, stepping into the office, passing under the pull-up bar in the doorway, and towards the chair. He walks with caution, his arms raised and combat ready. He must have been briefed about me; he works for the same people who mean to take me captive again tomorrow to use me in their sick house of horrors as another trafficked victim. *I believe* they don't know I know that or that I have a trap for their trap.

I watch his gait. He's left foot dominant and four steps from the chair.

I spin the cushion side with the notes to him.

"Here," I say.

He startles and pauses.

"Go, take them."

As he bends, I spin the cushion back to face me and grab and cram the notebook down the front of my jeans. I jump atop the cushion and jump again to straddle his shoulders, my pelvis in his face. While choking him with my thighs, I lean over his head, utilizing the momentum of my forward jump, such that his top half bends backwards, and now his stance is disrupted—these are simple physics.

I reach and grasp the doorway pull-up bar as he falls backward to the floor. I remain hanging; he lays beneath me, half in the stairwell landing, and half in Mother's office. I aim my feet for his face and jump down. All 117 pounds of hard me land on his nose, eyes, and mouth. I pop off and head for the stairs.

But I underestimate him. I thought, like Pink Skirt, he'd send his attention to his face pain, be distracted by it. But he doesn't even wince, doesn't raise a hand to touch his broken nose, his bleeding lips. He absorbs the injuries by ignoring them, stomach crunches, and pops to his feet. The cracking of his black boots and the creaking of Mother's wood floors echo around the blue walls of the open stairwell. Before I can escape, he pulls his gun and clocks me in a temple. Now I'm the one on the floor and sounds ring, bees return in my brain, stars blast in my eyes. A distorted and wavy vision tells me he's raising a boot, aiming to stomp me in the sore spot where his gun hit. And while I do have an instinct to touch my own pain, curl into it as if it would lessen the pulsing, I think of Sarge's chief lesson: *Your pain is your opponent's asset. Don't give your opponent assets.* It was the third time Sarge broke my nose when I stopped flinching. So I don't flinch. I don't comfort myself. I roll.

Sirens now fill the stairwell and the world outside. There is shouting down below, and running feet. I've rolled myself to the top of the stairs, and Asshole charges, his gun raised, like he's about to clock me again.

"Freeze," I hear at the base of the stairs. "Drop your weapon!"

I know if I move, this cop won't know what the fuck is going on, so I freeze too.

We're off plan now.

A rage is brewing and I'm trying to tamp it down. *Deal with this deviation.*

Don't fail like you failed Dorothy. Don't.

28

CHAPTER FOUR
LISA YYLAND: POLICE STATION

The East Hanson police station is housed in the same building as Town Hall. The entire town's governance is here, and it looks nothing like a place for governmental transactions or law enforcement. It reminds me instead of the southern plantations down by Nana's in Savannah—a white brick rectangle with white pillars and a grand porch. Big, fat ferns hang from eyehooks. The location shares the village's parking lot with users of the boat ramp. The boat ramp empties into an inlet, which holds rows of slips for Boston Whalers and speedboats. Out beyond the inlet and past a channel, over which a commuter train runs, is the harbor, where million dollar yachts and sailboats are anchored.

Mother's body is in the park adjacent the harbor. Her body likely under a white sheet by now. I stare out an open window in the Police Chief's office in that direction, waiting for the chief to finish reading a stack of internet printouts.

Naturally, my sub-par human eyesight can't travel beyond the inlet, through the bridge-covered channel, can't pierce the sails on the sailboats in the harbor, nor laser through all the trees in the park to Mother. But I do envision her body under a white sheet.

"Lisa…"

I picture a fold in the fabric over her toes.

"Lisa…"

Crawling my imagined vision over her body, I notice how the

29

white sheet doesn't move in or out on her face with her breath, breath that is absent.

"Lisa…"

The chief coughs to take my attention away from the window. Her name is Castile. I turn to face her, and she purses her lips.

"I'm sorry, Lisa. This must be hard," Chief Castile says.

This is a wealthy village's police station in a grand plantation-style building by the sea. There are no windowless interrogation rooms; there is no need. The station's one cell holds the Asshole who killed Barbara, but normally it is reserved for station-house card games. That's the information I gathered, listening to everyone squawking beyond the chief's office, while I wait for Castile to finish reading Google searches someone ran on me. Most of Castile's force and the State Police are at Mother's or the harbor, working the crime scenes. Chief Castile took it upon herself to speak with me, here, as the main witness and only living victim.

So here we go. Questions and no answers time.

She's looking at me, and I wonder how experienced she could possibly be in murder investigations working in seaside East Hanson. And even though I have a high degree of confidence that her professional life is tame and innocent and restricted to answering calls about tourists trespassing on private beach properties, I don't have verified and irrefutable proof that I can trust her or the people who have access to her files, so I won't divulge any relevant facts.

The taste of salt and the smell of low tide fills the room. A grayish seagull, who looks mangy compared to the ones swooping in the inlet, lands on Castile's windowsill. The bird looks like he's aiming for Castile's impractical sandwich, which has an inch of lettuce and two inches of meat. Castile stands, shoo's the bird, and slams the window shut.

"Vulture," she says, smiling at me. "That guy is always trying to take my lunch."

I look at a cabinet behind Castile in which Castile locked Mother's iPhone, which some cop sealed in an evidence bag on Mother's second-floor landing: it had fallen out of my pocket, right there between me and Laundry Room Asshole. Since Mother kept a sticker with her name and office number on the back, I couldn't claim it was mine. Mother's thin notebook is still in the front of my pants, beneath my "NOPE" T-shirt. I need that phone back. I believe Castile punched 8933 on the lock when she walked me in here and sat me in her guest chair, but I could be off a digit...or four.

Before the police corralled us out of Mother's house, Liu stopped yelling from the office phone at some point, and I trust started listening. "I am a victim," I kept saying to the officers who were cuffing the asshole and bagging Mother's phone. But since the cops didn't know what was going on, and they'd heard reports of me clawing Pink Skirt, who had fled the scene soon after I did, they didn't cuff or arrest me. They didn't search me either, but they contained me and asked that I answer questions at the station. It's faster to comply sometimes, so here I am.

"Did Boston call back yet? I want to make sure we get this phone to the right people for a forensic analysis. ASAP," Castile yells from her chair to someone outside her office.

"Not yet, Chief," some woman yells back.

"You don't need forensics on that phone," I say.

"Excuse me?"

"A forensic analysis isn't going to tell you what you need to know. It's unnecessary."

Castile bends over her desk, cups her chin, appraising me. The creases of the crow lines around her eyes are lighter, the rest of her skin tanned. Every part of her body, including her face, is muscled. The wall behind her, against which her evidence locker stands, is busy with certificates, a few degrees, a three-foot decorative surfboard painted orange, and in the center, a championship biathlon plaque—first place for sharpshooting while skiing. Her credenza is cluttered with framed pictures of a boy in various sports poses: soccer, paddleboarding, skiing, basketball, some with her arm hanging around his shoulder. All of his sports jerseys say he's #33. The images of them in various uniforms and sporting attire form a rainbow. Castile and her son could be me and Vanty, except her son's dull hazel eyes are not as brilliant as Vanty's blue crystals. Castile's gun is strapped to her chest.

I keep my palms flat on uncrossed legs, posture straight, sitting in the hard wooden chair on the guest side of her desk.

"Right. Right, right, right. You're the expert, actually, on all things forensic. And I know you know I don't mean that sarcastically, Lisa.

31

You do own one of the more renowned, and private, forensic labs in the country," Castile says while picking up the pages of internet printouts she's been reading.

"My company doesn't offer computer forensics. We mainly do physics and biology consulting, sometimes metallurgy and chemistry, for law enforcement and private companies. But I know you don't need forensics on that phone."

Normally I wouldn't talk this much or deliver lessons like this. But I have to find a way to stop her from sending Mother's phone off and out of my sight. I'm positive Liu is on his way, and I must be prepared to extricate myself and Mother's phone as soon as he gets here. I'm thankful in knowing that there are no photographs of Liu on the internet.

"Hmm," Castile says. She flips to another printout from Google. "A lot comes up when you search for Lisa Yyland. There's even a Wikipedia page. Says here you were kidnapped from your New Hampshire home at sixteen, while pregnant, and you escaped by killing your captor. The details of how you did that are pretty alarming, actually. Electrocution? Or was it drowning?"

Both.

"Hmm. I guess it doesn't matter, right? I suppose whatever you did makes sense since they planned on harvesting your son and selling him, right? I'd probably do the exact same thing, Lisa." She exhales a puff from her nose, taking a second to contemplate the rainbow of pictures of her son. "Yep. I'd do the damn same thing all right. Anyway," she says, turning back to me. "And then you led the FBI to arrest the rest of the gang. That all true?"

"Yes."

She goes back to reading, flipping through the pages.

"Chief," I say.

"One sec. Says here, another girl, Dorothy Salucci, didn't make it out."

Dorothy didn't make it out because I failed to save her in time.

"And now you own the building they held you both in. Wow. That's where your firm is. A former abandoned schoolhouse in Indiana you bought at a seizure auction. That right?"

"Yes. Chief, again, you don't need forensics on my mother's phone."

She sets the pages down. "So if I don't need forensics, tell me what I do need."

"A forensic analysis would mean you were seeking fragmented or deleted inactive data or metadata on the phone."

"But I need a forensic image in order to see any content, live or fragmented, so that we can maintain chain of custody and authenticate content."

Fine.

"But if what you want is to find her killer fast, all you really need is the password so that you can access her live email and text accounts. Her contacts, too."

"Do you have the password?"

Of course I have the password.

"That's my mother's password, not mine. You know she's a lawyer, right? At Stokes & Crane in Boston. I'm pretty sure all of her emails and texts, as well as her written notes, are protected by the attorney-client privilege."

"That doesn't apply. She, and I'm sorry, but Lisa, she is…"

Dead.

"Attorney-client privilege belongs to her clients, not to her. You should check with her firm Stokes & Crane first." A delay from a legal battle on rightful access is my backup. Just so long as nobody looks at Mother's notes within the next two days.

"This is a criminal investigation, Lisa. I'm sure those rules no longer apply."

I shrug. I could debate this with her to prolong the conversation, fight her with emotions and demand she respect my dead mother. I consider whether I should fabricate some tears.

Castile watches me, seemingly looking for some movement on my face. "Oh right," she says. "That's right." She sucks in her lips, picks up another printed internet page, scanning for whatever reference she's just remembered. "Right. The papers called you 'Terror Teen.' I'm sorry, sorry. But, they did, right? Says you can't experience emotions. At least, that's what the psychologist testified at one of the court hearings."

Wrong. The psychiatrist, not psychologist, testified I have a rare ability to choose emotions, or not choose emotions. Inability and choice are very different things. I most often do not choose emotions, because they disable and delay me.

Most emotions cause inefficiency.

"I would like to make two phone calls," I say.

She stretches her chin and circles her head. Her blonde ponytail swings. Her mouth is straight, and her eyes squinted.

"Two calls?"

"Yes. You haven't placed me under arrest."

"No, you're not under arrest. Right, right, right. But we'd like to ask you a number of questions here, Lisa. Maybe you're in shock still? Like I said before, I think we should call the paramedics down for you. They're just upstairs."

"No. I'll use your phone. You can watch through your glass door." I nod to her door as my direction for her to leave.

Castile scratches under her right eye. "Okay, then. Okay. If you're willing to stay here and talk, I suppose two calls are in order. Fine."

She stands and rounds her desk, passing me. I don't move, staring at the phone until she's gone. Out of the corner of my eye, I can see her standing outside the glass, watching. Whether this line is recorded will not matter in the immediate future.

Liu must have been waiting for my call on his untraceable burner, because he answers after one ring.

"What the hell is going on?" he says.

"East Hanson police station. They have Mother's phone. This hurts the plan."

"Fucking hell, the plan is done. Your mother was shot. Stop this shit. Sit tight. We're almost there. Five minutes."

We're: Liu and Lola.

Lola, which is not her real name, is the other agent who helped me save me eighteen years ago, and thankfully there are also no pictures of her on the internet or anywhere. She's not retired and working as a consultant like Liu, and the faction of law enforcement she does work for is confidential. We generally call it the Beta Agency, just to have something to call it.

"Get here. I'm going in early."

I make my second call. When I'm done, I turn to the glass door and indicate that Castile may come back in her office.

As she enters, a coffee mug now in her hands, she says, "Did you want coffee? We have that Keurig stuff, the capsule thingies, so it's no trouble. Hazelnut? Vanilla? Donut House? Decaf? Nantucket

Blend? What can I get you?"

"What are your questions?"

"Okay, then. No coffee."

She takes her seat again, and just as she settles herself, clasping her hands on top of her desk and hunching her shoulders so as to appear submissive—I know this technique, I've studied it—a woman barges in.

"Chief, some lawyer who says he's managing partner at Stokes & Crane is on the phone. He says he just got a call from here about the woman's phone. Says you need to speak with him before you look at anything. He's threatening to go to court to get an injunction."

Castile stares at me; I stare back.

"Two calls, eh?" she says, and bites her bottom lip the way my husband Lenny does when he says he's "frustrated" with me.

I continue staring.

"Chief, you better hurry. Sounds like other Stokes' lawyers are calling on other lines, too," the woman says, looking over her shoulder. "What's that?"

A man's voice is saying something to this woman in Castile's doorway, something about going to Boston.

"Chief already told you to get the chain of custody forms. Get those. I'll tell her," the woman says. And turning back to the chief, "They say to bring it all to the forensic lab on Clarendon. But what about these lawyers?" Turning away again, she says, "What? ...I don't know." Looking back to the chief, "Chief, where are the chain of custody forms?"

"Dammit," Castile says while hitting her desk. "Tell the Stokes' lawyer to hold on. Nobody takes this phone without the forms getting filled out. Dammit. The forms...forget it. Lisa, sit tight. I'll be right back."

Woman is dealing with amateurs. But this is the chaos I need.

As Castile rises to leave once again, I actually wish I could tell her everything. I wish I could trust her and trust that nobody would access her files. I wish she could help us ensnare the core of the group of people who led to my kidnapping and their awful customers, and help me free their current victims.

Castile could never understand, or believe, just how demented these monsters are and the horrible lengths to which they go to harm girls in order to sate their freakish desires. Maybe if I could tell her, she'd understand why I had to plan in such strict secrecy to bring them down by catching them in the act. Maybe she'd understand how dangerous it is for girls in active captivity to keep me trapped here with her. But I can't take a chance on Castile. I have no time to validate her innocence or ability to keep a secret.

CHAPTER FIVE
LISA & VELADA

Sure, I electrocuted and drowned my and Dorothy Salucci's jailer and imprisoned his twin brother, an incompetent doctor, and other pond scum accomplices long ago. But what I've never revealed to anyone, except Liu and Lola, was something someone said to me in the courthouse parking lot the evening I testified against the doctor.

There's more to the story that started eighteen years ago.

Nana says that sometimes in life you might shiver at the eeriness of how the universe throws mirrors in your path. Like the world, like life, like some all-being Creator is saying: *Look at this other person. This is how you seem to the world.* I never understood what she meant by this until I met Velada.

It was 1993, six months after I escaped. I was back in Indiana from our New Hampshire home to testify against the asshole-loser doctor. As it was winter in Indiana, the sky was cold, gray and dense, about to burst and bleed freezing pricks of ice-rain. Alone, I weaved through the cars in the courthouse parking lot, making my way to Mother's rental BMW. She'd be inside for another half-hour with the prosecution team, going over the completed testimony and the plan for the next day. I was drained from a day of direct and cross and re-direct examination.

Footsteps crunched the winter layer of salt and dirt on the lot's tar behind me, and since I was on high alert of being taken again, I broke into a sprint before turning to see who it was.

"Stop," called a female voice.

I kept going, weaving two rows over to avoid passing a green van. Indiana plate, number 677854. I'd learned the hard way to register such things on vans.

I stopped and turned and what I saw was no *physical* threat. A young woman, dressed in black, approached. At first, I didn't notice her feet. Gaging by where her head hit on the van, I measured her at five-feet-flat, about 100 pounds. Inches and pounds less than teenage, post-natal me. She walked in all-knowing, heartbeat steps. Estimating her at just over the edge of twenty, I inventoried her black hair, giant blue eyes, and thin, straight arms. Up closer, those arms became the muscled arms of a bat without the wing membrane; a perfect ball of bicep poked out each side of her black-cloaked arms, stretching through the tightness of her long-sleeve T-shirt. Skinny but muscled, no fat. A compact, efficient, lean machine. According to a *LiveScience* article, bats are more efficient than birds. So I should love the bat. I should revere the bat.

Something specific about her captivated me.

When I was in captivity, there were a couple of times when I swear a black butterfly fluttered in the pane of a high triangular window in my locked room. In times of weakness, when I succumbed to emotions and could not switch them off, I imagined this butterfly a savior. But I'm sure now, although I am confident my vision of the butterfly was real, the thought she was a savior was born out of the delusion that comes from solitary confinement. There's a medical term for it: Prison Psychosis.

This bat girl with the serial killer gait had a black butterfly tattooed on the space of her right hand between thumb and index finger.

"You're the girl who killed Ronald Rice and saved Dorothy, before she died," she said. Her affect was flat, her emotions drained.

"Yes," I said. Our bodies were still one foot apart. I was a few inches taller, even though I was a few years younger. I ticked my eyes a half-second on her black butterfly tattoo.

"I've been watching the trial. I wore a wig and sat behind the reporters, so you probably don't recognize me," she said, again in a monotone.

"I don't."

I made a note to correct this error in observation.

"You did it all on your own? Killed Rice, testified like you did today to nail the doctor?"

"Correct."

"I know you lied under oath. But you lied so he wouldn't get away with it."

I said nothing. Stared. Bat Girl had started a chess match with me.

"Then you're the only one I can trust," she said.

"Likely true." I have no cause for deceptions, no use for emotions, most of the time. I lie to my family about certain things to keep them safe. And I might have lied under oath against the doctor, but for the greater good. Most always, I tell it like it is.

Tiny Bat Girl with a big dipper of freckles on her forehead and a black butterfly tattoo on her hand, looked to her left and to her right, affirming we were alone. "You pissed off someone at the center of all this. He calls himself Eminence, and he tagged you. You'll be dealt with, he says, on his next visit to the U.S. I don't know when. It will be years, I know that at least, but I don't know how many. I'm trying to figure the timing out. For you. And for me. You ruined a source of Eminence's income by shutting down this little ring that steals and sells blonde babies. Eminence says you'll repay, and so you are tagged. My source is still on the inside. I've been trying to figure out how to expose or kill Eminence for what he did to me ever since I got out. I think, if you and I work together, we can get him."

"When did you get that butterfly tattoo?" I asked.

"What?"

"If you've been watching me, you've read the interview where I mentioned a black butterfly. Maybe you got the tattoo to ingratiate yourself with me, and you're here to lure me into some trap."

"I just like butterflies. Okay?"

"Possibly."

I wondered in that Indiana parking lot whether Bat Girl was lying about why she got the butterfly tattoo. While she didn't look up and to the left—the chief sign of a liar *creating* an answer, according to body language books—and her forehead didn't crease, she did focus a no-blink stare, as if forcing me to believe her.

"Besides, and I did read the article you're talking about, it wasn't a butterfly you think you saw in that room they held you in. Here in Indiana, the biosphere suggests that it more likely was a moth," Bat

Girl said.

She knows what a biosphere is.

"It was a butterfly," I said, because I needed it to be a butterfly. I needed to be correct. Precise about this.

"Yeah, well, you're the scientist, right?"

"I am a student."

"Look. If you want to be ready for Eminence, if you want to bring down the Center Ring, get real revenge for Dorothy, we need to work together." She reached around to her back pocket and extracted a forest green lighter and a single cigarette. As she worked the lighter and inhaled, which I considered rank rude—she should have finished her thought and not subjected me to second-hand smoke—she continued, "Are you listening? This is important. We need to work together."

"I don't work with other people."

"Neither do fucking I. You know." She paused to exhale. I held my breath to block her mouth smoke. "I'm sure you think you're rough as shit getting away from them. But they fed you, right? Didn't rape you, right? And you were held for just one month?"

"All of that is correct."

"So you have no idea what it means to be in the Lobster Tank."

"The what?"

The Lobster Tank: noted.

"You heard me. I have to go. I'm sure they've got people watching you now, and I've been exposed too long out here." She looked over her shoulder, then back at me, but kept her eyes low.

"The men who took you were like a subsidiary of a small but regnant corporation. Your guys wanted to deal in the kidnapping of only pregnant blonde girls, a very specific niche. But they had to pay a fee to the Center Ring, which runs a tight, but incredibly profitable, human trafficking operation that sells *experiences* to rich assholes. Powerful assholes. And these experiences are terrible. I was a Center Ring victim. I got away the night they put me in the Lobster Tank."

When she said Lobster Tank this time, she drew her eyes to her feet, indicating I should follow. In the cold of a December Indiana, she stood in flip flops. Raising one foot to a car's front bumper, she revealed burnt, wavy, puckered skin covering all toes, the forefoot, and up to her ankles. The natural length of her toes all lined up with the length of her big toe.

Keeping her foot in place, she continued, "They used me for their *experiences*, hooked me on heroin. And I've seen things you can't imagine. I need to take the Center Ring down, and especially Eminence. All I know is he comes in from Asia on some schedule, but I was too high while I was in to have anything but hazy details. Here's the plan for now, because it's all we got. I try to find a way back in with my source and I funnel you information when I can. It's going to take years. But we have to take them all down by catching them in the act, or it won't work. They're connected, have cops, judges, politicians, expensive lawyers to squirm them out of being pinned. You'll hear from me. But, be ready. You've been tagged. Be ready."

I cocked my head, replaying her words in my mind. She mistook me for questioning her.

"Did you hear me? Be ready." She inhaled a puff and exhaled particulates in a cancer cloud that hung in the cold air. I held my breath again.

Rude.

"Hello. You'll be ready, right?"

"Ready for what?"

"The Lobster Tank. You've been tagged. Hello? Are you listening? I don't remember much. I was fucked up. I remember my feet burning, and me somehow slipping away. So figure it out. Be ready."

"What is your name?"

"Velada is all you need to know."

And with that, Velada walked two rows over to the green van and entered. As she drove slowly past me, she stalled, rolled down her driver's window, and said in a taunt, "It wasn't a butterfly you saw. It was a moth. Be ready." She drove off, crushing her spent cigarette in an ashtray I couldn't see.

Next time get her cigarette for DNA testing.

Figure out the Lobster Tank. Be ready.

For a full two years thereafter, after the trial ended and we went back to life in New Hampshire, I battled with one persistent emotion: an enduring and debilitating love for Dorothy M. Salucci, the girl I failed to save. I worried I loved the butterfly, too—a being I might have wrongly identified—and so I feared the real possibility that I loved a mirage. *Did I really see a butterfly at all? Can we trust any of our human senses? Sight? Sound? Touch? Taste? Smell? Emotions?* In heightened episodes of trauma over these two enduring battles, love of Dorothy and fear of love for a wrongly-identified insect, I painted violent impressionist paintings in a birch grove behind our New Hampshire home.

But these traumas I too overcame, and grew more resilient at working my natural ability to switch off emotions and view everything as mere facts. In painting a weirdly-swirled birch tree one day, one with sad, melting, black eyes, I settled on a conclusion I could live with: *Love is a delusion.* And love does not dilute, it morphs and grows the more you allow it. Love does the opposite of dilution, love infests. Love is a nasty, virulent weed.

Who I thought I loved, I invented. Basically, I loved my own inventions. And inventions can, and should, evolve, be modified, reverse-engineered, retrofitted, re-defined, dismantled and rebuilt, and even destroyed. From that point forward, I controlled my inventions of love, because I realized love was a reflection on how I chose to view those around me, how I chose to interpret my world through human *senses.* Like what we see, hear, taste, touch, feel, and smell— our emotions are just our brains' models of perceptions. Our way of navigating the chaos.

I started focusing on figuring out the Lobster Tank full time. Thankfully, Special Agents Roger Liu and Lola had already begun running it down. Every minute since then, we've been gathering information and clues about what this Lobster Tank is, where it is, and when I was to be taken by Eminence. And I've been gathering assets so as to escape the Lobster Tank and trap the Center Ring and the very worst of their customers in the act, in one swoop. This is the plan. This is the team.

~~~

Now, eighteen years later in the East Hanson, Massachusetts police station, I think back to that time in the gray Indiana parking lot, Velada's butterfly tattoo, and her crazy, blue eyes drilling into me like she owned me. I wonder now how things would have played out for Mother had I said no, had I ignored Velada. Would Mother and her dogged ways have found clues about the Center Ring on her own? Did she find them on her own anyway? Her life was rocked to the core, she used to say, when I was kidnapped, and she often vowed to root out every "fucking demon" who ever had any hint of involvement in my kidnapping. She also devoted all of her *pro bono* time to human trafficking, all her free hours apart from her corporate litigation defense work. But I always considered her outbursts as no more than emotional fits with no merit; and I always assumed she, like everyone else, assumed we'd already strung the lot of them up. But with the words "Velada" and "Mariana Church" in her notes, my assumptions were wrong, and dangerous.

Outside of this office, Chief Castile is shouting on the phone with a lawyer from Mother's law firm. I hear a man's voice saying he has found the chain of custody forms and he's coming to grab Mother's phone from Castile's locker after he "hits the head." I rise, look out the window where the vulture seagull had perched, and see that Liu and Lola have arrived and are looking for a parking spot for their rented minivan.

I slide over to Castile's locker. I quickly press 8933—the numbers I thought I saw her press. Nothing happens.

I look around her office; the shouting in the station wanes. I have maybe two seconds to pop this lock. So I have one more try. That biathlon plaque, I'm closer to it, and it is obvious that it takes center place in her life, it being the most prominent item on her cluttered wall. She got the win in 1999. I look again at her son's sports jerseys: he's #33. I press 9933. Pop.

I'm sure she never realized how easy her passcode is—if someone were watching for it.

I grab Mother's phone in the sealed evidence bag, move toward the window, and along the way rip the top layer of bread from Castile's absurd sandwich.

I lift the window, step on a chair beneath it, climb out, and set the bread on the sill.

As I run to Liu and Lola, holding the notebook in my pants in place so it won't slither down, a green Prius pulls up behind them. Both cars are in one of the parking lot lanes. Mother's iPhone rings. I rip the evidence bag open.

While the Prius is behind Liu and Lola's minivan, it is offset, so I can see the driver. I'm staring at Pink Skirt, still in her pink uniform, but now with a brown wig and a stupid Red Sox hat. Mother's phone is still ringing.

Liu opens his driver's door, steps one foot out and stands, keeping one foot in. Lola doesn't move in the passenger seat; she's watching my every move. I place my finger on my lips to indicate they should not speak, but keep my gaze toward Pink Skirt.

I answer Mother's phone.

Liu doesn't turn, he's too frantic. I can tell by the way his forehead dances and his fingers skitter on the roof of the car. Lola still has not even shifted in her seat. Her face, her body, all blocks of gray.

"I have your son Vanty. Bring me those notes," Pink Skirt says in the phone.

Not only am I going to hurt this bitch, I'm going to maim this bitch for even threatening Vanty. She does not have Vanty. She can't.

I hang up, dial Sarge.

"Where's Vanty?" I ask as soon as I hear him answer.

"Right here with me. All is set."

"Move everyone to the spot," I say.

Sarge is in charge of making sure Lenny, Vanty, and Nana are secure while we're up here executing the plan. I will have to trust that he's doing his job; he's never failed me in the past. I had planned on securing Mother elsewhere, tonight.

The second I hang up, Mother's phone rings again; it's Pink Skirt again. "I will get Vanty. Notes, now."

Liu makes a hand signal: a V in his left hand, which he chops with his right. This is intended to indicate we're killing the plan. We had agreed that if any of the three of us took such a severe step, killing the plan, we would all agree. It was always intended in only the direst of circumstances.

Pink Skirt's face looks like a rat to me; she keeps saying, "Now, now," on the phone. I think of her saying these words in a different context, perhaps to young girls stowed in a windowless basement, as she commands them to undress for some customer paying for a sick *experience*. I hang up.

I still haven't collected critical assets: two tiny electronic discs from the lab my father set up long ago in Manchester, NH, that I planned on picking up tonight. (Also where I was going to store Mother.) I need these assets for the plan. If I ignore Liu, which would be a significant breach of our rules of engagement, could I get Pink Skirt to take me to my father's lab before what she thinks will be my confinement? I'm concerned. Concerned that with Mother's involvement and now murder, the Center Ring will cancel their own planned trap of me. I can't allow that. I can't allow eighteen years of planning to fail. I will force the early taking of me, force them to go forward with their own plan, so I can take them before Eminence returns to his hole back in "Asia." Also, I can't bear even the slightest risk of threat to Vanty. I have to go with Pink Skirt now.

Liu chops the V again; his chin is rising, teeth clenching, which I've seen him do a few times over the years when he's trying to curb spoken words.

A fluttering movement in the tree above catches my eye, and I watch as vulture seagull drops in a swoop to the chief's window. He grabs the bread on the sill and, given that the office must still be empty, enters.

I look to Lola. I believe she's reading my lips, noticing me looking beyond and behind their minivan. Lola, I can tell, is watching me decide whether our plan goes forward. In this moment, Lola is stalwart, hasn't blinked. She holds a chewed-to-the-nub finger in her teeth. I stare at her to indicate I need her answer, whether she agrees with Liu's killing of the plan.

She holds two fingers in a gun barrel up with her right hand, and at that, I run. In passing her passenger window, I say, nodding to the alley in the rear of the parking lot, "Alley, Vanty33. Pull hatch." To Liu, I say, "Secure Velada."

Commotion in the chief's office erupts; yelling from the chief is coiled with yelling from other voices, and a distinct cawing.

By the time I reach the back of the minivan, and only five feet from the Prius, Lola has reached over Liu's driver's seat and triggered the back hatch. I hold out for Pink Skirt to see Mother's phone, and also the notebook. I turn, reach into the minivan's back hatch, and work my magic. When I turn to face Pink Skirt, my hands are free.

I launch myself to her Prius.

"Drive," I say as I enter the passenger side.

I hold her arm to stall her as she rises to leave her own car to retrieve Mother's items from where she watched them disappear.

"Move it," I say. "Before they come out and see your car. Now!"

"Fuck!" she screams.

"Go, now!" I'm not giving her any seconds to consider me in this car or the items she saw disappear into the minivan.

She twists to look behind, jams into reverse, and guns the gas so we squeal backwards.

"You will die for this," she's muttering.

I roll down my window.

In a reverse doughnut, we swing toward the alley and she guns it again. I divert Pink Skirt's attention by pointing to the Knights of Columbus roof to our left at the mouth of the alley, and because she's fully immersed in the confusing endorphins flooding her brain in her choice to take flight, I keep saying, "sharpshooter." Meanwhile, my attention is fixed on a sub-alley between a dentist office in a rowhouse and a line of cypress on the right. My arms are outside my rolled-down window.

Once we're free and cruising out of town, Pink Skirt startles once she focuses on the fact that I'm in her car. I sense a fear in her, of me specifically, and especially my presence.

"So take me in, then. Isn't that the plan?" I say.

She's not prepared for this. She is not part of the goon brigade I know is scheduled to "surprise attack" and haul me in for torture tomorrow, but she is most definitely Center Ring. Perhaps Pink Skirt really doesn't have a clue I have an informant on the inside. Her right earlobe has half-moon cuts from when I grabbed her ears for handles down at the harbor; she rubs it.

"Cunt," she says. Her jaw clenches; her fingers shake.

The C word.

My right eye closes and trembles as though I just ate a sour candy; my whole body twitches.

I rehear the words she whispered when she held me to the oak, how intent she was to rid the world of Mother's thoughts and observations. I rehear the word *cunt.* I think of the torture Eminence has delivered to girls over the years, and those in current containment, his demented Lobster Tank, and how Pink Skirt is a part of all this. I relive her threatening to steal the only purpose for my life: my son. I think of Mother's body at the harbor, how her breath doesn't move a white sheet covering her corpse.

I turn hate on. I'm going to need hate for the remainder of the plan anyway. Sometimes hate delays me, clouds me. But most often it provides the added adrenaline I need to do what I do, and it sure served me well eighteen years ago.

I feel alive when I have hate on, like my blood boils in a useful heat, like my brain is electrified, but in an organized electricity, zapping along straight conduits on a precisely mapped circuit board. I feel like my senses are heightened. Like my eyes are crimson lasers. My auditory processing center a fine tuning fork, filtering out nonsense, grasping only what I need.

I side-eye Pink Skirt. Her red sunglasses are cheap, so I can see through the lenses when she looks at me. Her eyes are beady and squinted as she glares back.

You are going to suffer, bitch, and I will enjoy every fucking bloody minute of it.

CHAPTER SIX
FORMER SPECIAL AGENT ROGER LIU

Son of a bitch. Here we are in a fucking parking lot in East Hanson, Massachusetts, and some Chief of Police is yelling at me and Lola. We don't have time for any of this shit. I swallow three Prevacid OTCs. My throat is burning, and my heart is an erupting volcano.

Lola gave Lisa the gun barrel signal, the 'Go' sign. We're now committing total fucking obstruction of justice by denying seeing, with any reliable precision, what car just squealed out of here with Lisa—who obviously stole a very visible bag of evidence and left the empty bag in the grass. The chief's deputy fled out here three seconds too late for him to see himself. The deputy's black uniform shirt is untucked, his belly overhangs his belt, and his moppy hair flies in the sea breeze off the inlet. Lola's the one who said, "Oh my God, I think some kind of white Ford or something! This is so scary!" when the chief came running out.

Given all sorts of shit contingencies we have in the bag, I'm now Dakeel, an almost sixty-year-old, half-Vietnamese retiree, driving for Uber to fund bimonthly trips to Vegas; Lola is now Martha Tannhouse, my customer. And I know this because that's what fucking Lola said to greet the chief who froze us in place with her extended gun.

Look at Lola there, standing all square in her square gray pants and her square torso and her square head with gray hair and her square haircut. She's a pile of concrete blocks.

48

Son of a bitch.

"Chief, we don't know anything. My Uber driver was just dropping me off so I could rent a paddleboard at Phat Boards 'round the corner," Lola is saying. Lola offers the ID that claims she's Martha Tannhouse, a secretary at BetaAgency.Gov, which can be checked for false verification. I, too, am in some pre-planted phony employee database within Uber's cloud-based server farm. Many details can be implanted and hidden in the tangles of the cloud.

"Why did you open the hatch?" the chief demands.

"I was just trying to get my luggage. We saw that woman jump out of the window, it was very confusing. So crazy! Look in the whole car," Martha-Lola says. "Dakeel, let her look all over the car, okay?"

We're outside our shit minivan, so the chief walks towards the back hatch, which Lola, not I, had popped open for Lisa, right after Lola gave her the fucking 'Go' signal and they decided to fucking ignore me.

I say no words, pretending I don't speak English well.

This chief is not an imbecile. She's right to be suspicious. Look how we're dressed, me in gray pants, Lola in gray pants, and here we pull up right when Lisa jumps out a fucking window with stolen evidence. But right now I want to get out of here and onto whatever Lisa meant by "alley" and wherever Lisa sped off to, with God knows who.

"This is shady and I don't trust either of you," the chief says.

"Chief, a girl did jump out of that window there, and she was yelling to a car behind us. Really freaked us out. Right, Dakeel?" Lola says.

I nod.

The chief squints at Lola, appraising her, and I'm here dangling on the side like some slack-jawed loser, as if I'm not the senior member of this team. My stomach is a rock knot, and trying to think of my wife Sandra's soothing voice does nothing to calm the lava acid in my throat. Lola and her shit; she'll get Lisa killed, us jailed for obstruction of justice. And now the chief is delaying us. She continues looking through the back hatch, while I throw Lola all the anger I can through my eyes, which I'm trying to literally twist. Lola twitches her left nostril at me, but averts my eyes by a fraction. She's staring at my nose.

The chief looks in the spare wheel well, and I hold my breath. She's rooting around in there, pressing on the tire.

"Hmm," the chief says.

I can't believe eighteen years of planning, and now this. *Son of a fucking bitch.*

I look to Lola to indicate all of this is a total waste of time and if she had let me handle this, we'd be out of here and have Castile in our pocket helping. I say this entire tirade to Lola by the way I snarl my nose and shake my head.

"Martha. Martha, is it?" Castile says to Lola.

"Yeah," Lola answers.

"You fine with me opening your luggage?"

"All yours, Chief. Nothing exciting, I'm sorry to report."

The chief opens a black roller we have in the back. It's Lola's all right, but since she carries her badge in concealment, and right now her gun is strapped to her leg and hidden, I suspect all the chief will find are a couple sets of Lola's only uniform: white shirt, gray pants, white socks. Lord knows what the undergarments are. I don't care.

The chief abandons the search and trots back to us.

"Where are you staying? Your ID has you living in DC," she asks Lola. "And why was your Uber dropping you off here?"

"Four Seasons, downtown. I don't know why my Uber driver pulled in here. I just wanted to go to Phat Boards to rent a paddleboard. Maybe my driver wanted to park and use a bathroom somewhere? I don't know."

I stand like the dumb moron I've been assigned to play.

"I don't know what the hell is going on, but we'll need a statement from both of you. And your local addresses, numbers, all of it. I need you to come inside."

Walking inside, Lola slips me a ready ID for a Dakeel Rentower with an apartment address and landline in Lowell, Massachusetts. This is one of five backstories we have at the ready. It's been like this for decades working with Lola.

I speak up just as we are about to open a door to the station. In broken English, I say, "Girl tell woman to drive to mom house."

The chief raises an eyebrow at me, glares a beat, and then, with a mixture of urgency but also reluctance, demands her deputy take us inside to get our statements. Once he has us, she jogs to her own military-grade SUV. *Rich town.*

Inside, Lola and I double-team steamroll the deputy, Lola throwing half-baked legal jargon to avoid having to give over our own phones without a warrant, and pretending she's concerned about privacy, and insisting we're just innocent bystanders caught up in some "crazy ass shit."

A half fucking hour of this.

~~~

Now we're out and free. As we re-enter the minivan, I want to reach across this damn nasty rental and throttle Lola.

"Dammit. Fucking dammit. How could you? How could you?" I say, once we're pulling out of our parking space and heading into the alley. I check the rearview and don't see any patrol cars following. The chief, most all of her force, and the state cops, are still away at the house and harbor crime scenes, leaving the deputy inside the station.

"Boss, you need to chill. You know we need to go forward with the plan," Lola says.

Lola has always called me boss, even though I'm a consultant in the private sector now, and she's still a government agent. It's a holdover from when I was her boss at the FBI.

"You gave the go after I killed the plan? You fucking overrode me, Lola? And just launch straight into obstruction of justice without so much as even a glance to me? Just go ahead and do whatever you want, right? Right, Lola?"

"We're covered, Liu. There won't ever be an obstruction charge against us. My agency will cover us once we're done with the plan."

"Your agency doesn't know what the fuck we're doing right now. They have no idea. Lisa's mother was murdered. This has to end. Now. Murdered, Lola."

"I know. I know." She closes her eyes and bounces her head. "Boss, just means all the more we have to bring them down now. We'll be covered. My agency will cover us once we're done. Drive the car. Stop in the alley. Get to Mariana Church, stay on course. We need to make sure Velada is in place."

"Oh, you're just not getting it, are you? You just will refuse to get it. We're shutting this down, Lola. We are shutting this down and our chief mission now is finding Lisa and getting her out. How dare…. You're going to get her killed."

"Drive, boss," she says. And in a rare moment, I note her hands shaking. She takes and jams them under her ass, squashing her own trembling.

We've both been with Lisa since the day we saved her, eighteen years ago. She is like a daughter to both of us. We're both scared. We're both angry.

I shake my head and drive down the back alley. I roll to a stop and Lola pops out—knowing to look on the right, where Lisa was a passenger—and within fifteen seconds is back with the stolen evidence, Lisa's mother's iPhone and also a notebook.

Lola and I are not talking to each other as she punches in the password: Vanty33. As I press the gas to pull into traffic on East Hanson's main street, I consider making a sharp jostle of the wheel to throw Lola's balance and send her into the passenger window. Knock her head, bust her cheek.

But I don't. I won't. I wouldn't.

Because when it really comes down to it, after about three thousand fights with her, it doesn't matter how mad I get at Lola. For me, Lola trumps everyone, even her own infuriating self. She's seen things so horrible, put herself in such underground vulnerability, I owe the woman my soul—even if there are so many times, like right this second, I've wanted to throw her from a moving vehicle and watch her square, dense body smash its way down an embankment and dent the earth. I bang my steering wheel. "Dammit, Lola. Dammit! We are shutting this down."

She says nothing, continues scrolling through the iPhone. The notebook is flat on her lap.

I tell myself this is just what it's like when your decades-long partner is a miserable witch, a one-track-minded hunter who doesn't follow one fucking rule, but a woman who would do anything, literally anything, to save a child. I tell myself it's like this for all law enforcement partners. But I know it most definitely is not. I may have outranked her when we were both with the feds, and she indeed reported to me for a number of years. But the brave one among us is only her, only ever Lola. It doesn't comfort me to see her hands tremble, doesn't assuage my own fear and anger that she, too, has fear. To see her tremble ratchets up my fear, topples any resolve I might have had to plow through and bring these monsters down.

Lola can't tremble. Lola is the granite between us.

One such example was when she worked two years to figure out the most we ever could figure out about the Lobster Tank. And because the day she revealed what she uncovered was the sixth worst day of my life—one being when I failed to stop my own brother's kidnapping; three being his three attempted suicides thereafter; and one being the day we found Lisa and Dorothy, and lost Dorothy—I wish I could erase all of the knowledge she uncovered. The visual truth of the Lobster Tank is enough to make sinless mortals beg for mercy from all the Higher Powers, just for committing the sin of witnessing such evil.

CHAPTER SEVEN
FORMER SPECIAL AGENT ROGER LIU
THE LOBSTER TANK

Eighteen years ago, after a young woman calling herself Velada, with burnt feet, approached Lisa in the parking lot of the Indiana Courthouse, Lisa told Lola and me about the encounter and gave a sketch artist with the FBI (who Lisa made both Lola and I vow was trustworthy and the only one we'd involve) a detailed description. We also pulled grainy CCTV photos from the courtroom, since she had admitted to watching the trial in disguise. Despite pouring over runaway and kidnap and prostitution arrest pictures, we found no matches. Nothing. And we had a team, who didn't know why they were looking, run with this sketch and grainy court photos for months. The stolen green van Velada drove off in was found burned out, down by an Indiana river, between a highway bridge abutment and a scraggly bush decorated in balls of women's underwear as if ornaments on a Christmas tree. The name "Velada" was nowhere in our databases. We believed she made the name up on the spot when she'd first talked to Lisa. We had nothing.

I worried that perhaps Lisa might have been suffering post-traumatic stress or the lingering effects of Prison Psychosis. But we trudged on. Good thing we did.

Velada's reference to the Lobster Tank and the correlation to her burnt feet, again, revealed zilch from the entire history of archived FBI reports, and nothing was uncovered from any searchable state records. To this day, as old department and police files are digitized, we continue to search again and again for the girl's true identity and any reference to a Lobster Tank. And we find nothing.

As for any shred of evidence we might have followed from the splinter group that orchestrated Lisa's and Dorothy's kidnappings, one of the chief culprits was dead. The ringleader, Brad, was in prison and unwilling to talk with us about anything—wouldn't even use information as a bargaining chip to get parole. And the others involved were dumb pawns who were purposefully disconnected from information. The fact Brad wouldn't give us anything, and didn't even brag to fellow inmates (we had spies on the inside), told us Brad was hanging by a thin thread as far as the higher ups were concerned. They could murder him any second if they wanted. Part of me enjoyed knowing Brad lived in constant fear. Nevertheless, we got nowhere on this angle.

But there sure is underground knowledge about the Lobster Tank, all right. Just not in official records.

Given Velada's reported history as a forced sex slave, we focused on the sex trafficking trade. Under a variety of covers, Lola and I sniffed around the country's clubs, shitty motels, brothels, massage parlors, street corners, and casinos for six months. Nothing.

Until one day everything changed. The day that started Lola's descent into the underground.

We were, as we often are, eating breakfast at a diner. We were well into 1994. This time we were in a classic old-America diner, the kind that looks like a streetcar, under Highway 93 in Boston. A sad, paint-chipped, mechanical horse was tipped in a nosedive out front, waiting for kids with quarters. The scent inside was a mixture of musty rags and swamp-water mops, but you forgot about a wafting dump once the pungent coffee steam hit your nose. Settled in our booth, with the coffee warming our brains, I ordered my then intended diet: a poached egg and dry white toast. Lola ordered literally everything else on the menu.

"Boss, what are you slimming down for, a bikini?" she asked, while taking my wallet and extracting a ten from my money. "I got to go make a call. My burner's dead, and I can't use yours for this one."

"Why can't you use your own money?" I snapped back my wallet, like she was an annoying sister.

"Because you're the boss. Bosses pay."

Lola stood and shook out her thick legs in a wide stance, like she had to adjust balls in the too-tight crotch of her gray man-pants. Her holstered gun lumped the back of her gray jacket.

"You got eight quarters and ones to change out this ten?" she asked our waitress, waving the bill at her. I wished she'd leave the waitress alone so she could refill my coffee. Lola got her coins and pocketed the ones—*my* ones, now hers.

About ten minutes went by before Lola returned. In the time I waited, our food arrived. Mine took up one half of one placemat. Lola's took up her side of the table. She slid in the booth and started talking before she started eating, indicating something huge must be on her lips.

"Boss, I got some Pink Bear type of trash talk for you."

"Pink Bear" was my and Lola's inside term to mean bizarre evidence or strange coincidences. I widened my eyes. Whenever either of us has invoked "Pink Bear" it has always led to us solving a case, or causing a seismic shift in our investigation. I dropped my fork, straightened my back, and nodded for her to continue.

"That call I made. So, remember when we scoured the trafficking rings at the Super Bowl last month, asking about the Lobster Tank?"

"Yeah, go on."

"Well, one guy I cornered was the straggly-haired jagoff who had the job of mopping the floor of the inner room under the stadium hotel where they held the minors."

"You mean the ring Team Selig broke up? Saved the ten girls they air-shipped in from Cambodia?"

Lola and I were undercover at the Super Bowl, Team Selig was not, so they got the bust.

"Ayup. Mopper took my burner number, left a message for me to call just now. Mopper mentioned the Lobster Tank to his Ecstasy dealer. Ex dealer said he heard about a trash picker who found porno tapes in a New Jersey dump. There's all kinds of fucked up shit on these tapes, he thinks snuff films, and one tape the Ex dealer is hearing being referred to as 'Burnt Lobster.' Whatever this tape called 'Burnt Lobster' is, well, someone wanted it back real bad, because the trash picker was found dismembered in the Delaware River. Some Jersey gang went to loot the picker's cabin before the cops got there.

The story goes, when they got there, the place was already torn apart and the only thing missing was this mythical 'Burnt Lobster' video. Mopper thinks 'Burnt Lobster' is some kind of urban legend."

"Son of a bitch. What landfill? Where in New Jersey? What's Mopper's dealer's name?"

Lola flipped a finger for each answer to each question: "No clue. No clue. Mopper wouldn't say the dealer's name. And our only lead into this underground is tracking the dead scent of the trash picker."

"Shit. We got to do this one full undercover. In New Jersey," I said.

"Yeah. I'm thinking on more of my backstory." She brought her thumb to her teeth to gnaw at a hangnail. Her fingertips looked like pencil erasers. "We need home office to approve everything ASAP. So boss, finish your anorexic breakfast and work on all that admin shit you do." And although she had two orders of her own buttered toast, she grabbed my last piece of unbuttered white and alligator-chomped the middle in one bite.

I don't know what all Lola had to do or say or what parts she had to play, what lies, what necessary deceptions she doled out to gain trust of the worst of the worst. I don't know all she saw underground as a female bouncer in several brothels. She won't say. All I know is she'd surface from time to time to report she was getting close. A few times she surfaced to say she was giving up, but a week or two later, she'd plunk her head back into hell as the most indefatigable soldier on the field. Once she said to me, before slipping out of view down a dark street, "Liu, with what I got to see underground, how they murder the souls of girls and baby girls, hook them on all kinds of drugs, sell their bodies over and over, ain't no way I'm ever giving up; ain't no way we're stopping until we root them all out." She'd feed information to me about certain cells and sects and state-line-crossing kidnapper-pimps who I could arrange for FBI and local law enforcement to bust along the way. But always, through the years, Lola kept her nose to the lye in the soil, sniffing for any whiff of anything having to do with the Lobster Tank or 'Burnt Lobster.'

Two years in, so two-and-a-half years after Velada tipped Lisa off, Lola called me and Lisa to join her in a hotel room she'd rented near Lisa's college: MIT. Lisa's boy, Vanty, was nearly three years old and home in New Hampshire with his nanny, waiting on his emotionless mother to finish her studies for the day, drive home, and play with him—all of which Lisa did each day with the precision of a Queen's Guard at Buckingham Palace.

Lola booked herself at the Four Seasons in an upgraded, luxury room with heavy drapes of gold and blue, which was so far out of character, I assumed she'd lost her mind from all the undercover work. I said nothing in the moment I arrived, thinking I'd maybe address it at some more opportune, private time.

On that day, if you laid on her King-sized bed, you overlooked Boston Common in the throes of a full-blown summer. Green and deep as a rainforest with scatters and sprinkles of pockets of flowers, looking like Jackson Pollack had flicked brushes drenched in pastels over and between giant bunches of broccoli.

What odd luxury in our shared history so dire.

Lola answered her hotel door for me and Lisa, wearing a thick, white, terry-cloth robe with the Four Seasons logo on the chest. I scrunched my face, thrown back and shocked. This was the one and only time I ever saw Lola outside her gray costume as a boring Fed, or in non-descript underground fatigues as a brothel bouncer.

As I expected, she announced upon our entry, "Boss, you're paying for this room." When I didn't acknowledge that I would, for of course it was presumed the room would be expensed to the Bureau and I'd be the one forced to justify the cost, she added, "And this robe, too."

I didn't recognize this Lola before me. She rubbed the lapel of her robe in what I had to interpret as open pleasure, possibly her thinking of someone special. Freaked me out. But Lola's lapse into a sensible humanity broke quick enough when she snorted, and said, "Get on in here. We got some fucked-up crazy-ass shit to watch. You won't believe it."

Lisa, who had wormed her way into the room while Lola and I stood in the doorway, snatched a Snickers from the mini-bar, staring vacant-eyed at me as her way of saying I'd pay for that, too.

"Mother takes robes from hotels," Lisa said to Lola.

"Mm, hm," Lola said, as both women faced each other, nodding their heads in some sort of moment of respect for hard-ass women who take robes from hotels.

Many years later now, I think back on this minor moment, and given my Hyperthymesia, I recall the exact length of respectful quiet shared between the women in that Four Seasons' room—the creases in their solemn eyes, and them nodding four times in four beats of silence, all after Lisa mentioned her mother. They were then talking about hotel robes and Lisa's mother was still alive, but as I view the moment from the present day and overlay her current murder, that past moment becomes an eerie prophecy of mourning in a moment of silence.

In that Four Seasons' room in 1996, me stuck with the hard-ass women in my life, I longed for my loving wife, Sandra, and reminded myself that I was soon to offer my resignation to the Bureau. All I'd been working on since we'd found Lisa Yyland and Dorothy Salucci was paperwork on cold cases and supporting Lola underground. Lola snapped her fingers in my face to come sit and watch her presentation.

"I now know what the Lobster Tank is, and you are not going to believe this. That girl who warned you to be ready, Lisa, well…I don't know how you could be ready for anything like this," she said. And without any other ceremony or warnings, Lisa and I had to hurry to sit because Lola stepped to a VCR above the room's boxy television. Lisa took the comfy, upholstered armchair with embroidered tropical birds; I scrambled for the hard wood desk chair.

"The film quality is for shit. A rat who mules girls through an underground tunnel from a Philly harbor which connects all the way to armpit Newark, by way of various passageways and canal trails, says he taped this video off a TV in a room he wasn't supposed to be in. When the rat came upon this tape titled, 'Burnt Lobster,' uh huh, he took a camcorder in the room and taped the TV. I've never seen anything like this ever. And boss, I know you got a million questions about this rat and the room and the owner of the original tape and metadata on the tape, but we won't get anywhere with any of that."

Lola held up a flat palm to stem my flood of questions. "Hang on. Watch this. Worst thing I've ever seen."

Given how Lola and I had seen mangled bodies, charred bodies, drowned and gutted bodies, and watched a sixteen-year-old girl die while giving birth to a full-term baby, who also died, I braced myself, clutching the hardness of the lacquered chair, for I couldn't imagine what would be the *worst* thing Lola had ever seen.

Lisa took a bite of her Snickers.

The tape started abruptly; a grainy yellowish room became visible. No windows. It seemed the video started in the middle of something. Lola pressed pause. "This isn't the real beginning. See how the shot is straight and then rises fast? Seems like whoever is shooting put the camera on the bed for a bit of time and then picked it back up. Rat says he didn't get the whole thing."

"Keep going," I said.

Lisa nodded to join my command; Lola pressed play.

The camera angle was from one wall that was not visible, and in the center of the frame was a twin bed covered with white sheets. No discernable bedframe could be investigated as to place of purchase. A corner of what seemed to be a large square mirror appeared glued to the wall at the foot of the bed, beside the door. But since the mirror was to the side of the camera's shot, no reflection identified the videographer. About ten seconds of nothing rolled on in the stillness of this empty, yellowish room. Then the camera panned out and angled up to reveal the wall above the head of the bed. Out of that wall, a roughly-crafted glass enclosure protruded, about six feet tall and, although it was impossible to tell, about two feet thick. The camera stayed fixed on the middle of the tank. In it stood a naked girl of Asian descent, trapped. Her screaming was inaudible on the tape, but apparent by way of her open mouth. The ceiling was high, about fifteen feet up from the floor.

The camera shifted fast to the wall opposite the foot of the bed, but directed only to the door, so we still could not use the mirror for information. Two people entered the room: an enormous man with a sheer, but obscuring, black mesh hood over his head, and a naked Caucasian girl he pushed into the room. Her arms were tied behind her back and her mouth duct-taped shut. The man's face was indecipherable to the camera given his hood, but he could see out.

Lola pressed pause. "You don't want to see the rest. I can explain. I just wanted you to see the actual tank."

My shoulders stiffened and a wave of nausea rose from my gut to my throat. I knew this had to be bad for Lola to pause and offer us comfort.

"Play it," Lisa said, pointing her half-eaten Snickers at the screen.

I breathed in deep, knowing we had to watch, in order to be ready.

Lola pressed play.

The cloak-headed man tilted his head to the girl in the glass box in the wall. In a garbled voice, but discernible because he spoke deep from the back of his throat, and slow in a labored breath, as if in an exhausted slow-mo tone, he said, "You know the rules of the test. If you don't watch us, the tank fills with bleach. If you watch, then she dies, and no bleach. You decide who gets the gift to live in eminence."

Lola pressed pause again. "I think we should stop here."

"Play it," Lisa said, now on her knees, close to the television, tracing the side outline of the mirror. "And that's not Velada in the tank, or the naked girl being pushed in," Lisa said. "In case you're wondering."

"Oh, she's not Velada in the tank or the girl being pushed. Can't be," Lola said.

Lisa bounced her eyes at the remote in Lola's hands.

Lola pressed play. "Fine. You asked for this. This is terrible. The worst," she said.

Once done reminding the tanked girl of the rules of engagement, the mesh-headed man untied his black robe while pushing the hand-tied, duct-taped girl to the bed face-first. As he proceeded to sodomize her, despite her valiant protests, he choked her in a muscled head lock. I didn't see any tattoos anywhere on the parts of his skin that were exposed—only the middle of the front of his body down to his feet—and believe me, I've since dissected this film half-frame by half-frame.

Action on the bed stopped when the masked, open-robed man arched his chest to the tank and shouted, "You're. Closing. Your eyes. Bleach!"

Clear liquid appeared like a waterfall from both topsides of the tank and covered the tank girl's squirming feet. She tried to crawl up her own legs, but kept slipping back into the bleach.

Out of view of the camera, the man yelled, "Stop!" The bleach stopped. "Keep. Those eyes. Open." The camera shifted back to him on the bed and him once again raping the gagged girl, choking her anew. He abandoned her for a second and bent to grab a butcher knife from under the bed. Setting the blade to the knot of the start of her spine, he once again arched to the tank.

"Bleach!" he shouted, lifting the knife away from the girl's neck.

The glass box filled more, this time rising to the level of the caged girl's thighs.

"STOP! You keep. Your eyes. Open. So no. More Bleach!"

He flipped the gagged girl over, her back and tied arms on the mattress. She no longer flailed around in a fight: Her body had gone limp, but her eyes were open and watching. He raised the knife above her chest and plunged deep into her heart. Blood exploded when he removed the blade. He arched to the tank.

"Bleach!" he shouted. This time the bleach came up to the caged girl's chin. The parts of her that had been soaking the longest were now turning red.

Lola pressed pause. "This is why I believe they call it the Lobster Tank. The bleach causes the skin to turn red."

"I agree with that theory," Lisa said. "I've seen enough. I need a copy. We'll copy it at MIT. I have an ally in the AV department."

It's Lisa, so ally.

Lisa stood, a hand to her chin, as she proceeded to walk a circle in contemplation. She went to the freeze frame on the TV, which showed the middle of the tank with the girl in it, not the edges. Only a scant piece of the top edge was visible. Lisa sized the top edge with her fingers, as if they were rulers. She moved her fingers several times as if taking measurements.

"This tank is not straight. It's not hanging straight or it's not constructed straight," she said. "I'll try to study it further. I wish we had a clear shot of more than just the middle." She looked up to me, and said, "I need to be ready to escape, I'm theorizing, a homemade glass tank of bleach, while naked; thus, holding no weapon. I need to escape fast, before he rapes whoever the other girl will be. And then, after that, I have to disable him, avoid his knife, and get me and the other girl out. And we have to do this in a way that captures them, whoever here is involved, in the act, so all of them are unable to avoid prosecution. Velada was clear about powerful customers, so there must be customers for this show, and she's clear about catching them in the act. So where are they?" Her tone was factual, without any hint of fear or any notion I might disagree. It was the most words I'd ever heard her speak in one conversation.

"Lisa," I tried.

She held her hand up to stop me talking.

"Liu, we are going to catch them all in the act," she said.

I shook my head. "Let's talk. We'll talk," I said.

Lisa looked to Lola as her answer, and neither said a word in response.

We did go ahead and make a copy of the tape at MIT. I justified in my mind that Lisa might see things we wouldn't, or maybe she'd be taken before I could stop this and she should be ready. It's true, though, I did drive her to MIT to get it copied. I suppose, if I'm being honest, that was my first commitment to this plan we're dealing with now.

We weren't supposed to share such evidence with a civilian, obviously, especially a college student who three years before had been a kidnapped pregnant teen. But rules were like ancient text with no modern meaning to Lola and me as far as Lisa Yyland was concerned. And, given my own failure to save my little brother from monsters when I was thirteen, added with failures in following procedures up to and including finding Dorothy M. Salucci and Lisa, I didn't pay much heed to official procedure. I have always had an insatiable desire, which grows to this day, to get the bad guys, no matter the means. Lola, well…Lola has her own reasons, and Lola is Lola.

To sum up the remainder of the tape, the tanked girl is later shown dragged into the room with skin burnt toe to chin. We at the Bureau declared her dead. The gagged, raped, and stabbed girl, clearly dead. We never found evidence of who the hooded man was or who taped and/or released the bleach. We found no visible tattoos, and we never found the girls' bodies. No sounds in the room echoed in near silence for sound experts to identify a location.

We ran down every possible tank manufacturer—aquarium, terrarium, and so forth. We scrubbed the girl from a couple of stills to show the tank to manufacturers, but every one of them denied being the source, and every one of them said the contraption was an odd, custom-made piece, likely glued or welded together in someone's barn. They could not confirm, given the graininess of the film and how the tank itself was shot at a shaky angle, whether it was made of glass or what or how thick the panes were.

Even the video analysis experts at FBI headquarters could find nothing in the video that identified anything useful. And since it was a tape of a TV playing the original, and the tape was a common cassette you could buy anywhere and the lot number was scraped off, we had no definitive video forensics to run down. Even the underground rat who'd taped it disappeared. We had nothing. But that didn't stop Lisa Yyland from studying the minutia of each frame in her copy of the video for all the years until now.

~~~

Lola and I are right now entering the highway and heading south on Route 128, toward Mariana Church in Boston. This is the place where we must "secure Velada" and make sure "Velada is in place." Seeing as Lisa could be anywhere right now and not really headed to the plan's known location, Mariana is our one sure address for now. Lola is flipping through Lisa's mother's emails. She's muttering to herself about dates.

"Boss, the earliest thing in this notebook that seems related to what we're doing begins a week ago. Entry says, 'Stranger email directs me to check on Rasper in hospital.' So I go to a week ago in her email and search 'Rasper.' Earliest one is from a week ago, address is VVVVVVie at gmail dot com. Says, 'You don't know me. But I know you. You were a *pro bono* lawyer for a trafficked girl I heard about. You need to check the hospitals for Judge Rasper and ask him why he had a visit from the dentist. —*Vie.*'"

"Did she forward that email to anyone else?"

Lola switches over to the sent items. Searches. "Nothing. Unless she deleted," she says.

"Check her email folders."

"She got none."

"Lisa said her mother thinks this is connected to all this, that she mentions Mariana Church and Velada in there somewhere. How?"

"Don't know, boss. I'm still looking."

"We thinking Judge Rasper is one of the customers of the Center Ring? But who is the dentist?"

"Don't know, boss. But we really need to get to Mariana now and talk to Velada. This isn't right. Smells like shit."

"Oh, so now you say it. Now. Lola, we are shutting this down."

She shakes her head, exhaling through her nose like a bull.

"Who the hell is the dentist? Why is he visiting a Judge Rasper?"

I ask.

"Don't know, boss. Let me read."

CHAPTER EIGHT
JOSIAH OLIVE, VIEBURY GROVE

One week ago, in Viebury Grove, Josiah Olive, who goes by Josi, waited for Judge Rasper, watching from behind a rhododendron the size of a shed, adjacent to the metal arch that welcomes, or rather warns, those who enter the Grove.

A Massachusetts neighborhood set apart from the rest of Viebury, Viebury Grove is accessible by only one entrance, which hosts a twenty-foot-tall iron and copper arch, the copper aged in shades of antique green and moss. At the crest of the arch, antique cursive spells out, Viebury Grove. From there, one road leads in an upward spiral to a neighborhood on a plateau. At the top, there are a sparse amount of Victorians and Capes, many of which remain abandoned but owned by a secret trust, and one stone mansion—all of which are mostly obscured to each other, given the tall pines that weave between. There are inhabitants in the stone mansion. And some of the homes have elderly folks who want no trouble, no one bugging them, and have lived in the Grove all their lives. Josi Olive is the only anomaly; he lives in a little white Cape across from the stone mansion.

At the back of Viebury Grove's plateau, a full forest extends in a slope all the way to bogs, then a marsh, and then the sea. Along the way are dense sets of oaks, sugar maples, birch, and pine, stagnant streams, puddles, mud swamps, and a couple of granite outcrops, which shine under moonlight, given the plenitude of mica embedded on the rockfaces.

With the plateau-like setting, the forest behind, and the negligible population, Viebury Grove is separated from surrounding towns. Simply put, Viebury Grove is uniquely situated to host a criminal enterprise.

One hundred years ago, Viebury Grove was originally designed, and the arch created, with the intention of being a cemetery given the height of the plateau, thus safe from flooding. But thanks to a variety of East Coast politics, permitting was denied. Instead, a more lucrative path was followed, the land acquired, subdivided, and sold for residential construction. But the intended graveyard entrance arch remained, along with artful, ivy-decorated grave plot sketches, which were framed to hang in the library. These items, the plateau and surrounding forest, the arch, and the plot sketches, continue to give the small amount of residents the sense that they are merely ghosts in a separate plane of existence; the feeling that their homes are nothing more than elaborate mausoleums, and the fogs that rise from the earth in the forest beyond are spirits who escaped the soil, but who are unable to leave, trapped in the Viebury bubble. This sense was amplified when the burnt bones of a woman were discovered four months ago.

Two hound dogs flanking their master, a training triathlete, found a burned skeleton in the mud of one of Viebury forest's thin-water swamps. The skull's teeth were absent, given how a giant oak had fallen and crushed the burned skull, shattering it—allowing winds and waters and birds and animals throughout the season to take off with the teeth and several burned skull pieces. The fact it was even a skeleton at all was a guess, given how many bones were missing, again subject to nature's takings, and also due to the excessive heat that must have cooked the bones to mostly coal, which highly degraded whatever DNA might have been available, making amplification of genetic markers impossible. But forensic pathologists declared it a skeleton, and educated scientific conjecture said it was female. That was the best basis the medical examiner had to cement his opinion that the skeleton belonged to a beloved local woman, given "certain characteristics" he noted in the bones and articles of hers found pressed in the mud: a Sugar Magnolia coffee house T-shirt and a metal cuff with an engraved Dickens' quote. There was also her suicide note, rolled up in a bottle, found in a squirrel hole in a nearby oak.

Josi Olive didn't buy any of it.

The Sugar Magnolia T-shirt and the Dickens' cuff were items Josi Olive, the woman's newlywed husband, had confirmed to police when they hovered over her charred remains at the morgue. His identification of her "effects" called an end to any further inquiry, and since he said nothing to deny the validity of her suicide note, which claimed she'd immolated herself, and since he said she'd left him months ago, saying she wanted to live on her own and hike out west, for which he showed them two taped Skype calls where he was crying to her to come home and she refused, they gave him a number for a grief counselor and moved on. All this sealed the lid on any investigation, but sparked an unruly rage in Josi Olive.

The cops had stopped investigating. And that, he considered outright bullshit. "Sketchy as fuck," he said.

~~~

Things are not done, not sealed, no case closed, as far as Josi is concerned. Bitches will pay. His wife had said things in her sleep he'd never forget about the stone mansion where she'd catered from time to time, across the street. Vague, broken dream-speak about scumbags who party there. Terrible things about what they did, secrets held underground. Things she denied, insisted were nightmares, or Josi's own jealousies. And Josi said no words to nobody, because his wife said he'd fuck up her catering gig if he started saying shit about it. She also told him to keep to his own business for his own good and just work on his music.

Soon enough, after his wife whispered once again in her sleep, his wife said she couldn't take his paranoia anymore and was leaving him. That she wanted to hike out west, and not to bother her. Then they found her coal-fire remains, identifiable only 'cuz of her Sugar Magnolia T-shirt and the Dickens' cuff Josi had bought her for Valentine's. Ever since she went walkabout, Josi's waited out the men of the stone mansion; spied. Seen things. He's seen a few uniforms, that fucking Judge Rasper, too, so he knows to keep his trap tight and not fight how they stopped the investigation. He knows he's on his own.

One week ago, by the Viebury Grove entrance arch, Josi waited. He'd decided, whether it was wise or not, to bust up the worst of the motherfuckers. He had no real plan. Basically lost his shit that morning while looking at the long dead flowers he'd given his wife before she disappeared—and he stewed in his rage all day in his sound lab in his own basement. Couldn't write any music all day, couldn't calm himself with any chords. He figured finally he had to do something. He had a target. He'd start with Judge Rasper. A recognizable asshole since he was a pictured commentator on legal crap in *The Boston Globe*.

He'd seen the comings and the doings and the goings of the Judge to, in, and from the stone mansion. Having climbed a tree, Josi had watched through a window as Rasper tied and raped a girl—looked like rape, since she looked high and listless and under sixteen—so this, too, fueled Josi to act. Josi didn't trust the cops to do a thing about it; he'd seen a few uniforms going in and out. And they were doing fuck nothing about his wife. So wise or not, he decided to pick off these customers, one by one, himself. Josi knew he was out of his element; he was really just a rapper or hip hop artist, whatever the fans want to call his beats. Knew he should do none of this junk, should just run, and restart his life. Aimless, though, he chose to act in a disorganized rage. Nothing made sense, so why should he.

Josi passed the hiding time by stripping bark off newborn twigs and sitting on a bumpy boulder, growing a sore ass to match his sore mind. About fifty twigs cascaded and teepeed on the toes of his black boots, his right foot abutting a cordless drill.

He thought of her. How he missed her, still. And his stripping of a twig became more forceful; he snapped the twig. He recalled the night he proposed and how he'd tricked her. "How 'bout I take my baby to Top of the Hub," he'd said, referring to the fancy restaurant in the square head of the Prudential in downtown Boston.

"No way we'll get a table on a Friday night, Babe. Besides, I'm not dressed for it," she'd said. He sniggered to himself, for he loved tricking her away from the hour she normally took to prepare for dates with him—he thought she was perfect in her raw state, unedited, in the pair of khaki pants she read her nerd books in and a plain green sweater from the thrift store.

"Let's go home and play Scrabble," she'd said, for she'd moved in to his Viebury Grove home, an abandoned family property he'd inherited as the sole surviving member. Some distant uncle, or whatever, and Josi was an adult orphan, his parents crashed in a wreck when he was twenty-five. Once all the probate crap passed, Josi had gotten wicked huge offers to sell, some were sort of aggressive, which was odd to Josi, since he thought of the inherited Cape as a dump. But his dump. His very own dump. A dump with a yard, so much better than the shit apartment he'd been sharing with two dirty bandmates in Manchester, New Hampshire. And his very own dump had a perfect space in the basement to build out his "sound lab" for mixing beats.

Scrabble was Josi and his wife's go-to from 'Day One': they'd met in a bookstore, her buying the game and her surprising Josi by being the one to spark their conversation. They fell in love hard and fast—from Josi's perspective—while chatting in line. For them as a couple, Scrabble was never put away in the box. In fact, the board had its own table in the living room. They played so often, they made up screwball rules only they understood, and foreign words were allowed.

Josi clicked his tongue while checking her head to toe like he could jump her bones right there in the Prudential lobby in front of all the other jerks trying to get a table. "Sexy baby, we go to the Top of the Hub. We'll give that a try. We lose, we'll go the Scrabble-pizza route," he'd said.

Up to the 52nd floor of the Prudential Building they rose, crowds of tourists doing the same around them. He suggested she wait by a black vase holding stems of long flowers that looked like the necks of Viebury marsh birds. He waltzed over to the maître d', whispered something, and BAM, they had a table. Her look was a prize itself, her face glowing, showing her amazement that her boyfriend, who was really a club rat, could pull off a table in a classy restaurant. And it was a Friday, no less. Their table was beside a huge window, overlooking the Boston skyline. Her eyes filled with silvery glitter in the candlelight. They chitchatted through a course of chicken and steak, and she never once questioned why his fingers skittered like he was playing a banjo on his knees.

She excused herself to use the bathroom. The waiters hurried. Josi, for once in his life, felt like a commanding king, but he also wanted to hurl at the thought of her saying no.

When she returned, the plates had been cleared; in their place, a fresh white tablecloth was covered with her favorite blue petals, delphinium—not lame roses, she hated the cliché, he'd been warned many times in their one year of dating—and on top of those were the words MARRY ME BABE spelled out in Scrabble letters.

"Scrabble?" he said, referring to the letters, the proposal, and their favorite game all at once. He panicked when she gave him a confused look.

"Chill, baby. Our set's together at home. Bought an extra box from the White Elephant."

She was the one to go to her knees at his side, sobbing into his lap, as he curled around her like a mitt around a ball. He took her reaction as a big, loud YES.

All around, the diners and waiters clapped and awed. And when he produced a fake ring, which if it were real would have been sixty billion bucks but was in fact only glass, some highfalutin woman with dead fur around her neck coughed out an, "Oh. My. Lord."

"We'll shop for a real one together," Josi said. "Got this bling for ten bucks at the Maxx. Only the best for my girl, yeah," he said.

They waited one month and eloped. That was one year ago.

One week ago, at the arch to Viebury Grove, a tear formed in Josi's right eye but did not dampen his rage. The rage was so white hot, he thought of himself as the core of fire. *The core of fire, in the mire, in the muck, in my mind*, he thought, planning to drill the lyrics into some chords and slam out another song in his sound lab.

She deserved a royal death. She deserved the world and the sun. They smashed out her teeth—I know it. Wasn't no fucking fallen oak. Poetic fucking justice never knew poetic justice until tonight.

Josi likes to think of himself as a local Eminem, but with a bent to infuse the Blues in his works, and also political statements and declarations of love. Before he lost his girl, he thought of himself as a softie with no street cred. A rapper with a college degree and no stinger. "No guns. No drugs. No stereotypes. Just a simple boy, running rural rhymes through the times," he used to say, passing with a smile and in his slow, easy pace. But Josi doesn't feel any peace within himself anymore. Just buzzing and anger. He kicked at the boulder with his heel, a crashing *whack, whack, whack*, and he imagined a blood blister forming there, some kind of disgusting representation of the pain in his heart.

A silver Mercedes rolled down the steep incline from the Viebury Grove plateau, having just left the stone mansion. *This pig will be the first to suffer*, Josi thought. *Mutherfucking Judge Rasper.*

Josi clutched his drill in rising from his uncomfortable spot, the skinned twigs falling to the ground, wedging sideways and vertical in the patches of crabgrass and between fallen leaves. He poked around the fat-ass rhody to watch the Mercedes turn right out of the exit of the iron and copper arch. Two carved pumpkins stuffed with battery candles flanked the arch on top of two stone pillars. Yellow light pulsed through jagged mouths and triangle eyes.

Behind the silver Mercedes, which Josi tracked with hawk eyes, a black Audi blocked his line of sight for a couple of seconds. It was hard to see it anyway, because the driver shut out the car's lights, pulled over to the side of the road and parked under a droopy willow beyond the pumpkin pillars, outside the confines of Viebury Grove. If he hadn't been hiding where he was behind the big rhody, he would have never seen the Audi, 'cuz it was invisible now in the black night.

Josi dropped his cordless drill in an open space under the seat of his unmarked dirt bike, pulled on black gloves, popped on, snapped on his helmet, and rode along in pursuit of the silver Mercedes. He hated using this bike and the danger it posed, but the contraption wasn't licensed, wasn't traceable, some piece of shit he'd found for sale on the side of the road in Maine and hid in his garage. Riding it a week ago in pursuit of Rasper, Josi couldn't tell if his heart raced more from fear of crashing on a crappy lump of metal or from what he planned to do to Rasper. He promised himself to never ride such an unsafe vehicle again.

In passing the now parked Audi under the dark, droopy willow, he noted the back plate read 'SHARKK.' A woman, around his age, in her thirties, with a ton of blonde hair piled in floppy swoops, exited the driver door and made moves as if checking a flat tire. Josi considered her just another North Shore rich bitch who would call Triple A. He rode on, in pursuit, taking care to keep the bike level, his arms aligned on the handles, and his body balanced.

Josi followed along the snaky curves of the country road away from the base of Viebury Grove. When the Mercedes turned down an old dirt road no one ever used, which was a northern border on the base of the Grove, just as Josi had tracked this same driver the week before, Josi accelerated to buzz in front.

Once ahead of the Mercedes, Josi decelerated by fractions of five miles, five miles less, five less and, once down to twenty miles per hour, Judge Rasper began to honk. Five miles less. Five less. Now ten. Rasper yelled, having rolled down his Mercedes window. Josi responded by going five miles less, and stopped. The Mercedes screeched to a halt.

Josi didn't kickstand his bike; it crashed to the ground as a lump, on which he dropped his helmet. He flipped up the seat and pulled out the drill and a black ski hat. He pulled on the hat, one with eyes and nose cut out over his face, and popped up from the dust his crash kicked up. With cordless drill in hand, he jackrabbit hopped like a cranked-up gangster with a loaded gun, hips and knees locked, no hesitations, fast and straight to Judge Rasper, who exited his vehicle swearing like a fucking fool. Josi jumped up on him. Face to face, only one inch separated their noses.

No streetlights. No witnesses. Only the headlights of their vehicles shone like stage lights into the black night, cutting through the dumped dirt bike's cloud of road dust, and barely scraping the audience of dark trees. A wind ruffled the dry leaves, which sounded like a wave of applause in the club.

Once Rasper saw the drill at Josi's side, or perhaps when he heard the increasing sound of the drill's *whir-whir-whIR-WHIR*, coming in threatening pulses, he stopped yelling—stopped his dumb muttering, too. Placing a cautious hand on the hood of his car, he scurried back.

"Now, now," Rasper said.

"Get into the woods right now and you'll live. Don't even think of turning to run. Just do what I say, old man."

Rasper was grandpa-age to Josi, and had about fifty extra pounds on his shorter frame. The folds around his neck made him look like a grubworm, as did his freakishly small ears on the sides of his bald head. His eyes were rusty screw heads. His neck and chin vibrated as he spoke.

"Um, well, I never…what is the meaning of this? Do you know who I am? What is this, some ransom plot? What do you want, son?"

Josi slammed his forehead against Rasper's forehead to stun him, grabbed his spongy arm, spun him toward the forest, and pushed him into the trees.

"Yeah, I know who the fuck you are, bitch," Josi said. "Lean up against this pine."

Rasper complied, *like a pussy. He's a roll-neck pussy who takes it out on girls*, Josi thought, *as a way to justify his actions*. Josi believed he was more anxious, more outright freaked than this *pussy* could ever be. But his fury overrode his anxiety. He thought of his wife. He thought of the poor girl he'd seen assaulted in the stone mansion.

Josi shoved a tube sock in Rasper's mouth and tied his hands behind his back and to the pine with yellow rope he yanked from inside his zip-up sweatshirt. He did the same with Rasper's legs. Once done, he straddled Rasper against the tree, nose to nose. To the side of their nearly kissing mouths, Josi *whir-whir-whirred* the drill in pulses.

Whirrrr-whirrrr-whirrrr-whirrrrrrrrrrrrrrrrrrrrrr-whir-whir.

Josi sweat under the cover of his knit face hat.

"You're going to live, bitch, but in pain. I know you won't say a word or admit you were even near Viebury Grove. You know why. I have a whole hard drive, and uploaded backups to the internets, all the internets, baby, of pictures of you in that house with those girls. You sick fuck. Been watching you and the others for months. Yeah, I know who you are, Your Honor. Your. *Honor.* Is this what you make the girls call you when you rape them? Old Judge roll-neck Rasper, you're going to live in pain now. All your Judge friends in the Federal Fuck House of the District O' Mass, they are gonna wonder, though. Wonder what old scar face been up to, to deserve this."

Josi stepped back and *whirred* the cordless drill. To stop the Judge's shakes of the head, he jammed his forearm under the Judge's chin. With his drill hand, he pressed the sharpest point of the bit into Rasper's jaw and *whirred* on in, drilling into the man's jawline until bit met the stone of the Judge's teeth, and burst through. Josi did this two times, bursting through skin and two teeth, one on each side of the Judge's face, like he de-tusked a warthog.

The Judge passed out, slumping to the ground, his arms caught above and behind him from the yellow rope catching on rough bark. Josi inspected the crumpled form of the unconscious Judge and kicked his torso. Blood wove down the Judge's neck and onto the ground. Crouching to Rasper's face, and with his still gloved hands, Josi extracted a fistful of wooden squares from his pocket and a tube of superglue. He glued Scrabble letters to the Judge's forehead.

THE DENTIST

Having watched CSI re-runs with his wife all the time, Josi knew to take away anything that might have his DNA, even though he knew Rasper wouldn't give clues about nothing. So having gathered the rope and the tube sock, he popped back on his dirt bike and rode away, thinking: *Who needs plans? I'll do this forever with these shits whenever I fucking feel like it.*

CHAPTER NINE
LISA YYLAND RIDES ON

According to a psychological survey summarized by Eva Heller in *Psychologie de la couleur-Effets et symboliques*, everyone hates pink, with only brown, hated even more. So psychologically, Eva Heller would say I'm consistent with humanity on hating the color pink. This horrible non-human driving me in her green Prius, I have no clue what her name is, and I don't care. But I'll think of her as Eva now, given I have hate on and I do hate her and her pink outfit.

"The plan is to take you where, exactly? What is it you know?" Eva demands.

I don't want to give away Velada, or don't want to admit to Velada. And the reason is not because I want to protect Velada; I frankly don't trust Velada completely. But what I can't do is let on that I *think* I have a mole. I need them to think they have a perfect plan to put me in the Lobster Tank.

"What do you know?" Eva yells.

"You don't need to yell."

She raises her hand as if to strike me, but stops herself. She unconsciously rubs her cut earlobe. I can tell she wants me out of her car.

"I know what I know because I've been investigating all of you for years," I say, indicating in my tone that obviously I would have been doing that.

"Did your mother talk to anyone else about what she found out about Judge Rasper?"

"What do you think she knows about Judge Rasper?"

"Oh give me a fucking break. You know full well."

I shrug like I know. *I don't know.*

"I do not know what you think my mother knew," I say.

"You can't play fucking dumb. Here, open the glove compartment. We know everything."

I open the glove compartment and a manila folder pops out.

"Go ahead. See for yourself. We know everything. Your mother. You last week, Dentist. You're really a sick person. What you did to Rasper. We know everything. Nobody is going to unravel the Center Ring. Not your mother. And definitely not you."

I'm the Dentist? And I did something to Rasper?

Inside the folder are a series of photos. The first is a high-def glossy of a man in a hospital bed. His eyes are shut, tracheotomy tube in his neck, face swollen with two open wounds on the sides of his face. On his forehead, Scrabble letters spell out THE DENTIST.

"There's your Judge Rasper. That's what you did to him, Dentist. Judge has lock-jaw, sepsis, can't talk, can't eat. You're sick."

"How did you get this picture?"

"Please."

"How? They would need to cover those wounds soon after the trachea, and remove those letters."

"As if we don't have connections. Keep going. We know everything."

I flip to the next picture, and now I see a lower definition picture of Mother in profile, standing at the foot of Rasper's hospital bed. With her head down, she's writing notes in her moleskin notebook, the one I threw in the alley. Seems the picture was taken on a clandestine basis from the other end of the hall, possibly from a smartphone. The clarity is not as precise as the Rasper picture, but it sure is Mother.

"Your Mother. Comes to Rasper's room. Asking all kinds of questions. But he's been in intensive care a week and he isn't talking. Her asking questions is enough though. Enough to shut her up. Asking who did this to him and why. Please. She knows full well it was you, or she was tipped off by you. How else would she know to go there so soon after it happened?"

I'm not answering her, because I didn't do this, but also I'm stuck on her phrase *enough to shut her up*. Like a fire poker to embers in a fire log, my hate flares.

"Keep going, Lisa. Keep looking."

As I stare at Eva, I'm thinking about the satisfying release I will feel when I suffocate her. I turn back to the folder and flip to the next picture. Before I can look, I drop it when we take a sharp and fast corner to drive through East Hanson's cemetery. Cemeteries are scars, inefficient wastes of space. Like golf courses. Dead people on the right of me, dead people on the left of me, my dead mother at the harbor behind me, a future dead person driving the car I'm in. The fall air is warm in the day still, the sky crisp, the clouds uncloudy. The trees all over this town are still in rainbows of colors. Dangling from the rearview mirror, a cherry-shaped car freshener reeks up the interior with the chemical stench of cherry cancer.

I take a guess. "So Rasper is a customer of your sick enterprise. You wouldn't want to shut Mother up if not," I say, as I bend to pick up the picture from the floor.

She inhales, turning her head from me, and then back to me with raised eyes, like she's irritated. I have no idea what this expression means but, based on context, I believe she's confirming my guess.

I look to the picture that had fallen. I have to hold it closer because the image on it is sparsely pixilated. The shadows are dark, and the picture is of outside at night. Closer, I see Mother's Audi, the SHARKK license plate, and a blurry picture of a person moving behind it. Looking further, I realize that person is me.

"You. The night you drilled Rasper's face. We never would have pulled security footage at the Viebury arch had you not attacked Rasper," Eva narrates.

Chaos. Unimaginable contingencies.

"So where's the video of me drilling Rasper?" I need to know if they have video of me lurking around within the grounds of Viebury Grove. I assume they don't, because she wouldn't be so confident in accusing me of drilling Rasper, as if that's the only thing I did that night—which I didn't even do.

"Please," she answers.

"So you have no video of me drilling Rasper."

"Whatever. You were there. You did it."

"Caught me," I say, flipping back through the pictures.

"We'll get your mother's notes and phone from that car you put them in."

I consider her a moment. Thinking on her singular mission to get Mother's documentations and on what my singular mission is right now.

"You know she would have kept backups of everything in her firm's satellite office in Manchester, New Hampshire, right? You need to take me there. I'll get them for you." My father's lab is one block from the Stokes & Crane Manchester satellite, and that's where I need to get my two important discs.

"You are so full of shit," she says. "Right next to your father's lab, right?"

I pause, noting she knows this. "Yes," I say, something I can't deny. "Just go to my mother's office in Manchester."

She picks up her phone, texts something, but I can't see what she's written. Now she contemplates me as we slow behind a line of cars at a stop sign. "Hmm," she says, looking at me and smirking, seemingly confident now that she has her text out—like she made a dispositive decision. "You think you know Velada, don't you?" She says, in a tone that I believe she intends is meant to cut. I work hard not to react to the fact that she is the one to raise Velada's name first, which is somewhat surprising, somewhat not. I've always wondered if Velada is known as Velada within the Center Ring or just to me.

"I don't know any Velada," I say.

"Right," she says, and laughs to herself. "Velada, hilarious. Well we have you now. She was never on your side. So tell me, what is it you thought you were going to do? What did you think she would help you with? Whatever she's told you is a lie."

Nothing I say really matters right now in answer to her. What I want are my discs from my father's lab and to figure out whether Velada was just a double agent or a double-double agent. She's always been such a puzzle. "What do you think Velada told me?"

"Oh, so this is how it's going to be? We just keep asking questions, pulling on each other's dicks?"

Anatomical metaphors. So unnecessary.

"Or you could just take me to Manchester and I can get those notes for you. I would also like to know what my mother wrote."

78

"Your mother knew too much, and so she had to die, and I will get and burn everything she's left behind."

I'm rehearing this bitch's phrase, 'and so she had to die,' and I'm fighting back a powerful switch in my mind, one I've failed in the past to push back: Homicidal Rage. I jam it back in place and hold tight so it won't spring into action. I must stay on plan.

And now I'm thinking how Eva said Velada lied to me. I need Velada in place. But *they* don't know this even if Velada is a double-double agent, because Velada doesn't know my full plan. *Velada better be in place.* And whatever bullshit Velada might have shoveled over the years about her role in all this, working from the inside, the role *they* think she is to play for *them*, well fuck you, Velada. Be in place. You *be ready.*

And if you are a double-double agent, so be it.

Nobody knows, not Velada, not even Liu or Lola, that over the course of eighteen years I've been able to independently validate a few important items.

We pull onto the main road out of town and Eva jams on the brakes to avoid colliding with a black Tundra in front of us. An orange paddleboard wobbles within the truck's bed. The air freshener under the rearview mirror swings and twirls, scattering more air particulates of cherry cancer. I hold my breath.

I stare out the passenger window, ignoring Eva's intermittent attempts to jab questions at me, this shrill, false tennis pro in pink. We're in leaf-peeper traffic now, heading for the highway, and I can only hope she heeds my demand to drive in the direction of Highway 95 North. I stare on. She jabs her violent questions. I pull on a lock of my real and fake hair, which fell from my clip. This lock reminds me I am a weapon in full. I am an asset in this war, what with all my gadgets *en body*. I wish I could feel my two prosthetic toes, but I can't: they're made of molded rubber, magnets, and important retractable parts.

As we pass Saleo Country Club, Eva shoots Saleo a side-sweep of her eyes, as if checking to ensure nothing is out of sorts. *Interesting.*

She is not turning on any signals to get on 128, north or south. We're about fifty yards off from the decision point and are jammed up in traffic. We lurch forward as the traffic unclogs, and Eva drives past Route 128; she drives straight. This way could lead the inefficient way to Highway 95 north, where I need to go to get to my father's lab, but I suspect she plans on stopping at one of the secluded forest pull-offs, where no one can see.

I calculate what to do next.

Sure enough, Eva turns off the road and drives down a dirt trail. We come to a stop next to a red truck with multiple compartments built into the bed—looks like two stacked rows of red wooden caskets. The side of the truck is decorated in white paint:

RED'S HENS

SALISBURY, MASSACHUSETTS

Before I can yank the Prius door handle, exit, and secure a positional advantage, my door opens on its own, and a man grabs my hair to yank me out. Normally I would stomp his foot, lean out while kicking his groin, elbow his nose upwards when he bends, and escape, but I cannot have him harm the thick, synthetic locks woven within my hair, so I stand, lean into him to loosen the torque and create slack in my hair, and go along with his motions. In the seconds it takes for me to show this momentary compliance, another man comes from around the far side of the truck, and the two men flank my sides. They are bigger and taller than me and look to be jacked on heavy steroids. They drag me to one of the red boxy caskets in the back of the truck, pick me up, and stuff me in horizontal. I immediately scrunch down so that I can use momentum by pushing my feet on the end and spring out, but one of them reaches in, pulls me up and pins me still, while a metal U drops and clamps over my neck, holding me in place. Since I'm stomach down, I move my face to the side to breathe, moving cautiously so I don't rip any of my synthetic hair. I'm concerned the metal U has snagged an important strand.

After slapping my mouth with duct tape, they close the compartment door, which hosts a top-mounted, wire-mesh, breathe-through window. I can't lift and turn my head to look out.

"No one will find you, Dentist. Drilling faces, well…you'll get what's coming to you from Eminence," Eva taunts through the door.

I'm fairly uncomfortable in this shit truck, something not a rational thinking being would suspect holds a stolen human in transport. People likely think this contraption is filled with hens. The engine starts, rumbles my body and eardrums. We drive off. I hope we crash.

Once my hearing calibrates to the smoother rush of the tires when we hit tar, I hone in on a sound coming from an adjacent compartment. Someone is kicking. I hold still. The air is stagnant with a stench of sweat and hot wood.

"My tape fell off," a girl yells to me. She's hyperventilating, crying. I imagine tears clouding her vision. "They said I'm tagged for Eminence. What the fuck! What the fuck! What is going on? Help me!"

So here is the girl I put at risk in this ordeal.

I knew this moment would come. I knew there would be a time when I'd have to face the other tagged girl, the one intended to be raped by Eminence, while I watched to avoid burning in bleach. I've trained for this, and I do have an important role for her. But by meeting her so unexpectedly and in such a dangerous setting, I must admit, I suffer a jolt of fear and a higher jolt of guilt. I think of Dorothy. *I always think of Dorothy.* I wish my tape had also fallen off. I wish I could calm this kicking girl with the steps I'll teach her. But I can't, so I listen, and I think.

CHAPTER TEN

LISA YYLAND: VELADA'S SECOND VISIT
The Sciences of Light and Sound Waves
The Arts of Deception and Misdirection

The second time Velada came to me, unannounced, she crashed my dissertation celebration. Although I didn't predict she'd show that specific day, I'd been waiting on her, for I had something to tell her, too. Also, I was prepared to collect something from her. Ultimately, what she had to say to me in her second encounter was mind boggling. And what I said to her might seem at first to be irrelevant, but is central to the plan. My whole eighteen years of planning plays in, but especially information concerning a certain insect and other creatures.

According to the University of Florida, Entomology and Nematology website, "The Luna Moth (*Actius Linnaeus*) is arguably the most beautiful moth." And according to applied physics researchers, it's 'a smart motherfucker in outwitting bats by twisting its double tail to create confusing acoustics, throwing off a bat's otherwise superhero echolocation.' But these sound science facts are not why I was able to identify my guardian as the genius Luna Moth and not a basic black butterfly.

When I was twenty-three and a few years into owning the Indiana boarding school where they held me (a trust fund had vested when I turned twenty-one and I needed to own that building like I needed pink lungs), I was still bothered by Velada's attack on my Lepidoptera precision when I first met her in that Indiana courthouse parking lot in 1993. Since first meeting Velada, Liu and Lola, and I had figured out her warning about the Lobster Tank, studied and *started* investigating the 'Burnt Lobster' video, and I'd finished college and was well into my post-grad curriculum. All along, perhaps as part of a personal study, I'd been drawing sketches of the black butterfly so as to remember precisely what I saw high up on that triangular window when I was a pregnant, teenage captive.

One day, while sitting on a cushioned wicker chair on Nana's wraparound porch in Savannah, sketchbook on my lap and colored pencils on the armrests, Nana solved my vexation. White-haired, ghost-skin Nana who wears a rainbow of colors in her clothes.

The silvery Savannah sun poked spears through the fronds of fat hanging ferns and created a matrix of illumination on the wood planks and blue rugs of Nana's porch. And since we are a cat family, Nana's fattest orange feline snored like a retired circus lion at my feet. A warm breeze carried the scent of Nana's frangipani flowers, scenting the porch like a floral candle.

Eight-year-old Vanty was spending his days at a day-camp down the road called Pirate Camp. Didn't seem safe nor practical toward his future education, but Nana had explained that such a camp was good for Vanty's "social development" and was therefore both practical and productive.

"It's a Luna Moth, dear," Nana said, sliding an envelope, yellowed with time, over my shoulder. "Look there. In 1987, the U.S. Postal Service issued a Luna Moth stamp." On the envelope was the exact shape of my "black butterfly" on a stamp. Nana collects stamps. "But you keep coloring her black, dear. Why? She's green. Or blue. Or blue-green."

The thing you cannot mistake about a Luna Moth is the shape and pattern: it has a center tail, which at rest is split in two, but when evading the bat, twists together. It also has decorative ringed "eyes" on its wings. Both distinctions, the double tail and rings, I'd been drawing for years, for these are the attributes I saw when I was held captive. But can you mistake the Luna Moth's color? Is it possible to mistake green with black? I needed to solve these questions. I needed to experiment under the exact conditions I'd first seen this mystery.

I generated several instructions for Vanty's care on a printed spreadsheet and handed it to Nana. She put her overfull coffee mug on it and allowed coffee rings to blossom on the important rows about practicing the Heimlich and checking my boy twice daily for ticks. But I have never been victorious in a debate with Nana, so efficiency told me to move on.

I raced to my Indiana schoolhouse, which indeed I did purchase in a seizure auction. It was then in Phase II, in what would be hundreds of phases of renovation. My practice Lobster Tank room was under construction in one of the four third-floor wings, so I checked on the progress in passing. I wasn't pleased with the depth of the two glass tanks embedded in the walls, so I instructed my designer, who worked under a strict NDA, to start over. She thought I was building testing tanks for the study of reptiles and aquatic plants. I then returned to the third-floor room in which they'd jailed me and in which I'd cooked my jailer at age sixteen. By then, the 12 x 24 holding cell had been swept clean and emptied.

Outside, I asked a man in the renovation crew to scotch tape several perfect-colored leaves I'd scoured from saplings in the surrounding forest—the leaves either light green for the male Luna Moth, or blue-green for the female Luna Moth. I charted the appearance of color for twelve hours, at different levels of sunlight: always black. My prior perception did not account for the tree blocking and deflecting light waves that prevented me from seeing the moth's true colors. I have the handicap of human sight, human sound, human taste, human touch—my perceptions can model only to an upper limit. I'm no bat who can hear up to 100 kHz. No hawk who can scan the Earth from 15,000 feet for a rodent. Evolutionary scientists say human limitations allow for our species' survival, otherwise we'd go mad if we could hear so much or see so much. But it also means you can capitalize on this deficiency in others and leverage flawed human sensory perceptions. You can deceive humans by manufacturing a false sight, false sound. Misdirection. You can use their own prescribed definitions of the world against them.

Perhaps this is when I first realized that I'd have to use as assets to escape the tank, since I'd have to be naked, various sensory deceptions—sight and sound chief among them. Also, after identifying my insect as the Luna Moth, I awaited another visit from Velada so I could advise her of what I'd learned. The black butterfly tattoo on her hand was inaccurate. If it was based on something I'd said, she'd mistaken my meaning and walked the Earth with a lie.

It was the day I defended my dissertation for my PhD in Physics, specifically on sound waves, more specifically on the biophysics of using ultrasound to *attract* rather than *repel* rodents and other creatures. As with my dissertation, which came in handy in building the plan, I'm interested now in calling vermin to the cage and ensnaring them in my trap.

The day of my physics dissertation, I was twenty-five. Underage compared to the others. During the celebration, which had been a big deal and part of a press release (given my already issued patents and all the prior news about my kidnapping), I had a strange instinct that someone was watching me from the edges of the room. I sensed eyes on me, beyond those on me for purposes of the celebration. Maybe I was primed to feel this way, given my past, given my kidnapping, given my years' of wait for Velada to reappear. And I'd felt this ominous, invisible glaring before. Once in a park, while I fed Vanty, one by one like a mother bird to the most beautiful blue baby bird, one mandarin orange wedge at a time at a picnic table I had bleach-wiped so not a single germ would corrupt his perfect health record. Twice while obtaining Snickers and other work provisions, like coffee for Liu and toothpicks for Lola, from the supermarket. Once in a public gym while guiding Vanty to listen to Sarge, who'd clap his back and rub his hair and teach him useful life skills, like how to jam an assailant's nose bone into his brain and stop him dead. But whenever I'd sense this ominous glare and I'd put my "head on a swivel," per Sarge's instructions on protecting my and Vanty's "360 degree perimeter at all times," nobody was ever there to see.

And so, stewing in my bath of science at the celebration for completing my dissertation on sound science, wasn't it quite ironic (a concept Lenny has taught me to understand in explaining his poetry), that when I put my head on a swivel while a professor spoke congratulatory words about my work to use sound science to call, not repel, vermin, I saw her. Velada was indeed there, sending vibes to spike my instincts in feeling a glare upon me.

Velada paced, thumbnail in teeth, on the outskirts of the school cafeteria. She waited for me to break free from an unnecessarily large cake decorated with sound waves, which were incorrectly labelled in blue icing as "20 kHz ULTRASOUND." The blue icing was wrong, the peaks and valleys of the waves so not 20 kHz; they were more like 30 HZ, a lower frequency at which run-of-the-mill humans hear and not the higher frequency of ultrasound, which efficient rodents and bats, who all have superhero senses, hear. The sound waves depicted on my dissertation cake were scientifically inaccurate, also not super or special, and so, the sheet cake needled me to explain sound to my family and the faculty in attendance. But I said nothing because Nana whispered through clenched teeth, "Just smile, dear."

At first, a strange instinct forced me to want to make Velada wait, because I didn't like her thinking she alone scheduled our meetings. I believe this is a survival instinct and not at all an emotion. How many times Velada hopped on one foot and then the other and checked her watch, I know: 27 hops and 35 watch checks in the span of 4 minutes, 57 seconds. I supposed she was in a hurry, so I nodded her toward the single stall women's bathroom, followed in behind her, noted the shape of a lighter and cigarette in her back pocket, and locked the door.

Lighter and cigarette seem a constant with her. Keeping them in her back pocket is her pattern.

She wore all black again: a thin, tight, black T-shirt exposing her muscled bat arms, and the black butterfly tattoo on her hand. Again she wore flip-flops. I believe to remind me of the burning she'd been through. I again noted the natural alignment of all her toes, given by way of her personal genetic cocktail.

Nodding her into the women's bathroom like it was my office reminded me of The Fonz in *Happy Days*, a show my then not dearly-departed father would watch in syndicate. We entered one after the other, and I locked the door so no one would interrupt. She turned fast and leaned against a sink. I did the same, facing her.

It had been nine years since I'd last seen her. She'd set up for us a long-woman's game.

"Do you remember me?" she asked.

"Of course."

"Well then."

I stared back at her. Perhaps she thought I'd forgotten all about her, and that I hadn't obsessed over every one of her words for the last nine years.

"Whatever," she said, breaking away from our stare-down. "Look,

I don't have much time," she said. "I've been working with my inside source since we last talked. Did you figure out the Lobster Tank?"

"Yes."

"Okay. Great. Wow." She seemed to hesitate, stopped herself from asking another question in follow-up, I think. I waited for her to speak. She shook her head, pursed her lips, and said, "Yeah, I know now what they did to me. It's fucked up."

"Yes."

"But did you find out where it is?" she asked, stepping closer, seemingly intent on my answer.

"No."

"Hmm," she said, turning and hiding her face from me. I don't know why she hid her face, but I sensed something wrong about it.

Turning back around, she said, "Well. It gets even more fucked up."

"You can smoke in here if you want. There's no smoke alarm."

She widened her eyes.

"I said you can smoke."

"Okay," she said, more as a question. I watched as she reached around like last time and pulled out a forest green lighter and single cigarette.

People and their crutches, they mark themselves so easily.

She continued to smoke and talk, like she did in the Indiana parking lot. But this time she wasn't rank rude, because I told her she could do it.

"They burnt my feet two years before I saw you. And I've discovered that the reason the bleach only rose to my feet and I was able to slip past them when they pulled me from the tank, is because they'd erupted in some kind of big fight. They weren't supposed to do that to me. They were supposed to wait twenty years for Eminence to return. They'd already burnt a girl that same year. Apparently, whoever I saw on the night they put me in the tank, was not Eminence. Just some other demon asshole. My source says he was shot and thrown in the ocean for using Eminence's tank and trying to do 'Eminence's thing.' "

They'd already burnt a girl that year in the tank. That other girl must be the one we saw on video.

"Why were they supposed to wait twenty years?"

"One reason was the superstitions of the Center Ring leader, Eminence."

She coughed as a pause, and I thought superstitions, *you have a superstition too, about single cigarettes and a green lighter. Observe.*

"That's all I know. I don't understand it. Something about the number twenty. Everything being in increments of twenty. Twenty everything. The Lobster Tank every twenty years. The other thing is, if the *experience* of the Lobster Tank is only every twenty years, paying customers will pay the highest amount to watch live. You were able to figure out the Lobster Tank, like I was, because the Center Ring *wants* the underground to know about it. It's never proven, of course. They keep it boiling around as a vague urban legend."

Watch live? From where?

"There's more," she said, and paused to inhale her cigarette and exhale fast. "There's rules and you need to be ready for them. No electronics, nothing metal, no trackers. They'll scan you straight away and if they find anything they'll crush it. But they'll also hurt you. This is how they've kept off the radar for so long. Nobody, and I mean nobody, gets close to the Center Ring with any technology. No GPS, nothing. They are totally analog, old school. Also, you have got to figure out how to not let them stick you with heroin. That's the main way they keep girls hooked and quiet and compliant. Drugs."

"These are the rules of engagement then," I said and blinked slow.

Velada looked to the air beside me, as if a third person were with us, and flung her hands as if asking that invisible person to explain me to her. "What?"

"You're laying out the rules of the game you set for us. Every twenty years, no technology, heroin, so on."

"This is not game, Lisa. This is life or death. Hello, don't you get it?"

"Without emotions everything is a game."

"You think life is a game?"

"Yes." I paused because she looked again for help from the non-existent third person beside me. "It's a very complicated game, I'll grant you that. Requires more strategy than chess."

She blew air from her mouth hard. "Wow. Just wow. Whatever. I don't have time for a philosophy talk with you."

"This is not philosophy."

"You know…fucking what? You actually believe that, don't you? You're so fucked up. Whatever." She clenched her jaw, considered me a couple of beats. "No, wait. Wait. Hold on. So if life is a game, how do you win it?"

"That's one of the complications. It's subjective. Depends on how you choose to use your senses, your perceptions. But, no doubt, there are winners. And there are losers. And there are a bunch of people in the middle."

"Did you just point at me when you said losers?"

"My subconscious might have."

She drew her eyes away from the non-existent third person and stared at me, seemed to chew at something in her mouth. Flicked ashes on the floor.

"You are such a bitch," she said.

"Where is the Lobster Tank?"

"No more philosophy? No more insults?"

"Where is the Lobster Tank?"

She closed her eyes, acting like she was resetting her mood.

"I'll be so fucking happy when I'm done with you." She took another drag off her cigarette. In exhaling, by pointing her mouth toward the ceiling, she said, "I don't know where the fucking tank is. Okay? All I was able to figure out was that Eminence plans to put you in the tank twenty years after the last girl, that's his rotation. There's meaning in it somehow, I don't know. My source says Eminence hasn't forgotten you."

"Twenty years from when you were burnt is about ten years from now. But what month? What day? And where?"

"I have no clue what day or month. And my source hasn't disclosed the address yet. This Lobster Tank is more top secret than any shit at the Pentagon. They charge millions of dollars per asshole watching live. The bigger the urban legend, the more obscure, and the longer they wait, the more money they pay. It's a tricky balance."

Watching live. And paying millions. Noted.

"But you do have the general vicinity of where the tank is. You must at least know what state you were in when you escaped."

She flinched, puckered her mouth and took a drag off her cigarette. The stench of smoke mixed with the recent bleach of the bathroom. A noisy ceiling fan clattered above. "Look," she paused, rolling her eyes. "I don't have a fucking clue, all right? I remember being on a bus. Someone putting me on a bus. I don't know where I was for days. I woke up on the side of a Hardee's in Roanoke. We're getting close. Be ready."

The movements of her pupils indicate deception. Observe.

Velada nodded at me and started to walk out, still holding her cigarette. I grabbed her arm to stop her.

"I have to go. Now. Right now," she said, yanking her arm away.

"Hand me your cigarette. There are No Smoking signs out there."

Velada considered me a beat longer than I liked, looked me up and down.

"Here," she said, slow and cautious, like she was handing over a loaded gun.

"What aren't you telling me?" I asked.

I held the cigarette; she stared as if daring me to smoke, too; testing me. I stared back and didn't make any movements in my face. This went on and I would have let it go on longer, but eventually, she flinched.

"You're just paranoid, Lisa. I'm the one who's giving you information. What if I didn't tell you at all about the tank? Right? You wouldn't know to be ready. Are you going to be ready?"

I didn't like her obvious side-step. I considered whether fighting her on this point would be futile, and chose to work on gathering my own facts and validating everything, without her. I nodded at her to leave, holding the cigarette to my side. She walked to the door after a huff.

"It was a Luna Moth, not a butterfly. So your black butterfly is wrong. On your hand. It was a green, or blue-green, Luna Moth. The *Actius Linnaeus*," I called to her.

She paused and scratched at her false butterfly tattoo and turned back around. "I was right then. It was a moth," she said, wearing a smile that I registered, from a log of studied facial expressions in my mind, as prideful and taunting.

And then, she left.

I bagged her cigarette in the Ziploc I'd been carrying around in a pocket for years and rejoined Nana in eating the offensive ultrasound cake. In considering the blue icing again, in the distraction of wrong sound waves, thinking too on the trickiness of light in deceiving me to think a Luna Moth was a black butterfly, I considered several assets I'd need to work on in my labs in Indiana.

CHAPTER ELEVEN
LISA YYLAND: BACK TO THE LAB

Immediately upon graduation and obtaining my PhD, I packed up nine-year-old Vanty and finally moved in full-time to the renovated schoolhouse—now 15/33 headquarters—in Indiana. Lenny, my boyfriend, Vanty's father, my then not-yet husband, was studying poetry and teaching English in Johannesburg.

In the room with my two glass tanks, I set up a stainless steel worktable. I kept a keypad and also a biometric lock on the room's five-inch metal door, so I was confident nobody could enter while I worked or practiced or trained for the tank. Thereafter, except for a three-month intensive training period on one specific skill, after getting Vanty off to school, I'd spend one to two hours every day working on being ready for the tank. After that and until school pickup, I worked out with Sarge, worked on my various patents and building my consulting business in other labs and rooms in the building, and checked in with the visiting chef in the wing in which we lived as a family.

Within the practice tank room, I set about designing two higher tech assets and one lower tech asset to assist with the plan. All of which are in the category of sensory deception.

The portions of the walls around the practice tanks, I'd use as a canvas and would add layers and details to a painted birch grove as a way to work through thought problems. In the beginning, I had just one birch tree and some blue smudges of sky around. But through the years and as my studies and training and planning for the tank evolved so, too, did my painted birch forest on the walls.

On my stainless steel table, I sautered conduits and plastiques to create a host of prototype discs, discs that I hoped would register the right sound waves. Years of failure and testing ensued. One of my biggest hurdles early on was in figuring out how to power these discs and how to trigger them, too, seeing as I wouldn't have a power source to provide a constant charge. Nor could I be sure of how long they'd have to be charged or when they'd need to be triggered, precisely.

And so, I dragged into the tank room obscure and often foreign scientific literature (which I'd have to pay to get translated) about mechanical energy. Beside my scrap cuts of plastiques and frayed, sautered cables on the stainless table, I piled stacks of journal articles with such titles as, "The Harnessed Energy of Walking—Theory in Motion" and "Human Power." Boiled down, mechanical energy is the same concept as a windmill capturing energy from wind and storing it in large capacitors. Except here, with my line of study, that concept was miniaturized into wearable fibrous bands to capture energy generated from human movement. On my worktable, I created a flesh-colored band with adhesive that I taped across the side-spans of my knees. The first prototype required a lime-sized capacitor to hold the generated electricity from my knee bends, which I had to separately strap around my thighs. Really, it's not all that revolutionary or complicated. This technology is not only believable, but in use in small circles. But something nagged at me always about my knee band and also, obviously, the size of the capacitor. Even if I could shrink the capacitor, I just could never envision myself getting away with keeping the knee bands on my body while in confinement. But as it is with scientific conundrums, I came to a pinnacle where I couldn't see the solution, and so, I kept using and testing the knee band, trusting that someday the answer would come to me. I continued practicing and testing for the Lobster Tank in other ways, while creating smaller and smaller capacitors and sound discs.

As for the lower tech asset... Twenty is the OCD number driving this whole demented event. And it just so happens that "20" is a magic number for physicists. I'm not magic. Magic is not real. With enough practice, some people can harness skills that appear like magic. Magic is the combination of the laws of physics, physical skill, exploitation of human sensory limitations, and psychology.

And so, on this topic, I called to mind a trip I'd taken to New York City with Mother earlier in the same year of my physics dissertation. Mother and I were eating at a chain restaurant in Midtown. Mother was educating me about how the real New York is in SoHo and not "slime hole" Times Square, certainly not anywhere near "garish shithole Trump Tower," and how "pedestrian" the restaurant we were eating in was, with its "horrendous" red vinyl banquettes and "masculine" neon beer signs. But as it was a lucrative nationwide chain and her CEO white-collar-crime-accused client ran it, we had to meet him there in New York. Mother bristled and shrunk into the dark end of the booth when an entertainer popped at the end of our table. He called himself MagEEK, the International Star of Mouse Magic. He was a full grown man dressed as a mouse. Had Nana been there, I think she would have instructed that the entertainer was "humorous," but Mother didn't smile, and so, neither did I.

Although Mother scowled throughout, I watched MagEEK, and fell into study mode when he pulled Mother's wallet from a pocket in his brown costume, the same wallet she'd had in her Valentino handbag, the one pressed under her palm on the horrendous banquette and which she had not unclasped since we sat.

Back in my practice tank room in Indiana, I ran down the number for MagEEK and called him from a secure phone that hangs by one of the tanks. I hired MagEEK as my consultant, put him under an onerous non-disclosure agreement, and required him to live with me in Indiana for three months and train me night and day.

Now, three months is nowhere near enough time to reach the skill level of career magicians. But it was enough time for me to learn the core of what I needed to practice obsessively about object concealment and certain specific movement deceptions.

MagEEK never knew why he was training me; I never showed him the tank room. I, too, didn't know how exactly I'd employ these concealment and deception skills, but I knew I'd need to. Within our family gym in the basement, MagEEK made me practice for seven full hours every day on how to conceal objects with my hands. He'd hand me so many items: Vanty's tennis balls, dominos, rocks, bottles, apples, oranges, blocks of cheese, Snickers bars, anything and everything he found around the property that I would have to conceal from him with my hands and arms. He trained me on simple misdirection techniques, a thrown snap of the fingers, a thrown voice, here and there. The energy stored in my knee band capacitor on these days was always "full." MagEEK taught me how to flex my back just so, just enough to ripple a separate surprise there, so as to further distract from my real actions—say, for example, actions I might take once free of the tank.

CHAPTER TWELVE
FORMER SPECIAL AGENT ROGER LIU

The second time Lisa met with Velada, we learned the harrowing cycle of burning a girl in the Lobster Tank every twenty years. According to Biblestudy.org, "20" can mean a "complete or perfect waiting period." Numerologists and symbolists at the Bureau and Lola's agency agreed that, in terms of time, increments of "20" symbolize episodes of completion which require patience. In other words, in twisted cults, waiting 20 days, weeks, years, for whatever the cult places value in, can mean a symbolic rite of passage, a passing of an endurance or patience test. The achievement of some cultish enlightenment. Here, the Center Ring Grand Master Eminence had a superstition around "20," placing value in waiting 20 years for the rite of passage ceremony of the Lobster Tank, so we were obviously dealing with a fucking lunatic.

But who was Eminence and where was he? We embarked on figuring this out by researching the number 20. If we could find him first, we could shut this shit show down and destroy their whole enterprise in advance of them taking Lisa—that was my goal.

For quite a long time, flipping through a compiled federal database of cult and gang symbols yielded frustrating, dead-end leads. We ran down many different possibilities, some under strained theories, and found nothing. But one day, a symbologist with Lola's agency emailed Lola, saying, "No idea where this was taken, but an anonymous tipster sent this picture, scrubbed of metadata, to the Bureau with no notes, nothing."

In the photo was the brick wall of an alley. On the wall in faded white paint were the remnants of a rain-and-weather-faded circle, inside of which was a dragon whose one claw formed a "二" and his tail curled to form a "十," which together is 二十: or, to English readers, the number 20 in Mandarin. I kicked myself in that moment, shaking my head at the obviousness of it and my therefore embarrassing lapse. We never looked for "20" in a foreign language. Velada had said "twenty" to Lisa, and the man in the 'Burnt Lobster' video spoke English. But that's no excuse. Lola tried to comfort me by saying, "Even the head surgeon of a major southern hospital makes rookie mistakes sometimes; severing the wrong arm, for example." I thought Lola's analogy was oddly specific, totally random, terribly horrifying, and only slightly comforting.

"What southern surgeon?" I asked.

"Whatever, boss. Never mind," she answered. I did note, she walked away fast to end the conversation, her face suddenly flush and red. *Something personal, for sure.* An image of Lola in that white robe at the Four Seasons flashed across my mind in a quick second.

The agent who sent the photo had circled the 二十 and wrote "=20" in red felt ink, sparking my recollection of this image, something I'd seen in my past. In seeing the photo, my hyperthymesia kicked in to the point I had to sit and catch my breath. I recalled in excruciating detail, exactly the path to one brick alley. Chinatown, Boston.

~~~

Several investigations over the years have brought me to various U.S. cities, Boston being one. Given my memory ailment, or rather benefit, depending on when it hits and overtakes me, I walk city streets. I'll roam, aimless, walking for hours, looking around and storing images of what I see. Sometimes, as with the dragon forming 二十, these walks change in the future from aimless past walks to valuable detective work in the present. Like I'm my own Google image search engine. Sometimes. Of course, the year I first saw this alley painting, I thought nothing whatsoever of it.

Back when Lola's agency sent the picture, and after collecting myself from the hyperthymesia hit, I corralled Lola and we headed to Boston. This was eight years ago.

In finding the alley with zero mistaken turns, we entered, passing by a karaoke bar on the right and an all-night sushi bar on the left. Albeit faded with age and seasons of rain and corrosive New England sleet, the brick wall held our white-paint 二十 dragon.

As we were in the right spot, we entered a back door which, knowing the storefronts on the street, meant we were entering the all-night sushi joint. Immediately we found ourselves in a black cave. Hanging black fabric formed the halls of a corridor, leading us to a back pass-through abutting an all-black kitchen. Tinny music was muted by a gurgling water feature, which we found in an open, windowless room, empty but for three things: the water feature, which was a giant fish tank, one table with four chairs, and a man. Only black life swam within the tank: black sea urchins, a spotted lobster, and a fat black fish.

The man standing before the tank and holding a dripping net above the opening didn't turn to greet us.

"Sit," he said.

The man wore a brown bowler's shirt and brown pants, somewhat resembling a monk. He turned and stared at us with blank, milk-white eyes; blind. His hair white.

"Are you here for the games?" he asked, his vision dead, and thus his eyes aiming beyond us.

"Yes," I said, silencing Lola with my hand. I inched closer. He still held the fish net. Water dripped to the white floor.

"You audition first, with me. Did you bring the coins?"

Lola and I had no idea what he was talking about. However, given the context, I was pretty sure he hosted an illegal poker ring in another room.

We sat at the table.

"Lady to my right, man to my left," he said, nodding to each of us as he sat opposite. His eyes up close were surely blinded, so I can only guess what his senses were telling him about us.

"We are not here to audition," I said.

This blind man wasn't even trying to hide his gambling operation, meaning he had dirt on law enforcement or law enforcement was in on the take. Or both.

He didn't flinch. "Why are you here? Are you to take me to my maker?" He laughed. I estimated his age at about eighty-five, but his confidence at 1,500.

"No, sir, we're not here to take you to your maker," I said. "I'm wondering about the painting on the brick wall in the alley."

His smile dropped, he stood stick straight, and pushed his chair so as to take two steps back.

"You leave. Now," he said.

Lola hit the table, and the metallic slap reverberated around the room. "I will shut this stink hole down if you do not sit your ass and talk," she said. "Now, sit."

In returning to his chair, slowly, he asked, "Why do you want to know? What's the dragon painting to you? Are you Center Ring?"

Bingo.

"Maybe," I answered. I was glad he was blind, for my fingers trembled. We had not encountered anyone in all the years of searching who admitted to knowing anything about a "Center Ring," as Velada referred to it to Lisa.

"If you're Center Ring, then you know. I don't need to tell you."

"Tell us anyway," Lola said.

"What is your name, sir?" I asked.

"Reno."

"That's not a real name," Lola scoffed.

"Who gives a fuck what you call me! Call me fucking Reno, lady."

"Okay, fine, Reno," I said in a forced reassuring tone. "We just want to know what the painting of the dragon on the wall outside means. Why the number twenty in Mandarin is embedded in it, and who it represents."

"He will do worse to me if I say. He blinded me, the bastard blinded me the last time he was here. Twelve years ago. Twelve years I've been blind. How are you going to protect me? Fool. You can't protect me. I don't even know who you are."

"Nobody will know you told us anything. We are law enforcement."

I wasn't really with the feds anymore, at this point, and I didn't want to say Lola's agency. So I overgeneralized, hoping he wouldn't ask for specifics.

"Law enforcement, ha!" he said, laughing. "Good one."

"Please, you seem to be a good man. I see how you care for these fish. We want to help others, from whoever this man is."

Reno closed his mouth, dropped his head, and rocked in his internal thoughts. We said nothing.

Lifting his head, he said, "Nobody, all these years, nobody has ever come in here and asked about the painting. Never. Most of the time it is blocked by the dumpster." He laughed to himself, paused, and dropped his head again, this time swaying. I reached over to Lola, put my hand on her shoulder, indicating she should say nothing so as to allow Reno time to think. After a good while, he lifted his head and laughed again. "I'm dying. Doctor says I have the lung cancer. Three months. Bad luck for me, but I guess your lucky fucking day, whoever you are. So fuck it. He is to return in eight years. Every twenty years. I know nothing about what the Center Ring does. Twelve years ago, he had someone paint that dragon with the Mandarin 20 on my wall to 'mark his spot,' he said. Said my restaurant was his place now, that he owns some people in the police, and that they'd shut down my poker if I fight. So, I had to let him, and he played some poker. Then, one night, like I told you, he blinded me. I think it's because he thinks I saw his face, but I didn't. He poured bleach in my eyes when his goons held me down. When they held me down, he yelled at me to say nothing while he was back in Shanghai. He said his cops here would spy on me until he returned. He said the next time he comes, I better still be here and the dragon on my wall. He is a sick fucking man. Insane. Cruel. I passed out. I woke up, everybody was gone. The man you're looking for, his sign outside, look for a man in Shanghai obsessed with twenty. That is all I know. Now go. I can't describe him. He wore a black mask when he was in my building. He's the boss. He bosses everyone he brings. Two or three men were with him; those men, is all. Every visit. His men."

"Who else came with him? Any names?" I asked.

"Get the fuck out. I'm done now."

"We could subpoena video, you know. You must have some cameras in this joint," Lola said, which was a bluff, given how under the radar we were trying to stay in order to not tip off those connected.

Reno laughed. "Good luck with that, lady. I'm fucking ancient. No video. And so it is the same with everyone else on this block. We know this game. Get the fuck out."

After leaving Reno's, we did try our search anew, this time looking

100

for a man named "Eminence" in Shanghai obsessed with "20," in English and Mandarin. A few strained leads were hard to pan out given the distance and the suspicions and international diplomacy tensions aroused when we tried to get Visas—given our past and current positions in government or private consulting. I pled with Lisa to bring in Lola's covert unit, but Lisa reminded us of the need to keep things to us so as to finally capture the rich and connected watchers, the paying customers in the act. She raised great points about how powerful assholes had done insanely awful and unbelievable things for centuries, and no matter how hard law enforcement worked angles for years to make big busts, the big fish usually got away with the darkest of the dark crimes and high-level witnesses were always conveniently "suicided out." She reminded us how urban legends, no matter how awful or bizarre, all had rings of truth. And that if we ever wanted a chance to expose the strangest of them all, and get some big fish, we had to do something different, and we had to keep our group small. The plan concealed from all. Otherwise, we'd fail like they always fail.

Without the Watchers or the Center Ring's identities, it was impossible to determine around whom we needed to bob and weave. Lisa was right. And at that point, eight years ago, we had not yet discovered the location of the Lobster Tank. We were as blind as Reno.

CHAPTER THIRTEEN
LISA YYLAND: SHANGHAI PART I
THE SCIENTIFIC METHOD

According to Oakton Community College's online article on The Scientific Method, copyrighted by William K. Tong, "It may take many years of often acrimonious debate to settle an issue, resulting in the adoption, modification, or rejection of a new theory...There are rare examples of scientific theories that have successfully survived all known attacks for a very long time, and are called scientific laws, such as Newton's Law of Gravity."

Boiled down, in using the Scientific Method to develop my plan over the years, as facts and assumptions were verified, changed, or invalidated, I had to, as a scientist, adjust my method, my plan. I wasn't dealing with an immovable scientific law such as gravity; I was dealing with a psycho's idiosyncratic torture by way of a shitty homemade tank of bleach.

Prior to Liu interrogating Reno, all Velada had revealed was that Eminence "came in from Asia." Asia is seventeen million square miles and is comprised of forty-eight countries—each with a labyrinth of byzantine laws. Across Asia, close to 2,200 languages are spoken, and then a multitude of local dialects expanding from those. The population tops four billion people. There are trillions of nooks and hovels and high-rises, fields and farms and bamboo jungles, within which scumbag human traffickers could hide. The laws of efficiency, practicality, language barriers, and the reality of a multitude of governments, including the United States, corruption, kept me from wasting time on "Asia."

But then came Reno with his clue to Shanghai. A specific city, a tiny dot—by comparison to all of Asia, a bullseye.

Liu and Lola's searches in Shanghai were fruitless.

Mine were not.

I had figured out more than them about that 'Burnt Lobster' videotape. Back in 1994, after Lola showed us the tape, while awaiting the copy process to finish at MIT, and while Liu and Lola walked to the MIT cafeteria for cheeseburgers, I noted something and cut four key seconds off of a copy I led Liu to believe was Lola's original (easy, given the mass produced and widely available type of tape used and how the serial numbers were scraped off). In short, I kept a lead on Liu and Lola so as to protect Liu and Lola. Way back then, I'd formed a capture and revenge plan. Liu just wanted capture.

The real tape actually had a couple of hidden clues about one of the girls. And if you married those clues to the clue about Eminence in Shanghai, you could send out strategic feelers and rightly find a good lead. Took me three years of working in the darkest corners of the dark web, but I did ultimately unearth a solid prospect to run down, on the ground, in Shanghai.

"Liu. Lola," I said one day while we worked an unrelated case at 15/33 headquarters, a day when Lola was in for a visit from her "Beta Agency," and a free moment when Liu's wife Sandra had gone out to pick a basket of Golden Delicious in my Indiana property's orchard. Vanty was at school, and Lenny was off on a book tour for his latest chapbook of poems. "I'm heading out to Shanghai for some patent business. I'll be gone a week," I announced. "And Nana's flying in to help with getting Vanty around to school and basketball."

Liu, like Nana, always calls me on my lies, so he dropped his reading glasses on his desk and scowled at me. "Shanghai, Lisa. Really? Patent business? Do you think I'm a stupid idiot? How insulting."

I looked to Lola for help; she raised her eyebrows at me. I know Lola knows I don't think they're stupid idiots, they're just handicapped by emotions, so I directed my next statement to her. "Do you know anyone in Shanghai who might be good for driving?" I asked. "You know, from your agency?"

"Honestly, Lisa," Liu said, inserting himself on my question to

Lola. "You can really be transparent and insulting sometimes. As if we can't figure out you're tracking Eminence there. For God's sake, you're not going. And if you were to go, you sure as hell wouldn't be going alone." He pushed his rolling office chair back from his desk and leaned against the seat, arms crossed.

"I'm leaving in two days. You don't have a Visa, Liu, and you most definitely will not get one in time. Your employer—which is me, by the way—won't vouch for an emergency business purpose. You can't come. Impossible. And Lola would cause an international incident if she tried to come."

Lola popped her lips and exhaled while standing to pace the room. She does this when she's angry, she's told me it's how she releases tension. But Lola usually directs all of her anger, no matter who she's angry at, to Liu. So I was not surprised when she shouted, "Fucking hell, Liu. What the fuck with her? You just let her run all half-cocked all the time. I guess she wants to get herself killed."

"Yeah, guess she does," he said. He started chewing like he was chewing gum, like he does when he's angry—I know, because I'd asked about this strange action before.

I looked between them, calculating how to steer the conversation the right way. I was going to Shanghai whether they agreed or not, but I really could use Lola's help with a trustworthy contact on the ground to "drive" me. And she knew what I meant by drive. She'd helped me, privately, with "drivers" before.

"What did you find out, Lisa? What is it you think you're running down?" Lola asked, her teeth clenched.

It was important I stay ahead of Liu and Lola, that I know more than them, so the plan would play out as intended, so they would be protected, and so I could catch all the dirtbags and get revenge. I stared back at Liu.

"Lisa?" Lola asked.

"Liu, you can hold down the agency while I'm gone. I'm just attending to some patent work."

I left the room to the sound of Lola kicking a metal cabinet.

That night, Lola buzzed the bell outside my locked tank room, interrupting my practice, choreographed to the tune of Chopin's *Nocturnes in C-Sharp*. Standing in one of the tanks (the other tank was under important upgrades), I saw her square face on the monitor beside my side of the door. On the wall around the monitor, the birch tree forest I'd been painting was complete. I had just the opposite wall to complete at this point.

My practice tank had no front panel at the time, as I was in the middle of practicing jumps; also, although I'd soon start practicing naked, I was practicing in my surfing bathing suit—a blue and green one-piece with full arms and chest zipper—as I was using this practice for the dual purpose of a cardio workout. I jumped from the tank and landed on a twin bed, a replica of the one in the 'Burnt Lobster' video, in a manner that made me topple three whole inches too far to the right. It was imperative that I stick the landing and bend in control to fully flex my back in an arch, so I grimaced at my imbalance. I popped off the bed, barefoot, all my toes intact then, turned off Chopin on the wall knob by the monitor, opened and exited the room, not allowing Lola to enter.

She shoved a piece of paper and a tiny fob in my hand while walking into my space so close, I backed into the hall wall. Her eyes were bulged; she didn't blink. And she didn't make any of her regular "sarcastic"—she calls them—comments about my bathing suit.

"Lisa, don't you ever lie to me again."

I started to correct her, but she held up her hand.

"Nope. No sir-E. No, no. Nope. Listen. I know you think you didn't lie directly to me—I get it. I know how your brains work, girl," she said, tapping her own temple. "I get it. Ayup-de-do, I do. You tried, in your way, to say what the fuck you're up to by asking me for a driver. But you were sorta lying, yup. Don't you ever lie to me again."

"I will not lie to you, Lola, unless it's to save your life."

She hit the wall. I bounced, the *thud* was so strong.

"Nope! B*zzzz*. Wrong answer. You *never* lie to me. I get to decide how to save my own skins. You get that? How would you like it if I decided when to tell you the truth; that I got all the say in what you knew; that I got to decide, all by myself, how to save your life?"

Upon considering these hypotheticals, a vague sense of anger flickered in my brain, like it wanted me to turn it on. I closed my left eye to stomp out a rising heat in my body. Lola took a step back to the middle of the hall. I stayed plastered in my spot.

"Well? How would you like that, Lisa?"

"I believe that would anger me."

"It's easy then. Don't ever fucking lie to me, and then neither of us gets mad. Real simple. Okay? Deal?"

Seemed a denial of her proposal would not be beneficial for me and my objectives. And if she exited my life, mad at me, I wouldn't be able to protect her.

"Agreed," I lied.

Lola bubbled her lips and bounced her head, looking me up and down in my surfer's suit. "Hang-ten," she said, forming her right hand in the "hang loose" shaka sign, the one Vanty and my surfing instructor taught us during a Maui vacation.

She walked off, sniggering to herself, stopping two times to crouch and fling her arms in the manner of catching a wave, saying weird phrases like, "Surf Nazi's Must Die," and "Kowafuckingbunga," and disappeared down the dark corridor of the wing.

On the paper she jammed in my palm, she'd scrawled a dark web address and four pass phrases that would verify me to a Shanghai "driver," and the "driver" to me. Thereafter, the driver, who I called Dan, and I had coded communications on our separate encrypted laptops, accessing a restricted channel by way of four levels of encryption, the codes of which were constantly changing, but accessible through the tiny fob Lola had jammed in my hand.

~~~

It is the case sometimes that some people exist, waiting to die. Some wait to say one specific thing, some to see one specific person. To right one wrong. To atone one crime. Their time came and went long ago, they should be no more on this Earth, in the form in which they were born. They should be dust. And yet, they persist like a dormant siren in a locked tower, waiting to blare. These are the lessons I took from copyediting Lenny's history-inspired elegies and from reading original fairy tales to Vanty. This was the state of the girl I found in Shanghai.

Liu's mistake in following up on Reno's tip about Eminence being in Shanghai was that Liu inquired *only* on Eminence. He had concluded, like everyone did, that the burnt girl in the video had actually died.

In the last four seconds of the original, the girl who was dragged into the room from the tank can be seen breathing, her chest rising and falling. The breathing was delayed and shallow, nearly undetectable—could be easily missed, if you didn't watch in super slow-mo and add high resolution pixilation remastering from an MIT ally who had her own personal, super-advanced AV lab. Nevertheless, the girl was breathing. Seeing as I suspected her survival, I had a theory that the tank girl had been returned to whatever small cell Eminence ruled in Asia. Eminence's directives in the 'Burnt Lobster' video revealed his strange psychology, a twisted perception that the tank was a gift for the girls, a gift of who would survive, obviously, but also a gift of a chance to "live in eminence." Seemed to me that he would gift the survivor the *chance* to be near him or be special to him—this was my interpretation, one of my *theories* that I set out to validate.

Liu and Lola kept their contacts searching for a man named "Eminence" obsessed with the number 20. But nobody disclosed if they knew anything; seemed Eminence had everyone on his side of the world locked up, lips sewn. And again, we'd been told by Velada, and Reno implied, this was a small operation—only two to three men with him in the United States. That the Center Ring was small seemed a validated fact. Given the secrecy around the lobster tank, and the almost non-existent knowledge of it, and the archaic construction of the tank in the video, I believed Eminence's operation was, truly, small. Their customers might be more widely spread, but the operation small, the core management doling out limited and strategically-timed information.

~~~

After landing, I set out for a five-star hotel in city center, the Puli. Along the way, my tall and thin, quiet "driver" Dan drove us past fields stuffed with hundreds upon hundreds of unoccupied high-rise apartment buildings. The pictures on the internet do not convey the reality of what I saw. The blocks of apartment buildings coming into cities like New York and Chicago would need to be multiplied by the hundreds and all the paraphernalia that marks human existence—curtains in the windows, clothes drying on balconies—would need to be erased to recreate these endless fields of empty high-rise apartments. A true apocalypse. I'd use umber and shades of gray to paint Shanghai, and I'd mix dirt with varnish to convey my impression of the size of the air particulates. The thing that never leaves you when in Shanghai is the constant smog and burnt air.

I covered my nose and mouth in an N95 Respirator—not some flimsy mask like some common tourist. The N95 can filter 95%, down to .03 microns of particulate. I needed that, for I'd anticipated, in reviewing leaked manufacturing statistics and air quality reports, that the Shanghai pollution would be worse than the travel advisories, and it was. Secure in a robot's face, I watched the prophecy of mankind's ruins along the highway. I wanted to find the burnt girl, interrogate her, try to extricate her, and leave.

I made it to the Puli, confirmed plans with Dan, checked in to the luxury room I'd reserved, just how Mother taught me, and thereafter followed every medical advisory on overcoming jet lag: shower, massage in the spa, slept twelve hours, lots of water, exercise, and returned renewed to my same death-quiet Dan, who would multitask as driver, translator, and bodyguard. He had advised me to travel with my small bag and Visa at all times, leave nothing behind, so I threw all that in his trunk. He and I would protect my outside body, and the N95 would cover my pink lungs.

I wasn't surprised when Dan returned us to the highway that those fields of apocalypse came again. And I wasn't surprised when he exited the highway and maneuvered between a couple dozen blocks of the empty buildings, for I'd given him the coordinates from my lead. And I didn't jump in any surprise when he weaved between five towering empty buildings and we came upon an ancient hamlet of tiny shacks, persisting in the literal shadows of the towering high-rises, like rocks in a barren garden. Some had grass roofs, all were squares and rectangles of crumbling clay. And there was one concrete building, four floors high, in the middle of the shacks, which in my mind, I called "the boss building." I didn't jump, but I did not expect the scene of ancient living ruins between the blocks of empty modern dwellings. Here were signs of life: Laundry drying on lines, a washing machine outside, various mattresses lying on the sides of the dirt road with one on a roof, several stray dogs, and two barefoot boys playing soccer in Pokemon T-shirts.

My driver pointed to a thin, black door at the base of the boss building. We spoke our only words in confirming the plan we'd agreed upon.

"This is the prostitutes' base you identified. I've surveilled it for three days now. I've seen only women coming and going. I will tell them you're scouting a burnt girl we've heard of for a U.S. businessman, your boss, because he has a fetish for such things," Dan said.

"Yes."

Up a narrow staircase with a high-pitched ceiling we went. Long, red, pointy pendants scraped my scalp as I ascended. Dan knocked on a green, wooden door at the top landing; I brushed away two flies buzzing my arm. The pendants fluttered above our heads when the door opened, breaking the stagnant air. The scent that rolled out might have been of cooking meat, but since all I saw was dust and dirt, dried mud is the odor my brain perceived. The Mandarin scrawl of 20, 二十, was painted as the eyes of a dragon in the small part of the wall between the door frame and a cobwebbed corner.

A weak-chinned woman in a ripped, red dress peeked around the crack in the open door, eyed me, and directed a heated volley of Mandarin questions at my driver. He answered, passed her a fat stack of Yuan, and the crack widened enough for her to shoo us in. She slammed the door and locked it three times—a worthless act of imagined security, for all she had were hardware store chain-and-slide locks. Any fool could boot kick in this wasteland.

After the woman with the useless locks disappeared down a white hall with several doorways on each side, and between those, crooked hanging pictures of cats in fields, we heard Mandarin whispers roll to us in an echo from some chamber at the darkened end. No lights were on in the joint, but my driver and I had some illumination as we waited by a never-washed window in a den decorated with a piss yellow couch and a patchwork of twenty throw rugs; I counted. I'm sure bedbugs and body lice infested the floor, so I curled all my real toes in my shoes. My flesh-colored knee band stretched tight as I straightened my legs, and the by-then grape-sized capacitor connected to it poked into my thigh, under my REI hiking pants. My robot mask hummed away on my face.

Out of the dark shadows at the end of the hall of multiple doorways and crooked cats, my presumed tank girl—now a grown woman—edged out and approached, hunched and slow-shuffling.

She peeked up through her eye-scratching black bangs, nodded at us, her customers, then curled her finger for me to follow her back down the hall and into the bowels of her chamber. Recalling Nana's admonitions about polite society, I removed my N95 because the hopeful tank woman wasn't wearing one. I stifled a cough and blurred my vision to the drab navy curtains acting as doors along the hall—the curtains more like middle strips, as they were narrower than the doorways. Twenty doorways to twenty tiny cells, ten on each side of the hall. Most of the cells were empty, except for two, and each held one woman, lying on a floor matt. I counted twenty crooked pictures of cats in the spaces between doorways.

The woman and I entered a room in the back with an actual door. She shut it and pointed to one of two pieces of furniture in the room, a bed on a frame, and began to undress. I sat where she pointed. On the wall above her bed were twenty painted suns. My translator had told the weak-chinned woman that I'd need for my promised burnt girl to undress for me so I could confirm she was scarred enough for my sick-fuck, fake employer with the horrible fetish. I told her to stop after one sleeve was off; I'd seen enough. She was, I was near certain, the burnt girl from the video. Her skin had splashes of red wash, black spots, puckering, and uneven damage, all consistent with a chemical burn.

"I speak English," she said, when I motioned to get Dan to translate the rest of our conversation.

"What is your name?" I asked.

"Candy?" She answered as an offer-question, suggesting I could agree or disagree that her name was Candy. I did not agree.

"No, your real name."

"Never had name. My family called me Bucket once. A long time before. My customers call me what they want."

I probably should have suffered some inefficient pleasantries, per Nana's many instructions on how to properly ease into serious conversations.

"You were in America, put in a tank they filled with bleach, correct?"

Her back straightened, she shook, stared at me like I was fear itself, and started for the door. I blocked her.

"I am here to help you, please sit," I said. "I need to know all the

110

details of your day in the tank."

It took a lot of talking, all of the skills I'd been practicing and studying on the art of hostage negotiation. To me, the psychology was the same as between hostage negotiation and calming a captive. After an hour of me playing this psychological trust game, I poked my head out and directed my multi-purpose driver to pay for another hour of *Melanie's* time. Melanie, a name she'd given herself, a sharp departure from her younger years as Bucket.

"Yes, this tank. They burned me," she finally admitted, her head down, her body sitting, but curled into herself on the bed. Her bare feet appeared splashed with an uneven red wash. I wanted to jump into the several dozen questions I had planned out so I could drill into the minutia of her day leading up to the moments in the tank. I needed a granular step-by-step accounting and I needed independent validations of items I'd learned from Velada. But Melanie held up a finger to tell me to hold on, stood up, and walked to the other piece of furniture in the room, a three-drawer dresser. She crouched; her thin, yellow dress pooled on the concrete floor. Out of the bottom drawer, she pulled out a black cloth, balling it in her fist as she stood, turned, and walked to me.

The way she held her clenched fist in my space told me in wordless direction to open my hands, and when I did, she dropped the black cloth on my palms. It unfurled in a slow metamorphosis, stretching its nylon fibers.

I held up before me a sheer, black, fabric mask like the one Eminence wore in the video. An immediate instinct pushed me to look inside. Because nylon weave is like a sieve, I saw several embedded hairs.

"This is his, the man who burnt you, his mask?"

"He wears many. He leaves this here for when he come here."

"He comes here?"

"Yes."

"Where does he live?"

"Don't know."

"When does he come?"

"Anytime he wants."

"Are all his masks of this nylon, this fabric?"

"I think so."

I rubbed it, noting its cheap synthetic manufacture. I considered testing its flammability in my lab in Indiana.

"Could he show now, any minute?" I asked.

"Yes."

"You need to come with me. I can hide you somewhere in this country, get you protection. Whatever you decide. We must go now."

I still held the mask. She didn't answer.

"Why do you need these details of my day in the tank?" She looked to the floor, fidgeting her fingers. She sat back on her bed, this time on the edge, her head down.

"If I had every single detail you remember of that day, I might be able to save other girls," I said.

She flipped her face up to me and stared. Her fingers stopped fidgeting.

"He calls himself Eminence, right?" I asked.

"He says he is eminent, the highest being living."

"We can talk more once we are in a safe spot. Get your items together."

Her lips trembled and she stumbled on a few words. I thought she was about to agree to leave when Dan pounded his fist on the door and demanded I open.

"We have to go now. The patron of this house is coming. The woman who opened the door called him, told him you were asking questions of his 'Pride', she called her; I heard her on the phone. Couldn't stop her."

"You need leave," Melanie said, popping off her bed and moving fast to try and move past me. "They get you in a prison, you never leave. Eminence, he knows bad police. Embassy will not help you. Leave! I cannot come with you, they will kill all the girls here if I do. I am what he calls the Pride—the pin, he says, that keeps this house alive. He is crazy."

"Melanie, I saw only two other girls in the hall rooms. We can take them, too."

"You don't understand. There are twenty girls in this house, besides me, and the witch who opens door. The twenty are for rotation and they go to the city every day. They do sex in hotels. For U-S-A business men from factory offices. Regular customers. If I'm not here at night to send video to Eminence of them back, and count their money for him on video, he comes and he kills all of them. Those are rules. The two here now just have the day off."

I breathed in as much oxygen as I could, stared Melanie down, and determined I then had no other options. "I'm coming back, Melanie. I'm getting you out, and we need to talk."

When I looked at Melanie, I saw Dorothy. But I soon learned Melanie was her own force.

Melanie walked out of her room first; Dan and I followed her back down the hall. Along the way, she knocked once on the doorways of the two girls, presumably indicating they not move. Their navy door curtains swished as we passed, giving us the sight of them frozen on their mats. Then Melanie started shouting in Mandarin at the weak-chinned woman who'd called Eminence, thrusting her fist, and screaming at her. The woman immediately shrunk into herself, and I believe said, "I'm sorry," over and over in Mandarin.

"She is a stupid woman. I'll tell Eminence that she is a confused bitch. That she ran off a good customer for me. He will not know about you. Now go, you must go."

CHAPTER FOURTEEN
LISA YYLAND: SHANGHAI PART II
THE SCIENTIFIC METHOD

Dan and I speed-walked down the hallway, my adrenaline on fire, for, according to my reading of travel alerts, breaking out of a Chinese prison is at level 100 on a scale of 10 for impossibility. And if I wasn't to be framed for breaking some Chinese law by Eminence's crooked cops, being captured and held in China by Eminence, himself, seemed an even worse fate. Dan didn't wait for me to shut the car door before he jammed on the gas. I plummeted to the floor, scrambling to shut the door.

"I need to be able to watch that building," I shouted up to him.

He didn't respond.

We twisted and turned and sped around blocks of empty buildings. He checked the rearview mirror, said "clear," and without any warning, took the sharpest ninety degree left, and then slowed to a crawl. We rolled at about the speed of two miles an hour for several blocks, and I was so turned around sitting in the well of the backseat floor, I couldn't tell what direction we were going. Then he stopped.

"Sit here," he said. "Stay low, where you are."

He got out of the car, and I could hear him pushing or pulling metal, and then a slight creaking sound of metal rising. He popped back in the car, which was still running, arched his arm over the passenger seat backrest, looked over his shoulder, and backed us down a ramp. It grew darker and darker the lower we went.

"We're in a building opposite that hamlet. We need to get higher. We can watch from there. I have scopes. All these empty buildings have an electrical panel for access outside. I hacked it. Hacked the stairwell lock, too. Obviously, the elevators are not yet powered or are unreliable."

"Good. Let's go," I said. In my mind, I decided to pay Dan double for creating such an exemplary plan so quick.

Wearing my N95, I waited in the car while Dan worked the inside panel to shut the building's garage door and then went on to hack the door to the stairwell. Then he took a large, black bag from the trunk, along with my own necessities. He handed me the travel bag with Visa.

"We've got twenty floors to climb to reach my perch."

"Your perch?"

"Where did you think I did surveillance from for the past three days?"

I multiplied Dan's payment in my mind by three.

On the twentieth floor, I followed Dan through a maze of halls, wires falling out of plastered walls and no light fixtures anywhere. Plastic sheets blocked off some rooms and whole sections.

"They still have so much work to do to finish these monoliths," Dan said. "I don't think they ever intend to. I think this is all for show. Come on, in here."

Dan led me into what, I suppose, was a space that would maybe someday have interior walls and comprise an apartment. He assembled his .50 caliber with practiced ease, inserted a magazine, and rested the rifle's bipod on the sill. After adjusting his scope and sighting his target, he set up a second scope for me.

"You use this one," he said, pointing to mine; the one without the gun. "We'll watch from here. Don't worry, the windows are blackened from outside. Nobody can see us."

Next, Dan sat on the floor and pulled two bottles of water from his black bag. Setting one beside me and one beside him, he added, "I have protein bars for nourishment. For a bathroom, climb a floor and choose a corner. I've got a corner on a floor below. It's crude, but we can't come and go."

"Understood."

I liked how Dan talked: with minimal and efficient words.

Dan said no more, and we both took to our scopes. I checked the time on my wristwatch. Forty-two minutes later, a black SUV pulled up to the boss building. Out stepped a large man with a black mask over his head: Eminence. He headed into the boss building stairwell; his driver stayed in the SUV.

For me, having watched him so many years on video, I had started to question his existence—like, perhaps he was no more than a character in a movie. But then he stepped out of that SUV in Shanghai and validated the ugly fact of his existence in the real world.

"That's Eminence," I said to Dan.

"I know. I made us scramble out of there. We could have stayed longer. The traffic in and around downtown is atrocious, so I'm not surprised it took him an hour to get here from wherever he was."

"It's better we watch, and we plan," I said.

"Why wait?" Dan asked, nodding at the trigger adjacent his scope. "Two shots, easy. One for the glass, one for him."

I thought about all my own glass cutting and shattering devices back home in my practice tank room, all my trials and errors. How cutting a standing pane of glass, even if you know the type of glass and its thickness, and even if you're able to carry with you a large suction cup with a blade on a rotating arm, maintaining consistent pressure while standing in a tank with restricted movement, results are inconsistent and unreliable. I looked at Dan's long, sharpshooting, assassin's barrel, and while I appreciated the simplicity and efficiency of a bullet, I did not like the laziness of a gun, nor the fact that we'd kill my ultimate goal.

Without looking away from my scope, I said, "He needs to live so I can entrap him with others in the United States. We cannot eliminate him yet. If we eliminate him, another fungus will just take his place there, and I'll lose the one shot I got to take them all down."

"Understood," he said. And we continued to watch.

Eminence stayed for thirty-two minutes and fifteen seconds in the boss building. When he emerged at the base of the stairwell, he didn't look around, didn't look up, did not reveal any suspicion we were watching from on high. He entered his SUV and drove off.

"What do you want to do?" Dan asked.

"Watch for the return of the other girls tonight, like Melanie said. Watch again tomorrow to confirm that pattern. And figure out a plan."

"I know the pattern. They come back on a bus at midnight. And then many leave the next morning on that same bus at eight a.m. The bus remains all night. I do not know where the bus is during the day."

"I need to validate myself."

"So we watch."

"Yes."

And it happened just like Dan said. That night, an old blue bus, the short kind, came at midnight, parked behind the boss building all night, and the driver slept on the bus. In the morning, the bus driver took a piss behind the bus, and left with the girls at eight a.m., only to return again at midnight, and the cycle began anew. At no time did I see Melanie or the weak-chinned woman leave the boss building. At some point in our surveillance, I made a few phone calls and Dan and I hammered out the plan. On the third day at three a.m., when the whole hamlet was quiet and asleep, I stood facing Dan.

"Ready?"

"Ready."

He threw me his car keys.

Having already packed up his scopes and collected our bottles and protein bar wrappers, I assured my running shoes with perfect grips were tied tight; Dan adjusted his black micro-fiber pants and shirt and tightened his shoes. We slid down the twenty floors of stairs as silent as the air around us, and I waited in a shadow in the underground parking lot while Dan again hacked the gate. I set my travel bag and Visa in the trunk and locked the car back up, hiding the keys in a compartment by a back wheel. This time Dan left the gate open and the car parked inside.

Using night shadows and stepping lightly, we snuck to the boss building. I used a simple lock pick on the building's black door and entered; Dan circled the building and went to the bus, as planned, to disable the sleeping driver, tie him up, hide him somewhere, and take his place.

I crept up the stairs, listening for any movements of women awakening. I heard nothing. I extended my arms as I rose, touching the stairwell walls on each side, the width so narrow my arms bent. At the top, those red pendants hanging from the pitched high ceiling scraped my head again. I took a thin, metal sheet Dan gave me, slid it in the door seal and yanked up, knocking off each of the stupid lock and slide key chains. My first objective inside was to cut the phone cord in the kitchen from which the weak-chinned woman called Eminence. My second was to get to Melanie without any of the women seeing and thus sending them into alarm.

I went to the kitchen. The whole place still smelled of either cooking meat or dry mud.

And I was lucky, for here was the phone cord, but also unlucky, for here was the weak-chinned woman, staring at me and frozen by the sink. I went to her first, grabbed her in a headlock while slamming a gag from my pocket in her mouth, and then tying it tight around her head. Next, I knocked her out by stabbing my elbow in the soft spot on her skull; I caught her before she wilted to the floor. I tied her hands behind her back and tied her feet together—using zip ties, also supplied by Dan—after dragging her into a closet off the kitchen. I jammed a kitchen chair under the doorknob so she couldn't escape. Next, I grabbed a butcher knife in the sink and sliced the phone cord as I tiptoed toward the white hall with the twenty crooked cats.

Setting the knife on the counter as I entered the hallway, I felt a presence watching me.

I looked up. At the end of the hall stood Melanie in a spotlight by her chamber door, motionless and stiff-backed in a white shift. Her exposed bare feet were red with splashy burns, her arms the same, her neck, her chin, all burned.

Is she a ghost? That's not rational. She's not a ghost.

She held a finger to her mouth to quiet me. I tiptoed down the hall and did not see one woman stir as I passed. I entered Melanie's room, and she shut the door.

"I've been waiting," she said.

"My driver will take the women to a safe place I've secured. Once they're loaded in the bus and drive off, you and I will drive there separately and we can talk. Get ready. We're going now."

"They will not wake for many hours. We'll talk now, in case of a problem."

"Or we wake them now, get them on the bus. And go."

"That won't work. You have to get them on the bus with no suspicions. They're not supposed to have, but I think some have, cell phones. Some might panic. Call Eminence. We get them to safe place first, then the ones who want this life can choose to come back.

Most others just need a chance."

I didn't like the plan, but I had considered these very risks, the panic of some of the women, the cell phones they likely had snuck in. It wasn't a physical entrapment that kept them here, it was mental—they believed they had no other options, and the fear was baked into each of them that by leaving, they'd be murdering the ones who stayed.

Mental chains.

I had to agree that having them get on the bus unsuspecting of their new future was our best hope for the least static.

"What about the bitch in the front of the house? You handle her?" she asked.

I nodded. "I'll have to re-handle her. Do you have any narcotics?"

She went to the top drawer of her three-drawer dresser and fished around inside. Finding what she was searching for, she turned and handed me a bottle of Halcion, potent sleeping pills for insomniacs.

"I get these on the black market. One dose knocks me out for hours. Give the bitch three."

After crushing the pills and dissolving the dust on the weak-chinned woman's tongue, I locked the kitchen closet with a key Melanie had given me, and returned the chair to a kitchen table. All appeared back to normal.

I met Melanie on the piss yellow couch in the dingy den. And so…it was there, at 3:30 in the morning while everyone slept, that Melanie told me her life story and delivered important details in a way that surprised me, not only in details, but the strength of her conviction. She whispered so light, I had to lean my ear close to her mouth—so close, her lips grazed my earlobe dozens of times. As she spoke, she squeezed and fiddled with a roll of papers she'd brought with her from her chamber.

~~~

Melanie grew up in a lean-to shack outside of Guangzhou. Her mother died in childbirth when her placenta ripped from her cervix and she bled to death on the earthen floor of her and her husband's hovel. After throwing her mother's body in a shallow grave by an open-pit dump, the paternal side of Melanie's family said the woman's death was a just punishment for carrying the germ of a girl inside. For five days, the father and paternal grandmother hid newborn Melanie from everyone because the mother had violated the one child rule and, for shame, had doubled-down on violation by selecting a girl ovum from her greedy ovaries. I didn't correct Melanie on the horrifyingly wrong reproductive science she'd been taught, just like I'd been warned by Nana to not correct the cake decorator for creating unrealistic sound waves on my dissertation cake. "Some corrections are rude," Nana says.

On the fifth day of Melanie's time on this planet, her father tried to drown her in a bucket of mop water, but Melanie's paternal grandmother called her son a fool, explaining that in the very least, they could, once she was old enough to feed herself, sell the girl to sex traffickers. When Melanie turned 8, they reaped, in converting the Yuan to U.S. dollars, $80.99 for her life. Melanie had been told the story of her birth and near death every single day of her life until sold, because her father and grandmother repeated all the facts every morning as Melanie served them dumplings and tangerines. The agent of her almost death, the mop bucket, hung from a rusty nail over a drippy sink in their lean-to as a constant reminder of the gifts her family bestowed upon her by allowing her to live and serve them. "Bucket," they'd say while pointing to the bucket and then at her. "You are no better than the bucket. You are a bucket."

At age 8, Melanie left the lean-to shack, a space she'd never ventured beyond, and entered a black SUV, which drove her around and around a few hours and then landed upon a fenced-in, guarded compound. A man dragged her to a shed by her hair. In the shed, two men waited. One held her down while the other said, in halting language—which as described, matched the voice in the 'Burnt Lobster' video, "I am Eminence and I own you. You will learn English when you are fifteen. You will come to America to earn your keep with our greatest customers! If they reject you, you must pass a great test I am designing. If you pass, I'll let you live back here to serve as my Pride. And live in eminence."

Theory validated.

While waiting out the time until she turned fifteen, Melanie lived in the basement of the compound and was expected to practice English while stitching embroidered dresses that boys sold to tourists on the streets of Shanghai. Each dress had a sunflower with twenty petals: no less, no more. At night, Eminence would either rape her or one of the other twenty basement girls. Girls. Always under fifteen years old. And twenty girls. Always twenty girls.

I first thought Melanie's childhood background was irrelevant to the facts I'd flown to Shanghai to acquire. The facts I'd wanted were the microscopic movements Melanie made, every single sight and sound she observed on the day of her walk to, and time in, the tank. But I let Melanie divulge her past. I had concluded, from all the context, that no one had ever let her speak of them in such candor before. And Nana always says to not interrupt people who are in the middle of an emotion, even if I'm "not experiencing it," as she puts it. So I let Melanie talk. The more she talked, the more the asymmetrical injustice of it all bothered my executive function. There was so much waste in what she described, so much pointless barbarianism. I couldn't help but return to the hatred I'd allowed in my own captivity, which in comparison to Melanie's was as if I'd been riding Thunder Mountain like Vanty, in gap-mouthed, cotton-candy, Technicolor joy. So as Melanie went on, I turned hate on, and adding that with the loyalty and love for Dorothy that surfaced, I considered how my plan was now grander. It wasn't just for my own personal escape and total retribution for Dorothy now, it was something for all the Dorothy's, all the Melanie's.

"Eminence told me I was the first of his 'Prides' to take his tank test and if I passed, I live," she said. At this point in the conversation, having divulged her backstory, her hands no longer fidgeted with the roll of papers in her hands and her voice did not crack. Now her sentences came in a sharp staccato and her tone was one of anger. This sentence in particular resounded in me, as it verified a critical piece of Velada's story: Eminence designed the tank and it was his.

I motioned Melanie to continue, trying to get her to move it along. I had started hearing the stirrings of women waking. But Melanie was no longer looking at me for courage. She stared ahead and delivered her next sentence with a loathing monotone. "Eminence says another girl would *get* a chance in his special tank, but not for twenty years. He says, 'The power of twenty will free you, child.' He says this every day. Twenty is tattooed on his back in Mandarin. Everything in twenty. Even a piece of bread has to be cut twenty times." These facts verified

Reno's and Velada's warnings of twenty years, which only served to confuse me; I didn't understand, despite these verifications, why I still did not trust Velada. Melanie's facts and all the items and images in sets of twenty I saw in the boss building led to a psychological diagnosis: extreme OCD over the number 20, coupled with psychotic superstition. But the *why* of Eminence's sick plan is better left to the consternations of religion and philosophy. As a scientist, I needed Melanie focused on the critical scientific questions: *What can I know? And how can I know it?*

Women were definitely up now, the one bathroom door opening and closing. Melanie stood, still holding her roll of papers. She walked to the start of the hall and addressed the women emerging from their tiny cells.

"Kitchen woman will not make breakfast today. She's sick. You get ready now. Get on the bus. Eat in the city. Do not bother me. I am taking a new rich American client, talking out here. Nobody gets the day off today. All must go to the city on the bus," she said. After, she told me she speaks English to them as Eminence demands that they speak English to their western customers in the factory and corporate offices.

"Melanie, we have to hurry," I said when she returned to the couch. "Do you have everything you need to go?"

She didn't answer, just stared at the roll of papers in her hands. Melanie seemed catatonic to me then. She didn't flinch. "Eminence told me every day before the tank what every step would be like. And it happened exactly as he planned. He said it would always be the same. He said ceremony is key to supremacy. I wrote this all on scraps of papers for you. Here." She handed me her roll of papers, which felt wet. I noticed how sweat pooled in Melanie's hollow collar bones.

"Are you suffering a fever?" I asked.

"I'm just nervous."

"These papers have the details of your day in the tank?"

"That day is the day I died. I wrote it all. I never forget those details. You use these. Use these and save these other girls you talk about."

After some solid silence, I turned to Melanie, "Why does he use a dragon with twenty? Is that some Chinese cult?"

"No. Eminence is white. His parents flew here from America,

owners of a U.S. company factory for shoes. Rich owners. He wears a black cloth to cover burns to his face. From a house fire when he was a boy. His parents and most of his family died. He was left in a Chinese boy orphan house. No one wanted him he's so ugly, his face is very scarred. The orphan house had dragon toys, twenty dragon toys. And the main lady make him clean floors with bleach, every day. The twenty dragons, those were his only friends, he says. We girls hear this story all the time. His parents left him money in the U.S. though, and an old house. I think the money for him is in a track? Trast?"

"You mean a trust?"

"Maybe. That's how he got money once he was out of the orphan house. That's how he got his start."

A woman appeared in the living room.

"Like I said, I can add your boss to the rotation for three girls, starting next week. We will talk price now," Melanie said, not looking up at the woman as she adroitly changed the topic.

I took her cue to be deceptive. "I want to know the price for three girls first," I said.

Melanie shot her head to the woman who had appeared. She looked to weigh eighty pounds, dressed in a cheap lacy dress. "You get on the bus now! Do not offend our client with your face!" Melanie shouted.

The woman turned and walked down the stairwell.

"She will get on the bus now. They will all get on the bus now."

And so, it happened, they all silently filed out, down the stairs, and did not look into the den where Melanie and I pretended to converse about how I would hire three of her girls for my fake asshole sick-fuck employer. One by one they descended. They wore thin cloths and see-through laces; their shoes were simple slippers.

When the last one left, Melanie turned to me, tears in her eyes. "So many years like this," her voice broke. "So many years I must yell to them. Hurt them. Punish them. Or he would find and kill them. Please save my girls, too."

"You will save them," I said. Melanie shook and sobbed for the first time in our short time together, and I then considered her even stronger than Lola. We watched from the window while the women filed onto the bus. Dan would have told them their old driver was replaced for disobeying Eminence in the night, and given he was a native Shanghai man with the perfect diction, I hoped they bought it. He also would have made them turn in their cell phones to him, if they had one, making them plop them in a basket, giving them some convincible reason I was sure he'd concoct. The original driver, I didn't know where Dan hid him, and I didn't care. I trusted he'd been handled.

The bus drove off, headed for the safe place Dan and I had secured for them through our channels.

"Come on, Melanie. It's time," I said.

Melanie got a bag together while I pulled out the weak-chinned woman from her locked closet and cut her hand and feet ties. I laid her on the yellow couch; she snored, deep in a day coma from those pills. Melanie appeared and set a handwritten note on the floor by the couch for the woman. Melanie translated it for me: "Bitch, you run now. We escaped."

We started to descend those narrow stairs. Squeezing Melanie's roll of facts about her day in the tank, I went ahead with Melanie behind me. At the base, I waited for her, for she was taking her time, stalling on the treads, scraping her fingers down the walls.

"Hurry," I said.

"I never go down these stairs," she said. She was still crying.

"You must stop crying. You must be faster."

She did not stop crying. She did not move faster.

I heard the rumble of the earth, and the roll of approaching tires. I turned my head to the left and watched an SUV turn a corner around one of those damn high-rises. But sound continued rumbling to my right, too, so I turned my head that way and saw another SUV approaching from that direction. They sped, closing in fast on both sides, boxing us in. In front of us was the high-rise Dan and I had perched in for days. Behind us was the boss building and the shacks in the hamlet. Behind those…just an endless flat land with nothing. Miles of dirt. And Melanie was still straggling down the stairs in an inefficient stupor.

Motherfucker.

The only option was to buy a few minutes by barricading ourselves as best we could back in the boss building, taking the higher ground. So I turned, pushed Melanie to turn around, and forced her to run back up that meat-smelling, narrow stairwell.

We didn't make it far, given Melanie stopping and tripping twice. As I was behind her, I braced myself upon hearing his voice enter at the base of the stairs behind us.

"Stop now. You will stop," Eminence shouted.

"Melanie, go. Go, get up there," I said, pushing at her back. "Take these. Hide these," I said, handing her the roll of notes.

I didn't turn to watch Eminence storm up the stairs; Melanie was still two steps away from reaching the top. I set my palms on each of the narrow walls, just as I had when I walked up them earlier that morning, and pushed out as I jumped in the air, thinking I would brace one foot on each side and parkour up into the higher space from where the pendants hung. But as I jumped, preparing to fling my legs wide in a split, Eminence caught my legs and pulled me down. I crashed toward the stair treads and stopped my face from hitting with my palms, just in time. Melanie screamed at the top of the stairs, back in the upper entrance.

The round capacitor strapped to my thigh jammed into my skin and muscle so hard, it felt like it hit bone. I considered the bruise that would take over my entire thigh.

"You get her. While I deal with her," Eminence said over my head to another person I could hear climbing the stairs.

Eminence pinned me on my back with a knee; with a strong hand, he clamped my neck down, and with his other hand he managed to grab and hold both my arms. I estimated his weight at 300 pounds, all muscle, his hands the size of china plates.

I hadn't confirmed him by look of his face, nor seen him yet with his black mask on, like the other evening. It was his voice. That halting cadence. The tenor. The same one I'd heard in the video for so many years. His voice was more of an identifier than his fingerprints.

He pushed us to the side of the stairwell, still holding me as such, and another man squeezed past and headed toward Melanie.

"Run, Melanie. Go. Lock your door," I shouted. I hoped she'd hide those notes in her mattress.

"Shut. The fuck. Up. You bitch," Eminence said, holding me still. He let go of my neck, grabbed a fistful of my hair at the base, and before I could figure out his next step, he let go of my arms with his other hand. I didn't hesitate. I placed my palms on the stair tread to push off and back against him and his knee, hoping the torque would challenge his one-footed balance, causing him to fall down the stairs. But in taking his hands off my arms, he had also swiftly pulled a blade and placed it to the base of my neck, below where he held my tuft of hair.

"Move. And I slice," he said.

He held the blade there, and I paused to contemplate my next move.

It was a sick trick because he sliced anyway, taking a whole two square inches of skin and hair from the base of my scalp.

The sting. The flood of blood. The thick trickle down my spine. The searing heat on my neck. I wanted to touch it, stop it. I pushed off the stairs, pushing back against his weight, hoping again to destabilize him while he kept one foot on the stairs with his knee on my spine.

He didn't budge.

I pushed again.

"Where. Are. My girls? You bitch."

Dan got away.

"Where did you put their phones?"

Dan took all their phones. He'll crush them. Drop them. Avoid tracking.

I pushed again. Eminence didn't budge, kneed harder into my spine. Blood dripped from the head wound around my neck and onto the stair, pooling around my face. The pain rocketed through my whole body.

"My driver didn't check in with me. Where is he? Dammit, where is he?"

This is what tipped him off.

When he yelled this last line, he allowed his knee to lift a fraction as his voice rose in his emotion, so when I pushed hard this time, he toppled on his one foot, enough for me to twist, rolling out from under his knee. I slid, body straight, down the rest of the stairs. Landing at the bottom, I flipped forward, somersaulted on the earth, and found myself in the middle of the parked SUV's—their grills facing each other. One had a driver.

"Gun it," Eminence shouted as he emerged behind me.

I didn't have time to run out of the trap; the driver was only five feet from my body. I jumped up, hoping to avoid one grill sandwiching me with the other, and I made it most of the way, except for my right leg, which lodged between the grills when the SUV stopped.

I couldn't crank it out. Trapped.

I twisted while placing my hands on the hoods of the two facing SUVs, and looked up to watch Eminence walk slowly towards me. He was huge. Just like in the video. And wearing another of his black masks. I could not see the scars on his face from a fire, like Melanie said, given the mask, but also given the rising, blinding sun dispersing the smog around us.

"Where are my girls?" he thundered.

I smiled at him.

He stalled, tipped his head to the side, and seemingly took in my face. Then, he laughed.

He walked closer and pushed the air on the side of the driver, indicating the driver should back up. And when he did, just as my leg dislodged and I was about to fall back down, Eminence grabbed my foot and twisted my body, leaving me to fall backwards and crash, my leg in the air. He let go of my foot and jumped nearly his full weight to my chest, pinning my arms above my head as he landed. All in a smooth series of expert motions. My legs were in such a position that I could not kick from the ground, lying down.

"Bring me the tire iron," he yelled to the driver who, by the sounds of it, had opened and closed his driver's door.

Eminence leaned into my face, the black mesh scraping my nose. He laughed again.

"You are a little insect. I get pictures of you over the years. You are my gift. And you will be delivered to me, to my tank soon."

I am a gift? To be delivered? Is that different from him tagging me? But he verifies I am scheduled for the tank.

His breath seeped out through the mesh. Heavy, like the stench of waste. A pure halitosis.

A pair of boots stomped beside my head.

"I will stand her up. You hold her arms. Hold her in place," he said to the driver, who appeared, setting the requested tire iron by Eminence's feet. Once they had me standing and secured by the driver, Eminence slammed his own booted foot down on top of my left, pinning me hard to the ground. Then he bent and took hold of the tire iron, lifting his huge body slow as if sliding up my body. His skin and his stench were so close to vertical me, it was if we were slow-dancing lovers. He breathed in my face again. I gagged.

"Insect gift. I put in a cage," he said.

He pivoted a step back, keeping a foot on my left, raised his tire iron, and slammed down on my right foot. The shoe I wore offered little resistance. He slammed again. And again. And I saw him counting by mouthing numbers, "three," he said. I believe he intended to beat my foot twenty times. But Melanie screamed out of a fourth floor window in the boss building above us and seemed to stop the rotation of Earth.

Eminence stalled mid-swing, and we both looked up; her siren was so loud.

There she stood, like a ghost in an open window, still in her white shift. Wind pushed around the sheer fabric making it billow around her thin waist. I could see the roll of her papers bulge out in the waistband of her underwear—but I knew what to look for; I worried Eminence saw the papers, too. Then she dove headfirst out of the four story window. I knew before she landed, calculating the height and her trajectory, that she would break her neck on impact and die.

I held my breath the whole while, tightening my jaw and every muscle in my body, focusing solely on a pinprick of light above my head as a way of meditation—a method Sarge had taught me to get through torture, and also to avoid any emotions flickering in the periphery of my mind that I could feel fighting to be turned on. Bile rose in my throat. Sweat covered me everywhere. The pain in my foot, the sight of Melanie's broken neck, all I could do was focus on the pinprick of light.

I will murder Eminence in the most painful way possible. He will be eliminated. Every fiber, gone. He will become nothing. Fucking nothing. Zilch.

Eminence backed away from me, stumbling backwards and then towards Melanie, heaving for air and panting. The crack of her neck on the hard ground, that sound will never leave my mind.

Eminence crouched down to her and turned back to me, still held in place by his driver. I considered a few self-defense extraction moves, but I had to let the extraordinary pain in my murdered foot pass a couple of seconds before action.

"You killed my Pride," Eminence screamed at me. He fingered the hem of her white shift, lifting it slightly, and starting to roll it back, seeming from my vantage to possibly be aiming to take her notes.

I was about to try and extricate myself to stop him, when the man who had been up in the boss building with Melanie emerged at the bottom of the stairwell and indicated they all had to leave, ASAP. I'm not sure why. I can only guess they feared not having literally all the Shanghai cops in their fold. The man holding me pushed me to the ground. I noticed none of the hamlet residents came outside to watch or help.

Before driving off, Eminence rolled down his passenger window, and said, "I will see you in short years. You will fail the tank and burn. Insect." He sped off.

You will cry for me to help you. You will beg me, monster. And the only finger I will lift is to press into your pain.

Limping, I pulled Melanie's crushed and bloody, slight body back up those narrow stairs. She was a wisp of a human, so light. I dragged her down the hall with the twenty crooked cats. I extracted her notes and laid a white sheet over her body, her face. No breath moved her sheet as I stood there watching and waiting for four whole minutes, which is double the time the average person can hold their breath. In their tiny bathroom, I poured a bottle of hydrogen peroxide on my head wound, and bit into a face towel to ride through that added pain. Then I bandaged it with half a face cloth and duct tape I found under the kitchen sink. I didn't even dare look at my right foot as I wrapped an ace bandage, one I found in a cabinet, around and around the top half. I stole a larger pair of simple slippers from one of the women's chambers, big enough to hold my wrapped foot, so I could slide my way back to America. All of this took me a grand total of fifteen minutes, too many minutes, minutes of high risk, as I was sure someone from the hamlet had called the police.

I limped out of the building, around the high-rise where Dan's car was hidden and somehow drove away before any cops showed up. Maybe they never showed up. Maybe nobody cared about that particular hellhole on Earth.

There was not a chance I was going to a Chinese hospital. I wanted out of Shanghai fast. There was no point in fighting longer in China. I did not trust the US Embassy. Women, worldwide, we are largely on our own. I trust no one, anywhere. No point in trying to track down Eminence, to wherever he drove off to. I risked health and imprisonment the longer I stayed. No going to any embassy. No waiting for my scheduled flight to leave in three days. I drove straight to the airport and flew out of Shanghai on the first flight I could book to anywhere, and landed in London ten hours later.

By the time I landed, I had medicated my foot and head and thigh pain on the flight with ten shots of vodka and an emergency Vicodin I carried for extreme situations. In London, I took off my shoe in the women's bathroom and saw that a deep and alarming case of ischemic necrosis had overtaken my severely crushed Morton's toe—the second toe, mine longer than my big toe, thus called a "royal toe" given my genetics. Necrosis also appeared at the tip of the middle toe; red around both blackened parts signaled infection, and I diagnosed that I had a high risk of sepsis. Necrosis and sepsis are no jokes, so I went straight to a London ER and entered what they call, a "Casualty Department." I demanded the most aggressive form of casualty treatment and consented to the surgeon's offer to fully remove the unsalvageable necrotic and crushed Morton's toe and the tip of the necrotic middle toe. She put me on an IV of antibiotics, and as the medicine dripped in, I called an ally at MIT, a professor I once had who focused on biomechanical engineering.

As for my scalping spot, the London nurses treated that with topical steroids, topical antibiotics, and an icepack. I considered an evolution to my plan as my brain cooled on ice and I re-read the relevant portions of Melanie's extensive play-by-play notes:

*Day of death, they dressed me in red robe with wide sleeves.

*I must wear robe to walk to tank.

*In room for making pretty, no windows, basement, I sat with the other girl. The other girl he raped, he killed.

*Before tank, we ate last meal. We each picked our own food.

*I spent all day with the other girl. I

ate with her. Eminence said he wanted us
to bond.

I will have time to train the other girl, I thought while reading Melanie's notes.

*After last meal—I chose flat noodles with
lemon—they gave me any food I wanted. They
marched me down a stone hall. We were
underground.

*At the end, I climbed stairs to a place
they call the "Up Top." Other girls up
there, they were not allowed to look at
me. I kept my head up. They looked to the
scratchy wood floor. Up Top was windy inside.
Old house. Lots of fireplaces, all have fires.
Eminence tells me this has to be, because
fire is the "all power," so fire must be there
on my death day in the tank. I think three
fireplaces I passed. All in fire.

I liked how she wrote "all in fire." I liked how that sounded, that
something was *in fire*. It seemed like something Lenny might scribe in
a poem. When I mentioned this phrase to him (completely divorced
of Melanie's note, because he knew absolutely nothing about her
and never would), he shrugged and said, "Maybe. I don't know." He
didn't seem so impressed. So maybe I was wrong to like "in fire," so
much. Anyway, I do listen to hear if any musicians sing it, as songs
are the poetry I'm into—even though I'll read Vanty's chapbooks
when he asks for a "beta read."

*Man with a fast gun pushed me to empty
room. I didn't see no other guard anywhere
then. Like in China, only two men guard
Eminence. I wonder how he keeps security so
small. How come he's so powerful? I don't
see anyone else inside Up Top with a gun.

Just women. Just girls, I pass.

*Two women sat on the floor in the room he pushed me into. Another fireplace was in there. Another fire. Big square Brileycon jugs everywhere on the floor. X 25 says label. They pour X 25 on me to burn me. They lift up two boards in floor. They take my robe. They use my arms to lower me in the tank. I was screaming the whole time. Nobody helped. Nobody looked in my eyes. The man with the fast gun pointed the gun to my head from Up Top.

*In tank, I could turn sideways, but sides touched shoulders, so I turned to face the room. Nobody was in there but the girl with a video machine. At first. I saw a bed and a mirror. Gross old room. No windows.

*I feared I'd get stuck sideways. The glass was very thick. Very thick and not clear. Cloudy. Glue squished between the pieces in corners. Sloppy tank, sides not straight. Eminence made this tank by himself in the barn. He told me.

*Men came in to the room. They were naked, but all laughing, ha ha ha, laughing with the second guard who made sure they got in behind the mirror. But he had no gun, he acted like their friend. Laughing guard, he left and stood outside the door. I was screaming. Nobody cared.

*The girl by the bed videotaped everything. She put down the camera and locked the mirror shut with wood knobs, keeping the naked men within.

*When they pour X 25 on me, some dripped out
of corners where the glue was big.

The rest of Melanie's notes included other intermediary minutia and the details of her point of view on what we saw in the video, the bleach pouring in, and her post-tank physical recovery and return to Shanghai. While I have read these notes numerous times over the years to maintain a good level of lethal resolve, those additional details are redundant of what I already knew or not relevant to my escape and revenge.

I did not turn love on for Melanie at any point, for I'd learned the hard way to never do this with victims. But I did commit to Melanie and her legacy. *Melanie's life had purpose. She was no waste, no worthless bucket. She commanded me to save the other girls. She saved my life. Saved others' lives. I am nothing but a weapon in her war.*

CHAPTER FIFTEEN
LISA YYLAND: BACK TO THE LAB

Nana says, when the world gives you old bananas, "It's best you bake a banana cake." So with the verified facts, new facts, and injuries I sustained in Shanghai, after my scalping and getting my toes severed in London, I went back to my lab in Indiana to restructure the plan.

At the time, and this was five years ago, I re-entered through the red kitchen door of my work/home building on crutches. When I purchased the building, the kitchen remained as it was originally designed: industrial and boring and intended for serving students and faculty of the Appletree Boarding School. In remodeling, I kept the two long, stainless steel islands in the center but redesigned with vibrant colors and appliances, an apple green mixer and matching apple green refrigerator, red pegs for coats, an ocean blue hutch, a turquoise rug, and all of Vanty's school and artwork in painted, reclaimed wood frames, which hang all over the sky-blue walls. Psychology studies suggest colors promote natural endorphins⇒endorphins allow creative productivity⇒I decorate with colors.

Thirteen-year-old Vanty was waiting for me by the coral kitchen eating table, holding out a homemade cake. On it, he'd written, "Sry 4 Ur toes, Mom," in green icing and even drew an animated frowning foot in pink icing.

"You helped him with this, didn't you?" I said to Nana, who was still visiting from Savannah to assist with escorting Vanty around for his assortment of scheduled events: school, basketball, and time with

134

friends. Lenny was still on his chapbook tour, which did register to me as a long time for a poetry book tour. But, I wasn't sure. At some point in our relationship, and we'd been together since high school, I stopped keeping track of his comings and goings in relation to mine. Our wedding was to take place that year, so I noticed Nana had some bridal catalogues propped on the counter with Post-its to indicate items she wanted me to consider.

"Oh no, dear, the cake was all Vanty's idea," Nana said, walking over to me and hugging me, her arms scooping wide around the crutches bumping out my arms. She whispered in my ear, "You are home now. Vanty is frightened and worried for you. You need to turn love on and hug him."

So I turned love on for Vanty. As soon as I did, and as soon as I looked at that cake again and Vanty's earnest face, fighting away little boy tears in teen eyes, I nearly fell to the floor. All of the blood in my body heated to two hundred degrees and rushed to a lava flow up and down my chest. To have such uncontrollable love for a child, for the entire purpose of your life, is paralyzing, but also the source of life. I am not good at calibrating the hot blood and the swirl of joy with abject fear of loss when love is on for Vanty. I am, in a word, somewhat debilitated when it comes to him, my beautiful handicap.

"I'm fine. It's just two toes," I said, avoiding the topic of the bandages on the back of my neck. He rushed to me, and I collapsed on his shoulder, which he dipped, for he was thirteen, already well within puberty, and taller than me.

"Mom," he said, his face in my hair. I heard his voice crack. "Can you just not do these trips for your company anymore, where you're gone so long? And then you come home with no toes?" I know he was trying to hide his fear in humor by saying this, so I lied. Like I always lie to my family to keep them in their individual perceptions of happiness and safety.

"Vantaggio, this had nothing to do with my consulting business. I'm safe. This was just an unpredictable accident. A taxi ran over my foot."

"What about these bandages on the back of your head?"

"Obviously, when a taxi runs over your foot, you fall on the ground. I'm fine."

I leaned back out of our embrace, still propped on my crutches, and reached to rub his cheek. I looked to Nana, who nodded behind Vanty's back in approval.

"It's fortunate you made a cake, boy. Mr. Cam will be here tomorrow, and you know he likes baked goods. Coming from his off-campus lab. He's going to make me new toes."

"Sweet!" Vanty said. "He always brings me something cool from his lab."

"I know, baby. I know." I liked it when Nana called me "Baby" whenever I had love on for her, so it made me feel good to say that to Vanty in times like these, when he was *experiencing* for me. And since I was experiencing love for him, my heart felt present—I felt its mass, its valves at work, its chambers pumping, as I looked at my baby and felt how painful, but also how gratifying—both competing sensations, making me feel alive, like a real person—fullness was. Vanty has never let me down, never frightened me, never truly—or, for too long—made me question him or his intelligence, his abilities. Seeing him when I have love on for him means I see the physical proof for the purpose of my existence. I believe, in times like this, my invention of love is equal to his and so it is objectively validated and thus, a solid scientific law, as true as gravity.

"Let's get ready for Mr. Cam. But first, this cake," I said, handing him my crutches, which he leaned in a corner by our apple green refrigerator, as I sat on a red kitchen stool. Nana moved to the stove and put the kettle on, setting out three mugs for tea.

"Oh, Lisa, your father is coming in tomorrow afternoon too. Said he's going to visit and use your office to interview some new physicist for his lab in Manchester. She lives out here, I guess," Nana said. My father was then not a *dear departed*.

"Is Mother coming, too?" I asked.

"No, dear. She's still on trial, of course." Nana's "of course" was matter of fact, not the judgmental tone I'd detected when my father said this about Mother in a call we had shared a month before.

After the cake, I went to my practice tank while Vanty set off to work on chemistry problems I'd drafted for him, because his school chemistry was, in short, unchallenging. My walls of a painted birch tree forest were nearly complete; I still needed to perfect the cerulean of the sky and add fine details, like ladybugs on limbs and a cardinal in a nest.

136

I looked up at the wall with the glass panel tank, the one I practiced jumps from. Over the years, I had tested cutting so many variations of glass panels, all of which were lined up on the edges of the room. Elevator glass, which is typically constructed of ½-inch-thick glass. Aquarium glass, all different kinds of thickness. Just plain window glass, numerous types. Windshield, which is really just laminated glass with a thin layer of vinyl between. I had tried all kinds of shattering tools and blades to cut those panels, believing that once I figured on a tool that could destroy or slice a variety of different *standing* glass panels—not panels lying flat on an even surface (and that is a crucial factor to cutting glass)—I'd figure out how to steal in the right object.

But Melanie's recitation of facts did not validate that the tank was made of glass at all. Her notes describe cloudy, thick glass, joined in the corners by bulging glue. Based on this, I sharpened my hypothesis that the tank was actually constructed of polymethyl methacrylate joined at the seams by cyanoacrylate; in other words, thick plexiglass with a bulging epoxy as the corner-joining adhesive. And since cutting plexiglass would be even more difficult than glass, and it is near shatterproof—I also couldn't assure with 100% accuracy that it was plexiglass—I focused on the one fact I did gather from Melanie: the bulging glue in the corners. If the glue was "bulging," that meant there was likely a gap, filled with glue, between the adjoined panels.

I needed to exploit the glue, exploit the gap.

I sat at my steel table and conducted some internet research on epoxy and plexiglass adhesives. I ordered some products to test.

Next, I moved on to research regarding my toes.

After pulling up biomechanical articles on the evolution and current technology around prosthetics, I went to an unfinished portion of my painted birch forest and spent two hours highlighting sections of a cloud against the blue sky, thinking. According to a *Scientific American* article quoting Andreas Nerlich, a pathologist at Ludwig Maximilians University of Munich, the world's oldest example of a prosthetic is "an Egyptian woman…outfitted with a wooden toe prosthesis in approximately 1000 B.C."

Fortunately, for me, prosthesis technology has advanced a great deal in three thousand years, and I have an ally who specializes in the field: Mr. Cam. Mr. Cam is a scholar on biotechnology and just so happens to be one of the world's leading experts on prosthetics and medical devices. He once built four robotic paws for a hero dog who'd lost all of hers after jumping off a highway bridge to yank a boy by his collar from a burning car. Delegating the actual spring design and construction of my false toes to him was the most efficient route.

I had no choice but to capitalize on damage to my body: To *be ready* for The Lobster Tank, meant I had to be ready, *while being naked.*

Mr. Cam arrived the next morning when Nana, Vanty, and I were eating breakfast at the coral table in a corner of our rainbow kitchen. Above the table was a framed page of Vanty's first writing lesson in First Grade. He had to write an opinion and a fact, so he wrote: *Mondays shud be free. I kant lic my elbo.*

As soon as Mr. Cam entered, he delivered to Vanty a prototype robotic arm, some "extra thing," an "earlier version" of something he was working on in his own home lab. It looked so real, Nana screamed and dropped her fork with pancake still on it, shrieking about how Mr. Cam brought an actual human arm in the building. Both Vanty and I shook our heads at Nana in synch, our arms folded at our chests, Vanty smiling at Nana, while I smiled at Vanty smiling, because I had love on for him in that moment.

"You two," Nana said of us, tsking as she stood to clear our pancake plates and make Mr. Cam a cup of coffee and cut him a slice of my severed toe cake. The phone rang. It was Lenny. I said I was fine. He said he had one more week on the road. I handed the phone to Vanty to talk with his father and went off to work with Mr. Cam.

He and I spent up until lunch going over sketches in my office—not my practice tank room—and my objectives in what I wanted for prosthetic toes. With that discussion done, Mr. Cam took what seemed like a thousand measurements and pictures and four different molds of my foot. When he stood to depart for his lab in Massachusetts, he said he'd get to work on the project "straightaway."

As he drove off down our long, country Indiana driveway, passing through the grove of apple trees on one side and big oaks on the other, my father drove up it. I had buzzed him in to pass through the locked gate. Watching their cars pass each other midway on the security cameras off the kitchen, it was as if the two men had passed a baton. In the car with my father was a woman with long, red hair, who made me think of the actress Geena Davis. My father got out of the car and yelled to me, "Hey, doll, glad you're home from China. Hope Nana told you I flew in to visit and hope to use your place for an interview. This is Doctor…" His voice was drowned out by a wind. It didn't matter, though, because she was just another revolving-door physicist for my father's lab in New Hampshire. And I was only ever going to think of her as Geena Davis, anyway. I got them settled for their interview in about ten minutes' time while agreeing with my father, Vanty, and Nana that we'd have fried raviolis and baked ziti for dinner.

After all that fuss, I returned to my practice tank room, locked all the locks behind me, and pulled out my nanogenerator strands for generating mechanical energy. I rubbed the giant welt and bruise where the grape-sized capacitor had jammed my thigh in Shanghai. Sitting at my steel desk again, I held the bands in one hand and an earlier prototype of the capacitor in the other. Looking between the two, weighing their sizes, I reconsidered why I thought I needed them: to power my sounds discs. But then I thought about the evolution in remote control devices and evolution of powerful tiny batteries that had taken place since I'd started all the testing, designing, and practicing for my plan. I reconsidered the necessity of mechanical energy, sitting there at my steel desk in the middle, the two tanks on opposite walls, facing each other as if in a duel. I considered how I might get someone on the outside of whatever building I'd be held in to control remotes to power the discs.

So then I thought about how to get a signal out to the person holding that remote; the signal of *when* precisely to power the discs.

How to time it just right.

And I considered other diversions, too.

I thought of the fireplaces documented in Melanie's notes as I rubbed the bandages on the bald spot at the base of my neck. I thought of Melanie's words about being able to choose my own "last meal." I thought of her notes about the importance of fire in Eminence's history, thus in this tank ceremony. Those three fireplaces kept burning in my mind. And then I put all of that together: the need for a timing signal, my bald spot, fire, and my last meal.

I sat up straight. Pulled my laptop closer. Punched in a few queries, and read for about a half hour. I popped off my stool, slid to the secure wall phone, and called Mr. Cam on his cell.

"Did you board your plane yet?"

"No, just entering the airport now."

"Turn around. Come back. I'm going to need some thick synthetic hair strands that attach to the base of my skull as a tuft. Long, too. Thick enough to hold a powdery substance."

"Got it. On my way back for measurements," he said.

I looked at my nanogenerator bands and my prototypes of various capacitors on the steel desk. For a few seconds, I frowned over the feeling that I'd been wasteful and inefficient in designing and testing them at all. I looked to the second tank, the one I didn't use for practice.

I spun around my room, considering the mural on my walls of a painted forest, so vibrant the blue of the sky, some parts still needing work, the white of the birch trunks with black tiger striping, the yellow and the green of the leaves, the moss of the forest floor. I still needed a cardinal in a nest and some ladybugs on leaves, some other finer details. I spun and I thought and I looked at my bands, my capacitors, my practice tank, the other tank....

And it clicked.

A new use for my nanogenerators came to me in a flash. And, I admit, I turned on the emotion of homicidal rage and smiled with an evil joy in anticipation of the release that would come in using them; thinking, too, on all Eminence had done to Melanie and other girls over the years. I formed a whole new purpose for the use of my mechanical energy.

You will suffer, motherfucker.

I am your Devil.

~~~

It is five years later now, long past Shanghai and the scientific recalibrations of this eighteen-year-old plan, presently underway. I've been riding in the back of a red hen truck for so long, thinking back on Shanghai and Mr. Cam's visit in Indiana so deep, as a way to occupy my mind and distract from the discomfort of lying back here in this coffin-like compartment with a U metal loop on my neck, I near forgot I was here. I even tuned out the other captive girl, who's still screaming for help in the adjacent compartment.

Yes, surely I've been riding in the back of a red hen truck for hours, the girl beside me screaming, but then her voice dying away, and returning. We've stopped now. Those two men who grabbed me stopped this truck, opened her cage, dragged her out, and, by the sounds of it, disappeared for about ten minutes. And now, we're driving again.

I'm thinking back to this morning. To Mother's murder during our run. Her inexplicable entanglement with Judge Rasper. How Pink Skirt tried to contain me in the park, then I forced her to take me after escaping from East Hanson's police station, literally jumped out of Chief Castile's window with Mother's iPhone in an evidence bag. I think too on how I've named Pink Skirt Eva in my mind. I recall how Eva blamed me for being the Dentist and drilling Judge Rasper's face, which accusation makes sense, given Viebury's outside cameras catching me on the outskirts on the night he was drilled, but confuse me, seeing as I didn't do it. It's been, I believe, two hours since Eva stopped in the forest preserve and had her two goons drag and stuff me in this hen truck. I wonder where that bitch is now.

I'm dehydrated and my vision is blinded when they open my hatch door, my pupils accustomed to the dark interior of this red box. An arm reaches in, unhooks the U brace around my neck, and pulls me out like I'm a rolled rug. He drops me on the ground. It takes me a few seconds of blinking, but when my vision acclimates, I see we are in a closed barn. Next, the two men who stuffed me in one of the truck's red caskets drag me toward a hole in the concrete floor of the barn and drop me beside it. I'm too physically drained to fight them right now, and besides, it's more important at this stage that I not resist, save energy, and acquire information. Fortunately, I'm not blindfolded.

"Tie her arms," Eva says. "Wand her."

One of the losers walks to grab rope, while the other takes a rather advanced, slightly larger than a pen, wand, and roves it over my body. It beeps at my toe.

"Take your shoe off," Eva demands.

"It's just my toe ring. Keeps my prosthetic on. It's a magnet."

"A what?" she asks. "Give me that."

She cannot take the toe from me.

I hand her the magnet and make like I'm removing my fake toe as if I'll hand it to her.

"Just a prosthetic. I need the toe ring."

"That's disgusting."

"Idiots, tie her up," Eva says, while throwing the ring at me on the floor.

CHAPTER SIXTEEN
JOSI OLIVE: THE DENTIST

Josi Olive likes to walk with his cat, Cat, outside in Viebury Grove. Cat is like his shadow, this dark-furred beast who sticks to the sides of his boots like he's attached by glue. Today, the fall air is warm and the sky wicked blue, the kind of sky that beach jerks go crazy for, except the trees are all wrong, looking more like the bag of Skittles in his sound lab, with all the fat colors. Today is a day for strollin' and sniffin' wood fires and judging which Viebury house is decorated best for Trick-or-Treaters. There's only a couple occupied, and the unoccupied ones are creepy as fuck as is—so maybe there is no competition. Maybe some ghost grandma on a porch will offer him a slice of apple pie.

He steps out of his Cape with this daydream in mind, and Cat scoots around his boots.

"Cat, don't trip me, guy," Josi says, while he shuts the door behind them.

As he blades a hand in his pocket to get the house key and lock up, he turns to watch a red chicken truck with weird-ass boxes on the back pull into the stone mansion's big barn. Josi scowls, remembering his war with the people in that colossal pile of rocks. Remembering, too, his go with fucking Judge Rasper, which he'd really only forgotten about for a mere minute in thinking he'd take a stroll. Remembers now he's not allowed to have even fleeting peace. Remembers he's a fool to think he could just take a walk with Cat like it's nothing. Like his wife wasn't murdered in a mud swamp. Like her murder wasn't covered up by these pricks.

That fucking red truck again, he thinks. He knows that's how they bring the girls in. *Has to be.*

"Come on, Cat. Back in the house. I got work to do."

CHAPTER SEVENTEEN
FORMER SPECIAL AGENT ROGER LIU
MARIANA CHURCH

Lola and I are on our way into Mariana Church. This was supposed to be a simple igniter to the plan. We go in. Ask for Velada. Meet Velada. Tell her Lisa is ready to be taken. But our trip now to Mariana is to still ask for Velada, and my plan then is to shut this shit down. If we understand Velada's covert role in the Center Ring, Velada should know Lisa's been taken. She's told us she's been working this from the inside, as a double agent.

Now that the plan started earlier than planned, our waltzing into Mariana Church could be a trap. Lola and I are on guard. Maybe it was always a trap.

Mariana is typical of Boston churches. Old and made of granite. The original church itself is tiny, about the size of a double townhouse. But the whole of it, with disparate additions and adjoining buildings, is gargantuan. There's the granite church—alone you might find this building in some Irish field. There's the church's hip-thrust of an addition, a jutting-out box of more modern construction at a lower level, down an outside flight of stone stairs. Tall brick apartments with cantilevered back decks form a backdrop. And the strangest architecture in this jumble of rocks, bricks, and wood is a channel—a canal of sorts, running under the front third of the church, parallel to the sidewalk.

We head to the hip-thrust basement, down the flight of stone stairs. The jut-out addition houses a day shelter for the homeless. We've known this all for a month, when this location was given to us for purposes of meeting up with Velada. We've done surveillance, Lola and I, a few weeks ago, done some background investigation. Nothing popped up out of the ordinary that we could tell.

The shelter is a cafeteria-style, drop-ceiling basement room, set up with folding tables. Homeless folks play Ginny and Fish with decks of dog-eared cards, browse want-ads or housing ads in the classifieds, or sit with *pro bono* attorneys working on housing and disability forms. Lola in her gray pants and gray blazer, and I in my gray suit and white shirt with tie, don't fit in with the casually-dressed attorneys, who know better, and we don't fit in with the homeless.

A traditional black-and-white nun in full habit, veil, coif, and wimple, revealing only her non-dimensional front face, intercepts us, the obvious interlopers.

"What can I do for you?" She's miniscule, like a mouse-human, her facial features more like dots and pebbles. I search for a discernible nose, something's there, there are two spots for nostrils, but almost imperceptible. She could be, maybe four foot nine, maybe, and shorter by way of her hunch.

"We're looking for Velada," I say.

The nun drops her head, looking at her shoes. Her exposed face now totally obscured to us as the fabric of her veil falls down around her head in a curl.

Lola squints at her. I can tell by her look, she seems to sense something. But…from this? This dollhouse woman? When the nun is not looking, I flip a furrowed brow to Lola.

"Not nun," Lola mouths.

I shake my head at her.

The nun turns her face up to us. "Let's proceed into the chapel area," she says.

As we walk behind her, Lola grabs my hand and motions me to look at her own hands. There, Lola points to her wrist, as a way to indicate I should check out the nun's wrist.

When the nun opens a doorway that leads into a basement chapel, I catch only a brief flash of her left hand, but do not see anything suspicious.

I cast Lola a *'what?'* expression. She bugs her eyes at me and then at the nun's hand, but behind her back, as a way to say I need to look again.

The nun is walking in front of us, her hands clasped at her belly the way nuns tend to walk in holy contemplation. "This chapel is used for our homeless to pray, and also for community events," she says. Ahead is a stage with a true-to-life-size Jesus on a cross made of railroad ties. Jesus on his ties dominates the stage's back wall. Rows of brown-gray folding chairs fill the room, all of which have a degree of erosion by way of chipped metallic coating. Along an exterior wall are three confessional booths. Beyond those, another true-to-life statue, this one of a nameless saint, lying down and sleeping in an open coffin. I flinch at a swoop of air that hits my face, fearing a bat, only to find the swivel of a wall-mounted fan is in a rotation towards me. I look to shadows in corners, to swaying cobwebs above the bracketed fan, and wonder if it's mature of me to be thinking of demons and ghosts in a sacred place.

The nun turns to us, her hands still clasped, her fingers coiled together tight and half obscured by the length of her black cloak. Lola is doing that thing where she jams the point of her tongue into the outside of her bottom teeth. She has a tell. Lola smells high treason. I have to play this off.

"So, Velada? Is she here?" I ask with a smile.

The nun smiles back.

I ask again. Lola circles the nun, still picking her teeth with her tongue.

The nun chuckles, looking at her black shoes.

"Sister, I'm sorry. What is so funny?" I ask.

"Oh dear, my dear, your partner here is reminding me of a rough and tumble runaway we helped many years ago."

"Rough and tumble," Lola repeats in a scoff.

The nun looks up at Lola by stretching her hooded and aged eyelids.

Lola remains silent, openly evaluating the nun and then the lie-down saint in the statue coffin, like she wants to stuff her in it.

"What about Velada?" Lola says, standing to the woman's side.

"Velada hasn't been here all day," she says.

We were told that under all circumstances, Velada would be sure to be here every day this week, between the hours of 9-5, no matter what, specifically because, according to her, we'd need her help to save Lisa in time.

"Do you know where we can find her, Sister?" I ask, keeping a pained smile while Lola leans in and sniffs the nun's neck. The nun recoils.

"Excuse me," the nun says to Lola.

"You're wearing that powdery Crabs in a Tree lotion. My friend wears it," Lola says.

Friend? And it's Crabtree & Evelyn.

"Personally, I'm not a fan. Too powdery and too perfumy and too musty for my taste," Lola continues. "Like two days ago you clogged up your vagina with a cloth doused in baby powder and Chantilly and haven't bathed or removed it since."

Oh, my, God.

The nun steps back and frowns, curls her nose like Lola smells. I close my eyes and drop my shoulders.

Lola steps between me and the nun; she's now face to face with her. "Funny, because I've never met a nun who wears so much perfumy lotion. When did you take your vows, Sister?"

"When I was of age. I've always been a nun," the woman rushes to say. "But that's none of your business, you indelicate, rude woman. I don't have to stand for this."

"Where is Velada?" Lola says.

I'm edging to the side now, watching from the closest row of chipped folding chairs.

The nun stands taller, her hands unclasp. And it is now I see what has Lola so spun up. Under the hemline of her wide sleeve, which lifts when she unclasps her hands, there is a black tattoo of three overlapping L's in a circle on the interior of her wrist. The sleeve quickly falls in place again, but I caught it. The nun adjusts and pulls at her sleeve, unaware that I did, in fact, see. I nod to Lola; she nods back.

It all rushes to me who this woman must be, or rather, what she's been a part of. I see in my mind's eye a sketchbook of tattoos, a sketchbook Lola and I have had to reference several times in our years of investigating human kidnapping for trafficking. From the Women's Prison in Eastern Tennessee, three L's in a circle was the trademark of an inner-prison trafficking ring, wherein every Friday morning over breakfast, women pimp inmates auctioned off new inmates to senior inmates for the weekend. Getting a tattoo of the trademark on her left wrist meant "management."

This woman was, and I suspect is, in the management of human trafficking. She is likely keeping up the nun charade on days when she might come down to the church in her extreme costume to recruit homeless runaways. A unique scheme, but I've seen almost everything when it comes to ruses to lure runaways and the disenfranchised into trafficking, so I'm not calling Pink Bear on this one.

"Loretta Likes Love, the triple L's, the triad, the name of your prison gang," I say. "You were in management." I smile at Lola; she smiles back.

We surround the nun, who grins in an annoying *you caught me, now what?* kind of way. These people are able to doctor records and insert themselves in cash-strapped churches. Identity fraud like this happens everywhere. They say they've relocated, anything to get in past an initial scrutiny. And once in, they're in.

"Velada is not here," she repeats, this time stone cold.

Lola steps into the false nun's space, and I know what she's intending. She's intending to drag the woman outside, out through an alley door I see her eyeing, and force the woman to talk. But just as Lola's arms are rising to grab her quarry—and I don't flinch to stop her—a priest enters from a door off the stage and shouts, "What is going on here?"

"Father, these people are harassing me. Please, make them leave," the nun cries out, hunching again, and summoning a crackling old lady voice.

I suspect Father is not in on this drill and is indeed, a real priest. But since we can't pull any pins and call the nun's bluff, we step back.

"No trouble here, Father. Just having a difficult time accepting some bad news from Sister. Isn't that right, Sister?" Lola says.

The fake nun nods. She has to agree. She doesn't want her cover blown.

"We'll leave now. Sorry for the trouble," I offer. I'm figuring Lola will take the front of the church, I'll take the back, and we'll wait her out.

We make our way through the cafeteria, past all the card tables of homeless people with legal forms and playing cards. We exit out the side basement door and are about to step on the stone steps to reach the sidewalk and street. But in a simultaneous head turn to the right, Lola and I look down that weird canal running under the granite church and parallel with the sidewalk. This canal, channel... whatever, is not just some drainage culvert, it's a walking path, deep enough under the church to walk and not bend. It continues this way for several blocks, running under homes and buildings in parts, and out free in other spots with open air and power lines above.

A man stands about forty feet from us in the channel, whispering with our nun in the basement bulkhead doorway. He is a skinny scarecrow of a man in a red and black flannel shirt and dirty jeans about three sizes too big. When he sees us seeing him, he swivels his body and runs away, along the channel. Lola and I pursue—me down the channel, Lola up the stairs and along the parallel sidewalk. It's been a long time since Lola and I have been on a tandem hunt.

I'm close to sixty, but I'm in shape, so I won't sweat this chase too much. The skeletal man will be winded in no time. But we must hope he doesn't slip down some cutoff or into a doorway without us seeing. I've got a clear sightline on him so far, watching him yank up his crusty pants as he runs. Lola stomps the sidewalk to our left. When I near our nun in the bulkhead doorway, I anticipate she'll swing the door to block the channel and jam me. So I block the swing of the door with my hands hard, pushing her back into the chapel. I run on.

I'm in a groove in passing home basements and through parts clear of construction and mounds of dirt. And just as I'm gaining a thrill at the thought of clotheslining this fool ahead, he turns left, toward the sidewalk, and I hear a distinct clobber.

I don't need to see that Lola caught our mouse to know she caught our mouse. He turned the corner left—he had to turn left because the channel ends and a house blocks the right turn. Lola must have been standing there with her arms outstretched, waiting to clamp around his neck, for this is how I find the pair.

"Where is Velada?" Lola's shouting at him.

He gurgles and spits, losing air, losing breath.

"Lola, let him down," I say. She has lifted him in the air by holding his neck. She drops him, and his skinny ass crumbles to the ground.

We both tower over whoever this is. "Where is Velada?" I shout.

He hovers his scrawny arms over his head, shielding himself.

"Okay, okay. Look, man, I'm just a driver. I don't know nothing. I don't know no Velada."

Lola bends and sticks her gun into his ribs and jams. Calmly, she sinks to straddle him, stretching her gray pants as if torturing the seams. In a calm tone, while straddling him on the ground, the gun barrel still in his ribs, she says, "I will blow your black lungs out, *right here, right now*." Lola's *right here, right now* is sing song. "I don't really care. If you don't tell us what you're up to with that fake fucking nun, and where Velada is, right now, welcome to bye-bye time, Mr. Gangy Man."

I have no clue what Mr. Gangy Man means, but it sure sounds derogatory.

"Okay, okay, okay," he says. She pokes harder. "Ah shit, I'm fucked. Sister'll know I talked to you. Look, I'm just a driver, okay. I thought they had a load for me today, but no one's here. I don't know who Velada is. I'm just a driver. They don't tell me nothing. I wasn't even supposed to be here today. Needed cash."

"One of the drivers for what?" I say.

He juts his chin and bugs his eyes like we're stupid for asking what he obviously drives. "Girls," he says, and practically adds, *duh.* "I haul girls in one of the chicken trucks. They pay by the head. Other guys drive the main truck. I'm just new. I'm just a driver, man!"

Lola, still crouching over this Mr. Gangy Man, turns her head to me and purses her lips, shakes her head in a slight jostle, and closes her eyes slow and reopens them slow. I'm transported back in time to when we searched for kidnapped and pregnant Dorothy M. Salucci and ran across a key witness, a chicken farmer, so I am not surprised at all when Lola moves on in thought like I have to that memory, and she says, "Chicken trucks. Always a fucking chicken man, Liu. Fucking chicken men."

"And where do you take the girls?"

"One of the holding places. Depends on the day."

"Where's today's holding place?"

"No clue, ma'am."

"Don't you fucking call me ma'am, Mr. Gangy Man."

Mr. Gangy Man looks at me. I don't give him any apologetic sympathy. I have nothing but contempt for him.

"You have no clue where today's holding spot is? How can that be?"

"I'm telling you it's different every time. They hold them, the girls. Then they move them on to some other place. I don't know."

Lola, still crouching over him, shouts in his face, "Where? Move them around where?"

"Look lady, alls I know is we drive them somewhere to hold. Then someone takes them to a place in Viebury to get ready."

"Big stone mansion?"

"Yeah."

Lola nods at me. I nod back. We know the stone mansion in Viebury. This is where the alleged "Lobster Tank" event is supposed to take place in two nights. Again, we learned this last clue last month from Velada to Lisa, and it's something Lisa insists she "independently verified"—she refuses to say how. Lisa being held for periods of time in unknown holding places is also not new, and one of the reasons why we have to track down Velada to find Lisa before the tank—and for me, to shut it all down.

"Get ready? What are you talking about, Gangy Man?" Lola says.

"I don't know. I think. I think they get them ready. Like, girl stuff, ya know?"

"I do not know what the fuck *girl stuff* means, idiot."

Mr. Gangy Man gestures for me to explain, indicating I, the male, must know what girl stuff means. He searches my face to help him make this woman, who sits on him, understand.

"Do you mean do their hair and nails, like that type of stuff?" I ask.

"Yeah, I think. Like, girl stuff. I'm just the driver, man!"

"Whatever," Lola says. She twists her face at me, like she's so profoundly put off by this whole conversation. Turning back to Mr. Gangy Man, she demands, "Show us this chicken truck. And then you are going to take us to all these holding places."

She steps her legs out of the coil of the man beneath her, and says, "Get up, dummy."

Here, now, in an alley, with Lola pushing Mr. Gangy Man as he leads us to his red chicken truck, a migraine bleeds in my brain so fierce I am literally blinded by the sun. I close my eyes, wince, lean against a house for a two-second break, worry I'm having a stroke and breathe in. Once things calm and I scrape my feet forward, I try cracking my eyes open and read the side of the truck: RED'S HENS, FREE-RANGE EGGS, SALISBURY, MASSACHUSETTS. Built into the bed of the truck are what would appear to be rectangular cages or compartments for hens, but as we inspect closer, are tight, confined, empty caskets for human bodies; or, live girls in transit. Mesh high on one end for air flow. Gangy says the other chicken truck is the same.

Of all the unexpected shit contingencies, we're dealing with a barbaric contraption of cages. And red, like a huge middle finger to law enforcement.

CHAPTER EIGHTEEN
LISA YYLAND: THE BARN

The light is still tricking me as I blink to focus, having been blinded in that damn red truck so long. But I believe I see, through a crack in the back roller doors to this barn, where the sun is a flood of white, the form of a man with a knit hat over his head. He's spying, as Eva's two henchmen tie my arms behind my back. I'm still seated on the barn floor. With Barbara's murderer in jail, plus these two goons tying me up, that makes three fucking inbred, mouth-breathing guards. So unless Velada was lying in our visit a month ago, I've met the whole U.S. management group now, except for some second woman, and all I know of that woman is she's very short and much older.

I'm not sure if I'm hallucinating about the spying man in a knit hat outside. Maybe he's just another false perception, another black butterfly. But I have a sense I should not broadcast his presence. I look to Pink Bitch Eva, blink at her.

"I need water, bitch," I say.

Her two mouth-breathers are done tying my arms behind my back in a thin, sturdy rope, with lots of weaving around and between the wrists in multiple figure eights and tied tight. The most impossible to break out of without tools or help. They stand above me, looking down, both of their mouths open and exhaling in panting bursts. I'd like to spin on my ass and swing straight legs around in a fast circle, like a sickle slicing hay, to strike their ankles, chop through their top heavy balance, and then when they're toppling, push them head first down the hole in the floor of this barn—the one beside us—and listen as the bones in their necks snap. *Crack.* The same sound that came from Melanie's head dive, but this time the cracking sound of retribution would become my earworm, not the miserable sound of suicide.

You fucking pigs.

I've dialed hate up to rage.

"Oh you need some water, Lisa? Could I draw you a warm bath? Maybe get you your favorite chocolates?" Eva says in a sickening taunt.

"Just some fucking water, bitch."

She stares at me, standing there in her disgusting pink outfit. Her legs bare. She's a beast. The air in this barn with a high-pitched roof and room for several cars—tools dangling on walls—smells of a mixture of car oil and grass, the scent of a county fair.

Shaking her head while scrunching her nose as if I emit some toxic odor, Eva says, "I should have killed you when I shot your mother."

A flash of red blocks out all vision for me.

Next, pulsing black.

Pulsing black.

This bitch shot Mother?

My head twitches.

This bitch shot Mother?

My eyes are blinking fast, blinking, I can't stop them.

This bitch shot Mother?

My body jerks, I can't stop blinking.

The fucking tennis racket handle. This bitch shot Mother.

Through my rage, my face growing hot and fierce, I see Eva cock her head to mirror mine, as if mocking me and reading my thoughts. She grins like she did when she pinned me to the oak in the park.

This bitch shot Mother.

I'm watching Eva even though it feels like red blood fills my eyes. She's calling out to the mouth-breathers hovering above me. "Don't stand there with your mouths open, dumb fucks. We have to clean up this mess before Eminence gets back from golf and meetings. He can't know her mother visited Rasper. We have to contain this."

Rage is now dialed up to Homicidal Rage, and I can't turn it off.

I'm blinking mad, my body is jerking and twitching. I believe my arms are on literal fire behind my back, trying to burn through these impossible knots. In my mind, I'm performing violent movements. I'm slamming her fucking head on this concrete barn floor. Her pink outfit is stained with her splattering blood, in my mind, and I keep slamming, slamming, slamming her face in the concrete. It's hard to be precise here, between the rage and the vision acclimation and the dehydration and the flood of white light by the back roller doors and the visions of me bashing in her fucking ugly skull, but I think she just said, "We'll have to find the car she stuffed the phone and notes in later. Get the GTO. Cover my Prius. You," she points to one of the goons, "and I will take her to her mother's office in Manchester. We'll get whatever duplicate notes, even burn the whole fucking building down if we have to. Eminence will be back here past midnight, so we have some time. Unless the whore is lying." Now I believe she's looking at me, and in my mind I'm gouging out her eyes with her Prius car keys. "Whore, you lying about Manchester?" she says to me.

I realize the completely justifiable violent homicide playing out in my mind is causing me to rub my tied hands in a furious, and useless, manner, still writhing to get out of these knots. I'm also now standing, although I don't recall jumping to my legs. What's playing out for me is a separate mental dimension, disconnection, which I'm allowing to play out, even though my metacognition is pleading with me to stay on one level plain of reality. I stare as she says words, lava now dripping from my eyes, as I continue gouging out hers with her stupid fucking keys and then spit in her eyeholes. I must be screaming and spitting and frothing a hellfire.

"Shut her the fuck up. Knock her the fuck out," she shouts.

If I could see my hands behind my back, I believe I'd see her blood painting my palms. Movement approaches me, perhaps one of the mouth-breathers picks up a lead pipe from a corner. If my arms were free right now, that pipe would be mine and embedded in Eva's atrophied brain. I see only a spiral of red and pink, which is edged by a maelstrom of swirling black. I imagine I drop the pipe, that metal hits concrete and echoes of *tings* fill the open barn space as the pipe *clinks* in bounces, end to end, end to end, and settles and rolls. I snatch her brown wig in my clenched claw, like I scalped her. But my arms are still tied behind my back, and she's still in her wig.

156

She's walking toward a door on the structure attached to this barn with one of her mouth-breathers. I believe she's saying phrases like, "Check the Up Top…" "They're fine. They're high…" "Eight here in Viebury. Eight girls…" "Everything will be fine." "It has to go forward…" "Too much money to lose."

It has to go forward. Too much money to lose.

We're in Viebury Grove.

The mouth-breather whose movement captured a pipe is closer to me. I square my legs.

Eva stops in the doorway, turns to me, scans me up and down, stalls for what feels like an hour, but time is not measurable through these warped dimensions I'm experiencing. My senses are all scrambled. Finally, she says, "You're not Up Top quality. If you survive the tank, you'll be a Basement Bitch."

A crack reverberates in my mind, through my skull, as I hear Eva add, "Not so tough now, huh, Dentist?"

Black overcomes me.

I believe I wilt to the floor. I believe the asshole with the pipe disappears. I believe I am still murdering her in my mind, my eyes are red pools, her skull crashes and crashes. I scalp her, but feel nothing in my hands. I see black, nothing but black. Then nothing, maybe a long forever of nothing. It's possible a cat with yellow eyes is licking my nose, that birds flew in my ear canals and up my nostrils and have nested in my brain to chirp out the loudest bird symphony in the loudest tropical rainforest. It's possible I'm moving, somehow—flying or floating. It's possible I have died, my energy dispersing, becoming light. I'm in a heat in a tropical rainforest of birds. Light outside me, but black inside. And black is all I see.

CHAPTER NINETEEN
FORMER SPECIAL AGENT ROGER LIU
A HOLDING PLACE

"What the hell does 'Mr. Gangy Man' mean?" I ask Lola as we drive to one of Gangy's holding places. Gangy is in the backseat of our rental minivan, next to Lola.

Lola pretends to not hear me.

"Okay, so, you made it up? Some random name, Mr. Gangy Man?" I look to her through the rearview.

Lola tics her head to the side, a floppish wince. "It's just a name, Liu, don't worry about it," she says, shaking off something about this name. "Please."

"Sure." I sense this is now a serious topic, this name, Mr. Gangy Man. I'm guessing something to do with Lola's past, the one she never mentions. Then again, she doesn't mention her present either.

Our Mr. Gangy Man has an actual name, and we took it and all, but we're never going to call him by his real name: Rod Razen. Stripper name, if you're into gangly skeletons with possible scurvy and meth teeth.

In the back of our rental, Mr. Gangy Man sits in Lola's cuffs, which she jammed on his wrists. After that, Lola had read him a half-hearted version of reluctant Miranda rights—under the authority of her current employment.

We've been with Gangy Man an hour and a half now. The first holding place was an empty house in Lynn. We searched top to bottom, found nothing, and decided to move on. We're headed now to the second holding place, in search of Lisa, of Velada, of the tailpipe stink of another chicken truck. Lola insists we're on our way so as to ensure Velada is in place. But I am hell-bent on shutting this shit down.

"Hey, hey, here here, turn left," Mr. Gangy Man says, and sure enough, I see the sign of Saleo Country Club, outside East Hanson. Now I'm concerned Chief Castile will see our car back just outside her town, and she'll immediately haul us back in, because I am supposed to be Dakeel Rentower of Lowell, Uber driver, long rid of Martha Tannhouse, my passenger.

Gangy had said one of the holding places was a "punk ass club for bitches, the kind who wear fucking white on white and hit small balls," but he couldn't remember the name, because I'm finding he's a complete imbecile and also he's twitching, coming down from a meth high, so this guy's mental faculties are essentially fried. We took back roads to get here, following his often insecure directions, leading us to take several wrong turns and having to turn around. It is only now I realize we're right back to the adjoining town to where we started this morning.

I crank a hard left. We drive down a single lane driveway with tall maples bordering both sides. Between the trees on the left are clay tennis courts, dotted with two pairs of players in only white. Beyond tennis, rolling, rising green acres of golf. Two groundskeepers roam the holes with vacuums strapped to their backs like Ghostbusters, sucking up any colored leaves.

Ahead is a palatial mansion of brick with a crushed-stone circular drive. Giant clay pots of red mums flank a double door, which appears to be cut crystal in the dwindling daylight; the shine off the door fractures in prisms of a hundred thin rainbows and a thousand air diamonds. I count no less than three Rolls Royce and several varieties of land-cruising black SUVs. Two elderly, black-suited drivers read newspapers in their separate cars, waiting for their human cargo. Our blue rental minivan is a scar upon this scene of opulence. We're coming into evening, so the sun is falling, but people still dot the golf course lawn.

I wedge our scar car between a waxed GMC SUV and a shiny YUKON SUV, same car, different name. I exit and open Gangy's door, while Lola uncuffs him.

"Listen, asshole, you're going to take us where you go, and you're going to keep your mouth shut. Play along. Maybe they'll give you a plea then."

"Fine, man. I usually go straight in the Club, up to the bar. The barman gives me an envelope, then they have me drive around back and down to the basement service entrance. Sometimes I bring them coke. That's all. But, but…"

"But nothing!"

"Yeah, but, I ain't never been here in the day or night. They make me come before dawn, in the wee hours, so no one sees. Like the members and all."

"Well, they're seeing you today. Take us the way you go," I say.

"Wee hours," Lola mocks under her breath. But getting louder, she continues, "Wee hours. *Wee hours.*" She hits Gangy Man in the back of his head. "Wee hours? Shut up, Gangy Man. You're not fucking British."

We walk to the crystal-prism door, my hand in a vise grip on Gangy's arm.

None of us are in all white, like all the members I now see lingering beyond the door. And none of us are in all black, like the two drivers, who I'm sure are each named Jeeves. Lola in her gray suit, me in my gray suit, Mr. Gangy Man in dirty jeans and a red-check flannel shirt. We walk in. Heads turn.

A man in a thin cashmere sweater, white, and white golf pants strides up to us.

"Judge Frackson, nice to meet you. And you are?" Judge Frackson says with a fake smile and in the uppity accent of Kelsey Grammer on the show *Frasier*.

"Don't matter who we are," Lola says.

The Judge tight smiles at her, then wide smiles, obviously thinking better on his game. He attempts to humor her with a loud blast of a laugh, as if she were joking; he's forcing the joke, for us and for the members around him mingling.

"What can I do for you? Who might you be calling on?" he says as if a butler host, although it is clear he is one of the Grand Masters. I read in his subtle body language, the little twitch he gave when Lola blocked him, the way his cheek shakes from the inner clenching: he's nervous. Behind him, I note members whispering to each other, and lip read one as saying, "Looks like they got our coke dealer."

"There a woman here who might be in business with this coke dealer?" I ask. Several members drop their heads into drinks and step away. Many disperse, wanting no part of this.

"A woman? Part of the staff?" Judge Frackson says, confirming women cannot be members themselves. He keeps with the rhythm of an oblivious foyer conversation, all for the benefit of the listening members behind him, while keeping a growing viciousness in his face to us—the glaring pupils, the flaring nose. His skin is a perfect caramel tan, even and supple soft, like he uses his wife's creams. I note he won't look at Lola or Mr. Gangy Man, and I note further he's having a hard time keeping eye contact with me. Scanning quickly around at the members, of which only a few still linger, I see only men. None of black or Asian or other descent. Through a side door, I note a pool, and in a loungy pool chair, one woman, only one, reads a magazine under the shade of a floppy hat and blanketed against the fall temperature. Must be a member's wife. Lola would never be permitted to be a member. And I assume I, with my mixed race of Vietnamese and Rochester, New York, would likewise be denied. On a wall to our side are about two dozen headshots of present and past members, all men. And as they are aligned alphabetically, given the engraved brass name plaques beneath floating heads, I quickly find one for an Honorable Judge Malcolm Rasper.

"How does one become a member in this *cunt*, ry club?" Lola says, while sniffing the air, and not waiting for Judge Frackson to answer.

Frackson dismisses Lola by pivoting his head askance and keeping his eyes on me, looking me up and down as if I'm trash. "Perhaps you're looking for Sussex Country Club? Down the street?" He says *Sussex* as if *Sussex* is a stinkpot for stinkpots like me. "We are sometimes confused with the Sussex. We are a different club, though." And for the benefit of now two remaining visible members brave enough to step closer, he says in a louder voice, "We're *very* different from the Sussex, aren't we boys?" His sycophants gain a little closer on tender side steps and giggle and guffaw at this inside dis of some other country club. "You must be looking for the Sussex," Frackson ends in a cool tone and sinister smile.

"No," I say, conjuring the flat affect of Lisa Yyland, my young boss.

Lola is circling behind Frackson now, smelling the air without hiding her action.

"I think you're going to have to leave. I'm not sure what or whom you're looking for, but you will have to leave now," Frackson says, in a whisper to me, hiding his distress from the two listening members. *Not everyone is in on what's going on.*

Lola is sniffing and walking toward an open stairwell down. A door at the top of the stairwell is cracked open, which I presume is a mistake given the '*dammit*' wince Frackson gives upon sighting the door. Lola's so quick, Frackson doesn't have time to stop her. As she descends the stairs, she unholsters her gun and raises it in both hands. "Crabs in Trees," Lola says, hinting at the stink of lingering lotion she finds in the air, and which I now smell, given her cue.

I push Mr. Gangy Man to the stairs, force him down, and as I pass Judge Frackson, I whisper, "Whether you know or not what's going on in the basement, I trust you won't be calling the cops now, will you?" I look at the two members. "Make sure you and your buddies don't come down here or I will bring you all up on coke charges. Got it?"

The members throw up their palms and back step. "Whatever, Officer. We aren't involved in any of that. No drugs for me," one says.

"You, too," I say to Frackson.

Frackson, chin-up, agrees, which tells me, he knows what's going on in the basement. He does not want any cops here, for he wouldn't be able to gaslight the unwitting club members, and he wouldn't be able to dictate which cops come. Me suggesting I don't want him to call the cops is, to him, a welcome reprieve for what he thinks will be time for him to gather his own troops, which will take him some time. I note how this sleepy, wealthy, demented place has grown indolent: there are no bodyguards on site on this sedate fall day. The gentlemen drivers outside are just that: drivers. I noted on the way in no snipers, no hidden goons in corners. Complacent, too—*nobody* would dare enter Saleo's privileged grounds without invitation is the assumption they all must hold. The guards will have to be called in. We've got time, but not much. We follow the Crabs in Trees, *Crabtree and Evelyn*, scent.

Lola and her nose.

The stairwell is arched in plastered, faux paint. A facade of the cracked, tinted stucco of an Italian villa. We descend in formation, me with the added obstacle of Gangy in the middle. My gun is also unholstered, held up, and ready.

At the bottom of the stairs, Lola sniffs the air, and we go left, curve around some dark halls, and land in a lower area with no lights. A metal door painted gray and slightly open is where Lola leads. A dimly-lit, long hallway, at the end of which is a buzzing, neon sign in the shape of purple lips. On both sides of the hall are door after door after door, like a seedy hotel floor. Lola follows along the powdery scent, and I open a few doors along the way. In each room, the same sparse setup: a bed and mirrors on the wall. This is a hall for paid sex. No Johns in here at the moment, though. I suspect this is a nighttime place, and only used on special occasions. I'm guessing this, based on the outdated Fourth of July decorations still hanging crooked from failing tape. It's October.

Near the end, Lola stops by one closed door. This door is a louvered wood door, the kind with a solid frame, but the guts are like the fins of a fish. We hear muffled breathing seeping through the slats. Lola flanks one side; I flank the other, holding Gangy Man firm to my side. I could break his scrawny arm by squeezing a millimeter harder.

Lola inhales and nods to confirm her trail of *Crabtree and Evelyn* lotion once again, and even I now detest the thickness of the musty power. I believe our nun from Mariana Church is here. She must have fled here as soon as we ran after Gangy Man and wasted time on the first holding place in Lynn, and then all of Gangy's hazy fucking directions thereafter. And by the sounds of the muffled, anticipatory breathing behind the door, it sounds like she's got someone else in there with her.

Lola kicks the door in, her black boot breaking several slats.

We enter.

And there she is: Sister, still in her nun's garb, but with the wimple gone and the head shield down. She holds a gun on a short woman. A ceiling fan whirs above their heads, hanging from a single rod.

We look at the short woman's feet.

She wears flip-flops.

Her feet are burnt.

Lola stares at her.

The woman glares back.

I can't tell if she's in on it with Sister and they are trying to trick us, or if she truly is captive.

She's small, just as Lisa described all these years. Tiny…petite with muscled arms, the arms of a bat. This is the first time Lola and I have ever seen her in person. In all of our surveillance of Mariana, we never confirmed sight of her; although we were fairly sure she was the short woman hidden under a hat and hoodie and sunglasses who would come and go—too fast for us to intercept. During those times, Lisa's warnings rang in my mind: "Don't do anything to cause any suspicions, don't talk to her. Don't. We're so close now."

"Velada," Lola says, while pointing her gun at Sister.

"Where's Lisa?" I demand.

Sister laughs. "We have her now. Fuck off," she says, holding the gun firmer toward Velada, which, given the circumstances, we know is a direct threat to Lisa for what Sister doesn't know: we need Velada to be in place on the night of the Lobster Tank. Or *does* Sister know?

"Velada is done," Sister says.

Sister pauses to smirk at Lola, a mere fraction of time before, as it appears, she intends to press the trigger, and it is this pause to smirk that is a mistake. Lola never hesitates.

A crack fills the room when Lola fires at the ceiling fan, which causes Sister to drop her gun and jump back. Lola lunges and pulls Velada toward us, just in time for the fan—which dangled a few heart-stopping seconds—to crash between Velada, now with us, and Sister on the other side.

I cup Mr. Gangy Man's mouth to stifle his screaming. Lola rushes over to Sister, quickly subdues her by zip-tying her wrists together. I note several additional backup zip-ties poke out of a pocket from Lola's inner jacket pocket. I stand blocking the door and holding Gangy while Lola next unties Velada, which knots seem a little *too* loose to be totally convincing, I'm not sure.

"She just got here. She just got here. She's worried I'm going to ruin the event. They insist it go forward, too much money. And Eminence is crazy, doesn't care about risks. She was going to kill me. She just got here. You two freaked her out at Mariana asking for me. She didn't trust me anyway. She wasn't supposed to be at Mariana today."

"Why weren't you there?" Lola asks.

"Lisa fucked everything up is why! When she forced herself into that car at the police station, forced herself in early, everyone got freaked out. And why did you even go to Mariana after all that? I figured you'd be smart enough to stay away. I had to stay here to keep things calm, make sure everything stays on course, because he's…" But she stops talking because in this moment, Gangy Man torques and wriggles away. Snapping to, I give chase, the second time today with this asshole. We run down the hall of rooms, around some basement corners, and out through a basement well, and it takes no time because Gangy trips, and I tackle him on Hole One. Members in white jump back, aghast. The evening shades and shadows are thickening, and it must be the time of day for golfers to come in, for they all seem to be on pilgrimage to the club from the course.

I remove one of my own zip ties from a jacket pocket, thinking I'll tie Gangy again. I saddle his prone body, my knees on the green. It is a struggle, so I jam a knee in his spine, and an elbow into his neck. Once I have him tied, I sit back on my heels, keeping my body on his legs, and breathe. In so doing, I note a golf cart to the side with a two-digit license plate: "20." A black-haired man is a passenger, his back to me. He will not turn his face and reveal himself, like everyone else.

I stare at the number 20 on the golf cart license plate.

The golf cart has stalled, and the driver twists to see me, but the passenger, black-haired and sized like a WWE wrestler, still does not turn. Around them, a sparse scattering of other men dressed in all white, also stall and stare, but no one flinches or moves or shouts. They act as if nothing, no alarm at my distress, as if I am just an annoying bird who landed on their green and they have to wait for me to lift and take flight. Two men in the outer beyond speak, and given my eyesight acuity, I lip-read one as saying, "Guess we'll have to get coke from someone else now." And yet, the driver of the golf cart with the "20" on the license plate grins, a vapid grin of evil, like a despised President signing an Executive Order he knows the great vast majority of citizens despise—the type of grin that says, '*struggle and protest all you want, I hold all the power.*' The kind of grin you wish to kick in the chin and punch in the jaw.

I assess the crowd, loosening my leg grip on Mr. Gangy Man, so he is able to slither out from under me. I feel as if the great outdoors is distorted, the air full of melting sunlight and the sparrows scratching to stay in flight, as if time wishes to push forward, but the wind sends minutes back in a tug-of-war. It's warped, my thinking, this sense—my perception modeled ten degrees off the place in which I sit.

Most club members in the surround seem undisturbed, I assume because they think all I've done is catch their run-of-the-mill coke dealer and they can buy coke anywhere, these elite. A couple of men grin, like the driver of the golf cart and one standing man, who I recognize now as one campaigning to be a Senator. These are men of power, all of them. They are ambivalent as to what I do, some disdainful. They look down upon me, someone of law enforcement, many zeros behind them in monthly pay, not entwined in their enterprises, and thus, a lower lifeform. They see me sitting on my heels in my mass-produced suit, as if I am a pathetic fly. Whatever members here who are in on the events of Viebury Grove will go ahead with their plans because they are confident they will not get caught, will never be held to blame. They are connected. They believe they are in a secret society. They are in control. Some of these men are the intended Watchers of the Lobster Tank; I know it, I feel it in the way the golf cart driver looks at me. And I know it, I feel it, the golf cart passenger who still will not turn his black-haired head to me, despite all the other members in white stalling and looking, is Eminence.

Lola enters the scene from the basement. The golf cart driver's eyes note her incoming, and bounce back to me and wink. A deeper grin overtakes his smug face, one that says, *'make your move, no one cares.'* I am enraged, but the rage is futile, so I also feel impotent. I creak my cramped legs to stand and back-step to Lola. I do not leave the driver's stare. I do not blink. Gangy, now that I no longer pin his legs, struggles to his feet, turns to look at me, and runs off into the woods, his hands behind his back.

"Liu, what the fuck? Go get Gangy," Lola says, but doesn't prepare her body to run herself. She must sense I am not alarmed by his departure; she must sense I've moved on in thought. She stands beside me.

"Velada let me tie her to a pipe in the basement because I said I didn't trust her. She's waiting on us. The nun, same thing, tied to a pipe," she says.

"Let Velada go," I say.

"I thought you wanted to shut this down? We'll make her help us find where Lisa is this minute. We'll shut it down. Things are too off."

"Velada needs to be in place. It doesn't matter what we do. Shut Sister up. Drag Velada elsewhere. Find Lisa. Stop this. Interrogate Gangy. Arrest them. It doesn't matter. They will win and go forward with their special night or other special nights after that. They have all the power. Look. And if they can't, he'll never stop hunting Lisa. He'll kill her. Look."

In one last glance, I sear the black-haired golf cart passenger's head to my mind's eye.

"Get back in the basement before Frackson has a chance to talk to the nun and find out about her suspicions on Velada."

"Don't worry about that. I knocked that stinkbug out."

~~~

"I was trying to tell you Eminence was here, but then that idiot runs. Here, take this. You need to get her out of here now and keep her from talking to any others," Velada says, indicating Sister, while shoving a bag of blow in my hand.

"Listen, missy, if you are fucking with us, if one fucking hair is harmed on Lisa, I will personally hunt you down and grind your short ass into woodchips, got it? And I do indeed have a woodchipper," Lola says to Velada. "I mean that *very* fucking literally."

"Yeah, I got it. You've said that like five hundred times. You guys need to go. Now," Velada says.

Lola's got the nun slung in her arms like a baby, her limp hands zip-tied. She's still out cold. We go up those basement stairs with the Tuscan, stucco arch. Velada is going to her office way at the end of the basement and will pretend she's doing Saleo's books, with her headphones on and door shut. Like she heard nothing. That's what she tells us.

At the top, Frackson is waiting. I hold up the bag of coke to him and say, for the benefit of any listening members, "Tell your boys the DEA is not going to like how we found blow just sitting out in the open down there and two coke dealers just milling around your grounds. The one got away, but we got this one. She's notorious. So we'll take her in now."

Frackson looks me up and down, somewhat of an approving, but annoyed look, as if we're playing chess and I made a move for "Check" but not "Check Mate."

"Unfortunately, we do have a couple of men who have their demons. Trust me, we'll ensure there are no more problems at Saleo, Officer. Here, let me walk you out."

In walking out to our rental, Frackson takes care to keep us far from the others. I'm on guard that Frackson disobeyed my warning and slunk into the basement while Lola and I were outside with Gangy Man and he saw Velada tied up, but that window of time was short. As we reach the minivan, I know Frackson didn't do any such thing.

"You must understand that I need to protect my club. Ensure strangers aren't packing explosives in their vehicles, and all. You understand," he says, when he sees me noticing the back hatch popped, the cover to the wheel well gone, Lola's black roller open and her clothes strewn everywhere.

I draw up close to Frackson while Lola shoves our old, slumped nun in the backseat. "It's going to be fun visiting you in prison, asshole. They don't have tanning beds there, so you'll be just another pasty prison runt."

Judge Frackson smirks. "Must be sad for you. A sad life," he says, throwing me a look of mock pity. "Toodle-oo," he says, waving.

Lola, on the passenger side now, having secured Sister, flips off the Judge.

I enter the car. I flip him off, too. Slam my door, back out fast.

"Dakeel, take me to your place in Lowell. We'll stash this trash human there until this shit show is over," Lola says.

"Yes, ma'am," I say, playing my part as her fake Uber driver.

In pulling on to the main street, I look in the mirror to see an East Hanson police SUV.

"Duck. Get down. Now," I say to Lola.

The SUV slows behind me the further we drive from the border of East Hanson.

I'm pretty sure Chief Castile is driving that SUV. Maybe. Hard to say.

"Can't be Dakeel's place in Lowell, Lola. Pick one of our other backups."

"Go to that shit trap we got in Magnolia."

"We got a different car there?"

"A beater, boss."

"Fine."

CHAPTER TWENTY
LISA YYLAND

I've been through this before. The awakening from a blackout. The first time, I was sixteen. My monster jailer walked me to a quarry and showed me one of his cut-up teenage victims, bloated and drowned and sliced in the womb, tethered and tied in the water, as some macabre trophy or warning or other demented reason. I fainted then, crashed down, out cold, on granite rocks in the Indiana woods I now own. Back then, when I came to, the living world feathered me in waves of white and flickering grays, then jumping colors and disjointed sound. Then color and sound invaded in a rush of wakefulness, then stopped quick, leading me back to black for a respite, followed by another rush, longer, then black respite, and so on until I agreed to awake. Here now, eighteen years later, I'm going through the same cycles of white waves, flickering grays, jumping, rushing colors, but this time, sound comes in the rhythm of singing. This time, my head throbs from a metal blow.

I feel cold leather on my cheek, feel a warm blowing above my body, like from a heat vent. If I move my cheek, it sticks a bit to the leather, which is soft, and my body is also softened on whatever I lie upon. I crack the upper eye. A blur of images invades my brain, browns with blues—a shape of a man, singing, headphones the size of hamburger buns on his ears. I close my eye. The singing is more distinct now, and the beat is modern *thuds*, like my workout rap.

I crack the upper eye, the bottom one, too. Now the browns I saw before are not waved and braided with blue, now the browns are brown-paneled walls and the blue is his shirt, denim, unbuttoned to his sternum. He sits in a chair, headphones on, rapping to himself. A soundboard, black with levers and knobs and buttons is before him, and behind that, a glass window, into which, as I sit taller and come to life like a daisy at dawn, I see a standing microphone and walls padded with black, egg-crate shaped foam. A sound booth.

Outside of the sound booth, but in a sound studio, I am not tied. I am free and sitting and rubbing the back of my skull and feeling a large egg bump. I go to the fake tuft of false hair at the base of my neck, check the quantity and tension on all, and all are intact. I exhale.

I set my free palm on the cushion of the black leather couch. I am in a basement, given the lack of windows and the coolness of the concrete floor, the parts I feel with my naked, real toes. Inspecting my right toes, I note that the magnetic rings around the fake parts are there, the false toes, too. I exhale again. Someone took my Keds or they were left…where was I last? In a barn? Yes, in a barn. Am I in that basement, through that hole in the floor?

Someone carried and laid me here, propped me in a comfortable position, even placed a fleece blanket on me that now slithers to the floor with my movements.

Other parts of the basement floor, beyond the couch, are layered in a variety of misshapen red, blue, black, and purple handwoven rugs, the kind you might find at Ikea or rolled in a woven-grass basket at a Bangladesh bazaar. This underground space of cool concrete floor with foreign rugs must be the rapping, head-phoned, blue-shirt-wearing guy's sound studio, and he is a musician. But what is this? Where am I? My arms were tied before. My arms are no longer tied.

The walls are male, I know from the faux-wood paneling for one. Also the splayed-leg-crouch poster of Li'l Kim taped to a side wall above an army-green filing cabinet. Li'l Kim's music is part of my workout playlist. Missy Elliot, Eminem, M.C. Capone, and Mackelmore in a fur coat glare around the room from other posters, these ones tacked, not taped, into the paneled walls. I run a list through my mind and match all of these artists to my playlist as well. And, as I home in on what Blue Shirt is singing, I find I like his rhythm too. My head throbs. I don't know him or where I am, and yet, I note a conflicting wash of calm and familiarity, like my mind was in a knot and fire red and is now melted and blue, like what my subconscious registers when Vanty and I are home reading or outside skeet shooting. Perhaps I'm not yet fully awake. I strain my eyes to focus on Blue Shirt and clear my thoughts.

Blue Shirt notices me now and is starting to remove his headphones. I note a hint of marijuana wafting in the air. On top of the soundboard back brace is a propped box of Scrabble, which leans against the glass window to the egg-crated sound booth. Also propped there is a framed quote: "*We forge the chains we wear in life. – Charles Dickens.*" Next to the quote is a blown-glass bong and beside that is a black knit ski hat.

When I was on a barn floor, did I see a man spying into the barn? Yes. Yes. I remember this now.

Strewn beneath the back brace and threatening to spill to the levers and buttons of the soundboard are a variety of paraphernalia and clutter, including a Red Sox bobble head, a pack of orange Tic-Tacs, and a bag of Skittles, which I want to pour into my mouth as a rainbow waterfall of medicine, for I feel dizzy and need to boost my glycemic index. There's also a dog-eared journal, which is an open-faced sandwich of black-ink scrawls. Zeroing in on Blue Shirt's fingers, I note the stains of black ink. He is like my husband, Lenny, the poet. They are the same in having stained fingers from writing. Lenny, the poet; Blue Shirt, the musician.

Get back on plan.

I have a weakness for lyricists, writers, masters of the linguistic mind, for I do not hold such sorcery. Now, right now, I acknowledge a special weakness for musicians in barely-buttoned blue shirts, ones who apparently untie me and set me gently on a soft couch. What a strange glimmer of joy I feel and did not consciously turn on, as I awake from a blackout, which he might have played a part in, but I don't care. This glimmer must be the surge of adrenaline and wakeful endorphins, upon appreciating survival. Or maybe it's the weed. Or maybe it's all the music I like and how he's looking at me, smiling, revealing a dimple in his cheek. Maybe it's all of it. I shut it all off.

Don't allow Stockholm's now.

"Who are you and where am I?" I demand. I don't dare stand, for as I speak, my eyes fight my mind and flicker, blurring the world. I strain my eyes to stay straight.

172

"Oh yeah, here she be, raging girl trying to murder fuckers with her hands tied," he says, sly and slick and grinning at me from his chair. He sets his headphones on his soundboard.

"Tica, tica, tica, tica, Cat," he says, curling a finger toward a corner of the room. He keeps saying, "Tica, tica, tica, tica, Cat, Cat, Cat," faster and faster, like an auctioneer.

Out from the corner to which he's directing his curling finger, a blur of fur bounds and jumps on his lap. He strokes the cat's chin. I recall yellow eyes staring at me, something licking my nose.

"Where am I?"

"You're safe is where."

"Where!"

"Those fuckers bashed your skull, you fell, they left, I dragged you out before they got back. The end. Got it? You're safe."

"I was safe there. I had it under control."

"Fuck you did," he says, raising an eyebrow and one side of his mouth. He stands up, moves over to a refrigerator in the corner by the foot of the couch, extracts an icepack from the top freezer, and hands it to me. "Here, cool your brain."

I take the pack from him and compress it on the egg coming out of my skull.

"I've been after these fuckers from that big stone shithole for months. And I've seen that red truck coming and going. I couldn't take it no more."

"You fucked everything up. I need to get back in there."

He looks at me with a squint and a smirk, sits back in his chair. "Look. Let's skip ahead, Terror Teen. That's what they called you in the papers, yeah? I know all about you. Saw your name tattooed above your butt, your shirt rode up, along with your blood type and social. Smart. Survival technique. Yeah. I googled your ass. I know all about you, Lisa Yyland. The savant, they say, perhaps with, what they say? Psychopathic tendencies? So, at first I thought you might'a been one of the poor-ass girls they steal. But you, not you, no, you're up to something. I can help you. We can snag them together."

We?

Did he see the rest of what's printed on my back? Must not have. He would have commented. He seems to like to talk.

He's still talking.

"You're the one who fried some fuck who stole your teen ass. Eighteen years ago. Cat likes that. Right kitty cat, Cat," he says, taking his eyes off me and nose-to-nosing with his cat, coaxing Cat to agree that it likes me. Of course the cat respects me for killing a monster. Cats are ruthless murderers.

"I watch them, you know. Watched that witch who called you a basement bitch, watched her from high in a tree drag a girl into a room upstairs in that stone mansion, made her attend to some man. And I know, okay. I know. Let's just say I got a vested interest." He drops his voice on this last line and flares his nostrils. His tone changes to one of anger. "I want to ruin them. So, let's skip ahead. You and me, we team up."

"I already have a team. No."

He tsks and returns to grinning. "Here's the thing. This ain't me askin'. This is me tellin'. You and me, we teaming up. So let's not waste a bunch of bullshit time on wondering whether we gonna team up. We gonna team up, Terror Teen."

"How long have I been out?"

"Two hours."

I can still salvage the plan.

I try to stand, but wobble, so I sit again, calibrating my thinking and my breathing. I look around the room again, the egg-crate sound booth, his soundboard, the rapper posters, a file cabinet. Now that I'm on the edge of the couch and leaning forward, I note a black object hiding behind the file cabinet. I shift my eyes up to him: he's watching closely where my eyes fall. I shift them back to the black object. Then, back to him: his mouth is tight, he's breathing in small inhales through his nose. I shift my eyes back to the black object, rove my sight over the handle, the battery compartment, the drill bit. I look back up to him and stare.

"You have a vested interest?" I ask.

"Sure do," he says, staring back and serious.

"This cordless drill here, that part of your vested interest?"

"What cordless drill?" he asks, no smile and staring straight at me.

I stare back and mirror him.

He smiles, nods his head. I don't need a literal admission, just this acknowledgement is enough, but he keeps talking anyway. "Well now, Lisa Yyland, if I had a cordless drill, which I don't, I understand they have many off-label purposes. You got a problem with that?"

"Do you have a car?"

"What you think? I got a sweet pick-up named Cassie with a covered bed."

"Do you live here alone?"

He drops his smile in a flash, doesn't answer. I wait. He looks to the floor and whispers, "Yeah, I live here alone."

"Let's go get your truck. We have to complete something and then get back here and I need to get back in that stone house."

"Don't you want to know my name?"

I can just call you Blue Shirt in my mind.

I stare ahead. I'm keeping all emotions but hate for Eva and Eminence and all the motherfuckers off. I can't allow anything, as I allowed Homicidal Rage, to throw me off course anymore. I'm reset. I have renewed drive. As I come into a refreshed consciousness, I realize Mother's murder was a nuke bomb. Everything until now was me floundering around in the great plumes of nuke dust. This respite with the intervention by Blue Shirt was, as I reflect, a welcome level-setting, the settling of the nuke's aftermath. I am coming into real focus now, seeing the plan achievable again. I will remain on this level. *Grief is the most destructive distraction agent. Requires you to take inefficient time to redefine your new world. Here's the sterile definition of my new world: Mother was murdered, and I can't quit the plan.*

I'm still staring; he's still talking.

"Ah shit. Psychopathic tendencies. All right. Okay. Even though you don't ask, I'm Mr. Josi Olive, at your service. And this is Cat."

I blink at the cat to acknowledge it. "Let's go now," I say. "And where's your phone?"

"Don't got none."

"Give me your phone."

"Don't got none. Don't want no one ringing me, breaking my concentrations. And I accidentally drowned my cell in the tub a month ago, and I ain't gone to the store to get a new one. Don't talk to no one. No phone."

My greatest enemy in life is all this inefficient chaos.

"I got a Mac, though. Want to email someone?"

"He won't trust an email. He needs to hear my voice."

"Can't you use Skype then?"

"He'd never agree to a video chat. Too risky."

"Who's he?"

He is Liu.

"We need to drive to Manchester, New Hampshire," I answer.

"Whatever. Whatever the plan calls for. Now come on, get up. You want to go to Manch-Vegas so bad. Let's go. This is good, us a team, and us going to Manchester. I got to collect my check from a club I worked last month anyway."

We're not going to some stupid club. You are not part of this plan. We're getting my discs and getting back to Viebury.

Josi rises from his chair, and as he does, his unbuttoned blue shirt shifts, so I see more of his muscled pectoral region. Also, the rolled sleeve on his left arm raises, and I note a navy-blue, toile-like tattoo wrapping his forearm. I dislike toile, toile on china to be specific, but as Josi's toile tattoo appears to be of spear-carrying women warriors on a field, and as it is on his olive skin and fierce, I will allow his toile. He extends his toile-patterned arm to my hand to guide me, and I'm wondering if I should be thinking of my husband Lenny instead.

I stand and tamp down reproductive biorhythms sending blood to my breasts and lower core. I grab Josi's open bag of Skittles from atop his soundboard and pour them in my mouth to spike my glucose level. He upticks his head, shaking a tiny yes to indicate approval. We catch each other's eyes and stare. I don't blink; he doesn't blink. His eyes are shiny sapphires and white squares sparkle in the pupils. I wonder if he sees the Christmas tree cataracts in my eyes, refracting light everywhere. But this goes on three beats too long, so I speak.

"Move it," I say. He turns to proceed to a thick, noise-cancelling door.

"Where are my shoes?" I ask once the door is open and he's moved into the stair landing.

Josi looks at my feet and makes a confused look.

"Hmm," he says.

"Where?"

"They must'a fallen in the woods while I was carrying you. Huh."

He bites his bottom lip and shakes his head, not taking his eyes off my feet. To himself, he mutters, "the feet, the feet."

I have no idea what he's indicating and I don't have any past Nana lessons in my mind that apply. I think he seems sad or nostalgic, maybe, I think that's what Nana calls it, about feet.

"You got sneakers I can borrow? I'm a six-and-a-half," I ask. I'm hoping some woman he's slept with or is sleeping with left some shoes in this pit.

"Actually, I got women's sneakers, that size or 7's, close enough, upstairs," he says in a deflated tone, his head bent. He stalls on the stairs not moving, shaking his head.

Holy fucking shit. Just get me the fucking shoes.

Finally, he moves and up a carpeted staircase we ascend, entering what appears to be Josi's rectangular living room. To my right is a galley kitchen with a sink full of dishes. To my left and where we're headed, the living room has the longest orange couch I've ever seen, likely purchased from a yard sale. The T.V. opposite the couch is housed in an unstained, Ikea-like T.V. cabinet, the scattered wood knots of the piece like a colony of areolas. The rug is a faux oriental of red and navy blue, one brownish blotch stains a corner; I'm guessing red wine. On top of the areola cabinet is a cluster of framed photographs of a couple, and while I do not inspect these photos, because the people are irrelevant to me, I note the metal and wood frames and shiny glass fronts are the only items devoid of dust or some greasy film. I hypothesize that Josi is missing someone, given his tone and unintelligible pauses about the shoes and the cleanliness of the picture frames. *Who cares? Move on. Get to the lab. Get the discs.*

Josi hands me a pair of purple Nike's and a pair of white crew socks.

"I bought these for my wife. She's gone now, she died. But she never wore them. Said they hurt her feet," he says, as I bend to put them on. "Huh," he says again, still shaking some thought he's having in his mind.

As we pass through the living room, I note a small card table under a window to the left of the orange couch. On the card table is a Scrabble board with Scrabble letters sprawled out in words, collectively in the busy horizontal and vertical line pattern of complex piping in a chemical factory. This game was left, it appears, to freeze-frame in perpetuity, for here, too, is a layer of dust over the lines of word pipes.

I catch my breath at one of the words. A vertical one.

I spin, jog back to the areola T.V. cabinet and the row of shiny

SHANNON KIRK

photos.

And there she is, hugging Josi.

I spin, return to the Scrabble board.

Josi is beside me, screwing his eyes.

"Who played the word Velada?" I demand and point.

"My dead wife, Carla," he says. "She said Velada means *soirée* in Spanish."

"When did she die?"

Josi takes a step back. Then another. He's not answering.

"When did she die?" I say louder.

"They killed her months ago, months. They killed her." He's pointing out the window in the direction of the stone mansion.

Josi's wife is Velada. He thinks she's been dead for months—so, another layer to her. I saw her one month ago. When I unraveled one of her other layers.

CHAPTER TWENTY-ONE
LISA YYLAND: VELADA'S LAST VISIT

Heroin, formally known as Diamorphine, chemical compound $C_{21}H_{23}NO_5$, is an antique drug created in the 1870's. It was first concocted to combat Morphine addiction. But irony stepped in to play its fucked up games with the world, making Diamorphine more addictive than Morphine. On top of debilitating addiction, a serious side effect of $C_{21}H_{23}NO_5$ is depressed respiration, and I do not ever allow risk to my perfect pink lungs. So I'm going to take a Hard Pass on allowing any of these assholes to jam even a drop of 'hero' into my veins. I may be able to control emotional switches in my brain, but I can't control the strong-arm bully of a flood of dopamine, the baddest motherfucker of all the body chemicals.

These heroin facts weighed in the back of my mind as facts I had to address in advance of me being taken for the Lobster Tank. Also, I still needed the date and location of the event, and to advise Velada of information I'd validated *after* Shanghai, information I needed to tell her to her face so as to judge her reaction.

So, with all this on my mind, ever since returning from Shanghai five years ago, I awaited another visit from Velada. But year after year rolled by, and I grew concerned that she waited so long and so close to the event. In this last year, before she returned, I've lived on a constant trigger, not venturing beyond my building much without taking adequate precautions. I've had a thousand contingency plans ready if anyone invaded my headquarters, many such contingencies, including the poisonous venom of tanked life forms I keep in one of two Dorothy M. Salucci terrariums in the building. But these contingencies have proven unnecessary. I've lived paranoid, as Nana would call it, that I'd be taken at any time. I set Sarge on round-the-clock Vanty detail, and generally monitored the comings and goings of the rest of my family. It's been a physically and mentally exhausting year.

And then. Just like that. She showed. One month ago, brazen and bold, Velada intercepted me at 15/33 headquarters, buzzing for admittance at the locked gate at the end of my long drive. Nine years since her last visit at my dissertation celebration, she rings my bell, as if she were a friend-neighbor. Like she belonged in my life. Like she was invited.

I think she must have waited and watched to see that Liu and Sandra had not driven in, and that Lenny had driven off with Vanty for a day out. She must have also clocked that no lab employees had come in to work that day—it was, after all, a Sunday. She didn't even try to sneak in, which I would have known because she would have tripped several of my invisible fence sensors and several dozen of my one thousand and four cameras mounted in trees, circling the perimeter. I buzzed her in and rushed to my office to retrieve a document from my driftwood desk, as she drove past the orchard on one side and the oaks on the other.

Velada pulled up in a rental and parked beside my kitchen's red door, where I stood waiting in the open doorway. We didn't say hello or any other nonsense small-talk greeting as she got out of her car. I walked into my kitchen; she followed.

I watched her move around one of the two stainless steel center islands, her black bat arms still thin and muscled; her feet still in flip flops. She basically looked exactly the same, just nine years older. Same weight, same compact body, same black hair and haircut. The hair had thinned slightly, maybe there were a couple of gray strands. Same big dipper freckle on her forehead, which had deeper lines in her late-thirties, early-forties face. Some crow lines were added around her still blue eyes. The black butterfly tattoo was still plastered flat, and wrong, on her hand. And I confirmed she still carried a lighter and cigarette in her back pocket, but I did not give her permission to smoke on my property. I would never allow second-hand smoke to poison Vanty. Besides, I already had her DNA.

"Heard you went to Shanghai," she said.

It wasn't a question or anything I was required to confirm or deny, so I stood straight, my hand near the knife drawer, in which I kept a sharpened set of professional chef knives, but also where I'd slipped the document I had retrieved from my office.

"Well," she said. "You killed his main pride, he called her. So now he really wants you in the tank. But you must have known that already?" I detected her tone as a forced calm, like she wasn't really calm, but was pretending to be. She walked, trailing a finger lightly along the surface of one of the stainless steel center islands. I stayed fixed by the knife drawer.

"He says I'm a gift," I said.

"So you actually talked to him? I hadn't heard. Wow. What's he like?" she asked, stopping her stroll in my kitchen and turning to face me while raising her eyebrows. But her physical movements were a beat off her words, meaning her acting was terrible. She gave away several body language signals of lying, so I didn't answer.

"Fine. Whatever. You must know everything now, right? Did his pride tell you everything?"

"Her name was Melanie."

Velada raised her eyebrows a tic higher, put her hands behind her back, and started weaving through the two center islands while looking up at the high ceiling. Seemingly evaluating, like the real estate agent in our New Hampshire home when my father became a dear departed. She then roved her eyes over the kitchen's sky blue walls with the rainbow of Vanty's framed artwork and schoolwork, the ocean blue hutch, the coral dining table, my full-figured cat on the turquoise rug. She nodded as if approving. "Nice," she said. "A caterer's dream."

Then, with her head tilted back up and pointing at the ceiling fan, she said, "That where they kept you, right? Right above the kitchen, eighteen years ago?"

"When is the night of the tank?"

She swiveled her head down to glare at me. "Oh, Melanie, Melanie, was it? Not Pride, right? Melanie didn't tell you everything? You still need my help?" she said with that same sarcastic, eyes-blinking-in-fake-innocence tone I'd logged in a couple of the teen romantic comedies Vanty used to watch.

"When is the night of the tank?"

"October thirteenth, of course," she said in a way that suggested I already knew. She picked up her meandering stroll again, this time coming back toward me. A center island between us.

"October thirteenth. His birthday, right?" I said, and this made her wince and trip forward—almost like she'd been pulling on a rope and then I yanked back. When she dropped her smug face, it felt like I'd slid my Bishop into the most threatening spot on the chess board.

"You figured that out?" she said, allowing a shake in her voice. Our palms were flat on the opposite sides of the center island, and we stared at each other.

"It's obvious."

It wasn't obvious. But given the symbolism and ceremony, and given that Eminence said I was a "gift," it did make for an educated guess. I could tell from Velada's wince, and her nervous body leaning away from me, that she hadn't wanted to confirm this personal birthday detail about Eminence. Because if I knew it was his birthday, I might know his identity. And his history. But I actually didn't need his birthday at all.

I turned and pulled open the knife drawer.

"What the fuck?" she said, moving fast down the length of the island and toward the door. "A knife?"

"It's a document. Stop."

At ten feet away and nearer to the door, she turned and faced me. As I walked to her, I kicked off my left slide-on shoe. When I entered her space, standing two feet from her and both of us beside the door, the sun shot through the upper glass panels in several angled rays, spotlighting the floor by spilling in a puddle of light on the kitchen tile. In that puddle, I looked to our feet.

"Do you see how my second toe is longer than my big toe, and then the rest of the toes get shorter and shorter?"

"Oh my God, what is this? You're such a fucking psycho. It's like you're not even scared about the tank. You go to China and you talk to…Melanie, you want me to call her Melanie, and what did you talk about, anyway? What leaves you so chill and talking about feet? What, Lisa?"

"Why does it matter to you so much what I talked about with

182

Melanie?"

"Because we're a team here, Lisa. And if we're going to catch them, then I need to know we both have the same information."

"If you're so worried about it, why didn't you come sooner? I went five years ago."

She rolled her eyes, crossed her arms. "Obviously I was fucking nervous when I heard you went there. I worked forever for us, for *us*, you and me, to get myself back in on the inside. To a point where even Eminence calls me. So when Eminence called me screaming about you in Shanghai, I freaked the fuck out. I had to make sure the coast was clear, that they wouldn't track me meeting with you, trace any of it to me. I had to make sure that you didn't go and alert all sorts of law enforcement. Give me a break, it's obvious why."

Again, she displayed several body language indications of lying, but also some indications of truth.

"And yet, you come here pretty brazen today. You must know I have a thousand stills and video of you now, on this property."

She snorted into a laugh. "Having an image of my face hasn't helped you figure out who I am all these years. Please. Right?" She paused, seemed to fight off some other thought. "Right? And what does it matter anymore, Lisa? The event is in a month. He arrives in three weeks. Tell me, do I need to worry about anything? What did you learn in Shanghai? What have you done? Who have you told?"

"You will know what is necessary. Now, look at my foot. Do you notice how my second toe is longer than the big toe?"

Velada crossed her arms and took a step back toward the door.

"I'll just leave then," she said, taking another step back.

"No you won't. You need to know what I know, and you want to know if I'm going to blow this whole fuck show up."

She flinched, stalled.

"Answer my question." I extended my left foot toward her.

"Yes. Whatever. It's longer," she said.

"Now, what do you see about your toes that's different?" I pointed to her feet.

"My fucking toes are fucking burnt."

"What about the alignment?"

"This is ridiculous."

"If you would just answer my questions when I ask them, we

could finish this conversation and you could leave. You're wasting time."

"My fucking toes are all aligned and the same height. Happy now? Psycho."

"Correct. This means you have Germanic heredity. I, however, have heredity that is obviously mixed. With my blonde hair and blue eyes, you might be thrown by the fact that my toes are of Mediterranean, Greek, Italian ancestry. But you, with your black hair and blue eyes, and straight-lined toes, and this," I handed her the document I had pulled from the knife drawer, "your heredity is solid German."

"What is this?" she asked, looking at the document.

"Read it."

I stepped backwards to the subzero refrigerator, opened it, extracted my recycled glass bottle of spring water, and guzzled hydration while she turned her back to me to read the document.

"Do you want me to interpret it for you?" I asked. Her back was still to me, her body bent over the document, so I couldn't read her face. "That's a DNA assay on hair from Eminence, your full German brother, and also a comparative DNA assay from your saliva on your cigarette. You'll note in the conclusion how the two samples indicate siblings. But this assay was a simple objective validation. I'd already formed a theory about your familial connection by comparing the visual of your toes with Eminence's toes. And other physical characteristics." If she weren't agitated, she might have inquired how I'd seen Eminence's toes, which might lead to me divulging the existence of the 'Burnt Lobster' tape, but her breathing grew heavy, and she snapped out of her act of ignorance to turn to me. Her face indicated rage.

"Don't move, Velada. I will snap your neck if you enter my personal space," I said, as I set the water bottle back into the refrigerator while opening the door in her face.

"Fuck you, Lisa!" she screamed, rushing toward me and slamming the door shut, making the condiments on the door shelf rattle and crash. She stood opposite, leaning in on me, breathing hard in my face and baring her teeth. I tilted my head to the side and watched her, evaluating all of her clenching and face contortions and breathing. I blinked twice.

"This is interesting. This act of yours," I said. "Are you truly surprised I figured out that Eminence is your brother?"

"Nobody would ever imagine you'd figure this out and go all the way to China. I've given you nothing. Nothing to go on. You don't, and could not possibly, know my real name. So yeah, I am surprised."

I looked around the kitchen, inventoried in my mind all the changes in my building.

"But you know I run this consulting business for law enforcement. I think you always knew I'd figure this out."

"You do physics and biology. You're not a fucking spy. I figured you'd dig out of rumors and street talk the urban legend of the Lobster Tank, and that's all you need to know anyway, by the way. So you dug into my life. Good for you. You're just a scientist."

I am a mother. Also an artist. Several other sub-identifiers, too. Science is my profession.

"I had to dig into your life because you're a liar," I said.

"So what else do you know, huh? What else did Melanie tell you?"

"She dove out a window before she said anything relevant."

"Bullshit."

"You will believe what you choose. Just as you choose your sense perceptions. It's simple psychology. Simple biology."

"Fuck this. I'm done. I'm out. You're on your own. I'm not sticking around for his show. Fuck this. Fuck this," she said, as she torqued fast around and headed for the door again. I found all her emotional upheaval tiring. But I should have, and did, expect she would uncoil like this once I pulled off a layer of her cover and exposed her. This was also tiring because it was the longest conversation I'd endured with someone I did not emote for in a long while, but I suffered through it by telling myself I was talking to the upside down image of myself in a mirror. Just like Nana said, the universe sometimes throws mirrors in your path. So I treated Velada as a mirror, but one that was dysfunctional.

"Don't be absurd. You are not out. You can't be out," I said. "I have things for you to do." I watched her cross her arms at the chest and hold her breath. "You need to control your emotional responses, Velada. You'll not evolve mentally if you don't."

"I fucking hate you," she said.

"I find you useful for specific things. Come back over here. What's the other thing you see about your burnt feet?"

"I see fucking burnt feet. Fucking. Burnt. Fucking. Feet."

"I can tell you don't understand the question. Here, look. Your burn patterns have caused the tissue to pucker, fold, and divot, the interior pockets to turn pink and some edges to callous. Have you ever seen how skin appears from a chemical burn?"

She didn't answer. Her eyes widened.

"Melanie's skin appeared as though she were washed in a red dye, uneven pigmentation in some parts; some parts were puckered, some patches blackened, scarred. Very unlike your fire burn. Your feet were burned in a fire. Not by bleach. You were in the same fire as your brother. The one that killed your parents."

Velada seemed to choke, her eyes bulged.

"You know nothing about me," she said, shaking her head.

"I know you started the fire." This was a wild theory I had, but I wanted to test out possibilities so I could evaluate how much of my plan I could trust with Velada. I was actively judging every twitch she made, every bit of body language she threw out, her tone, her words, her eye contact. All of it was necessary, which is why it was necessary to throw her lie and a wild theory in her face.

Velada looked away, turned her back to me again. Said nothing. Then she curled her body into herself and threw her hands to her face. I could not evaluate her facial movements with her turned and bent, but next came the wracking noises of her sobbing. "You don't know. You don't know. You know nothing," she said between sobs.

"Turn around," I said. I needed to determine if this was an act. "Turn around."

She continued sobbing and added disjointed phrases between heaving for breath: "…they found girls in factories…smuggled… He learned from them. From them…"

These words seemed dualistic to me. One part of these words seemed rehearsed, but another part seemed based on truth. She turned around, her face full of tears, her eyes red; she wiped her face, stood straight, and breathed in deep as though steeling herself to plow forward with some crucial admission. And when she then said, "I was only ten. I had to burn it all down," I concluded that I could not know at this juncture how much was rehearsed for her eventual alibi in all this, and how much was true. So I determined to tell Velada only what was absolutely necessary.

"Where is the Lobster Tank when all this happens on October thirteenth?" I asked.

"That's if we go forward."

"You've waited this long to trap your brother—jail him and his powerful customers. So we're going forward and you know it. Stop delaying. Where?"

She ground her teeth, flared her nostrils, and whispered, "A stone mansion in Viebury Grove, Massachusetts."

"What time?"

"Evening, but I do not know when. Could be any time."

"What time?"

"Lisa, I have no clue. He says it's when he believes the fires feel right. Nobody knows whateverthefuck that means."

"Fine. It's at night. Close enough."

She flung her hands in the air and rolled her eyes. "Yeah. Close enough."

"And this lobster tank. Still the same as it always was?"

"Yeah, it's still as crazy as always. He is really sick, Lisa. He's obsessed with things being the same, things going on ceremonial cycles, tradition. Obsessed. I have to ruin him."

Now that I finally had a date and location, I could take a moment to throw an accusation at her, something that had needled my executive function for years.

"You knew all these years where it was and you lied. I am troubled that you allowed so many girls to be taken and tortured for so long."

"Please."

"You are, in many ways, a monster like your brother, Velada. Actually, what is the name you really go by now?"

"You're so fucking smart. You couldn't unravel it with what Melanie told you, huh? You could have intervened sooner."

"I did try to find more about this fire, so I could get your real name and then unravel more. But, as this fire happened somewhere in China, where? And happened, when? Thirty years ago? There's nothing I could find in any accessible Chinese papers which, by the way, are written in Mandarin in some areas, Cantonese in others, and so on. I didn't even know which region to look in. Didn't know how or where to look in off-line, archived, foreign-language, local papers." And what I did not say to Velada, the further truth, was my driver on the ground, Dan, couldn't help because after he secured the girls on the bus in the location we'd scouted for them, he got sent on assignment to some other undisclosed location. The most he disclosed in our last encrypted communication was he'd been sent to "the lower part of Earth." I've never talked with him again. And I couldn't involve Liu and Lola, given that I'd intended to stick with my patent lie about going to Shanghai in the first place, something I convinced Dan to also stick with if ever asked by anyone, including Lola: Dan and I became close colleagues in those three days in the high-rise. As for any follow-up with any of the girls on the bus, I had none of their names, and they all dispersed.

"I don't care."

"The fact remains. You knew and you did nothing. For years."

But could I have worked harder, involved Liu and Lola, and discovered the 'where' sooner? I reminded myself I was not to blame; Velada was all to blame.

"First off, psycho. I couldn't tell you because I figured you'd be a dumb bitch and get all sorts of fucking feds involved and shut it all down too soon, tip them off with their moles in law enforcement, and they'd wiggle away, like they always wiggle away. You do know we have to get them, Eminence and his customers, in the act, or this does…. Not. Fucking. Work. All of this would be a waste. We have to, we have no other choice, take this up to the very last minute. We need irrefutable evidence of involvement."

"You withheld location to the detriment of many girls. That's unacceptable."

"Those girls had to be a part of all this so I could end it forever."

"You don't get to make decisions about other people's skins."

She shook her head, her forehead creased while she cast me a confused look. "Skins?"

That's how Lola says it.

"Whatever," she said, smoothing her facial expression to flat. "Well," she said and paused before adding, "we disagree then."

"We do."

She closed her eyes, shaking her head, and appeared deep in thought. When she opened her eyes, in a resigned tone, she said, "Fuck it. Are you going to be ready?"

"It's important that *you* be ready," I said, winking at her. I had turned on rage a smidge, rage at her lies and delays and for allowing the torture of girls for decades, so it did feel pleasant to see her squirm at my wink and directive for her to be ready.

"One. How do they get the bleach?" I asked.

She stared at me.

"Do they order it?"

"What does that matter? They order the bleach."

"How?"

She stalled, biting her bottom lip. I waited.

"I order the bleach, okay? I do all the ordering. And I keep the books. That's my big inside role. A family enterprise. But didn't you figure that out, Lisa? As soon as he got out of the boys' orphanage, he got the trust money, all of it, because my parents were assholes. He found me in my girl orphanage, got me out. I had no choice."

I didn't care about the *why*. I just cared about the forward-working facts.

"Did you already order the bleach?"

"Actually, Lisa. I haven't."

"If you're truthful about wanting to entrap your brother, then here's what is going to happen. I'm going to send a shipment of the bleach. Every single jug is to be left in the room where they drop me in. You give them that instruction. I'll know immediately if you don't do this, and I will not back up whatever alibi you've concocted. There will be blood, you will be jailed. Remember, it is possible that I know way more than I'm telling you, and also, you've seen me lie under oath before. So, you'll be in place to handle my delivery of bleach?"

She bounced her head, apparently doing calculations in her mind. It seemed she was listening closer as she said, while pacing, "But, there's a specific brand. You don't know the brand."

Brileycon. Industrial strength.

"What's the brand?"

"Brileycon. Industrial strength."

"Fine."

"It has to be a specific size."

Twenty-five liters.

"What size?"

"Twenty-five liter bottles."

"Fine."

"And you need to order fifty jugs of it."

"Done. So, you'll accept my delivery and make sure they're *all* put in that room?"

"Yes. Yes."

"Perfect."

"Is that all?" she said, turning agitated again.

"There's something else. But first, I want to confirm something. Your brother and whoever he has working for him in the States, they know you're reeling me in?"

"Well, yeah. I mean. They didn't know before. They think this trip is the first time I'm contacting you. They think you have no idea I'm connected to Eminence. And Eminence has no idea how you found Melanie in Shanghai. I convinced him that you are probably just crazy about following all kinds of leads on what happened to you eighteen years ago. I said maybe it was something that guy Brad said in prison. Anyway, they think I'm here now feeding you information about some totally unrelated human trafficking ring run by the feds and that you agree to meet with me in some yet to be determined place in Massachusetts on October twelfth, the day before, so I will give you some more information. They think you'll believe it's really the federal government running this ring and won't involve anyone else because of that."

"You convinced them of that?"

"Yes, I did," she said, her tone and body language not indicating any signs of lying. Her pupils were straight and did not flicker, her tone assured. But frankly, that can mean absolutely nothing. A liar's going to lie. Whether she was or was not lying in that moment was a 50/50 split. "Look. Remember. This is a very small operation. I've told you before. Eminence has to keep it small so he can totally control everything from Shanghai and so he can do these insane experiences with the most powerful of fucked up assholes. It's like this...." She took a step, turning a circle, now delivering me a lecture. "You know all these countries collect extortion level intel on their powerful enemies, right? How do you think they get that intel in ways they can disavow any knowledge? They use little cells like my parents' cell, like my brother's. They buy whatever dirt these cells dig up or, in our case, create. It's all over the place. A black market for dirty intel. Okay? China, recall. He lives in China. So on the U.S. side he's got me, or so he thinks, and he's got these two other women to manage what is typically just a run-of-the-mill, illegal brothel with, yes, some pretty fucked up experiences in the basement. True. They tape things. Extort people, sell those tapes to interested governments, competing political parties, sketchy consulting companies, *etcetera*. But it's small and there's no hidden camera or electronic evidence, except for what only the core of us use. Has to be this way, otherwise, the whole ring would blow. In the U.S., there are just three guards. Then, of course, me. And then two women managers, one of whom is this really short, older crook of a woman who my brother kept around because she used to do the same shit for my parents. And then a couple flunkies working on the periphery to do odd jobs and runs. But those flunkies know nothing about how things are run. So convincing Eminence and the women and guards on the U.S. side of things was not all that difficult. Lisa, you may be the boss of your world. But I am the boss of mine."

"Well then, here's your second assignment. You're going to make damn sure none of those assholes comes anywhere close to putting a needle in my veins." I walked over to the ocean blue hutch and extracted a skinny manila folder amongst others hanging in a pull-out bottom drawer. "Say you stole these medical records from my office. They say I'm allergic to components of heroin. Or don't use these medical records. Say whatever you want, just make extra fucking double triple sure no needles come near me. Understood?"

"Are these records real?" she asked, snatching the folder from my hands.

Of course they're not real. Like I'd tell you a real vulnerability of mine.

"Of course they're real. This is serious. I'd experience anaphylaxis."

"Fine. Geez. Don't worry about it. I'll handle it."

"Good."

I'm the boss.

"Excuse me?"

"I didn't say anything."

She took a step back, her voice with a shakiness in it I had never heard before from her. "Whatever. I work some days at an office in Mariana Church in Boston. That's part of my cover. On the week of, I will be at Mariana every day, nine to five, no exceptions. Have whoever you have on backup stroll in and ask for me. I know you must have at least some backup. Unless you're an idiot psychopath. Won't do them any good being on backup without connecting with me. They need me to get anywhere close to Viebury Grove and they'll have no clue on the exact timing. Remember, you can't have any metal or electronics on you. No GPS, nothing. Got it? And remember, your backup can't come busting in all hellbent until we have the Watchers in place. The timing is critical. Don't fuck this up, Lisa. When your backup comes to Mariana, this will tip me off that you're ready to be taken in. Okay? Deal?"

"Deal." I paused her from moving away toward the door by holding up my hand. "Wait. Why does Eminence refer to me as a gift? A gift from whom? From his sister?"

"I would never gift you to anyone. He thinks you're a gift from the universe, which is himself. He is the most eminent, so he gifts himself. He's fucking insane. Anyone else would have called this whole thing off after you went to Shanghai. But that only emboldened him more to go forward. He hasn't said a word about you going to Shanghai to any of the paying Watchers. They'd back out if they knew. So we're going to exploit his insanity and greed."

"Who are the Watchers?"

She smiled. "Now there is my insurance, Lisa. My insurance that you'll play this out and trap them in the act. I am holding that information. Are you going to be ready?"

I looked into her blue eyes and considered whether I would ever feel a release if I were to smash the smug off her face. But I had no emotions on, so I went with practicalities.

"You have your instructions. Now go," I said.

She shook her head, turned to the door, walked out, and drove off. *Bye, Velada.*

Who does this? What kind of moron criminal trusts some double-agent sister-woman to feed me intel and wait until the day before his big event to snatch me? Maybe Eminence always had another girl to drop in the tank and it didn't matter if he caught me, and that I was to be a mere bonus. A gift from himself, or from the universe, or from his sister, or…who knows? I reminded myself that whatever his and Velada's insane intentions were, they did not matter. What mattered was I was tagged for the tank, other girls were in jeopardy,

192

wealthy, connected men needed to be caught red-handed, and I had to be ready and solve this.

CHAPTER TWENTY-TWO
LISA YYLAND: HER FATHER'S LAB

I'm finding it difficult to accept the fact that Velada lived across from the stone mansion up until a year ago as some false wife named Carla. And Josi is clueless. What a cover. *What another cover, Velada. I despise you, but I'm intrigued by your bold acts.* I haven't talked with Josi other than to give left turn, right turn directions, even though he is peppering me with questions. I can't believe this guy doesn't have a fucking phone.

He's driving with two hands on the wheel and wearing a seatbelt. I noticed he checked and adjusted, by microscopic movements, all the mirrors of his pickup truck, one with a top on the bed, when he entered. He also made sure I was belted before he backed out. He talked to his truck when he started her by saying, "Keep us safe, Cassie," while patting the dashboard as though that were the truck's head. I appreciate all of these efforts to reduce risk, even the inefficient superstitious ones. Josi seems like a person full of contradictions: a puzzle.

I watch him ensure through all the mirrors that it's okay to pass a car in front of us. Once he does and we're cruising precisely at the exact speed limit, he turns to me. "I'm going to keep askin' until you tell me. Why did you freak out so bad over my wife's picture and the word Velada?"

"I thought I knew her. I don't. Drive."

"I don't fucking believe you."

"Keep your eyes on the road."

"What, you don't like how I'm driving?"

"I appreciate your careful driving." This is a true statement, so I don't understand why he shoots me such a weird face in response.

"Gee, thanks," he says, shaking his head, back to looking at the road. But then in a softer tone says, "Thank you. I don't want to end up a pile of dead bones in a highway wreck like my parents."

"Understood. Take the next exit." I stare ahead; we're almost to my father's lab.

Josi blows air out of his mouth in a loud way, but I don't look at him to see what facial expression accompanies the sound.

Now here we are, at my father's lab, a corner square building off of Elm Street in Manchester, buried and obscured between higher buildings and the fact it is nearly windowless and painted sand brown. The building's shape, set back just so off the sidewalk, with the desert-sand color and mid-rise height: it is city camouflage. Across the street is the Center of New Hampshire Conference Center and Hotel. I hate the inefficiency of the redundant use of "Center" in the title. I've always called it The Hotel. The Hotel hosts a front-face banner that welcomes antiquers to the "Fall Antiques Festival," in a four-foot, block-letter, all-caps font.

Josi stays in his black pickup with a white cab. He tells me he'll wait, as if he's my husband and I'm running in to CVS to fill a strep prescription for Vanty and not running into a state-of-the-art research lab where scientists study the effects of micro-doses of radiation on cancer tumors.

My father's camouflaged building is locked down by military-grade security, given DOE regs the PhD's who work here must follow in order to have radiated seeds—literal grains of radiation the size of rice—on site. The grains must be counted and accounted for three times a day, and are otherwise under strict lock and key in lead pigs. Radical terrorists should be targeting this joint, so security is as multi-layered and complex as an *Ocean's 11* casino. All of this security I have infiltrated and breached by myself; I didn't need ten other team members, like George Clooney. *Amateur.*

Multiple levels of precautions are in place, for these seeds of radiation could be left under the seat of any driver and give her cancer of the ass. Fast. I want nothing to do with these radiation seeds. I want something else, my two most special discs: a flesh colored, highly potent sound disc, the strongest of all the other sound discs I've already set in place; and a flesh-colored signaling disc. Something that sends Liu a message. I've kept these two discs the most secure in the most secure place I know on the East Coast, planning to keep them secure until the very last minute. I swiped my father's lab partner's key one year ago. The same red-haired woman he interviewed in my Indiana headquarters five years ago. The one I call Geena Davis. That woman doesn't have a clue, since she's on a leave of absence, scouring a rainforest down in South America for some lost city, her "hobby" ever since she read "The Lost City of Z."

My "dearly departed" father is with her.

Or, so I thought. He must hear me scraping at the door, for he opens to let me in. He's as surprised to see me, as I him. His eyes are bloodshot, red. He's been crying. He takes me in his arms, sobbing, "Oh Lisa. Lisa, my God. You're okay. The police are looking everywhere for you. Oh Lisa, I can't believe your mother's been shot. She's dead. Oh Lisa. And Barbara, too!"

Fuck.

A year ago my father revealed to Mother he was in-love with Geena Davis. I follow facts, facts are what I understand. And if someone tells me to treat someone like they're dead, like a "dearly departed," like Mother did a year ago, I'm likely to take that directive literally. I don't keep love on for Mother or my father—too disabling when I do. And when Nana, my father's own mother, heard what he did, even she advised I should probably listen to Mother for a while to show Mother "loyalty and support." I haven't talked to my father in a year.

I move inside the building and quickly shut his door; it locks behind us.

"Where's Geena Davis?"

"Oh please, Lisa. You need to stop calling her that. Her name is—"

"Where is she?"

"She's still in Brazil."

"Why aren't you there?"

He throws his arms up in the air. Paces in a circle.

"Lisa, honey, I'm so glad you're okay," he says, while pressing his hands in a prayer position. Now he crouches to the floor and shoves his face in his hands, weeping. "Oh my God, your mother. And they could have gotten you. Oh Lisa, I miss you so much. Oh Lisa."

"Dad, we do not have time for this right now. Why aren't you in Brazil?"

He sobs more. And when those sounds start to lighten, I ask again, "Why aren't you in Brazil?"

He murmurs something into his hands I can't hear. He may have used the words, *Mother called* and *your kidnapping* and a bunch of other words.

"What?" I ask.

He looks up to me; he's still crouched. I'm leaning over him. "Dad, what did you say?"

"I came home because your mother called me about a tip that she followed and how she found a connection to your kidnapping."

"So you…"

"So obviously, Lisa, I came home."

We stare at each other. He stands.

"There's more," he says.

I nod.

"Follow me," he says, walking into Lab 3. This is the same lab in which I'm hiding my two critical discs. I'm concerned he's found them and I'll have to explain them and then he'll try to shut down my whole plan.

We go to a computer on the side, diagonal to my hiding cabinet.

"Who gave Mother this tip?"

"Hold on," he says, typing. My father is powering through his emotions, he's turning himself to steel. I've watched him over the years do this when he's working. He can erupt, but immediately focus. It is a valuable quality I've observed.

"Look here," he says.

On the screen is an email forwarded from Mother's personal, not work, account. I note how Mother still had not changed her married name; it is dated three days ago.

Ms. Yyland, do you see what I mean now about Judge Rasper? Do you understand yet why The Dentist did that to him? Surprised me that Rasper mentioned in his Boston Globe column last year the Essex Law Review article he wrote years ago. He

slipped, is what I think. And of course, nobody saw the clue. They all think I'm illiterate, a useless illegal woman in Velada's house of fun. That Globe article might be a good way for you to connect the dots, without involving me. I have no recourse. But my girls need a shot—I can't care for them much longer. These men need to be caught red-handed. Please, unravel this.
—VVVVIE

I take a step back. *Velada's house of fun? It could fit with what I know about her. But it could also mean she's still lying.* And anyone could have written this email. Could have been Velada, herself. Could have been an undocumented woman in the stone mansion.

"What *Essex Law Review* article Judge Rasper wrote?" I ask.

"Hold on, Babe." My father's forehead is creased, he's breathing hard through his nose, wiping his eyes with his sleeves. "Here."

I step to the screen again.

"Just go to footnote 39."

I scroll to footnote 39.

[39]Notes of interviews with trafficking inmates, B. Rice (Indiana), T. Caldwell (Indiana), S. Renfeld (Tennessee), and C. Highsmith (New Mexico), retained separately in personal archive.

Brad Rice, the orchestrator of my kidnap, and T. Caldwell, the asshole-loser doctor they hired to deliver and take my Vanty. That teeny, tiny footnote, just two-lines in 10-point font, from a law review paper written fifteen years ago when Judge Rasper was a new judge, having just left private practice (that's what his bio at footnote 1 says)—*that* footnote says it all.

"When your mother called me in Brazil three days ago, she read me that footnote. Her theory is that Rasper wasn't doing an interview at all. He was checking in on inmates, making sure they kept their mouths shut about a larger enterprise. The perfect cover: a researching judge."

"Mother's theory is sound. They killed her for it."

"Oh Lisa…" His face melts again into a variety of emotional indicators.

"We need to get in your panic room now. That's why I'm here.

I was going to hide out in the panic room until the coast was clear. We can't trust anyone yet. The Judge was connected."

Had I known he'd changed his scheduled flight back, which when I last checked he hadn't, he'd already *be* secured like Lenny, Vanty, and Nana. I should be calling Liu with updates. I should be getting my discs. I should be getting back to Viebury.

"The cops are on the way here to ask me questions," he says.

"You're not answering any questions. We don't know who to trust."

Also, because I was still in the aftershocks of Mother's nuke-bomb murder, I mentioned my father's lab to Eva, or she mentioned it to me. So, even if cops weren't on their way here to question my father, and even if all those cops were innocent, surely the Center Ring "guards" are in the area looking to reclaim me, waiting to pounce.

"Move it, Dad. To the safe room. Now."

"Lisa, this is insane. Stop. Just stop."

"No. Move it. You want to end up like Mother?"

"My God, Lisa, how can you be so…"

I look at him, waiting to hear what adjective he'll use, what adjective I'll have to match in my mind to lessons from Nana.

"Never mind, baby. You're right. I'm sorry. You're right. We can be safe in there and we'll call a lawyer I know. Someone we can trust. If that means you'll feel safe, let's go."

"Yes," I lie.

We move to the safe room I made him install in the basement. He heads in, turns on the lights and air, and sets the temperature. I note the stainless steel toilet in a corner and the shelves are still stocked with cans of food and jugs of water. Two cases of Snickers are in the freezer, in case I ever had to be confined. I shut the door on him from outside and input the secret code I programmed: the one that locks people in and also disables the interior phone. This is a safe room and a cage. I plan for prisoners, too. The ironic thing is, I had meant to get my discs here tonight by convincing my mother I needed her to come with me, and I was going to lock her in this same panic room. If something happens to me, I've set a special timer on the door to unlock in three days.

I have no idea if he's pounding on the door for me to let him

SHANNON KIRK

out. It is soundproof. And I did not install a monitor on the outside because, frankly, this is mainly a proper panic room, and it looks like just another wall.

I make my way through the white and steel of Lab 3, swipe Geena Davis' card in the locked locker. *Pop.* I fist my two remaining discs, push them deep in my SEVEN jeans' pocket, making sure my gray "NOPE" t-shirt falls over the bulge. I don't have time to make, nor do I want to risk making, a call to Liu. I'll have to do it at Josi's club. Some joker's got to have a phone in that joint.

I scurry back out to Josi's truck, taking cover of my head for any goons who might be slinking in shadows and moving quick. I press the flat, round discs in my jeans' pocket, they are deep and tightly held. To Josi, I say, "Drive. Fast. Go. To your club." I look to my purple Nike sneakers, *Velada's sneakers*, and remember that Josi is clueless as to the level of danger he's in with me, clueless about his "dead wife Carla."

It feels odd as I acknowledge how I don't like a disconnect between what I know and what Josi knows, to identify I don't like Josi to be clueless.

The club is about three minutes from here, he says, down at the river, in one of the old brick mill buildings: Club Bub, a place for fun. But tonight it was meant for making an update call to Roger Liu and also taking cover to ensure the heat is not on us. While I may be fine with being taken in now, I need to ensure Josi is safe.

It's a hell of a lot easier when I have to save just my own skins.

As we drive, I don't think I detect anyone having spotted us, but then again, Elm Street is busy with cars and I cannot be 100% sure.

"Take unexpected turns, Josi. Drive fast and turn a lot, take the long way to the club. Use some alleys. It is okay to be less careful this time," I say.

"Got it," he says. "Buckle up. Come on, Cassie girl, keep us safe."

I watch the muscles in his toiled arm flex as he cranks the wheel around corners. He checks all the mirrors constantly, and at times when we're going straight, he pats the dashboard and says, "Good girl, good girl."

200

CHAPTER TWENTY-THREE
LISA YYLAND: CLUB BUB

"Go, go, go, go," I say to Josi as soon as we park in a shadow beyond Club Bub, which takes up a ground floor corner of one of eight long brick mill buildings along the Merrimack River. The mill buildings have been repurposed for modern eating and shopping. In the same building as Club Bub, restaurants and boutiques take up other ground floor space, while the upper floors are devoted to architects, interior designers, and lawyers.

It's a warmish fall night, people are smoking outside Club Bub, leaning against the exterior brick in t-shirts and skirts with no hose, girls in open toes. Spilling out the bouncer-guarded metal door, is a sea wave of pulsing bass, shouts and roars, which informs me the patrons inside just plain fucking love tonight's headlining band: *Sons of Kalal.* By the untethered frenzied tsunami of noise, I expect to walk in and see women ripping their tanks to bear their padded breasts for the lead singer, who someone introduced through a bullhorn as "Uncle Monk, the one and only, M.C. Capone!"

Josi throws a pair of silver aviators at me as he rounds the hood of his truck and says, "Put these on and hide your crow lines. You look about fifty years older than the babies in this joint."

"You're my age," I say. And I know this because I took his wallet in the truck and read his license.

"Maybe I just want to see how you'd look in glasses," Josi says in a dry, disconnected way, something I can't quite decipher. Maybe he doesn't know what to choose to feel—sadness, fear, maybe he's trying to say something right. Maybe he's struggling like I do when I don't have Nana in my head.

But this is war. I need a phone.

I put on the sunglasses.

We enter a seriously disturbing collection of bouncing humans. The crowd shares sweat and saliva, and I'm calculating the rate of risk of catching mononucleosis and a fungal infection. Herpes Simplex to the left of me, genital warts to the right, a staph infection at the U bar in center, and four strains of flu in line for the one-stall bathroom. A slam-dunk case of Hepatitis-C at the stage with strobe lights.

Thanks, or no thanks, to black Lycra, I can make out the entire shape, curves and grooves, of about twelve women's reproductive systems. Two boys of "twenty-one" have so far ground their groins on my "tight sweet ass." And I've only passed the bouncers and am still in the vestibule.

"Got the boys up in yo' junk already," Josi teases, but dry, as he's been since he mentioned his wife's death. No smile. And his face with the dimple seems made for smiling, like in the pictures with his *wife*.

"Oh yeah, Lisa's a hottie," he repeats, nodding at a third boy who wishes to grind his testosterone into me.

I'm no Basement Bitch.

My aviators hide my squinting. I search for a phone I can swipe. After I scan the swarming dance floor, I rule out swiping from the girls in Lycra: they don't have room for their own vaginas, let alone a stealable phone. About 20% of the crowd has phones in their back pockets, 50% of which are poking out.

Uncle Monk yells from the stage, "Yeah, yeah, y'all, Master Josi is in the HOUZZZZ, and don't he want to jump up on this bitch and slay a beat with me?!"

What is this language?

Josi acknowledges the call-out with the first authentic smile I've seen on him (I've catalogued the differences), which stuns me as unexpected. I kill the light emotion by dousing it in a bath of hatred. Josi weaves through the thick, pulsing crowd to the stage. I'm on my own.

A *tha-tha-tha-thump, thump* of a rapid fire electrical drum sends out several hummingbird beats, followed by a deep canyon of a horn, three riffs of electrical guitar, accompanied by notes from an acoustic guitar by Josi, who holds the instrument, which is another surprise, and Uncle Monk and Josi are off, rhyme-singing in a duet about conspiracy theories and mindless drone-people "livin' they lives like sheep." As in Josi's sound lab, the scent is of smoking weed but, here, it's mixed with sweat and heavy steam.

I often listen to hard-core rap and hip-hop, also mind-altering classical, when in my practice tank room. So I appreciate the passions this type of music can generate. My muscles twitch in the rote, self-defense movements I've been practicing to tunes like this. Several dancers around me grind in cycles and touch my skin. I fight back the urge to cringe from having their sweat comingle with mine, and instead decide it's best to blend. I whip out a twerk and ass grind a fellow ass grinder. I may have appeared when I first entered Club Bub like an old giraffe in a pool of piranhas, but I'm the piranha, and this is a coy pond. People are cheering.

I see my quarry ahead. Some brunette who must want to mate with Uncle Monk, by the way she's peacocking for his attention and pointing. She is rewarded, for Uncle Monk pauses his designated lines, like a cliffhanger to his song, points back at her, winks, and says, "This here for my shortie, Dani-Pants." Dani-Pants squeals and winks back, a signal that in their mating dance seals their pact to have sexual relations tonight. I snatch her dangling phone from her bouncing ass. I make my way to the fire exit ahead, which seems a decibel less loud there, in order to ring up Roger Liu.

I'm in the fire exit landing. I throw Josi's damn aviators to the ground, and they smash apart on the concrete floor. I need 100% accurate vision. Or, at least, the best my human eyes and occipital nerve neurotransmitters will allow me to perceive. Above me is a coil of fire hose twenty-five feet high on the brick wall of this stairwell shaft; the mounting wheel is bolted to brick near the tin ceiling. The hose's brass nozzle is reachable by an iron hook, which hangs lengthwise beside it. Club Bub must have mounted the hose high so the mass of dancing viruses wouldn't do something stupid with it, like uncoil it for fun, or whatever impulsive decisions come with heated peacocking for sex. Or maybe since we're below grade here, in the fire exit, the water source is higher. Also, we're on the river's edge, so perhaps the high hose is to account for flooding. No clue.

Don't care. But some sense is pushing me to inspect the hose's high placement and, more specifically, its necessary accessory: a long, metal hook which hangs vertically on the brick wall.

I thank Dani-Pants in my mind for not locking her phone.

I start to dial Liu when, in a flash, Josi crashes in on my quiet; I hadn't heard him stop singing. He rushes in, bumping me, and I drop Dani-Pants' phone to the floor. It obliterates. Disassembled phone and aviator parts create a mixed media collage of debris on the vibrating concrete floor.

"Watch out!" Josi screams. Two men in all black are making their way through the crowd and are close. These are the same mouth-breathers as in Viebury Grove, the same men who drove me in their chicken truck and tied my hands together in the barn: Loser 1 and Loser 2.

I grab the hose hook, thread it through the door handle just in time. Losers 1 and 2 pull and yank on their side. The staff of the iron hook clanks and clatters against the brick wall and metal door; the musical thumps and electric drums vibrate the floor; human cheering and shouting blossoms in sound mushroom clouds: an acoustic whirlpool in this fire escape. *Sound. Electrical, wonderful, sound. An asset.*

"Run!" I say, pointing to the exit door. "I'll be right behind."

Josi stalls.

"Go! Go!"

He opens the exterior door and leads up the well of stairs and waits outside. I consider whether I should let him run, while I let the Losers take me in now. But I look out the porthole again and the Losers are heading out again, presumably, they'll circle to where Josi is now. And I need to be sure Josi is safe, so I launch out the back door.

"RUN!" I'm yelling to Josi as we run.

Go, go, go, go, go, go, go, go!

Josi and I sprint.

We've covered several blocks and near my father's city-camouflage building once again. By now, the heat-seeking missiles Losers 1 and 2 appear some distance behind, but they're gaining some ground. I check the discs in my pockets; they're there.

"In the conference hotel, look, a side door's open. Let's bust in there," Josi says.

The Hotel.

I follow. It's much faster to do this than fumble with the key card for my father's building. And besides, I won't lead Losers closer to my family.

Inside is a typical conference hotel. We've got two choices on direction: down a hall towards all the conference rooms; or, straight around a bend, and cross in front of reception. We head toward the conference rooms which, as we near, I note are all merged into one gigantic room, holding booth after booth after booth of antiques, a mad variety of stuff: painted cabinets, hutches, innumerable amounts of wooden chairs, glass boxes of primitives and folk art, chests, more chests, rugs, and quilts. And, with all this stuff, like in Nana's attic in Savannah with all her finds at flea markets over the years, we have numerous places to hide.

I recall the banner out front of The Hotel when we parked at my father's building: *Fall Antiques Festival.* And in thinking of my father again, I cringe that it was my statements to Eva about having to come to Manchester that brought the Losers to find me.

I hear Loser 2 enter through the side door. I poke my head out of the antiques conference room, look down the hallway and see him searching for us; he holds a gun and speaks into his wrist, saying something to, I presume, Loser 1.

I'm guessing whatever slack-jaw hotel receptionist has the late-night shift is napping or lending all his brain waves to posting selfies on social media, because I'm not hearing or sensing anyone who works in this moldy joint giving one care about the security breach to the side door. Or the fact that we're in here amongst all these antique treasures. If I were renting this space for my *Antiques' Festival*, I would raise serious concerns about the lack of security.

The conference room is dark, alight in pockets of orange-red around Exit signs. The apocalyptic light filters into muted grays from there, over booths. I'd use crimson, tangerine, yellow, Payne's Gray, black, and white to paint this scene.

I push Josi forward. "Hide," I whisper.

As we tip-toe, passing booths, I note many, many things. Many assets, and I log several of interest in my fast-growing, *ad hoc, ad lib* escape plan. Josi and I hide behind a corner hutch, painted colonial red. A patchy-haired porcelain doll the size of a toddler googles us with her round eyes from an oak highchair. A whaling knife lays under her porcelain hands on the tray of her highchair. Her right pinky is broken off.

Vanty was the first doll I had, and he turned out perfect. No practice necessary.

We wait.

We hold our breaths.

We wait.

With a violent break, Loser 2 slams open the conference room door and enters. He is followed by Loser 1.

"Lisa, we know you're in here," Loser 2 says.

No shit.

"You're cornered. Time's up," dumbass Loser 2 continues.

"Josi," I whisper. "Go across the aisle. Hide there. Go."

Josi crouches and soft-shoes across the aisle; he hides between two tall hutches.

I stand in an opposite shadow with the whaling knife I took from the doll. If one of the two Losers passes through our shadow line, they'll either miss us in the shadows, or see us and suffer our respective attacks from each side. The Losers' first reaction won't be to shoot because I am their lucrative bounty, and if they kill me, their boss in the Center Ring will kill them. In fact, they're morons for even carrying guns. Either which way, whatever way the Loser turns, to me or to Josi, the other one of us will be in position and jumping to slam our weapon in his back or side neck. I'm trying to say this whole plan telepathically to Josi through our eye-to-eye line, and son of bitch…the amount of people I have to trust in this ordeal.

I again consider exposing myself and letting these Losers take me in, as planned. But I have to ensure Josi, a civilian, escapes. And I don't trust that if I pop out into the center of this aisle, he won't too. He'll just keep inserting himself in my life.

Loser 1 starts down the first aisle, eight over from us. Loser 2 starts down our aisle. He scrapes forward, pointing his gun at shadows in the different booths. He shouts at a carved wooden Indian, until his eyes focus. He moves on. Five booths away now. Josi crouches and is hidden in his spot between two high hutches. I hold my whaling knife, ready to chop this Loser's neck up close, or thrust it at his back if he tries to harm Josi. A real blacksmith banged this thick, black blade over a raging fire long ago.

Loser 2 is now three booths away. Loser 1, still over in the first aisle, shouts for me, "Lisa, time's up. Stop hiding." He is farthest away from the exit door, which is directly at the end of our aisle.

Loser 2 steps in the center of my and Josi's across-aisle sight-line, and this is when I notice Josi staring at a power strip by his left foot and under the claw feet of his left-side hutch. I watch as his eyes crawl along an extension cord plugged into it, and I follow the cord, too. Josi has a far better vantage to follow the cord; I can't tell where it leads. From my point of view, in the direction of the cord, and several booths away and at the end of our aisle, I see several electrical items that could be plugged into this extension cord: lamps in vendors' booths, a stereo, a big fan, and a speaker on a pole. But there is one other item plugged into this power strip, and I note Josi's eyes follow along a thin brown cord, up the side of the left-side hutch, and to one of those old-school PA speakers sitting on a hutch shelf, about chest high.

Josi stands up out of hiding but stays to his side of the aisle. This causes Loser 2 to swivel toward Josi, keeping his back to me. I note the power strip's light is now red, indicating Josi pressed it on before standing. But the fan did not turn on. Neither did the stereo. And none of the lamps. Could be that some of those items need to be switched on, but could be that it's just the speaker on a pole that's plugged into the extension cord.

I stand slow, choking the whaling knife, and watch Josi's face.

He presses down on the PA speaker with his elbow. And although his lips don't move, I hear him, using a high voice, projected loud out of the speaker down at the end of the aisle. "I'm down here, I'm down here," he's saying, as if in a girl's voice.

As soon as Loser 2 looks that way, confused obviously, Josi takes the PA speaker and bashes once, hard, into the side of Loser 2's temple, and we do not wait while he falls.

We run.

Fast.

We are out of the building and not looking back. Sprinting again. We take a side street without lights, just when I hear the hotel side door bang and them shouting for us. I'm almost sure they didn't see which way we ran. But we keep sprinting anyway. And even though we're sprinting, I have to comment, because I admit, I am intrigued that Josi didn't panic and used simple assets around him. Also, he used sound. "You used a sound diversion. And with ventriloquism. Impressive."

Josi doesn't lose his stride or breath when he turns to me, "What can I say, I'm a musician. I'm good with my mouth." It's possible he winks at me.

Josi is simply a tool in my arsenal. Nothing more, I say to myself. And yet I find I can't take my eyes off him.

"Whoo," he says to the dark air ahead. He jumps too, after looking behind us; I do as well, but there are no Losers in pursuit. "Yeah, that's right, they'll learn," Josi says, as we continue to sprint. We are far out and around several corners, and I don't see anyone behind. Nevertheless, we keep up the fastest pace we can.

Josi shouts now, "Fuck," and I can tell he's full of adrenaline.

This is the quality Lenny shows sometimes and that my mind finds attractive on some measurable chemical level: this wildness, this uncontrollable, unpredictable, emotional hurricane of happiness colliding with rage. Like the beautiful catastrophe that is nature. The opposite of me. Untamed.

"Whoo!" he says, not winded, even though we're going very fast and our heartbeats must be at near maximum beats per second.

He's so proud. I'm impressed. We continue to run. He keeps up. And here is my opening. Here is my chance to tell him. Won't be a time better than this, a time when we're running for our lives, toward the darkness of the river's edge, on a warm fall night, and Josi's alight in some wild passion I can register, but do not feel. I need to tell him the truth about his life because I detest imprecisions and people believing fake news. Just like it troubles me that Velada tattooed an inaccurate, flat, black butterfly on her hand in honor of me, when it should be an elaborate Luna Moth.

"You were avenging your wife Carla?" I say. "Drilling one of the ones you think killed her?"

"You fucking bet," he huffs out. He can keep up with me all right, but I'm not breathing hard like him. I turn and check to ensure we lost the Losers, and since I don't see either of them yet, I stop running and hide under the night shade of a large tree. Josi realizes ten steps ahead that I'm no longer at his side. He slows and circles back. Beside us is a thin alley between two brick apartment buildings.

I swivel such that he must face me by standing in the alley's mouth.

"Take a step back, further into the alley," I say.

"Why?"

"Just do it. I have to ask you something."

"Fucking now?"

"Yes, now. Get in the alley."

He steps into the alley and faces me under the tree.

"How long did you know Carla before you got married?"

"A year."

I look to my right to see if the Losers have emerged. I'm out in the open, but shaded under this tree. Josi remains opposite me, further into the alley.

"Take another step back," I say.

"Lisa, we need to get going. We need to get back to Cassie."

"You didn't know your wife before you met, right? She just came out of nowhere?"

"No, I never knew her. What the fuck?"

"Did she approach you when you met?"

Josi jostles his head, acting confused by my question, and yet seemingly thinking on it anyway.

I wait.

"Yeah. So what? So she came up to me at a bookstore."

"Did you already own that house in Viebury?"

"I'd just inherited it. So what? What the fuck?"

"Your wife *is* Velada. She staged her death. And she used you as cover. I think she was spying on you to see how much you knew, how much you cared about whatever was going on at the stone mansion and, *or*, she just wanted a good cover. The cover being, a nice, young, married woman living in Viebury. She helps to run that whole funhouse in the stone mansion. You were set up. You have the perfect house."

Josi's knees sink. He places his palms on the opposite brick walls of the alley.

"What?" he says, full of indications of anger, as if I'm the one who set him up.

I'm calm, because I speak the truth. "I met with her a month ago. She duped you. Used you. She is not dead. She is a liar."

"Who the fuck do you think you are? She's dead. How dare you?

She's *dead*. The medical examiner said it was…." He screws his eyes, as if noting the gaps in the analysis.

"Judges are caught up in this. Cops. You think the medical examiner isn't paid off or bribed to say whatever they want? This scheme has been going on for years. They're masters at this shit."

"Whose body was it then?" He pauses. "Wait. Wait," he says. His voice is dropping. He's whispering to the ground, coming to acceptance faster than I expected, likely because he already suspected suspicious details anyway. "The body could be any girl," he says to me, as if he needs to convince me. He's looking at me, but he's not really seeing me, I think.

"Could be a runaway. Could be any girl," I confirm.

Mumbling to himself, Josi repeats incomplete phrases that I patch together in my mind to say: *They left Carla's shirt and bracelet on the girl's remains. Throw everyone off. Carla tricked me?*

It is illogical to not accept that Velada lied and tricked Josi. Carla is Velada and she duped Josi. So I will push him along in his acceptance. I need him to leave soon.

"Did you ever meet her family?"

"She said she had none. Said she'd run away."

I say nothing.

Josi looks to the ground. When he turns to face me again, I detect movement to my right. Josi can't see, he's too far in the alley. The Losers are running this way.

"What's out there? What's that you see?" he asks, but in a tone that is angry. He rises to stand, using the walls as his brace, and steps forward toward the mouth of the alley.

"Stop," I say, curt. "You'll get me killed if they see you." This is a lie. He'll get himself killed, but I suspect he doesn't care much about his own skins right this minute. I have to manipulate what I'm sensing in him: an emotional drive to protect.

"What the fuck is out there? What do you see?"

"Nothing. We need to separate. Go now. Down the alley. Hide. You're making us unsafe by sticking together. Hide for the next two days. Go!"

His eyes, although shadowed to me, seem to dance in a fury. I don't know what he's emoting or thinking.

"Go!" I yell.

He skips backwards, turns sideways, shaking his head, and before bolting down the alley, says, "You're a fucking liar. Carla didn't dupe me. I'm out. Good luck with whatever bullshit you're up to."

I watch Josi disappear into the darkness, while I remove the two, flesh-colored discs from my pocket and kick off my right shoe. I remove a protective sheet off each of the backs to reveal their strong adhesive, and stick them to the bottom of my right foot. Once my shoe is back on and I am sure Josi is gone and cannot be seen, I step out from under the tree and over to a spotlight off the back of one of the brick apartments. In that pool of light I stand straight, raise my arms with palms up like I'm calling a crowd to bow before the cross. "Come get me, bitch. I'm ready to be taken now," I yell.

These two dipshits run to me fast. Loser 1 pulls the specialized pen wand from his back pocket, wands over me everywhere; it beeps on my right foot again.

"It's just her toe again. Let's go," Loser 2 says.

And here we go, I'm ready to be taken in now. So I am taken in now.

CHAPTER TWENTY-FOUR
LISA YYLAND: TRAINING ROSA

"We can take them
We can shake them
We can break them down."
—Sons of Kalal: *How Low They Are* (feat. Apeshit)

They call this a spa. A windowless rectangle of a basement room in the stone mansion of Viebury Grove. Cinder block walls painted in several chipping coats of dingy ivory. I'm in a pedicure chair; Rosa's in the one next to me. Nail station across from us, but there are no tools there, only a box of nail polish. A massage table is folded in a corner, along with two folding chairs. A hanging blue curtain caps the long end of this rectangle room, behind which are stacks of paper towels.

Otherwise, seems they pulled out of here any objects I might use as assets.

After the Losers dragged me back to Viebury, I was locked in a room with nothing but a sleeping bag. I stayed in there the remainder of that first night, all day yesterday, and last night. When they threw me in, they gave me a bucket, a loaf of French bread, and a jug of water, and said I was on my own.

This morning they collected me, dragged me to this basement room with the pedicure chairs. And then they brought in Rosa. Today is the 'Day Of.'

I'm supposed to be "bonding" with Rosa, perhaps painting each other's nails. But all I've been doing is training her.

Rosa has a name. Rosa is a runaway. Rosa is the girl who yelled to me in the back of that red truck. Rosa has black, twisted hair and gold-speckled, brown eyes. She sits in the pedicure chair beside mine breathing hard, taking a break from our last practice round. We've been at it for hours. Rosa could be Christine, Amy, Masie, or Molly. Rosa could be Dorothy. Dorothy M. Salucci. Rosa could be Melanie, Candy, or Bucket. Doesn't matter why Rosa ran, why any of them run. Rosa could be Black. Hispanic. White. Asian. Eastern European. Greek. Rosa could be every race balled together in a mash of DNA. Rosa could be tall. Rosa could be short, medium, classic, or strange. Rosa could be an addict, running a con, innocent or damaged, or all of that. Rosa is almost always between 13 and 17, fleeing a childhood that was no childhood, suffering something and certainly damaged emotionally. Rosa didn't swallow horse pills of self-esteem from her mother, like the ones I was fed. Or, Rosa could just be a regular teen with a still developing frontal lobe, who made a dumb mistake.

When taken, fresh on the streets, Rosa will believe what any collector with a roof and a bed and food tell her. Rosa wants to fight, but can't. She lacks resources, support, and something she should have had, a childhood that gave her the chance to seek other options. Sometimes our Rosa, who could be any girl, *any*, gets taken and hooked, drugged and beaten, held against her will and threatened. So she stays with the life of the underground and lurks in short skirts on corners, in cheap motels, satisfying her keeper, her pimp with the gun, who reminds her he loves her, after he beats her, and buys her steak dinner take-out once a month, after he forces her to suck his dick in a way to prove she doesn't enjoy her Johns' dicks more.

In my preparation for this day, I've interviewed several dozen human trafficking victims in safe homes around the country. And the story is always different in detail, but the same narrative. Same plot. With common cycles of malevolent kindness after physical assault.

Usually, the pimp keeps Rosa well addicted, and thus controlled. The public might call her a whore. Everyone has seen 'Rosa the Whore.' Rosa is everywhere. Even in the quaint suburban strip malls. She's there, lingering between delivery trucks or by trashcans outside a corner Bier Garten. Rosa won't approach the pink-lipped mom in her Volvo and pastel J-Crew sweater, but Rosa might want to. She might want to curl up beside the mom's plump children in the back, like she's one of them, and ask to be taken to Planned Parenthood for treatment of an STD. The public might scorn her as a cockroach prostitute. A plague. Wives might blame her for ruining a marriage. For disease. For blight on the city. Some say Rosa chose this life, that she pushes her pussy for money and drugs. They're wrong. She is Rosa. She's a girl.

It doesn't matter *why* Rosa ran. Rosa could be rich, poor, immigrant, documented, undocumented, American, pretty, ugly, sashaying in a masque of perfection. It doesn't matter. It does not matter. Rosa is a girl human. And that girl human could have been raised in a way to benefit society, or at least her own self, on her own personal journey. And since I don't like to waste resources, and since I suffer a plague of loyalty for my beloved Dorothy, and I have been programmed by Melanie to save these other girls, to place value on Melanie's violent death, I have ample motivation to aid all the Rosas—get revenge for all the Rosas. Rosa is Dorothy. Rosa is Melanie. But Rosa is not me. I'm just a weapon in their war.

This exact Rosa before me with the black, twisty hair and the gold-brown eyes, she was taken three days ago, had run away just three days ago, thinking she'd been invited to join a modeling troupe headed to L.A., a plan presented to her by a man who approached her in a mall. *Snap.* Just like that. A common scheme. Rosa's single mother prohibited this plan as foolish, and, of course, Rosa defied her mother, snuck out after midnight when her overworked mother passed out on the couch, a full ashtray on the floor under her dangling hand and a bottle of rum tipped on its side. Rosa was tricked, naïve; she is sixteen. A virgin. She is tagged as Eminence's rape victim for the Lobster Tank show. After that, they'll intend to hook her on heroin and sell her over and over again, if she survives.

Today's work, if the plan is successful, will hardly make a dent in human trafficking worldwide, but it's a start and that's something. You lay one brick at a time. You set one puzzle piece at a time. You destroy one trafficking ring at a time. You keep going. And you never, never, never relent. Never.

Right now, a real girl human named Rosa, and her name is indeed Rosa, sits beside me in her pedicure chair in a basement spa in the stone mansion of Viebury Grove. Yesterday, she was hidden in some attic closer to what she believes might have been a golf course. Before that, they held her in a different basement in Maine for a night, after they stole her from a Braintree T-Stop, where she'd been told to go to meet her modeling contact. Rosa wants to go home.

The only positive news in this room right now is that Rosa has fight in her gold-brown eyes and a strong, compact body with muscular thighs—she does the 100 and 200 meter dashes on her track team. I can use these assets. If she'll trust me. I have to give her the choice. It will do her and me no good if she's not fully committed. If things go wrong, one of us will die, or both of us will; or, one of us will die, and the other will be burned in a bath of bleach.

I'll give Rosa an option to cop out. But I promise her, and I do have full confidence that, if she trusts in me, she'll be the one to take them down. She'll be empowered, and she'll crush them.

"You ready to try it again?" I ask.

We've been locked in this room now for nine hours together, not tied in place. Loser 2 paces outside our closed door in the hall. I've given Rosa assurances, speeches, and explanations. I've explained to her several moves, and one key twist, and made her practice on me several times. She has her mind now, she controls her body, and she does not cry.

"Yes, let's try it again," she says.

She stands. She no longer shakes or cries, like she did for the first two hours we were in here. When she sobbed through telling me her backstory, just the same way Melanie did.

"You know you can do this, right Rosa?"

She doesn't answer, just side eyes me and bounces her head. Her mouth frowns in an indication of sadness.

"I should never have listened to them. I'm an idiot, an idiot. My mother was right," she says. "Oh my God, I'm going to die." Her voice cracks.

We don't have any time for emotional upheavals again.

"Rosa, stand. We need to practice again."

She sniffles. Nods harder. "All right, all right. Let's do this." She stands.

I tie her hands behind her back, using the tie from one of the two wide-sleeved robes they gave us.

"You trust me?" I ask.

She nods.

A black curl blocks the glitter reflecting off gold specks in her right brown eye; her left eye, however, glitters unencumbered by the dankness of this den like a bath of light, revealing a font of natural intelligence and fierce defiance. Intelligence and defiance are Rosa's two greatest assets, and we are going to exploit them.

Assets. Assets everywhere, in abundance, in humans, in objects, in senses, in light, in sight, in sound, in taste, in touch. In gravity. In space. Underground. On earth. Within wind. Generated in mechanical movement. Everywhere, assets, literally everywhere; every square inch of the planet and beyond, littered in assets.

What a messy, chaotic universe. Beautiful. Loud. Quiet. Sight full. Blinding. Useful.

Rosa and I practice for another solid hour and she's willing to go longer, but I can tell she's aching, so I untie her arms.

"You need to rest again. You're doing well."

Rosa and I return to our pedicure chairs.

"Time to put in your meal orders," a gruff voice shouts through the spa door, jostling Rosa and me to attention and signaling the game is on. Loser 2 walks in.

"Eminence says it can be anything at all you want and that you have to eat. So, you know, order whatever you want. You?" he says to me.

"A bowl of tangerines. Not peeled. I want to peel them," I say. "I won't eat them if they're peeled."

"Fine, whatever."

"You?" He turns to Rosa.

"The same thing," she says.

CHAPTER TWENTY-FIVE
LAST MEAL

Two hours later, Rosa and I remain in this room with the pedicure chairs. A woman, mid-forties, deep olive skin and wiry hair, comes in, unfolds the two folding chairs and sets them on either side of the manicure station.

"Sit here," she says. We do as she says. She's hunched a little, and I believe she's trying to shoot me some look in her eyes. Hard to tell with her hair in her face. And hard to tell if she's got green eyes.

Eva walks in with a bowl of tangerines. Drops them in the middle of the manicure table, sending one bouncing out and rolling across the floor. Tonight Eva is dressed in a black dress with a high collar and horrible white pearls around the neck. Mother often ridiculed pearls. She hated pearls and I hate them, too, because I have hate so totally on.

"Here's your damn fruit. Finish up fast. We need your hero to set in."

Eva pats a needle in her pocket.

"The hell you're sticking us. We're both allergic," I say.

Eva laughs. "Please. Velada told me, and we both had a great laugh over that."

Before I can protest more, Eva walks out, and the slightly hunched woman lingers a second. She shoots me a definite look this time, like she wants to say something. And she does have green eyes, just like my former nanny, Gilma.

"Doris, come on. We need to get things settled," Eva barks at her.

"Hey," I say to Doris. "I really need a spoon. That's the only way I can eat tangerines."

"Holy fucking shit," Eva says.

I stare at Eva. "Fine. Doris, get her a spoon. But fast."

When they shut the door again, Rosa whispers, "I don't want them to stick me with hero...what is that?" Her voice is trembling.

"Heroin. Let me figure this out. Your only job is to stay strong and suppress all of these emotions. You must focus on your one job. That is all. Got it?"

"Okay."

"No, Rosa. Not okay. This is definite. You must be solid. You have no other choice. You get it, right? No wavering, no matter what they say or do. You own this."

"I know. Okay."

"Who owns this, Rosa?"

"I own this."

"Say it again."

"I own this."

"Again."

"I fucking own this."

"That's right. Don't forget it. These people are beneath you."

Doris walks in, hands me a spoon. In leaning to set it beside our bowl of tangerines, she whispers, "I wish your mother had been able to follow my clues in time to stop this. I trained to be a nurse in Colombia." Doris sets her hand on my bicep, clamps it tight. Her palm is hot. She quick releases and leaves fast.

As Doris walks out and shuts the door behind her, I'm trying to calculate what her words mean, but I'm also using the spoon to scalp a portion of the rind off three tangerines. *Doris is the one who emailed Mother. The one who takes care of her girls in Velada's funhouse. Doris may be good, but she's also the cause of chaos and the cause—unwittingly, maybe—of Mother's death. I can't have any more chaos.*

I scoop out the guts of the tangerines and slide them over to Rosa to eat. I scoop complete, can't allow any of the squishy, acidic, wet middle to remain. Just the rind. I wish I had time to let my hallowed tangerine balls dry.

I bend to my right foot, remove the stabilizing ring magnet, unscrew my long, fake toe, spring the inner, small, but incredibly sharp blade, and pull and slice three separate fat strands of my fake blonde hair from my inner tuft. Only this blade could cut through the reinforced skin of these strands so quick, and in a manner that no powder within them spills. Now the strands are like those fat Pixy Stix, open on one end and full of powder. I pour a different powder in each of the three, hallowed tangerines.

"What are you doing?" Rosa asks, watching while eating tangerine guts. "Holy shit. What is that?" Pointing at my toe on the table, she pushes back in her chair.

"Just a fake toe."

I secure the toe and toe ring back on my foot.

"Do you take chemistry in school?" I ask.

"Yeah. I mean, yeah."

I pick up one tangerine. "Borax, makes a light green flame." I pick up the next. "Sodium Chloride, makes an orange flame." I pick up the third. "Potassium Chloride, makes a purple flame." I set down the third and ensure none of the tangerines roll while I slip out of my underwear and the tank top they gave me and into my red, wide-sleeved robe.

"Now, these are super, highly concentrated versions of those chemicals, of course. Pure-grade, specially prepared. It would be a great demonstration for you on chemical reactions if you could see the show when I throw them."

Rosa's eyes are wide, trying to feed this intel to her brain, I can tell.

"Throw them where? I don't get it," she asks.

"In the fireplaces, of course."

Rosa scratches her scalp; her dark, curly hair bounces. "Look, lady, I don't know what you got planned. But it's really fucking cool that you had chemicals in your head and a fake toe."

Rosa tempts me to turn on some kind of emotion for her, but I don't. Instead I ask again, "Who owns this?"

"I own this."

"Exactly."

Rosa settles into her robe while I hide the three chemical tangerines in the box of nail polish and then set to eating more of the ones in the bowl. A good half hour passes before Eva and Doris return. I note when they open the door that Loser 2 is guarding outside still, but now with an AR-15 across his chest.

Mouth-breather.

Eva stands at the end of the manicure station to my left. She hands Doris, who stands to my right, a loaded needle. I remain seated.

"Doris," Eva says.

Doris takes the needle in one hand, and I note a balled washcloth in her other hand. She yanks my right arm fast, toward her, which is away from Eva, and pushes up the wide sleeve to my bicep. Without any seconds for me to pull away, which I will do in a simple second and disable her, smashing this vile, she stares into my eyes. "If you move even a millimeter, this won't go right." My former nanny, and then Vanty's nanny, Gilma, had green eyes like Doris. Had olive skin like Doris. Had that authoritative Spanish accent like Doris. When Gilma used to stare into my eyes with her green ones, she would hypnotize me with a pure trust. So I am hypnotized into a pure trust by Doris. And I trust this most primal sense. I don't move any muscles. No shaking.

She keeps her balled cloth to the side of my inner elbow and sets the needle point toward my cephalic vein. She presses the plunger.

I flinch my mouth, but keep the arm just as Doris holds it. She pulls the needle away and places her thumb to cover the spot where she had pointed the tip of the needle, pressing down. Next she moves the balled cloth over that spot.

"Hold this cloth there for a few seconds," she says.

I do as she demands.

"I sure hope you're as tender with my friend's veins," I say to Doris in a tone of hatred. "You fucking bitch." I rub my arm.

"I'm a professional," Doris says. "Even for you dirty cunts."

Doris looks to Eva and laughs. Eva has been looking around the room, trying to gauge, I think, if I found any weapons in here; but she, somewhat distractedly, laughs along with Doris.

Doris moves on to Rosa. I nod to Rosa, hoping she understands to do exactly as I did and not move a muscle. Rosa winks at me.

And it is this moment when a lightness hits me. A fluttering. Bees in my brain. I turn homicidal rage firmly on and smile.

Doris slipped the needle like a magician pro into the cloth.

Rosa knows this, and Rosa owns this.

I've got my chemical tangerines loaded and ready to fly.

I'll trigger both of my extra-special discs next.
And. It is. Fucking. Go time. Bitch.

CHAPTER TWENTY-SIX
LISA YYLAND, DAY OF: THE WALK

I'm walking down a stone basement hallway on my way to the Lobster Tank. I'm in my red robe with wide sleeves, my long, blonde hair—along with some remains of my synthetic tuft and something coiled within that—is hanging loose. I time my steps in a slow-motion cadence, setting my stride to match the *thumps* of a rap in my mind, one I've practiced to many times: 50 Cents' *In da Club*.

Some silent worker-bee woman ahead is meant to guide me, and Loser 2 holds the laziest of weapons to my back, his AR-15. Only complete losers without confidence in hand-to-hand combat skills would use this lazy weapon to control and intimidate. The woman ahead is slight, a fruit fly: She won't hasten my stride down this granite basement corridor. She's also a victim and doesn't want to be here, I can tell by her apologetic looks. I'm holding a motivational musical moment in my mind. We turn a corner; I see a set of stone stairs leading up, up, up to the Up Top. All of this *exact* to what Melanie described in her notes.

With the red robe and the chemical tangerines concealed up my right sleeve, lined up like bullets in a barrel, and the burning in my body, I am fire. I can only hope that Liu and Lola are in place. I triggered them back in the pedicure room by pulling the battery tab on my signaling disc, no longer stuck to the bottom of my foot (now stuck to the bottom of the manicure table like chewed gum). With the signal, I triggered Liu to power the sound ring I set around this house a week ago. The same night as Josi's "Dentist" night.

The sound discs outside form a calling circle, a ring for corralling and calling rodents and bats and other creatures by using sound at a frequency inaudible to regular humans. The most powerful of these discs is the second disc I retrieved from my father's lab, and that is now adhered to my back shoulder.

I step up, up, up, and now I'm Up Top, passing one of the stone fireplaces Melanie promised. *Check.* It's to my right. *Phew. And it is, "in Fire."*

Using my magic techniques, I distract to the left by snapping my left fingers and turning my head left to say, "Green!" Simultaneously, I have rolled the first chemical tangerine to my right palm and flick it fast and precise to the fire. The flames sizzle, I slow my walk, I look that way, and sure enough—science is very cool—the flames burst into a bright, light green.

"What the fuck!" Loser 2 behind me yells. "How did you do that?"

"I didn't do that. You saw it when I did."

"Keep fucking walking," he says, and there's so much doubt and confusion in his voice, I'm afraid he might have a stroke when he sees the next fireplace.

There are a variety of women standing around watching. The floors are wood and old; the interior constructed and decorated like a typical New England Victorian.

Liu, he's duped. He thinks the remote he should have pressed by now is a vibration signal back to me to tell me he's in place and that it's *okay* to get in the tank. He thinks it means he's to wait twenty-two minutes, exact, and then bust in with Lola to arrest the entrapped Watchers. He has no clue about the sound discs.

Here we go. We pass the room with the second fireplace and, just as Melanie's notes detailed, there is another raging fire. *Check.* Using the exact same methodology, I flick fast the second tangerine while yelling, "Orange," to my left.

"Holy fucking shit, you're a witch," Loser 2 says.

The woman ahead hides a smirk; it's possible she saw my flick of the wrist. She's clearly on my side, given how her smirk is contained.

Loser 2 pokes the barrel of his gun into my spine. "What the fuck did you do?"

"Nothing at all."

"Move it. Move on," he says.

The sound ring should be zapping now, calling and corralling rats and mice and moles and other New England dirt dwellers—calling bats, too, that I hope are in the old attic—to fly and tunnel and crawl and slither through these walls and foundation to me. Things can't deviate now.

I hear the vague possibilities of scratching in the walls. None of the women in the room we've entered now notice. This is the room with the third fireplace, *check*, where the women are removing wide pine floorboards so as to drop me in the tank. I hear the definite beginnings of scratching in the walls.

AR-15 Asshole Loser 2 immediately looks to the third fireplace expecting a color now, he's been trained fast, what with his sheep-mentality and easy manipulation as a Pavlovian mutt. He's paused there, waiting, his back to me. I throw the third tangerine from behind him while I drop to the floor, pushing the door shut as I fall. He watches the flames burst into purple, and I take this time to sweep my legs into Loser 2's legs. And as his legs bend, I kick the backs of his knees, one, two, and as he falls to the ground, I elbow the top of his skull, grab his stupid gun, throw it to the ground while whipping the tie off my robe, set it around his neck, and choke him the fuck out.

I slip out of my robe and grab the Brileycon jug I marked with a red dot before shipping. Again I remove my toe, spring the blade, cut the score line, and *bam*, they're there: the items I left inside, and my secret tamper-resistant seals have not been tampered with. Had they been tampered with, I would have taken the gun, extracted Rosa, and failed at catching them all in the act. But, no tamper, so game on.

I look down through the floorboards, look into the tank.

Still the same. Same piece of shit as in the video. As Melanie described. Check.

This also means I don't need to shoot up all these idiots to save Rosa, which means we can take this to the limit, and hopefully entrap the Watchers.

I look to the women who are meant to pour the bleach; they've been stunned into silence in the minor seconds I took to do all this.

I whisper, "When he says pour the bleach. Just pour the bleach. Say nothing. And keep that door shut."

They nod in agreement.

With my items from the jug now in my hands, I jump straight into the tank, my feet splayed just right, bending my knees just so on the landing, as I've practiced to jump into a narrow space, several feet down.

Thud.

Velada did as she was told with the jugs. Noted.

Is she the one who had Doris slip the heroin needle? Unconfirmed.

Although I trust body language, microfacial tells, and also my instinct, which has never failed me. And although I do have an instinctual trust of the women with the jugs, I am still not 100% convinced of Velada's innocence. I need triple confirmation on that—I have a nagging that won't leave.

And here she is now, the only one in this room, readying her camcorder, just as she did twenty years ago.

Of course. She's in place.

She nods to me; I nod back. My two items from the jug are in my hands: two cans of aerosolized refrigerant, which I got at Home Depot. No big deal. Standing A-Frame, I point the nozzles to each gluey front corner. From the inside, I can tell this aged, homemade tank, is decrepit and poorly constructed. I spray both corners simultaneously, from top of the glue to all the way down, using an ambidexterity I practiced many, many times. Refrigerants can cool the existing state of epoxy glue, and quickly, such that it will crack and crumble. And given that this particular epoxy is old as fuck, I can already tell it's working. I spray again to be sure. I thrust the empty cans of spray up to the Up Top, which is five feet over my head, three feet of which include the tank. They land up there. I consider how, if everything goes wrong, I will use my backup plan of parkouring up and out, but that plan B, no matter how often I practiced, is really difficult to do fast and in the first try, given the dimensions and slipperiness of this tank and the two-foot gap from the top of the tank and the floor above.

Velada has her constant lighter in her back pocket. *Check.* She points her camcorder toward the door and nods towards it.

The door opens.

Loser 1, also with a lazy AR-15, marches in a line of naked men; they are all laughing and smiling, and some point to me in the tank. Velada catches all this on tape. I hear one of the men say, "Whoo,

225

boys, we've waited a long time for this show." Another says, "I'm already hard."

One looks to Velada with the camera. "We really have to tape?"

And another man says, "We need to know you won't talk. You knew that when you signed up, Bill."

And now we have you in the act, mostly. I want a little bit more though, just to be absofuckinglutely sure.

I'm focused on the fact that Loser 1 has an AR-15. This was never mentioned to me before; in fact, Melanie said the other guard walking in the men specifically didn't have a weapon—because they're all a friendly, chortling bunch. We need to get rid of Loser 1 with the AR-15.

I am no longer fire, like I was outside the tank. Now, I'm slicing ice.

I hear rodents scurrying in the old walls, even through the glass, for their scurrying is all around me in this side of the basement wall. This side is bumped out from the cinder blocks, which form the outer shell on the other side, in the spa, and the back wall of this tank. In the tank room, the cinder block is obscured by sheetrock, which I suppose covers the framing which holds the tank bolted to the cinder block. And within the guts of the framing and behind the sheetrock, I do hear claws scraping and vermin mouths keening, screeching in excitement at the false noise my strongest disc sends out. There is a mixture of ultrasonic mating sounds and food sounds, designed for the preferences of rodents and earth dwellers, and I had even threaded in some sounds attractive to bats. The sounds are irresistible to them: nutrition and sex, all any *body* really wants.

I hadn't hoped for many creatures. All I needed were a couple to cause chaos in the tank room and in the different floors of this stone mansion. I may have upon me an abundance of chaos. It is an old house in New England, I shouldn't be surprised.

The gross, laughing, naked men are being led to a small space behind the open mirror at the foot of the bed—just as Melanie's notes described. Same. *Check.*

I'm watching them through my long hair, which I keep over my face to obscure my identity. The refrigerant is fizzing on the epoxy and the fumes are toxic in here. In practice, I increased my perfect pink lungs' ability to hold my breath up to 2.2 minutes.

The men are quickly shuttled into the space behind the open mirror—a closet, basically, that holds five wooden chairs, one for each one of them. Eva, in her fancy black dress and awful string of pearls, walks in behind AR-15 Loser 1 and enters the closet space with her own camera. *Her camera is for a lifetime of kompromat and extortion, as is Velada's.*

Velada films Eva filming the men in the closet as she directs each one of them to say their name and how they got here this evening, how much they paid, and from what account.

Once done, Eva says, "Okay then, we all have a deal?"

The men nod and smile.

Velada walks to the closed mirror, and what was not visible in the 'Burnt Lobster' video, are three wooden bars on one side of the mirror that Velada now swivels over the side of the mirror, as old-school locks. They can't get out.

Showtime is coming.

AR-15 Asshole Loser 1 moves outside the door to this room; the door remains open. We all wait.

I'm itching to remove an item I have coiled in my head. *Tick tock,* the time is coming.

I don't move a muscle; I keep my head down and listen for Eminence's footsteps to approach and also to the vermin in the walls.

Right now it's just the silence of the Watchers, whose voices don't break through their mirror wall and the tank, and the vermin scratching, having been corralled closer from outside given the outer ring, and now closer to me, aching for the sound coming from the potent disc on my back. I listen, too, to my heartbeat, which is loud, but at a slow rhythm—loud because I am holding my breath.

It's been two minutes and twenty seconds, so I take a quick sip of air with my mouth and resume holding breath.

I take this pause to stable my thinking on my chief asset: sound.

I got the idea for the rodent and bat ring when I visited the Fermi Lab in Illinois in 1999. At Fermi, there is the Tevatron ring, which is an underground ring used by physicists to spin and smash neutrons and electrons and study their decay and guts, such as quarks and other particle matter. Same thing as the more famous CERN. I merged the Tevatron ring with the myth of the Pied Piper, a man who lured rats from the town of Hamelin, Germany, with his magic flute. There are contrary theories about the Pied Piper and whether he saved Hamelin of the rat plague; or whether, having not been paid, lured children away with his flute. There's always some truth to urban legends, and I suspect the truth behind luring rats or children was in sound science, not a magical flute. And so, merging Fermi's underground particle ring with the sound science underlying the Pied Piper, I came up with my Viebury ring, made of sound discs, to surround the stone mansion so as to call to my bidding: nature—the greatest asset of all time.

I look at Velada now. She's holding her old-school camcorder. She nods. I nod toward Loser 1 with the AR-15, indicating, I hope, that she needs to get rid of him. I hear footsteps approaching. It's go time. I uncoil the tightly-wound package in my false hair tuft.

CHAPTER TWENTY-SEVEN
LISA YYLAND: IN THE TANK
Set to the rhythm of 'Nocturne in C-Sharp' — Chopin

50 Cent's rhythm accompanied me in my walk to the Tank, but now as I stand here, the original musical gangster takes over: Chopin. *Nocturne in C-Sharp* begins in my mind, sound-tracking the dance I'll take. I ensure my hair remains fallen over my face so the Watchers behind the mirror can't see me. I will remain nameless to them like this, especially now that I uncoil from the underguts of my woven hairs, my mask. My mass of hair and these woven strands have proven worthy of several key things: hiding my face, hiding my color chemicals, and holding my tight-coiled nylon mask, one I collected in Shanghai—Eminence's very own.

Each key of Chopin's piano is a slice in my mind. Sharp knives slicing slow, one, two, three, four, *slice*, as if the pianist is making love to murder, a bloody knife raised above a heart for a deep plunge. This is what I consider as the sound in my mind, and the image in my mind, as I stand here stock still, naked, arms spread, legs spread, like I'm da Vinci's "Vitruvian Man." In a tank.

I give the Watchers locked behind the mirror this image as a warning: me still, my hair obscuring my face, my arms and legs wide, no shaking, solid, my body naked. The bottom corners of the tank notably have major gaps given the sloppy alignment of this makeshift construction. The epoxy corners where I sprayed refrigerants sizzle and crack. *Piece of shit.*

This pause is timed to the brilliant silence Chopin gifts, a freeze between first chord and second, in his most murderously sensuous song, like a lover hovering and holding above the lips of an anxious woman, making her wait for his precise lunge and thrust.

Velada steadies her camera.

The bustle of butterfly flutters of Chopin's piano keys signal the exciting shift of energy Chopin gives me, his thrilling taunt of anticipation. I unroll Eminence's mask with one hand, nimble-fingered, for I've unrolled replicas of this mask so many times. I've caught my fingers working to this motion upon waking, upon breaking from thought, in the shower, while driving. Unrolling this mask is like a tic to me, part of my being.

I settle the mask over my head as the door widens. I do not look up.

The door creaks.

I hear a heavy foot.

"What the *fuck* is this! My mask!" Eminence screams.

I do not look up.

"You look up now." He slams the door.

I do not look up.

"You *will* look up now!"

I do not look up.

"What the fuck is this! Some sick joke? My gift a fucking sick joke? Taunting me? Mocking me?" He howls towards Velada.

"No!" she shouts.

Back towards me his voice shouts, "You take off that mask now!"

I do not look up.

"Tell Brian to go up top and help that other shithead get her under control," Velada yells to Eminence.

Eminence, holding Rosa's arm like he could squeeze through it, turns to the door, opens it, and tells Brian, *aka Loser 1*, to go up top and handle me. Then he slams the door shut and screams, "Bleach!"

Bleach pours in, rising to my ankles. *No worries. I'll be in here only long enough to have superficial burns.*

"Stop!"

I hear cheering from the men behind the mirror, they are loud, thrilled about this.

And now we have you so totally red-handed, fuckers. The rest is extra frosting.

Rosa, in the room and still held by Eminence, is bawling. Screaming and crying.

The epoxy is crackled now, pieces of the bulging glue falling off.

I look up for the first time and direct all my vision to Rosa's gold-brown eyes. She meets mine back. This is Rosa's signal. And like a striking viper, she stomps Eminence's bare foot with the German toes, slips down fast, breaks his hold on her arm the way we practiced. *Check.*

Rosa should become an actress. She's not crying now.

Naked Rosa, free of Eminence's grip, drops to the ground in the position of hopping frog, hops forward, swivels and somersaults toward Eminence's legs, and in a jiujitsu leg sweep, unearths Eminence's feet out from under him.

Meanwhile, as Rosa works her magic, I've bent my knees and push my feet up against the glass, my back pressed against the back wall; I push hard. Jam my feet. Push. Jam. After four intervals of such, the panel falls forward, only to hang…dangling, still attached by epoxy on the bottom. Rosa rolls sideways to the wall, pops to a standing position, and runs out the door. All of this takes a total of eight seconds.

I wish Eminence and the Watchers could hear the lovely song in my head, for his steps into the room, his bewildered and aggressive screaming, him falling from Rosa crashing into him, all fall in lockstep to the *Nocturne* in my mind. It's like he's performed this part with me all these years.

We're dance partners, Eminence. You and I. Us.

The once subdued scratching of the rodents and the beating of wings break through, also in time to the now furious portion of *Nocturne* in my mind. I've released this, the most powerful of my sound discs, into this room, flung it free from my back as the panel fell. Sound waves flow through hidden holes in walls, and attract the squeaking and the clawing; everyone above is running crazy, screaming at the chaos of rodents. Here come a few lovely creatures into the tank room; they must invade the Watchers' enclosure, too, for I hear those naked men screaming in their confinement.

A single bat swoops in from above through the tank as I jump and land on the bed, and I presume she flew down from the rafters in the attic—the fireplaces are all raging fire colors. I set my false toe and stabilizing "toe ring" on the bed in a mattress divot. I'll reattach it later. Industrial-strength bleach rains down on Eminence's head on the floor.

I didn't expect a crazy swarm of thousands of rats and bats, like Batman's conjuring of his namesake in *The Dark Knight*. That was sci-fi. And since this is real sound science, I estimate I've Pied Piper'd a grand total of a dozen bats and rats and mice and other New England rodents, like moles and perhaps even a chipmunk—at tops, fifteen creatures total throughout the whole house—which was likely infested anyway, given its age and drafty walls. But you don't need thousands of rats and bats and mice and moles and chipmunks to descend chaos upon a house of mostly women. Even one spastic rat can cause panic.

I curl into my landing on the bed in a bending crouch, my long hair down around my neck and pooling on the mattress. I arch my stomach over my knees and reveal in a slant my transformed back in full. Only Velada and Eminence can see it; none of the Watchers. This is the moment. This is the moment when I reveal my true new identity to the world, and specifically Velada, the videographer, who stands to my side, between bed and wall. She thinks I give her one second to see my new identity but this, too, is a magician's diversion, for every molecule of me, every painted fiber on my back, every second I use is all a diversion, a trick of sight. Moths and bats have been engaged in warfare for 60 million years. She is a bat. I am a Luna Moth. She's transfixed by my jump, she's catatonic about the image on my back. She has no clue I swoop my right hand to grab the butcher knife, where it's always been, from under the mattress.

I was a mere caterpillar before. Pupa. Larvae. I was germinating in a cocoon, attached to a host. They thought I spun myself in, waiting on my predator, a willing victim. But I'm like the moth in the moonlight who tricks the bat. Wings spread in my new, true, identity. I give one second to fill my lungs by arching my back even more—I need full lungs for this next part. At the pinnacle of a breath-sucking arch, I stretch my back's tattooed skin and show the fine fibers of the Luna Moth. My master artist spent weeks pricking me with needles, painting my Luna, shoulder blade to shoulder blade, wings stretched to each flank, and the moth's tricky double tail down each side of my spinal column and ending above my coccyx. She's blue-green, her ringed eyes black, her split tail and wings outlined in a beautiful reddish purple, her antennae black. She's no simple, tiny, black butterfly tattooed as a lazy afterthought on someone's hand, like Velada's. My spinal Luna is a statement. She is power. I have metamorphosed.

One rat, a mouse, and a bat screech around the tank room. The bat swoops and swoops. All around me I hear screaming, in the room, behind the mirror, feet jumping. Eminence struggles for balance, his distraction evident in his shaking head, wiping at bleach from the netting on his face, taking in the creatures in the room, the screaming all around, the noises Up Top, me on the bed, holding his under-bed butcher knife and hosting a giant moth on my back. I bring the chaos. I own the chaos. For me, this is pure order.

Rosa is clear and free, disappeared. And so, I resume being a weaponized human.

I pop to both feet on the bed, knees bent to absorb the motion and the cushion—butcher knife in my right hand. This takes one second.

I step to shocked Velada, her mouth agape, she's popping on her feet from the rat and mouse, who can't escape now, desperately searching for mates and food, trapped in the sound ring. The bat is furious, fluttering around the room; Eminence wipes it away from his face. He's to his knees now. Men behind the mirror are screaming and pounding on their side of the mirror.

I spin Velada with one free hand, grab her lighter out of her back pocket.

"Keep the camera on the mirror and don't move a muscle," I yell to her as I roll away on the bed, her lighter in one hand and the knife in the other, and land on the other side. I square my feet to faceoff with Eminence.

This series of actions, including launching from the tank, showing my tattoo, and the time I took to gather the butcher knife and the lighter, takes a total of seven seconds. Exactly as I've done 3,488 times before.

It is beneficial that Rosa was able to do as I said and frog-crouch-roll-swipe to topple Eminence. That ended up being a bonus. I had accounted for her failing and me having to go with my backup plan of popping out of the tank, grabbing the knife, and stabbing Eminence in the head to free Rosa.

I slide to the light switch. Shut off the lights so the men can't see this next part.

I know exactly where Eminence is and I know he's regained his balance and is out of the swoop of the bat. He is so huge, he takes up nearly all this room, so all I need to do is wait here by the light switch, by the door. And because he can't control himself, he lunges toward me in the dark, and I grab that damn mask of his, and light it with Velada's lighter. Immediately the entire thing combusts. He jumps back from me, his head visibly engulfed in flames in the dark, and the netting melts into his hair and scalp and face skin, mixing with the bleach from the floor, which has soaked into his mask. He's furious to remove it, crashing about the room like a bull.

This is only phase one of your painful death, asshole.

I switch on the light.

"Seems he's immolated himself," I say.

I estimate Liu and Lola will enter in about five seconds, seeing as that above, on the first floor, I hear Liu kick in the door and women who work above screaming and running.

I hear one bullet fire, which means Liu or Lola shot once at Loser 1 Brian, the only one of the two guards conscious. And since I don't hear the rapid fire of an AR-15, I'm assuming it was a kill shot.

Brian's dead.

I move toward the mirror of Watchers. Eminence is banging behind me into walls and the bed.

"Film the floor for a second," I say to Velada.

She turns the camera to the floor. I note she doesn't twitch or shake or refuse my commands, even though her brother's face is burning off.

Fully nude except for my black mask, I stand before the Watchers, my legs in A-frame again, my fully waxed pubis in full view, my eight-pack stomach, my low-pile breasts, my long blonde hair coming out of the bottom of the mask, and my arms out wide. I am twice now before them da Vinci's 'Man.' But I am a woman. And I am a moth. And I am the one with all the power. While they have none.

Velada called me a psycho, so maybe I am. I don't care.

Rumbles of running feet approach the door. We are now fifteen seconds since I landed on the bed.

So.

Right.

All of Liu's worry was for naught, just like I told him. I suppose I could have stayed in the tank until they came. But then I couldn't have stress tested all my assets and my skills and my artful performance in the field. And what if I had waited to see if they'd come and save us and they failed? Anywhere along the way they could have failed to get here on time. Precisely on time. What if I wasted precious seconds and Rosa was raped? No, I couldn't wait for Liu and Lola.

I jump back up on the bed, reattach my toe, and wrap the top sheet around me like a toga. Eminence writhes, on fire, to my side. Velada returns to taping the mirror.

Liu enters, heads to Eminence, snuffs his flames with his suit jacket, and zip-ties his wrists. I turn my masked head to the right to watch Liu with Eminence. Liu looks at me in my toga and mask, looks at Velada with the camcorder to my side, notes the rat, mouse, and bat, sees the lighter on the floor, the butcher knife in my hand, and looks back up at me with an indication of horror, like the first time he saw me eighteen years ago…when I was trapped in a car, submerged in a quarry, one of my captors out cold to my side.

I can see in his eyes now acceptance. Acceptance that, of course I'd duped him into thinking the plan was a simple trap.

And now, the Watchers.

Lola shoots a corner of the mirror; the glass shatters.

All of the men inside, all of these Watchers, five of them, naked. Eva shrinks into herself in a back corner. Two rats are in their closet room, running between the wooden chair legs. All five men shake upon the chairs and cup their franks and beans. Lola stands like a federal agent with her gun in their faces, a GoPro strapped to her head. She's taping too. Velada filming with the camcorder from behind. Eva's camera in the closet, which we'll seize. *These dirtbags have for sure been caught in the act.*

Liu joins Lola, having zip-tied Eminence's wrists and left him panting, almost passed out, and sitting in a corner. The burning nylon has been ripped from Eminence's nose and mouth holes, so he can breathe. Portions of his face and neck skin and hair meld with the nylon. The pain must have weakened him, for he falls fetal in his corner, half-awake in a stunned and low-moaning shock.

Good.

Now Liu and Lola point guns at the five Watchers and Eva in the closet, mirror glass scattered and jagged in the room and on the closet floors. The Watchers remain still, frozen to be under the command of two guns pointed at their heads. They stand on chairs.

Lola bellows, saying each word clear and distinct, as if narrating, for that's exactly what she's doing, working as the announcer for this *bust film*, not *snuff film*, we're making.

"Boys! Raise your hands in the air! Today is motherfucking showtime. Say hello to your *faaaaaaannnnnnns.*" Sounds of chairs scraping and shouts do not overcome Lola's repetition of her opening phrase. Three times she says the exact same lines, drawing out the word "fans" like a WWF announcer and huffing out an imitation of a crowd cheering. She has them corralled and under her command, for she begins to pace, crunching mirror glass under the soles of her black boots.

"Good afternoon, Ambassador Howell. Stop cupping your balls and raise your arms back up. In. The. Air. Your speech about family values was great last week. The one when you protested same sex marriage." Lola pops her lips and clicks her tongue. "Do you think *your family* values you masturbating in a closet to the sight of another man raping and killing? Is that what you mean by family values? I'm confused." Lola pauses in what I register as a pitch perfect delivery of sarcasm. She continues, "And hello there, Mr. Wannabe Senator, or *was* going to be Senator Falsenhoff. Saw you on the golf course today. Are you crying like a raped little girl? Hmmm? And Judge Frackson, such a prick. CEO Adams, you were driving the golf cart for that fuck in the corner with the mask. I remember. And, Sergeant Rockford. Sergeant Rockford, please stop peeing yourself."

"Bitch," Judge Frackson says. I cringe, expecting a bloody brawl to break out, Lola the vicious instigator against them all. I expect a volley of roundhouse kicks to temples and money-shots to guts and broken noses, or perhaps even the sound of her shooting every one of them in the forehead. *Pop, pop, pop, pop, pop.* All done and dead. But that's not what happens. Instead, Lola laughs like a mad crazy megalomaniac, proud and happy and wild in humor. And then she stops and yells, "Don't you fucking snarl at me, bitch. You're all under arrest…you have the right to remain silent…"

As Lola and Liu are zip-tying the five monster Watchers and Eva, I move quick to Liu's back pocket, where he always keeps car keys. I take the keys, move to Eminence, force him to stand. He's whimpering and wailing and groaning, and I do not give one fuck. I push him to walk forward, out of the room.

"I'll hold him outside," I yell to Liu, who, as I suspected he would be, is struggling with his arrestees, deputized by Lola. Lola is calling in to Beta Agency agents, now that we have video to thwart any insiders, if there are any, who might want to thwart these arrests.

"Beta will be here in ten. I didn't tell them where or what. But I had a few good ones staged close," she yells to me. "Hold him here." She means Eminence.

"Okay, I'll hold him out here."

"Lisa, do not fucking move another muscle," Lola yells, but she's distracted, because at this moment, Frackson kicks her below the belt. Liu is likewise struggling with Sergeant Rockford, who happens to be six-foot-five.

"Oh fuck no," Lola says to Frackson. I don't stick around. They don't need me. Liu already has Rockford on his stomach, Liu's knee in his back. And Frackson is a lily-livered baby man compared to thick tree Lola.

No one stops me and Eminence as we move through a separate basement corridor. A door at the end leads to the backyard, which is really a bowl of property, the backside of a scooped-out hill—Vanty would love it as a snowboarding half-pipe. Still wearing a sheet as a toga, I push Eminence forward, keeping the butcher knife on a knot in his spine.

"Freeze, Lisa Yyland," I hear shouted at me from my side. It's a woman's voice. As I turn, Eminence twists, head butts me, and runs off into the woods. He doesn't have his hands to brace him or level his uneven gait. But he is gone, and fast, into the dark woods.

I turn, my vision blurred a moment from the head butt, and find I am face to face with Chief Castile of the East Hanson police department. Rosa is wearing Castile's deputy's coat and sitting in the squad car with him way around to the front. The deputy apparently didn't see Eminence run off, and Castile is so confused, she's keeping her gun on me.

Fucking Castile.

CHAPTER TWENTY-EIGHT
FORMER SPECIAL AGENT ROGER LIU

Seconds ago, Lola and I emerged out of the basement into the backyard, Lola and I having zip-tied all the fools and locked them back in the closet while we await Beta. Lola's got Velada by the arm, because we aren't letting her free without questioning and possible booking.

And what did we fucking find? Chief Castile, who I knew had our number, holding Lisa against a tree and cuffing her.

I told Lola we'd get rung up for obstruction. *Shit.*

There's a rumble in the earth. Sounds of sirens.

I turn, and it feels like slow motion. Heading toward us now are several black vehicles, all bulletproof.

Lola looks to Castile.

"Chief, sorry about the little white lie earlier, but it's all authorized by Beta, and here they are now. Lisa is deputized by me, so you're going to have to let her go now."

"She let Eminence get away," Lisa yells to us.

CHAPTER TWENTY-NINE
JOSI OLIVE

Josi can't go to his Cape. Can't appear seen in Viebury with his truck, Cassie, which they must know now. They did find them at Club Bub. And fuck, they've seen him now, totally interested and involved, not just some unaware neighbor any longer. But he can't stay away neither. He's pissed as all fuck at this Lisa who gives vile news as if it's nothing. But he also knows she's right, and he also suspects, whatever her game is, she likely needs a hand.

There's a good tree. The tree he can climb and watch things happen in that stone house. And this is where he is now. Hiding high up in his tree, having left Cassie parked on the access road, at the side base of the hill of Viebury. No streetlights there. Where he drilled Rasper.

They got fires going in the stone mansion, he can see through the window, and also the smoke from the chimneys. They got women running around all over in there. He thinks he hears screaming. Not much is real clear, except there does seem to be screaming and lots of movements.

And it is now, when all breaks to fucking hell, and Josi near falls off his sitting limb, when a naked girl comes screaming out a back door, her arms tied behind her back, and she circles to the front, only to be met by a woman cop who pulls up at this precise moment.

Also, coming out of fucking nowhere from the back lawn, two cop-like people in gray suits storm an upper back door, enter, and

240

within a flat second, Josi hears a single shot.

The naked girl is screaming to the woman cop out front, while the woman cop's partner unties the girl's arms and wraps her in his coat. The girl points the woman cop to go to the back lower door, around the house, the one she exited from. The coatless partner settles the girl in the squad car out front and stays with her.

"Ah, fuck," Josi says to himself. He's frozen on his limb.

Holy shit, he's thinking, as now Lisa in a sheet comes out into the night pushing ahead of her a beast of a man with a burned head. Black netting pasted to his reddened skin.

The woman cop detains Lisa, the beast head butts Lisa—*ah hell no, fucker*—and runs off into the woods.

When the beast passes under Josi's limb, Josi doesn't give his next move a second thought, doesn't plan what he does or what he'll do next.

He jumps.

CHAPTER THIRTY
LISA YYLAND

I'm standing here as Beta takes each of the vermin into custody. Lola's off to the side trying to explain things to Castile, who I'm really pissed off at—my homicidal rage is surely still on. Before Castile inserted herself, I was going to claim Eminence got away, shove him in Liu's tinted-window rental, which I knew he'd park down at the front gate at the base of Viebury, knock Eminence out, and once Liu and Lola were preoccupied with Beta, say I had to get clothes at Mother's by borrowing Liu's rental. But now, Beta is forming a search group to head off in the correct direction of where Eminence ran. And I'm also wondering if this plan of mine would have worked anyway, because as I look at Liu's key I swiped, this is for a Ford, not the rental they had earlier.

At the edge of the woods, I note Josi stands as if he's just a curious neighbor. He nods to me in a way that indicates he has information.

"Lisa, where the hell you going," Lola says as I'm halfway to Josi.

"That guy, I think he saw something. I got this."

"Hold on," Lola says, but she keeps talking to Castile. The Beta agents are forming into groups.

I run to Josi.

"He's in my truck," he says.

"Lincoln, by the cemetery, East Hanson. Tonight," I say as fast as I can.

Lola joins us.

"You see something, guy?" she asks.

"I think so, yeah. I think I saw like some huge dude run toward the back swamp."

Lola beckons the agents to run that way.

"Can't one of your agents take me to my mother's house to get clothes? This is absurd," I say, indicating my sheet dress. "They can ask me questions on the way."

Lola looks me up and down. "You do look ridiculous. Hal," she shouts over her shoulder. "Go take Lisa to East Hanson. Take Picard with you, do a prelim on the way. And then let her get some fucking sleep."

"Thank you, Lola," I say.

"Yeah." And she trots off. She stops midway, turns around. "Hey, guy, I'm going to need…"

But Josi disappeared the second she trotted off.

I lift my arms like I don't know where he went.

Lola considers me for a second in a way that is almost anger, but then a Beta agent pulls her away. Beta agents Hal and Picard come up to me, and we're off to Mother's.

On my way out of town with Josi and Eminence tonight, after I change and get my phone, I'll text Liu that I freaked out and needed to take a drive back to Indiana to process things in my mind. After all, I'm not under arrest. I'm deputized.

~~~

Josi and I had an appropriate level of relief, at least I did, in driving from Massachusetts to Indiana, keeping Eminence sedated with a variety of needle sedatives I'd stashed back at Mother's. In our drive, Josi explained how he had intended to break into the stone mansion and save me, but then he figured I had a good plan, I must, and he waited and watched as back-up in his tree.

When he said this, I turned on a glimmer of joy: joy that he would get me, joy that he would trust I had this under control, joy that he was patient enough to trust this trust and lend himself as back-up. Joy, too, that he didn't give a fuck that I intended to harm them bad. Didn't give a fuck all the way to enabling me, like a real partner.

243

Lenny had no idea what I was up to, nor that I'd had this game playing in the background for eighteen years.

I chose not to tell Josi the full truth about Velada until we hit Ohio. He took it as well as you might expect. I listened. I didn't talk. And then when I thought we were done with all that, he freaked out in Columbus, Indiana, which is a reprehensible pit I prefer to sleep through when driving. Josi pulled over and forced me to use a Columbus, Indiana payphone—horrible—to call Liu and get an update on Velada. My cell had died and Josi's truck didn't have a workable lighter chamber.

I rolled my eyes.

I was done with my use of Velada, and I wished Josi would just move on. While she may have come through in our arrangement, there are unforgivables about her: 1. She actually did tape the first event twenty years ago and did nothing to help; 2. She was involved with the trafficking house for the last twenty years, didn't tell me where it was, and allowed all those girls to suffer; 3. Because of her silence, Mother was shot. Above all, my gut still didn't trust her.

But Josi refused to leave Columbus without me calling Liu for the update, and since my skin was beginning to crawl with the feeling of centipedes to have to remain in Columbus any longer, I called.

Liu reported that indeed they'd booked Eva, and since I had her photo on Mother's iPhone at the crime scene, and since a number of "Up Top" girls and "Basement Bitches" provided witness statements connecting Eva to the stone mansion, she was easy to charge with a million different crimes. *Whatever. Obvious.* I'd get my retribution on her for Mother's murder one day, another day.

As for Velada, Liu said she was proving to be a hard case. A "twisting, convoluted knot," he said. She's claiming she had to play the role she did and lie to me and not admit she was Eminence's sister, because there was no other way to get me to save myself in a way that would trap her awful brother and the powerful Watchers. She insists I had been tagged by Eminence himself and that if she hadn't inserted herself and fed me intel, and controlled with her brother when I could be taken in, I would have been taken by surprise, tortured, and likely killed in the tank. Also, she says she won't testify against the Watchers without immunity and protection.

Liu said Velada's claims about why she disappeared and staged her own death to trick her husband are details that he didn't want to discuss right then, as he was busy.

I looked over at Josi and indicated I had just one more minute on the phone.

Josi paced around the phone booth, waiting for the update, like Lenny did when he was waiting for me to deliver Vanty.

Josi heard me say enough words on my end of the conversation with Liu to get the gist. And having obsessed by that point over his new reality for several long driving hours, he stopped pacing and hung his head: his wife was at least for some years a willing—by active volition, indifference, or inactivity—human trafficker.

Liu went silent, and I could tell he was going to have some pointed questions for me, after I'd pulled from him all he had time to discuss about Eva and Velada.

"So, why is it you chose to leave Massachusetts so fast and go back to Indiana?"

"I needed time to think, Liu, in my own private space. Imagine what I went through."

"Then why didn't you fly?"

"Again, I wanted to be alone. To think."

"You didn't take your mother's car."

"Beta said I couldn't take anything of Mother's. I Ubered to a rental."

"Mmm, hmm. And nobody's with you?"

"Who would be with me?"

"Don't know. You tell me, Lisa."

"Nobody's with me, Liu."

"Hounds lost the scent of Eminence in the middle of a dirt access road. You have anything to do with that, Lisa?"

"Like I said before, he ran off when Castile fucked everything up."

Liu's throat started to gurgle, and I could tell he was rising to a level where he'd scream about how I didn't exactly answer the question. So I hung up.

Liu, I know him, he's going to remain quiet on his end; he'll say Eminence "escaped." He needs to know no more. He won't do anything to know the truth or bust me. And I will ultimately have to pay for his purposeful ignorance. Lola, the same with Lola.

As Josi and I returned to his truck, him now resigned to the dark news of his not-dead-duping wife, I demanded he peel out of Columbus fast before I vomited for having to be there any longer. But what I was thinking was: *Perhaps this life and death game with Velada is not yet done.* So I'm not sure if my internal acknowledgment about her caused me to actually vomit out the passenger window, or if it was because the hypocritical biblical clouds over Columbus compressed my pink lungs.

CHAPTER THIRTY-ONE
LISA YYLAND: THE SECOND CLUB BUB

Above the door to my practice tank room on the third floor of 15/33 headquarters is a sign; I painted it last night on a floorboard, one taken from the room in which they held me when I was sixteen and I used then in my escape. The sign declares the new name for my workout room: CLUB BUB. Although it was only minutes Josi and I were there, I felt a measure of fun in Club Bub, even with all those bouncing viruses and fungal infections and the aggressive exit.

I enter my now fully-painted birch grove practice room with two tanks on the walls. I lock the heavy steel door to *my* Club Bub. Nobody will be joining me today in here, except my test subject, who's in *my* Tank. Most of my family is still in hiding with Sarge. I called my father on a hidden intercom I programmed for remote access in his panic room in Manchester and gave him the code to escape, but told him to keep an invisible profile, perhaps go back to Brazil with Geena Davis—after we're done burying Mother. Josi and I—and Eminence in the bed of his truck, tied up and drugged—arrived in Indiana last night, after driving straight from Viebury Grove in Massachusetts. I'll need to conduct this final experiment/revenge phase and advise Sarge to release my family. My father is building the itinerary for Mother's funeral, so I need to return to Massachusetts for that, too. Josi is going to wait and drive me back, but I sent him off to stay at the local Stork & Crane Inn until later tonight, because I can't have him lingering around here today and having any part in what's about to go down.

Busy, busy, busy.

I'm in a crop top and sweat-wicking workout boy shorts. All my hair is coiled into a tight twist. I will sweat soon.

I whip out my iPhone with the perfect workout Playlist: Missy Elliott, Chopin, some La Bohème songs, Pitbull, Sons of Kalal, 50 Cent, and Josi Olive, or rather, Master Josi, his stage name. On my steel desk, I find my blue headphones, which match the blue sky above the painted green and yellow treetops. I wink to a painted ladybug on a green leaf who converses with a cardinal in a nest, as though they are cross-species lovers. I start a sweet jam for my ears and my mind and my muscles: endorphins rocket under the spell of thrilling riffs, electrical drums, and Josi's tender voice in rhyme. *Sound magic.* His songs are first in rotation.

I've turned on in myself homicidal rage and pleasure. That's all. The only emotions I need. I am a Molotov cocktail.

I check the adhesion on the twenty bands all over my body, all there and connected to a capacitor to collect mechanical energy. I look up to Eminence, naked in my *very* upgraded version of his tank. He, too, has twenty bands adhered all over his body, parts where his body parts can bend or flex. His capacitor is strapped to his belly. Strapped to his back is a high impact, but very tiny, bomb. His arms are bendable, but tied at the wrists so that his arms are held in place and anchored to each top corner. Point is: he can't remove the bomb or the bands because he can't use his hands.

I pick up a remote control on the steel table and point it behind me to two digital monitors mounted on the wall in such a way, it appears as though they are televisions propped on two birch branches. Each reads: 00 in red. And so. The game. Begins.

"These are the rules of the game," I say, mocking his manner of speech. "If my capacitor maintains a stronger charge than yours for three seconds, you will detonate. You have twenty bands to create a charge. I do, too. Moving makes the charge go up. I'll start slow. Remember your charge must stay higher than mine. Watch the monitors."

This is my game, so I withhold from Eminence three key rules to this game. One is that he doesn't know when I get dancing, especially now with how much I like Josi's voice and rhythm, I am incapable of slowing down. The second thing is, I have motivational music and I keep it contained in my earphones. I handicap him by denying him any sound at all. Here we go.

I press play. Josi sets up this song to begin with a sample of an old piano solo. It is so perfect. It's like Chopin in duet with Eminem. I take very slow and subtle sways of my body along with the slow beat. My monitor rises to 01; Eminence sees my monitor at 01 and his at 00 and bends his knees. His rises to 01. I sway a little faster and go to 02. He sees this, and like a dumb lab rat, he smells the cheese quick. He bends his knees faster now and rises all the way up to 05.

"You are getting it. Good. We'll go faster soon," I say, and because I remind myself about Dorothy and Melanie and Mother and all the others, I escalate my homicidal rage and pleasure. I smile wide and wink at him. My heart fills with a flood of heated liquid, and butterflies storm my brain. I feel I could fly, I'm so light in pleasure.

Now I lift my shoulders in a bounce, getting my body to get in the groove of the faster pace of the song now, Josi having added an acoustic guitar and also electrical drums and other fusions of electrical and natural sounds. His voice joins, too; smooth. The lyrics come in rising speed and are reaching near an almost fever pitch. My monitor reads 18; Eminence is moving as many muscles as he can and tossing his head about; he is at 19. And this isn't even the climax of the song yet.

Ah...here it is, here it is, it's almost like right before I orgasm, and fuck this feels good. I bend my knees fast and deep so my legs are splayed and I twerk down low. Now I shoot my body straight up, as if a reverse pencil dive. My monitor soars to 55 in two seconds. Eminence is working his large body as much as he can, but he doesn't have music, and his body is huge, and his quarters are cramped. His monitor is at 42. He's got two more seconds to get above mine, he thinks, or else *kaboom*.

The third key rule Eminence doesn't know is this: he doesn't need to have his capacitor reading maintain above mine. The very second Eminence gets to 53, his bomb is going to blow.

I slow all the way down to a light jog in place. My monitor shoots down to 25.

He slows a little like an idiot.

"You should not stop. You need to keep going. Play the game.

Don't you want to live?"

I wish I could bottle and sell this pleasure I'm allowing right now. I typically deny myself, because according to Nana's cozy mysteries, murder is wrong. But I do enjoy, I *really* do enjoy killing fucking monsters. It's not about attaining justice or vindication or retribution, if I'm being honest. The truth is, I dislike clutter and viruses and infections—I like to eradicate harmful things for the health of the whole. Like I'm a criminal sterilizer, a societal antibiotic. And since I have rage and pleasure on, and I can be honest with myself here alone in this closed room, the real truth is, this is the greatest high I could give myself. My brain has dissipated into fluttering butterflies and helium and all my organs are balls of light.

I start to bounce my shoulders again, again timing when to match my body with the music and thrust—like timing myself to jump the fastest jump rope. Eminence is moving as much of his body as he can.

"I gave you twenty bands to get your energy up on the monitor. Twenty. Can't you use all of them? Twenty gifts I gave you in this game! You are ungrateful!" I am not breathing hard as I say this, even though I am grooving now in dance. Eminence is breathing hard. My monitor shoots back up to 50. He's at 50.

Eminence makes for a large subject. With his mass, his death and decay will take longer than those of average size. He's naked and huge in my upgraded tank. If the Center Ring's tank was analog, mine is a robotic, futuristic, automated, plumbed spacecraft from another planet. Remains of a replica of the Center Ring's archaic tank are on the wall opposite my futuristic tank, the replica blown open from the last time I practiced.

Even if his arms were free, Eminence has a hot chance in hell he'll find a way out of my temper-resistant, triple-laminated, bulletproof, three-inch glass. I checked all his toes and digits, and he doesn't have any false appendages with retractable diamond-point blades. Also, the top of his cage is not open. Steel bars, like the automatic bolts locking jail cells, locked in place after I forced him in from above in the attic. Over that, I engaged the soundproof seal. And over the soundproof seal, I replaced a floorboard. The Center Ring...the Center Ring is more like the Center Ring of Antique Folk Art Torture Chambers. They should put their tank in a booth at the *Fall Antiques Festival* in the center of the New Hampshire Conference Center.

I've pumped in air for Eminence to breathe because I don't want lack of oxygen to be a contributing factor to his failure in this game.

Once he blows, his dead, waste of flesh, asshole, rapist, murderer body will dissolve in liquefied, concentrated Sodium Hydroxide, which I have primed to pump in through pipes built into the tank. Sodium Hydroxide? Oh, *absofuckinglutely*. But the Center Ring used bleach? *Please*. Sodium Hydroxide is what you use to burn skin and muscle, then organs and bones. It's the chief component of drain cleaner—the stuff that unclogs human hair balls.

I'll clock how long the dissolving takes. This is no childish Lobster Tank. This is a Magic Tank. Soon, Eminence will be invisible. The disease of him, eradicated. He will be literally nothing. Obviously, I can't avoid the calcium shell and red sludge that will remain after I drain away the liquefied Eminence, but no bother, I've designed this tank to self-clean.

Josi is a master of the beat and lyric, and my hips swing in uninhibited thrusts now, minding Josi's rhythm all on their own. I guess Josi and I are plutonic "friends," something Nana once explained to me is important to understand as between men and women, even if my animal body is demanding that I mate.

"Baby, no. Yes, you may find a man attractive, but you are in a relationship with Lenny, your child's father, right? And so, you need to be platonic, just friends, and not have sex with just anyone you find attractive," she said once, right after I told her I wanted to have sex with a man who walked by, and before I married Lenny, but after we had Vanty and lived together as "partners." I think I was nineteen, so my hormones were mutinous against me.

"But it's a biological urge, Nana. Why not?"

"Honey, I know that. And part of these urges might be explained, for you, as biological, and part of these urges, for you and for others, might be explained by some mystery we just don't know. I get urges too. But fidelity in a consensual monogamous relationship is a rule we follow in polite society. Doesn't Lenny expect you to be monogamous?"

I later asked Lenny if he expected me to be monogamous. He cried and wouldn't talk to me for a whole week to even ask such a "stupid and hurtful question." He screamed, "Yes, be monogamous," at me before slamming a door in my face.

This physical, sexual urge is not an emotion at all, so I cannot simply turn it off. I have to take other measures to follow Nana's lesson.

I note on the calendar that I am ovulating, and this means my biorhythms are a challenge, making me think too much on Josi's arm tattoo and how his chest looks in an unbuttoned blue shirt. So when I sent him off to the Stork & Crane to rest there today, I told him to pick out two audiobooks for the ride back to Massachusetts. We'll need to not talk and we'll need to focus on some thriller storyline to patch us through until my body is done throwing estrogen everywhere and dumping an ovary that must remain unseeded.

Right now, in my own tank room at 15/33 headquarters, Josi off at the Inn and picking out audiobooks, I'm sweating in a multiple 8-count, double-grind routine. My monitor is at 52. Eminence is at 52. One more digit to go until he blows. I speed up my moves, encouraging him to dig deep and work harder to surpass me. This is a good game. A game where he doesn't even know the real rules. And one where, bonus, I get to stress test my mechanical energy bands.

And, tick. He hits 53, enough energy to trigger the bomb.

A grand explosion overtakes the tank and all turns red. I don't hear the blast, for the tank is soundproofed and I have the headphones on. It's like when an insect hits a windshield and immediately vaporizes into a blood blast, but the impact is silent.

You insect.

The morning is on schedule.

Still holding the remote, I press a button, and Sodium Hydroxide waterfalls in from portholes on the top sides. I keep dancing.

I'll soon be rid of Eminence for good. The tank will drain down dedicated pipes to Biohazard barrels in a hidden and locked room in the basement; the barrels will then drain, over the course of three months, ever so slow, a trickle, directly into a sewer line that leads to my own septic field. Winter will come, whatever vapors come off the sewer steam will melt it, and as such, Eminence's entire existence will dissipate into the atmosphere.

Bye, bye.

My mini workout is done. I slide to the secure wall phone and call Sarge to release my family. We'll meet in Massachusetts for Mother's funeral.

Later today, after packing and making arrangements for family and work, I'll meditate by painting in the rose garden, the site of the former quarry for dead bodies on this property. I'll mix hues of reds and pinks, and I'll finger frame the placement of a real cardinal on a real branch. He lives out there by the quarry, this cardinal. An artist from Maine makes beautiful birdhouses made out of license plates, so I bought him one. My lonely, fire-feathered friend lives in this licensed home like an overlord, guarding my roses, which cover the dread, long since dredged.

Annie Lennox sings a song called *Why*. At the end, I think she whispers as a final line—maybe I'm wrong in what I hear, but what I choose to perceive as camouflaged along the lingering rhythm of the final chord is, "You don't know what I fear." Maybe she says something else, but I choose the word "fear." I consider that one line the truest statement anyone could say. Maybe even truer than saying water is made of two hydrogen atoms and one oxygen. Nobody knows what someone else truly fears, another's most personal fear, and nobody knows what I fear most, when I allow fear. I might say I fear the devil, but that would mean I fear myself. I might say I fear that God does not exist, but that means I fear that I and everyone else do not exist. I might say I fear nothingness, that my energy will vaporize and I will have no use, no purpose after death. Or worse, that I will become zero energy, inefficient and wasteful, wafting about like stench with no flesh and no senses, but in the worst of hells because I'll hold conscience: I'll know I'm zero energy and can do nothing to change anything. But how could I test such a theoretical fear? How could I rationalize it?

Perhaps what I fear is the intersection of all these possible fears...the devil, no God, nothingness, zero energy, that intersection coalescing into something tangible and specific. For now, I do not wish to delve into such matters. I do not allow fear. If I even think about this intersection of fears, there's a possibility someone will discover and have me at my most vulnerable. I'm not sure I could work my way out of the Gordian's Knot I won't let myself think of, and I certainly will never tell anyone the answer, the one controller of all my emotional switches. I've figured out what the one controller is, the only thing that could make me feel everything and have no ability to flip switches off, but I will not say what it is.

As Sodium Hydroxide rises, boiling away the blown mash of Eminence, I pause in a brief moment of silence for Mother. Head bowed, I take a knee, and switch love on for two solitary seconds, fight through the panic that is instant, and send out to her afterlife energy all around me, a whispered: *I love you.*

AFTERWORD
SEVERAL MONTHS LATER
FORMER SPECIAL AGENT ROGER LIU

I drive to this cryptic address, as provided by Lola with cryptic instructions, in the company of Sandra, Lisa, Vanty, and Nana, all of us in Nana's bulletproof Escalade—purchased for her by Lisa—after convening at Grand Nana's in Savannah. Lola told us to all meet there and then drive, to her specifications, twenty minutes outside of Savannah, to where we're headed now. Lisa's husband Lenny is absent. "He's moved out for now," is all Lisa will tell me. I've learned to not press for details.

I know we're headed into some kind of surprise party involving Lola's early retirement, but there is some secret about this, and the address is new to me. Actually, I've never been given any address associated with Lola. We've always just met up for work. And this whole surprise thing is throwing me extra sideways because I have an urgency to pull Lola and Lisa aside and to the back of the Escalade where I need to show them something I just uncovered this morning. We have some unfinished, and I fear, dangerous business with Velada still to attend to.

Sandra, my ever-polite wife, gave Nana the front passenger seat, so I look to Nana.

"What's this all about? Come on, tell me," I speak low to her.

"Now, Roger, you'll see soon enough, dear," she says.

Both Lola and I have known Nana for years. Full name, Mila

Yyland, authoress, Nana to Lisa, Grand Nana to Vanty. She's been at
15/33 headquarters many times and encountered all of us working
late. While pulling a late shift, or when interacting with Lola who
came in from the underground, it's often been Nana in the kitchen
at 2:00 a.m. making one or both of us snickerdoodles and fudge
and tea. So it was a little bit of a jolt a number of years ago, but not
earth-ending surprise, when Lola announced she quite liked Savannah
after popping in on Nana and decided to find her "own place." Lola
never said where exactly, and she never invited me. Never talked
further beyond the one sentence, "I'm getting my own place down
in Savannah, near Nana's."

What *is* earth-ending surprise is when we pull up to the address
Lola gave me last week and I see, over a cut-out in a property-
wrapping, seven-foot high sculpted hedge, a banner that reads:
"CONGRATULATIONS LOLA AND SHERRY!"

Who. The fuck. Is Sherry? Seriously, who the fuck is Sherry?

I slam on the brakes, and a gentleman in a black suit and bowtie
motions me to roll forward to a team of valets. I forget for a moment
the burning issue I need to raise ASAP with Lola and Lisa. Something
far separate from this party and whoever the fuck Sherry is.

What?

Nana's soothing, authoritative voice enters my swirling conscience
from the passenger seat. "Roger, I'm sorry that Lola insisted you find
out in such a stark manner, but she made me promise to keep this
under the strictest confidentiality from every living soul until the final
moment. She's so worried about security. Sherry is Lola's wife. They
were married in a private ceremony in 1997."

I'm transported back to the weird day in the Four Seasons in
1996, when Lola rubbed the collar of her terry cloth robe in personal
happiness. She was in-love.

"They met in 1996, didn't they?"

"So you knew *then*?"

"I most certainly did not."

It doesn't surprise me that Lola married a woman. What surprises
me is she married a human. I figured she lived out of an abandoned
warehouse and cooked hotdogs over a garbage can fire because she
wouldn't need plates or utensils for such a hound dog's meal. I figured
she waited on me to buy her real meals.

I've been working with Lola for 100 years.

No, 1,000 eons.

And even if Lola didn't live in an abandoned warehouse, I never expected she lived with, much less married, another sentient being and not a dead lizard in a cage. So please, I hope no bystanders are offended, as I step out of the car, limp-drop my keys to the valet without aiming, miss, not bend to pick them up, and stand here like a fool with my mouth in slack-jaw while my wife Sandra nudges me to close my clap-trap quick.

Sandra pulls me to cross through the hedge opening, and we run immediately into Lola, whose arm is locked with the arm of a woman bearing long, silky, raven hair. Someone introduces us and states how this woman locking arms with Lola is Sherry, Lola's wife, and how she's retiring her post as the Chief of Surgery at some *whothefuckknows* local hospital. I cannot process all of this information.

Lola.

And her wife.

A fucking hot, son of a bitch, WOW, goddess with long, black hair and violet eyes. Long legs and high cheekbones, like a comic-book warrior queen.

Flawless.

Fucking flawless.

Is my mouth still open?

"Honey, shut your mouth," Sandra whispers in my ear.

What the fuck is my name? How am I supposed to greet this bombshell? I don't even know my name. And wait, she's the one who decorated this fern-filled wraparound porch like we're at Nana's house, or on the cover of *Southern Living*?

Lola lives here? This isn't a toxic, rain-dripping, abandoned warehouse with open trashcans for fire. How so? I blink my eyes.

I must have been silent too long because Lola repeats the introduction. "Liu, this is Sherry. Sherry, Liu," Lola says unceremoniously, like she's introducing some meaningless transient. I note their arms are no longer locked.

Sherry hugs me, tight, pulls away, holds me at arm's length, and let's go to pluck a cold lemonade from a passing server's tray. She hands the frosty, perfect glass to me; I gulp for three full seconds. I'm sweating.

"Roger, so nice to finally meet you. It's been many, many years I've wanted to meet you. But Lola, you know Lola, she's so worried for my safety and all. Too worried." Sherry raises her eyebrows toward Lola, indicating a familiar marital squabble. "She, of course, fought me on this party, but I told her if we didn't have a retirement party and if I couldn't meet the people she's worked with, I wasn't going to retire too."

Lisa, who I forgot was here because I forgot I was standing on planet Earth, says, "Well played," tipping her own cool lemonade glass toward Sherry in a sign of flat, naked respect; no smile.

"What was your surgical specialty?" Lisa asks.

"Neurosurgery, and sometimes just general surgery, filling in in trauma. We're short staffed. Low funds."

"So, a brain surgeon?" Lisa says, stepping closer.

"Yeah, I guess so," Sherry says, very casual and easy, smiling. It's obvious she loves the practice of medicine. Maybe the reality of retiring hasn't quite settled in.

Lisa resumes her study of the woman, evaluating. She's not thinking about shock. Not thinking about how you can never really know someone. About benevolent deceptions. About broken trust and loyalty. About being winded by your closest friend, your partner. Having to redefine everything you know about her, and yet act politely at a garden party as if hiding the love of your life from your best friend, partner, *colleague-who-would-fucking-die-for-you* is normal.

Why couldn't Lola have told me?

I'm not mad. I just feel unworthy. Like she couldn't trust me.

My vision scatters around the yard as I try to find some mental foothold so I might regain a civilized attitude and remain a functional guest. Beyond a wildflower garden is a row of white bee homes, and beyond the bees is a wooden fence holding back the longest and skinniest mule I've ever seen. I'm guessing, given the white ring of fur around his mane, this mule is ancient, an elderly pet. And I'm guessing he's beloved, given the shine of his coat and the red ribbon around his scrawny neck.

Sherry catches my gaze and giggles. "So, you've found my little love. That's Mr. Gangy Man. I've had him forever. I just love him. He can't gain a pound though, no matter what we feed him."

The others in our circle pepper questions about Mr. Gangy Man, as a slight smile starts a slow creep on my lips.

Mr. Gangy Man is a long, skinny, old-ass mule. I look at Lola and smirk, and now we have another inside joke. Lola straight-lines her lips and shakes her head at Sherry, indicating they must have a difference of opinion on how much love Mr. Gangy Man deserves. Obviously, by her body language and the fact she named a scumbag criminal the same name, Lola doesn't think much of Mr. Gangy Man the mule. My wife and I have a similar squabble over a pet she adores and I, well, *tolerate*. Sandra's white lab, Dexty Boy, has eaten one too many hams off the counter to be in my good grace. He crop-dusts rooms with farts so toxic we have to clear out for a good half hour. He always has a tick or skunk spray or porcupine needles to clean up. And he seems always wet, from a pond or a puddle or a swamp or…who knows. Still, I do feed him under the table when no one's looking and I do like it when he curls up next to me on the couch—when he's clean and not toxic. Knowing Lola, and knowing me, I bet Lola sneaks this pain-in-the-ass mule pieces of pie when Sherry's not looking. We're hypocritical enablers.

Whatever, back to this shocking new reality I'm finding myself in, in Savannah.

What the hell is Lisa studying? Why is she evaluating Sherry like she might buy her? *Shit.* Sandra is going back and forth with Sherry about the flowerbeds, thank God, as I continue to try to force the blood back into my brain.

Sherry cuts through my fog and addresses me, "Roger, I want to thank you for keeping Lola safe all these years. And caring for her when no one else would. You're the only one who stood up for her at the Bureau and gave her a chance. Without you, she wouldn't have a career."

This snaps me out of my shock, because now I have something to say. "Well that may be true, but that's a crime, Sherry. Because without Lola, I'd be dead in a ditch and countless children and women would be lost to hell. She's the best investigator this government ever had. I'm damn proud to have worked with her."

Sherry starts a little weep, dabbing her ridiculous violet eyes with a linen handkerchief, because she's a perfect, exotic Southern belle. "Oh Roger, Lola loves you. She'll never tell you that. But she sure as hell does. The only picture we have framed in this house from the

259

entire side of her life—well, it's not any family members, that's for sure. And it's no college friends. It's you. Some candid blurry photo she snuck of you."

Lisa coughs and breaks the sentimental moment. "You're a brain surgeon?" she asks in a tone that is meant to cement this already confirmed fact.

"Sure am. Well…was, I guess. This retirement and all."

"You ever do freelance work?" Lisa's not joking, and thus doesn't return a polite little laugh when Sherry giggles at the question. Lisa's been especially non-emotive ever since Lenny moved out.

I turn around, hurrying my search of the crowd for Nana. I find her with Vanty at a bocce court. *Lola's fucking southern bocce court. What the hell?*

"Nana, yo, Nana," I'm calling, waving her to come over and help out. I nod to Lisa in a way that, between me and Nana, means I need her help on redirecting Lisa.

Nana joins us and redirects the conversation to normal things by tapping her index finger on Lisa's spine and whispering a few words in her ear. As the conversation mellows into banter about the caterer's award-winning spinach tarts and how Sherry calibrates the pH level in the soil to maintain the periwinkle of the hydrangeas that apron the porch, I slip back to my worry. My urgency. I, too, have something to reveal to my small band of compatriots. I think the shock of Lola's true life is settling, for on some subconscious level, I must have suspected *something*. Besides, she's not going to engage in any conversation with me about it, so I suck it up, swallow the pill, and plow ahead. Lola rifles five spinach tarts into her mouth, one after the other, and I see she has three more in her hand and on deck.

"Maybe the three of us could have a quick talk?" I say to Lola when everyone else is focused on Sherry's little nieces, her Senator sister's daughters, who are performing an impromptu Irish Dance on the walkway's pavers. Lola does not fight me, doesn't try to avoid a private conversation, perhaps thinking I'd want to discuss this whole Sherry thing. She knows I won't push, I learned too many times too long ago to not do that. And because we're a longstanding tap-dance team, she takes the bait and moves me and Lisa over to a vine-draped pergola by Mr. Gangy Man.

"We need to go to the back of Nana's Escalade. Can we go over there?" I ask.

Lola looks at me like I'm crazy. "Shit, Liu, what's with all the secrecy?"

I look at her with a *'you for real?'* look and throw an arm in the direction of Sherry, indicating all of Sherry as a symbol of secrecy.

"Fine. Touché," Lola says. And this. This is the one and only time Lola has ever come this close to apologizing for anything. So I take it as an apology and will not, of course I will not, hold a grudge. There would be zero point in holding a grudge against Lola.

"Congratulations, by the way," I say. She winces. I look away from her, won't give her the satisfaction, or torture, of a reaction, and walk on toward the back of the Escalade, which one of the four valets parked in *one of the two* side lawns along *Lola's fucking tree-lined driveway.* Fortunately, the back of this side lawn faces the surrounding forest, so once we have the hatch up, we're blocked from onlookers. I can see why Lola chose this property. It has a great perimeter, and now I note the several dozen cameras mounted high in trees everywhere, cameras I'm sure Lola mounted herself.

"You have an electric fence all the way around and even through the woods, don't you?" I say, looking up at the cameras in the trees.

"Of course I do, Liu. This whole joint is wired and trapped. What's this bug you got up your butt you got to tell us about? Hurry up, before all these freeloading fuckers eat all the tarts on me."

"We need to talk about Velada. I think we need to run something down ASAP before your retirement from Beta takes effect. I know Beta and the FBI, ATF, all of law enforcement, are running down all sorts of leads on the Center Ring. They've interviewed Velada, left, right, up, down, whatever. Here's the thing." I pause to catch both Lola's and Lisa's gazes, ensuring they are anchored into this conversation. "I remember a split second of a look Velada gave to Judge Frackson and then at Lisa that night. It was like a message with Frackson about Lisa in a quick, almost imperceptible, look. Like this." I demonstrate for them, using Lola as Frackson in my recreation.

"I hope you got more than that, Liu," Lola says, skeptical, her face screwed.

"Listen. Hold on. Listen. So, I pushed that look out of my mind because I figured it was all just part of the chaos, and here they all were, Frackson included, caught dead to rights, cuffed and under arrest and on several forms of film in the act. But, son of a bitch. Just yesterday, I get a call."

I reach for my briefcase in the back of the SUV and pull out a folder. Lola reaches to take the folder, so I clutch it to my chest.

"Hold on. Hear me out. Yesterday, I get this call. Guess what? Of all the fucking monsters, Frackson cuts the best deal. He walks. Totally walks. And, as you know, he was the only one of the crew who got to be on house arrest awaiting trial. So yesterday, he cuts the plea and they cut the ankle monitor." I snap my fingers. "Free. Just like that. And of course, Velada is free, too. She has everyone convinced she was a prisoner—which is a thin claim, but her testimony against her brother and everyone else, plus her vigilante work with Lisa, all now blessed by Beta, is her deal. So now, I hear this about Frackson and, right, I suddenly can't get that look Velada gave to Frackson and then at Lisa out of my head. Then, something hits me. It was so quick and so long ago my memory failed to connect it right away when we first saw him. And it was long before we ever met him at Saleo."

Lola furrows her brow, remains quiet, listening. Lisa stares at my face, following my eyes.

I turn to my briefcase and pull out a grainy black and white photograph, one out of dozens the three of us studied for hours many years ago. This particular one we'd sorted into a "not helpful" pile and really hadn't studied long.

"Do you see what I mean?" I ask.

Lola picks it up, moves to a sunnier spot by the taillight. Lisa looking over her shoulder.

"That's from the day in court. When I testified against the doctor. This is one of the CCTV stills we pulled after Velada visited me in the parking lot," Lisa says.

"Yes. Do you see what I see?"

Lola bites her bottom lip. "Motherfucker. Are you sure?"

"I'm fucking positive. Look at these." I spread four color photos I printed on Nana's color printer this morning. I narrate through the pictures, "This morning, I pull up images of Frackson. Found ones of when he was in law school at Northwestern, these; and then when he was a young associate at Miles Thorburough in Chicago, these. Miles Thorburough is only a few hours' drive, just a day trip, to the Indiana courthouse. And you didn't have to sign in back then, and don't now either. There's absolutely no record of Frackson there that day, except this picture."

Lisa picks up the associate photo and takes the courthouse CCTV still, nudges past Lola to take the sunny spot by the taillight, and studies them both, back and forth.

As she looks, I say, "We never cared about this CCTV still."

Lisa cuts me off, "Because there's only a sliver of Velada's leg visible here. But, what's important now, is her leg is next to Frackson, and he's fully visible. That's him."

"There's more," I say. "Within just the past week, I confirmed this morning, actually...guess where Velada lives? She's not living back with that husband she duped in Viebury, by the way."

Lisa does an odd snort and smirks. I raise my eyebrows at her.

"Go on," she says, making her face emotionless and blank again.

"Right," I say, side eyeing her. "Anyway. Guess where she got an apartment?"

"No clue, Liu," Lola says, squinting her eyes, not giving any inch on what she thinks about what I'm saying.

"She's living in an apartment two blocks over from Frackson in Cambridge. Here's my theory. I think Velada orchestrated this whole thing as a way to get rid of her brother and his most powerful, long-term customers, mainly Rasper and Sergeant Rockford, and also the two women who helped manage—the Sister and the woman Lisa calls Eva. Somehow Velada got twined up with Frackson long ago and they hid their own plan from everyone from the start, pretty fucking well. The only shot she had was waiting for the weird-ass, fucked-up Lobster Tank, and her pretty remarkable bet that she'd be able to manipulate her brother's insanity. And her one ally all along, the lynch pin to whatever her larger plan is, was always Frackson. Who knows what contingency plans they had up their sleeves if things went sideways with Lisa.

"It's never sat with me okay that she allowed all that trafficking, holding out knowledge on where the operation was, for so many years—years when I'm sure she was free to skim all the money she wanted from her brother's operation, with him in Shanghai. So many girls abused, raped. It's not right. She's not innocent. The biggest indicator is that the family trust says if her brother is incarcerated or dies, she's the sole beneficiary. And I'm concerned for your safety,

Lisa. Now that Frackson is out of home arrest, they'll wait a little longer, stay low. Wait for the trials to finish, play their part in testifying. But this doesn't sit right. I sense something."

"I see how Velada's probably dirty. Especially with this whole Frackson bullshit. But, you're worried for Lisa's safety because of a half-second glance she gave her on the night we busted those assholes?" Lola asks.

"Yes. Absolutely," I say.

Lisa nods an agreement to me and, standing side by side, together we look to Lola to validate the consensus. Lola snags the CCTV still and leans sideways into the sunspot to look at it once again. She sticks her tongue out to pick at the top of her teeth.

"Shit, boss," Lola says. Her serious tone and use of "boss" cements our tri-party agreement.

~~~

Lisa and I have been walking Lola and Sherry's grounds for about ten minutes now. From a distance, Lola nods to me to point out that my favorite song is up in rotation in whatever mix they have going for this early retirement garden party, perfectly calibrated in sound level and wafting through speakers disguised as boulders. Lisa and I haven't said a word to each other. We walk, both of us with our arms behind our backs, keeping our steps in synch. This is what we do when we get a new case, when we set out to plan something. We walk outside together in contemplation. She says me being by her side helps her to sort through the chaos of a new pile of facts. And I, for my part, have learned that this method works for me too.

The song surrounding the world of Lola and Sherry's southern lawn, with the ferns and moss-dripping trees all around, is Ray LaMontagne's *The Man in Me*. So I start to hum and sing along, soft so only I can hear, and Lisa too, for I can't help myself when this song plays.

Lisa looks up at me, not breaking her stride or moving her hands, bladed in her pockets. It is her look of study, her pupils tracking the micro-creases of my eyes and forehead.

"You always sing this song out loud. What is the emotion it brings you?"

"Truth," I say. "These words feel like truth to me."

"You equate truth to emotion?"

"I guess I do."

"Do you think trust is an emotion also?"

"Probably. But, you're the boss, Lisa, so you tell me."

She doesn't answer for a moment, looks ahead. We do not trust each other, and so, whatever that emotion is between us, is truth.

"Trust is a sense. It's like sight, smell, sound," she says in a mechanical, fact-giving way. "I've never trusted Velada. We need to run this down. I think whatever enterprise she has planned is worse than even her brother's. I trust my sense on this, and I trust yours."

We keep walking, I keep humming. She watches my micro facial twitches and creases like I'm an animal in a zoo and she's the zookeeper. Things are back to just about as normal as they've always been.

JOSI OLIVE
A NOT SO CHANCE ENCOUNTER

After spending the day in his sound lab mixing beats and thinking on the strangeness of his life over the past several months—the discovery about his fake marriage, the trip out to Indiana with Lisa Yyland, their communications since then—Josi works up enough agitation to *need* to walk around Viebury Grove. But in the evening and in the woods. He's thinking maybe it's time, time to forgive Carla, Velada, whatever her fucking name is, was...whatever, for her deceptions so he can move on and feel the love with someone else. He again envisions Lisa and her weird distance, but also their sometimes sweet closeness. Or is he imagining things? And she is married. *Is she still married?*

Josi walks with Cat while smokin' a damn fine cigar, stepping over logs, pausing where they found not-Carla's burnt skeleton, and beneath the grave marker he'd made for her, spelling her name in blue paint on a plank of wood he nailed to a pine. *Fucking lies.* Today is the day, he's going to do it. He starts to sand away Carla's name with sandpaper he'd stuffed in his back pocket. Rubbing and scrubbing hard, like he's the washboard man in a jug band, he works up a sweat. He can't erase her name completely, but enough of her name is faded now, the blue of the paint blended into the pine. Nobody's been able to find the real name of the real girl whose dead body was dumped and burned here—all they know from the living victims is she was a poor-ass, undocumented, runaway teen who died of untreated

266

pneumonia, or something else for which she kept hacking up a lung. So Josi glues the following, GIRL, in Scrabble letters. Below that he writes with a black sharpie in the free space on the plank of wood: SOMEONE OUT THERE LOVED YOU, GIRL. I'M SORRY.

He lays Girl a dozen wilted wildflowers he'd plucked from Carla's garden, and which he'd tied in a bunch with a garbage tie and carried here in his other back pocket. These from the garden under his and Carla's bedroom window where she said their future rug-rats would sometimes call up to them on Saturday mornings to come outside and play. The "flowers" are brown and appear as weeds, given the season.

Someone once told Josi they weren't wildflowers, they were scallion and basil plants, for he'd plucked them from Carla's "chef's garden." Back then, back before he knew Carla was a lying scammer, he'd told whoever said that, that his bouquet wasn't a bunch of flowers and to fuck off and that he'd leave his girl fistfuls of "fucking beautiful grass" if it meant she might know up in Heaven he still missed her. But now as he sets the flowers, he thinks, *I'm sorry about the weeds, Girl. Next time I'll bring peonies.*

Josi moves on to lighter places in the dark forest behind Viebury Grove. Along the way, he finger-juggles the super-glue tube in his pants' pocket. The sound of the *whir-whir-whirrrr* drill into the Judge's jowls still reverberates in his mind like an earworm. He tried all day to turn this sound into a beat in his lab on the MPC, layer in some lyrics, slay the mood with rippling guitar chords. He figures he'll have to convince Jam-Bone's girlfriend Keelia to sing high soprano, giving the illusion of crying in the background. To rid the rhythm in his mind of the *whir-whir* drill, he'll need to purify it in poetry, like he buried his wife, rather, no…buried Girl, in pages of poetry, literal lines on paper atop her coal remains.

Josi snakes between the pines, Cat close to his side, as always.

This fucking cigar, fuck, I love this cigar. Fat ass wood fire pipe in my mouth, keeps the 'squitos away from my face. He bends to slap a couple of suckers gnawing on his exposed shins, between the hem of his black jean shorts that fall to his knees, several inches from the rims of his boots. The fallen leaves and rust-red pine needles carpet this spot. So dark, an oil drum, in the middle of the forest. *Shit, there's a line: dark as an oil drum, in the foggy forest I strum. I'll use that. I can use that. What's the beat? Da-Da-Da-Draaaaaam—da-da, yeah. I'll check it in the sound lab after this patrol.*

"Come on, Cat, move it."

But Cat doesn't move, and as Josi listens closer, he hears feet scraping further ahead at the granite outcrop.

Probably fucking teenagers smokin' weed. Maybe they'll give me a hit.

"Cat, go up ahead, disarm them with your awful cuteness."

But Cat is already moving ahead of Josi, something he never does. He used to do that, used to run to Carla, the only other person Cat would leave Josi's side for.

He reaches the granite outcrop. Cat is standing next to a woman whose back is to Josi. He can't quite tell what her hair color is or any other specifics, given a shadow that falls on her from an overhanging limb.

She turns around, and Josi freezes.

"Josi," Velada says.

And fuck, it's all back in a flood: the anger. He thought he was past this, this rage at her. He thought sanding down her name meant he'd put this rage in the past. But he's a fool to think it could be that easy, especially now as he's looking at her and he wants to scream. He has so many questions. So much to say.

"Carla," Josi says, widening his eyes. "So they cleared you? You're out."

"I've been out, Josi."

"Your letter said you had to stay in an undisclosed location. Witness protection."

Velada stares at him as her answer.

"Oh, so that was a fucking lie, too?"

"Yeah, Josi, it was a fucking lie, too." She shakes her head in a manner that is half-sarcasm, half-embarrassment. Her snide demeanor only feeds into the rage he's damned for months. He's about to blow.

"How could you?" Josi snaps.

"How could I what?" Velada says, snapping back.

"Fucking A, Carla. I won't even ask about how you could possibly lie to me for so long and marry me with a false fucking name. We're annulled, you know. We ain't married anymore. I got it all documented."

"So what is it you're asking me, exactly? How could I what?" Skipping Josi's mention of their sham annulled marriage.

"I'm asking you, Carla, Velada, whoeverthefuck you are, how could you let those girls be tortured by those fucking monsters for decades? How could you? How could you allow some other girl to burn and make us believe it was you? You murdered her."

"I did not murder her. The cops cleared me of that and you know it. I took that opportunity, yes, to stage my own death. So sue me."

"I would if I could."

"Oh you would, would you?"

"How could you? Answer the question. How could you let this stink hole operate for so long in Viebury?"

Velada breathes in long, through both nostrils, straightens her back. "Look. I had to disappear, make you think I ran, so you wouldn't be caught up in any of this shit. Things were getting scary in that house. The closer we got to when my brother was returning for his big event, the other women started asking too many questions about you. And what you knew. I had to do it, Josi, to protect you. I had to disappear and live under their constant eye at Mariana, to prove you knew nothing and didn't give a shit. They bought it. They left you alone. And then that girl died in the house and I left my shirt and the bracelet in the muds, to prove to them that I was really gone to you, dead to you, and was telling you nothing. I knew you'd never let them know you suspected anything. You're too smart for that. I did fall in love with you, Josi. That was real."

"Don't fucking patronize me, Carla. You fucking scouted me at the bookstore because I had just inherited the house in Viebury. Because I wouldn't sell, you swooped in to control me and what I knew."

Velada looks to the ground. Shakes her head.

"So when you think I know jack shit, you weasel out," Josi continues.

"You're wrong. When they were asking too many questions about you and what information I was feeding you, I left, like I said. And also, I couldn't control what I was saying in dreams; we'd already fought about all that. I had to run, I had to stage my death, to spare you. I watched over you, made sure they left you alone. I did fall in love with you, Josi. I did." She steps to him, tries to take and hold his hand.

Josi pulls his arm away and takes a step back.

"Bullshit. Answer the question. How could you?"

Velada clenches her teeth, balls her fists tight, obviously angered at failing to trap Josi into a conversation about love. Josi recalls moments of fighting with her, when he did let her trap him, manipulate him. He refuses to fall for it this time, so he asks again, "How could you?" He wants her anger to rise, make her feel how horrible he feels; he won't, like before, try to make things smooth.

"Did your pal, Lisa, put these thoughts in your head? That I'm somehow some monster who let girls suffer for years? That I should have told her the location sooner?" Velada says, walking into Josi's space, her tone full of hatred.

"She's not wrong."

"Oh this is just plain fucking rich. So Lisa's still harping on about how afraid she is that I'm a big fat liar."

"You are a liar. And I don't think Lisa's afraid of anything."

"She's got to be afraid of something, Josi."

"Yeah, nope. I'm sure you're wrong about that. I think she can avoid fear totally."

"She has a fear all right, and I bet it's pretty specific," Velada says, staring off over Josi's shoulder as if setting her intention on something.

"What the fuck's that supposed to mean?"

"Nothing," she says, raising her eyebrows. "Jeez! Paranoid much. What? You like her, or something? Want to protect your girlfriend?"

"She's just a friend."

"Right. Sure, Josi."

Josi stops himself from responding, from denying, which is a surprise to his own self. He thinks about how before he would deny any of Carla's crazy jealousies, run up to her and pepper her with a hundred tiny kisses all over her body until she giggled herself out of being cross. He lifts his hands, resigned. "Whatever, Carla. I mean, Velada. I mean, whatever your name is."

"Goodbye, Josi," she says, staring him down. Josi doesn't flinch or stare back. He flips his hands in the air to indicate he has nothing further to say.

Velada turns and walks off into the shadows of the trees, and Josi doesn't stop her. He is surprised at the relief he feels in seeing her go. He is even more surprised by two additional senses: a sense of relief and hope that this is the last time he'll see her, but also a competing sense of fear, perhaps an obligation to protect, in replaying how she seemed so intent on Lisa Yyland having a specific fear.

ACKNOWLEDGEMENTS

This is a work of fiction meant to entertain. But the serious issue of human trafficking should not be taken lightly in the real world. I encourage people to seek out local organizations and safe homes for human trafficking victims, and inquire as to their needs. Trust me, they have needs. You can help.

As for the science depicted in this novel, again, this is a work of fiction, and I am absolutely sure I've twisted science into some warped delusion for fiction's sake. I underscore, this is a work of fiction meant to entertain. Nevertheless, I did attempt to educate myself (I'm sure I failed) and used some truly excellent resources. I encourage folks interested in sound science to read, "The Universal Sense: How Hearing Shapes the Mind" by Seth S. Horowitz, Ph.D., which I found to be very approachable for a lay person and fascinating. As for the powers of mechanical energy (Lisa's bands and capacitor), I was inspired into that idea after I read the 2016 *Advanced Materials* article (*pp. 4283-4305*), "Flexible Nanogenerators for Energy Harvesting and Self-Powered Electronics," by Dr. Feng Ru Fan, Dr. Wei Tang, and Prof. Zhong Lin Wang, who at the time of the article's printing were with the Beijing Institute of Nanoenergy and Nanosystems. While I've launched myself into fictional ideas from the article's grounded explanations, this true and revolutionary science should be, in my opinion, part of an active conversation on renewable energy options.

Thanks to Dr. William K. Tong, quoted in Chapter 13, for his great summary of The Scientific Method, which can be found on the

Oakton Community College website at *http://www.oakton.edu/user/4/ billtong/eas100/scientificmethod.htm*.

Thanks to Chris Holm (award-winning author of the *Collector* trilogy and the *Michael Hendricks'* thrillers) for his time in trying to guide me along the right words to describe the use of guns in Shanghai. I'm sure I butchered what he tried to teach me, but I hope I got it close.

Thanks to Kimberley Cameron, my agent. Look at our lives now, Kimberley. How did we get here? How wonderfully strange and awesome this all is—you make me feel like Joan Wilder in *Romancing the Stone*. I'm the desperate author superbly supported by her indefatigable agent. Love you. Thanks to Whitney Lee (foreign rights) and Mary Alice Kier and Anna Cottle (Cin/Lit agency), the remainder of the agenting team, who have always supported the *15/33* series. xoxoxoxoxoxoox.

Thanks to the EdicionesB/Penguin Random House team for the excellent support for the *15/33* series (and the awesome translations and covers).

Thanks to Shannon Raab and John Raab of Suspense Publishing for giving *Viebury Grove* a home in the English language. Thanks to Shannon for the spectacular cover—love the green with gold and the Luna Moth. Thanks to Shannon Raab and Amy Lignor for their invaluable edits and guidance. It's been a thrill working with the Suspense Publishing team, a joy for me as an author to have such excellent attention and care.

To my beta readers, you've seen this story changed dramatically over time, and I could not have done it without your tough love and your excellent direction. Beth Hoang, Mom, and Dad, I honestly owe you the world for the time you've given me and my work, and especially with this one. David Corbett, my private editor for this novel, man you were tough, but you were so very right. I went through the fire on your edits, and you, as only the best of instructors do, taught me a great deal and made me see things I'd grown blind to— and, in the end, made me love writing again. Thank you.

Lastly, to Mike and Max, you are my whole world. Max, you are my perfect Vantaggio.

ABOUT THE AUTHOR

Shannon Kirk is the international bestselling and award-winning author of *Method 15/33*, *The Extraordinary Journey of Vivienne Marshall*, *In the Vines*, *Gretchen*, *Viebury Grove*, and short stories in four anthologies: *The Night of the Flood*, *Swamp Killers* (TBP, 2020), *Nothing Good Happens After Midnight* (TBP, 2020), and *Border Noir* (TBP, 2020). Shannon is also a contributor to the International Thriller Writers' Murderers' Row. Growing up in New Hampshire, Shannon and her brothers were encouraged by their parents to pursue the arts, which instilled in her a love for writing at a young age. A graduate of Suffolk Law School in Massachusetts, Shannon is a practicing litigation attorney and former adjunct law professor, specializing in electronic-evidence law. When she isn't writing or practicing law, Shannon spends time with her husband, son, and two cats.

To learn more about her, visit www.shannonkirkbooks.com.

CPSIA information can be obtained
at www.ICGtesting.com
Printed in the USA
BVHW030128240922
647858BV00028B/439